Boiling Point

Frank Lean

Boiling Point

WILLIAM HEINEMANN: LONDON

First published in the United Kingdom in 2000 by
William Heinemann

1 3 5 7 9 10 8 6 4 2

Copyright © Frank Lean 2000

The right of Frank Lean to be identified as the author of this work has
been asserted by him in accordance with the Copyright, Designs and
Patents Act, 1988

William Heinemann
Random House Group Limited
20 Vauxhall Bridge Road, London, SW1V 2SA

Random House Australia (Pty) Limited
20 Alfred Street, Milsons Point, Sydney, New South Wales 2061, Australia

Random House New Zealand Limited
18 Poland Road, Glenfield
Auckland 10, New Zealand

Random House South Africa (Pty) Limited
Endulini, 5a Jubilee Road, Parktown, 2193, South Africa

The Random House Group Limited Reg. No. 954009
www.randomhouse.co.uk

A CIP catalogue record for this book is available from the British Library

Papers used by Random House are natural, recyclable products
made from wood grown in sustainable forests. The manufacturing processes
conform to the environmental regulations of the country of origin

Typeset by SX Composing DTP, Rayleigh, Essex
Printed and bound in the United Kingdom by
Biddles Ltd, Guildford and King's Lynn

ISBN 0 434 00743 9

For Agnes Mary McClean

The author wishes to acknowledge gratefully the help of James Byrne, Tim Holden, Peter King, Wayne Watkins, staff at Associated British Ports, Fleetwood and Thomas Wilson at Random House.

1

Whatever else you said about him Insull Perriss wasn't long-winded.

'The entrance . . . Tarn Golf Club . . . be there,' the captain of industry snarled before slamming the phone down. You'd have thought I was the one blackmailing him.

For me, a journey to Tarn has a special meaning. I have two children in Tarn . . . twin sons I've sworn never to see. I never have, either.

Still, you can't have everything. The sun was shining after months of gloom. Long, slanting, low rays which meant driving with the visor down.

When I reached the exclusive club I discovered that Insull Perriss meant exactly what he said . . . the club entrance and not a foot further. I spotted his distinctive pear-shaped frame as I searched for a parking space. This was even harder to find than a place on the club membership list. I couldn't have slipped my mud-coated Mondeo among the ranked Rollers, BMWs, Mercedes and Jags even if the stewards had let me. I parked on the approach road.

The industrialist was hovering at the top of the imposing entrance steps. He looked nervous, as he should. You can do serious time for circulating child pornography, not to mention the disgrace. For now, though, he was a man with a position to protect and there he stood like a robber baron at the gate of his fortress. Only it wasn't *his* fortress and they'd evict him before he had time to blink if they caught one whiff of what I had in my parcel.

Perriss knew what he was doing. The annual Pro-Am Golf Tournament was on and the place was buzzing. I wasn't the only errand boy around but was probably the best paid.

The deal wasn't much . . . hand over the material I'd collected from the ex-employees who were screwing all they could out of their former boss. I didn't like what he'd done but the stuff was freely available on the Internet. Anyway, I wasn't his judge any more than the tabloids he was threatened with were. Bold before, Perriss was scared speechless now and I guessed it would be a long time before he surfed the net again.

I passed him the parcel, but as in the children's game it was no sooner in his hand than it was out of it, carelessly knocked from his fingers by a passing couple.

The pair were quarrelling bitterly: he, red-faced and blustering, in his late thirties; she, much younger, redheaded and voluble. They swept past us, almost shoving Perriss into the shrubbery. Floppy disks fell out of the bundle as it bounced down the steps. I rushed to round them up and handed them to Perriss. He looked as if he was about to wet himself but my attention was reclaimed by the brawling couple.

The florid-faced citizen was trying to detach himself from the shrill female. It wasn't just a battle of the sexes but of opposites: she was trim and light and had a good figure; he was heavy, with dark features, a fleshy forehead, a big nose and wrinkles of flesh on his face like a day-old puppy. He turned on his heel to come back up the steps towards us. Poor Perriss flinched and positioned himself behind me.

'You stupid bitch!' the rowdy yelled over his shoulder. 'You had to get yourself plastered.'

It was a mistake; the woman had no intention of being dumped. She sprang onto his back and grabbing a handful of his black hair jerked his head to and fro like a big floppy pumpkin.

All around the car park normal motion ceased: jaws descended, eyes popped out on stalks. Such upsets might be routine in some quarters but here at leafy Tarn they held an audience enthralled. A golf tournament was one thing, an opportunity to showcase success, but this was real life.

Red-face was a big bloke, at least six foot three. He peeled the redhead off with an easy shrug of his shoulders, and then, turning, shook a clenched fist the size of a cauliflower in her

2

face. He swung but thought better before the blow landed. Perhaps the massed gasps of disapproval put him off. Perhaps not. He didn't look the sort who gave a damn what the gallery thought.

Instead of belting the woman he gave her a push on the shoulder and sent her sprawling. Then, as if ashamed, he changed his mind about going back in the club and headed for the car park.

The redhead struggled to her feet. 'Brave man, aren't you!' she shrieked, and then, putting her hands on her hips, gave what I think was intended to be a derisive laugh. At least I don't think the sound she made was a symptom of some medical condition. The peal of laughter was normal, though loud, but it was followed by an ear-shattering gargle as breath was drawn back into her lungs. It was a show-stopper. In the car park at Tarn Golf Club it was as unwanted as nettle-rash at a nudists' picnic. Red-face paused for a moment.

'Bugger off, you boring, bloody lush!' he roared, whipping out car keys and zapping a mud-stained Porsche.

I focused on the victim again. She was having trouble standing up. From what I could see she had better exterior curves than Red-face's silver-grey Porsche. She had the sort of glow that spells money; money and trouble.

'Don't call me a lush, you second-hand sex machine!' she screamed. She was game. Once back on her feet she was ready for another round. I turned to Insull Perriss but he'd already disappeared. I also decided to go, mission accomplished. There was nothing to keep me in Tarn. A paternal visit to my offspring was out of the question.

Meanwhile, Red-face seemed anxious to conclude his encounter on a high note. Whirling round towards his drunken companion, he gave her another mouthful.

'Listen, you pathetic part-time prostitute's get . . .'

'Better than a pimp's leavings!'

That was it. The would-be woman-beater started forward, fist again raised for action. Sensing that he was for real this time, the redhead scrambled away, but her high heels hampered escape. Big-boy cornered her right up against my car.

3

A social scientist might tell you how quickly it takes the average English crowd to respond to provocation – hours, days, and weeks, for all I know. But the golfers of Tarn were up for it. A posse of angry ladies began heading towards the couple, golfing umbrellas poised like lances at a pig-sticking contest. Somehow I found myself in the vanguard of the advance. Mucky though my car was, if it needed cleaning I'd rather do it myself than let this bozo wipe it with his lady friend.

Your man had the redhead by the shoulders ready to loosen her teeth when I barged into him.

I thought he was going to take a swing at me. I was firing adrenaline on all cylinders. Things might have got interesting but he surveyed the advancing throng with a beady brown eye, then turned back to me.

'Don't you know who I am?' he gasped.

'You're not Lennox Lewis.'

'Carlyle, Charles Carlyle.'

'Am I meant to be impressed? Keep your hands off the lady.'

'Lady! Hah!' he sneered, then he wheeled round and strode towards his car. Seconds later he was burning rubber out of the car park.

In the interim his intended prey slowly collapsed. My half-hearted attempt to hold her upright ended before it began. A kilted lady golfer elbowed me to one side and caught the redhead before she fell. The rescuer's raised umbrella clattered onto the bonnet of my Mondeo.

'Whew! Had a bit too much to drink, have you, love?' she said, turning away and fanning the air with a pudgy hand. Her knowing look and shaking head stopped the approaching reinforcements in their tracks. Gathering up her brolly, this not-so-good Samaritan propped her burden against my car and bolted. I had no time to gape because Carlyle's victim resumed her collapse into the Cheshire clay.

I grabbed her arm first, but that was as limp as a string of sausages. The woman was a dead weight. I put my arms round her and held her up. It must have looked as if we were practising waltz steps – not that anyone was watching. I

4

looked for help but all I saw was the middle class in retreat, tasteful tweeds and kilts blending into the scenery like ptarmigan into heather.

'Oh, great!' I mumbled under my breath. 'Just what I need.'

'Hang onto me for a minute, please,' the redhead said. She wasn't as blotto as I'd thought. 'I'll be all right in a moment. It's just one of these funny turns I get.'

Her previously closed eyes opened. They were a startling, almost vivid, green. I looked at her warily, alert for I don't know what. She was as calm and cool as a hillside lake on a still, clear day. There was no rage, no shock, nothing.

Awkwardly I tried to hold her at arm's length. She just slumped forward against my chest.

'Give me a minute,' she repeated. I wasn't about to dump her in the mud but I heard approaching footsteps with a sense of relief.

A blazer-clad individual sporting a badge certifying that he was an official steward moved into my line of sight. I didn't waste time on social niceties.

'Give me a hand to get her into the clubhouse.'

'You must be joking, pal!' he snapped. 'She's barred.'

'She's ill!'

'It's just a funny turn,' my dance partner commented faintly.

'Funny turn! The only funny turn is you turning up here on tournament day in this state! How dare you? You know you're barred!' Before leaving, the man gave me a hard stare as if to warn me that I had no more right to be in his hallowed precincts than the target of his scorn.

'A warm-hearted gang, aren't they? This event's supposed to be for charity,' she murmured.

'Frankly I'm not remotely interested in the club or its activities,' I snapped.

'Sorry to be a nuisance to you. I'll get some strength back in my legs in a minute.' There was a faint trace of a Dutch or German accent in her voice. Her eyes had shut again as if she was concentrating all her energy for the next move.

The nearest bus stop was at least a mile away, taxis even further.

5

'You'd better sit in my car for minute,' I said resignedly.

Her only reply was that peculiar laugh – a crescendo of mirth followed by the disconcerting choking sound.

Luckily, our mad tango had taken place on the passenger side of the Mondeo and by sweating and struggling and becoming closely acquainted with her anatomy I managed to wedge her in the front seat. I looked back at the club. There was now a posse of blazer-clad stewards gathered on the steps, all favouring me with angry looks.

'What's your name?' I asked, in hopes of getting on to her address but that was another plan that didn't work. Her head lolled back against the car seat. She really was senseless this time.

I let the seat back as far as it would go and strapped her in. She'd mentioned a 'funny turn' and the sweet smell on her breath could have been diabetes, or God knows what, but I was too familiar with the effects of alcohol on an empty stomach to be worried. She was just pissed – pissed and passed out. I wound the window down on her side and headed back for Manchester at a cautious pace. By the look of her designer jeans and fawn jacket she'd be well able to afford the taxi fare to Tarn when she landed back on the planet.

I was driving along the A556 back towards Manchester at no particular speed when the silver-grey Porsche showed up. One moment I was on my own on an empty road and a second later it was alongside me. Carlyle nudged his car towards mine until it was almost touching. He signalled me to stop. The imperious way he waved got right up my nose.

I smiled politely and shook my head. The section of road we were on was a dual carriageway which ended at a massive roundabout where the road joined the M56 interchange. There was about a mile to go. When Carlyle saw that I wasn't about to obey his lordly command he went mad. He swerved the Porsche into my path and tried to force me into the side of the road. I looped around him onto the outside lane and kept my foot on the accelerator.

His next manoeuvre was more effective.

Coming up on my offside he hoisted a shotgun into my line of sight, quite a feat in such a small car. The twisted hatred in his face suggested that he was crazy enough to use it. Presumably I was supposed to be frightened. I wasn't. Exactly why, I don't know. I've been told I'm stubborn to the point of stupidity so I expect that's it. 'Where there's no sense, there's no feeling' as my old man tells me often enough. I should have been scared witless by this nutter but something made me want to frustrate him. I slammed my foot hard on the brakes and he did the same, but with only one hand on the wheel he went into a spin which took him into a 180-degree turn. My ears strained for the welcome sound of glass breaking and metal being crushed but heard only the characteristic whining, waspish note of one of Ferdinand's little beauties at full stretch. I took advantage of the seconds he spent turning to race towards the junction.

He caught up with me at the roundabout and now we didn't have the road to ourselves. The risk of gunplay was reduced but the chances of an accident increased a hundredfold. The highway was jammed with vehicles coming off the motorway. We jumped over the white line together and raced into the path of an oncoming five-axle truck. Carlyle had his horn blaring as did the truck, which swerved violently. Carlyle used the Porsche's greater acceleration to overtake and block me when I reached the motorway slip road so I went round again, this time dodging a stream of cars emerging from the exit lane. It was bedlam. The deep throbbing scream of the Porsche engine was joined by the fanfare from a dozen car horns. Accelerating round the curve and getting friction burns from my steering wheel, I couldn't help noticing that my passenger was still slumbering away peacefully.

Then I got a lucky break. A huge trailer was just in front of me. I shot inside it and used its bulk as a screen for a turn towards Altrincham. Carlyle was blocked this time. My wild turn might have gained me as much as twenty seconds, not enough to reach the first junction on the Altrincham road. There was a garage on my right. I heaved on the wheel, and, bumping across the low barrier, reached the shelter of the garage forecourt nanoseconds before Carlyle came racing into the road. I might not have been scared of him but my heart was thumping painfully as I turned into the car wash area.

7

Carlyle shot past, on towards Altrincham, no doubt judging my powers of acceleration by his own.

'You need a special card to go through there,' a white-coated attendant said. 'It's not coin operated.'

I looked at him blankly.

'Pay at the office and put your card in the slot,' he explained patiently. 'You're in the queue here.'

I took in my surroundings. I was parked behind a car waiting its turn at the automated car wash. Even as I looked another car pulled up behind me. If Carlyle arrived I wouldn't be able to get away.

'Had a long drive, then?' the attendant asked chattily. 'Your friend's right out of it. I'll get the card for you if you like.'

I handed him a tenner and he strolled slowly off towards the office. The car in front of me moved into the wash and pulled up by the control unit. The friendly attendant soon returned with a piece of plastic and a handful of change.

'Here you are, mate, I got you the full works,' he explained. 'Your car looks a bit travel stained.'

It did, but when it emerged from the wash it was a different shade of green – different enough from the car Carlyle was seeking for me to risk creeping out and driving back to the motorway interchange. I was able to make the left turn onto the motorway without any trouble but the exit going the other way was completely blocked by a furniture van lying on its side. A yellow-jacketed patrolman waved me on as I looked for casualties. Fortunately, there were no corpses lying around, just a bunch of drivers scratching their heads. I went on my way.

2

My passenger's 'funny turn' lasted all the way into town. I parked the car at the back of my place, almost blocking the narrow street, and considered my options. There weren't many. I helped her into the back room of the office. She stretched out on the couch like a tired tiger and fell into an instant sleep. Fortunately, Celeste, my secretary, wasn't there to witness this scene. She must have been taking one of her extended lunch breaks. Leaving my unwelcome guest as comfortably settled as I could, I nipped out and parked the car in a nearby multi-storey. That took me ten minutes and when I got back I checked on the sleeper. She was snoring noisily. I retreated to the reception area and began reading through the mail which Celeste had sorted into different piles.

It was getting on towards two and I was beginning to wonder if Celeste had finally jacked in the job or been kidnapped, when the door was flung open and a woman stormed in.

'Janine!'

'Dave,' she said fiercely. 'I couldn't stand another minute in the office. You don't mind me calling, do you?'

'Of course not. You know you're the light of my life.'

'Oh, don't start all that again. I had to get out of that place if I was going to stay sane.'

'What's it this time?'

'That bloody editor thinks I'm going too far.'

'Outrageous!' I tutted. 'What was it he objected to this time?'

'Oh, you can laugh, but women are still treated abominably. How many women editors can you name?'

'All right, Janine. I'm on your side. Calm down.'

Janine White has been my next-door neighbour, on-off lover and constant source of frustration for over a year. She's divorced and has two children and from my point of view would make an ideal partner. The trouble is she doesn't see it that way. Since being deserted by her husband Henry Talbot, father of Jenny and Lloyd, she's maintained a front of mistrustfulness towards the whole male sex.

'Look, love, tell me what he's done and I'll go down there and smash his face in,' I offered.

It was the wrong thing to say.

'Hmmph! Typical,' she snorted.

'Janine, you know what I mean. I'm tired of just being your accidental next-door neighbour and part-time mother's helper. You can chuck up the job at the paper any time you like and come and work with me.'

'Thanks a bunch! Exchange one dominant male for another. At least on the paper I have my readers to back me.'

'I wouldn't count on them.'

'They're more reliable than the whim of some testosterone-soaked man.'

'You'd be a full and equal partner with me, biochemistry notwithstanding. No decision made without your consent.'

For a moment I thought she was considering the idea but she tossed her head back and swept the hair off her forehead. She looked round the room, taking in Celeste's empty desk. Not for the first time I admired my partner's style. If you wrote down her description it would come out all wrong. Janine adds up to a lot more than the sum of a few ordinary characteristics. Fair enough, she's of average height, with a rather full figure, mousy brown hair, and blue eyes. Marks & Spencer's could probably use her as a template for a million outfits. But that's not her, at least to me it's not. Whatever the opposite of nondescript is, that's Janine. You'd pick her out among ten thousand. She radiates a certain wavelength of energy that's entirely her own. She moves quickly. She doesn't accept situations. Patience on a monument, smiling at grief, she is not.

'Where's the coffee?' she barked.

I nodded towards the back room and she strode in.

10

A second later she was back. Her eyes were glittering. They seemed to be generating enough electricity for a small lightning bolt.

'What's going on?' she asked coldly.

'Nothing's *going on*.'

'Where's Celeste, and why is that woman asleep on your sofa?'

'Celeste's gone walkabout, and as for the woman your guess is as good as mine.'

'Don't play games with me, Dave. We all know what your favourite recreation is.'

'Oh, what is it?'

'Who is she?' This was delivered in a rising tone.

'I don't know. It's a long story . . . I found her at Tarn Golf Club. Some man was going to beat her up and they wouldn't let her back into the club because she was drunk.'

'So you just happened to bring her here,' she said in a slightly softer voice. 'God! Dave, I never know whether to fall for what you say or punch your lights out. You're the most manipulative pig I've ever met. You're just saying that about the man wanting to beat her up to get on the best side of me.'

'I'm not, honest,' I said, putting my hands up in surrender.

'You're not honest, that's true.'

'When have I ever lied?'

'Just now when you said we were accidental neighbours. There was no accident involved.'

'I had nothing to do with Bob Lane buying that lease and giving it to you.'

'Yes, and male chauvinist pigs can fly.'

'No,' I said firmly. 'How many times have I got to tell you that was Bob's clumsy attempt at matchmaking? I had nothing to do with it. He's like you. He thinks I've only to look at a woman and she goes weak at the knees.'

The very faintest, wraith-like shadow of a smile crossed her face at this. Her expression was unreadable. Did she believe me? Only time would tell.

She shook her head and then looked at her watch. 'My break's almost over. I'll have to return to the fray,' she muttered. 'I'd thought I'd call in for a cup of coffee and a few

11

words of comfort from the only man in Manchester who's even been halfway to treating me like a human being since I got here, but what do I find when I arrive? He's entertaining some floozy in the back room.' She started for the door.

'Whoa, lady!' I said. 'You're stretching things a bit there. More than a spot of the old hyperbole. Is that what's frayed your editor's nerves?'

'Stay out of my face, Dave.'

'Tell me why you've suddenly developed an aversion for the whole male citizenry of Greater Manchester.'

'Greater Macho-chester, you mean.'

'Rubbish! We're all kind and gentle and touchy-feely up here. It's you metropolitan types who're hard as nails.'

'Just remind me. How many people who have got in your way have ended up dead?'

'How many times have I told you? It was pure self-defence in those cases.'

'But they're just as dead, aren't they?'

'I didn't murder anyone.'

'So you said. Listen, Dave, I'm thinking of making a move. There've been feelers from a paper in London.'

'A national?' I had a sinking feeling as I said the words. I'd always dreaded that Janine was bound for higher things.

'I don't really want to go into it now, Dave. I'm thinking things over.'

'At least let me walk back to the office with you, if you don't think it will ruin your image to be seen with a man.'

'Come on then, killer,' she said in a more reasonable way. 'You can tell me just who that woman is. She's worth a quid or two by the look of the rags on her back.'

'If you know that, you know as much about her as I do,' I muttered, following her out into the street.

3

After I'd dropped Janine at her office on Deansgate my mind reverted to its customary fallow state. For want of anything better to do I decided to find out what I could about the mystery woman. I patted my pockets: no mobile. I was too impatient to wait until I returned to the office, and anyway it might be difficult to make enquiries if the woman was still snoring noisily on my sofa, so I dialled Clyde Harrow from a public phone box near the John Rylands library.

This turned out to be a bad plan. I hadn't reckoned on the amount of time it would take me to persuade one of the TV big shot's assistants to put me through to the famous little man.

'We can't just connect anyone,' she whined in a nasal South London accent.

'Dave Cunane, tell him it's Dave Cunane. He'll speak to me,' I said more confidently than I felt. I was one of the people that Harrow needed protection from, though his assistant wasn't likely to know that. Good old Clyde, the bright-as-a-button TV newshound, had crossed my path more than once. He found it hard to understand the meaning of the word 'private' in connection with the word 'detective'. Clyde thought that whatever I uncovered should belong to him and the whole wide world. Still, we maintained an arm's length friendship on the basis that I occasionally passed him useful tips while in return he kept my name out of the news.

After an interminable wait the rumbling, fruity tones of the TV journalist filled my ear. 'Clyde, Dave Cunane here,' I said.

'Dave Cunane, do I know anyone of that name?' he boomed crustily. 'This had better be good. I'm preparing an interview with unmarried mother-of-octuplets Mandy Mawson and her brood.' I could hear the squalling of infants in the background

13

as the latest products of fertility technology aired their lungs.

'That's a bit old hat, isn't it, Clyde?'

'Perhaps you can come up with something better, what's your name?'

'Oh, come on, Clyde.'

'Am I speaking to *the* Dave Cunane? The crapulous curber of the criminal classes? The cape-less crusader of amateur crime prevention? The gentleman, and I use the term figuratively, who, when last we met, cruelly sped my egress from his premises with a kick from his size-ten detective's pampooties? I'm not sure that I want to speak to that person.'

'Now Clyde, don't get carried away,' I warned. Failed actor, former sports reporter and now successful TV 'feature' presenter, Clyde was frequently swept to giddy heights by his own grandiloquence. 'You've had your fun, but I have a serious question for you. Do you know anyone called Charles Carlyle?'

What they call a significant pause ensued. I could hear Harrow's adenoidal breathing in my earpiece. A very quick brain was making some rapid calculations.

'"Carlyle", the youth says. How could I fail to be familiar with the name Carlyle? How could you, unless deep in your usual mire of clotted ignorance? The infernal family have a not inconsiderable interest in the company that employs me.'

'Oh, those Carlyles,' I muttered.

'Am I to take it that Charles Carlyle has come to your attention in some less than creditable context? He could hardly be one of your social acquaintances.'

'You could put it that way,' I murmured.

'Speak on, worthy Cunane, or forever hold your peace. All is forgiven 'twixt thee and me.'

'I was out at Tarn Golf Club . . .'

'And what, pray, could have lured a benighted denizen of the inner city such as yourself to such exalted quarters?'

'I was on a job . . .'

'Ah, a job? A job involving the Carlyle family? The capitalist cabal who've closed a thousand companies?'

'Don't exaggerate, Clyde.'

14

'Exaggerate! Tell that to any of the thousands they've done out of a job.'

'My job needn't concern you . . .'

'Indeed? We shall see . . .'

'Yes, m'lud, I was in the car park going about my lawful occasions when I saw this big lubber setting up to knock nine bells out of a good-looking redhead.'

'And being Dave Cunane, you intervened, presumably on the side of the good looker?'

'Not quite, but I suppose that's approximately what happened.' I briefly filled him in on the events that took place in the car park, and the car chase that followed.

'Tell me, good Dave, where is this unfortunate Titianesque wench now?'

'It wasn't her I was asking about.'

'Where is she, Dave?'

'She's in my office, sleeping off a drinking bout.'

'Hah! Inimitable! I take it that the aforementioned "big lubber" identified himself as Charles Carlyle?'

'Yes.'

'Describe him and the fallen female – worse for drink, you say?'

I described the pair.

'Charlie Carlyle and his missus to the life! Is she still at your office?'

'Yes.'

'Any visible bruises?'

'Not that I've seen.'

'Come, come, Dave. Surely, by now, you've managed to persuade Mrs Carlyle to reveal herself like Venus rising from the Cypriot foam?'

'I told you, the woman's drunk!'

'I wouldn't expect that to stop you, but a scruple's a scruple! They'll be the downfall of you yet, those scruples. Hold her at your office. Detain her, ply her with more ardent liquors, use whatever feeble stratagems nature has equipped you for, but keep her there until I arrive.'

Harrow hung up. Pulsating with horror about what I'd done, I hurried towards my office.

15

4

To my immense relief my unwelcome visitor was gone when I returned and Celeste was back at her post. She wasn't on the phone to her friends for once but was buffing her fingernails instead, boredom oozing from every pore.

'Where is she?' I snapped.

'Who, ba-aass?' Celeste drawled, extracting a wad of gum from her mouth and positioning it beside her word processor. Celeste, a pretty black girl from Old Trafford, knows to within a millimetre just how far she can test my patience.

I searched her opaque but perfect features for the hundredth time, looking for a clue as to whether she was sending me up. For the hundredth time I decided that with Celeste, what you see is what you get.

'The woman . . . the woman in the back room. Where is she?'

'No *wo-man* here when I came in, boss. No, but you left the outside door unlocked.'

'Oh, hell! She must have let herself out.'

Irritation mingled with relief. I could have done with an explanation, and a full-time secretary would have been nice too.

'Where were you?' I asked.

When it comes to enigmatic smiles Celeste makes the Mona Lisa look like an amateur. The smile turned into a scornful grin.

'You told me to take my lunch late . . . I was waiting for you to get back, but when you didn't arrive I decided to go out. I'm entitled to my lunch, you know.'

'Sorry,' I muttered, 'but didn't you even catch a glimpse?'

'No,' she said and then turned to her desk. Considering the number of private phone calls she got through in a day, her

16

desk top gave a good imitation of a scene of hard labour: bits of paper and files were scattered everywhere, and little notes were stuck to various surfaces. I was about to leave when Celeste swivelled round. 'Oh, there is this.'

She passed me a crumpled sheet of copier paper. There was a message scrawled on it in red biro:

'Thanks for rescuing me but I decided I'd better not wait around. I heard what your partner said. Are you really a killer? It sounds interesting. I know one or two people I could use your services on. Anyway, thanks again, MK.'

MK, not MC, not Mrs Carlyle.

I allowed myself to breathe a sigh of relief. Harrow would find that he was barking up the wrong gum tree and I wouldn't need my size tens to eject him this time.

I went through to my office and read MK's note again. One trouble was immediately replaced by another. God! My father and his retired police friends say I'm a stirrer, a troublemaker. It's not true. I don't need to look for trouble, it finds me without any assistance. Now this female had me down as a potential hit man, thanks to Janine and her big mouth. I could do without this. The business was at last showing signs of taking off. I'd even started subcontracting. I don't know whether this was down to a better location for the office, just off South King Street, or that I'd become more widely known, but the work hadn't stopped rolling in.

Publicity from Clyde Harrow was bad enough but the last thing I needed was this 'MK' bragging to her boozing pals, and drunks always have pals, that she knew a bona-fide hit man. What a sickener! The truth was that there were one or two other little problems that had been souring my mood lately. Janine was one. I could see a future where Janine and I settled down together. All right, got ourselves a house and a mortgage in Cheadle or Handforth or any of the other southern dormitories, if you like. What's so terrible about that? *'Semi-detached, suburban Mr Jones'*, there are tens of thousands of them. Why not me?

Circumstance was twining us together like the bindweed holding up an old fence. I'd had fifteen years on my own since my wife died. Now Janine was calmly announcing that she

17

was thinking of moving back to London. Great!

My other big problem was the old trouble – my parent Paddy Cunane, former pride of the Manchester CID. Recently he'd got a bee in his bonnet about the Lowry painting that I own. I was given the picture by Dee Elsworth, mother of twins that she assured me were mine. The Lowry had been hanging in Paddy's living room for six years when he happened to read that a smaller Lowry than mine, owned by some private school, had been sold for a six-figure sum.

He came over all funny after that. Where did I get it? Did the person who gave it me know its value? Shouldn't I give it back? Should we sell it and put the money into a more secure business than private detection – a McDonald's franchise, for instance? I couldn't think of anything worse. I'd rather give the picture to an art gallery. It might have been better if Dee had never given me the Lowry in the first place, but she knew I'd admired it and as I'd agreed never to see the children I'd casually fathered she must have thought the sight of the painting would be some consolation. It was only now with Janine on the point of disappearing that I was discovering that a six-figure sum is no compensation for never seeing your own children, no compensation at all.

Paddy was capable of picking away every trace of flesh from the Lowry issue until the bare bone of 'fact' was left. And what was that? That two killers, both professionals, had been in the process of raping Dee, prior to arranging my own permanent exit, when I terminated their tricks. They now lay deeply buried at the bottom of Dee's garden.

A joke, you think?

How often have I wished it was and how often have I regretted telling Janine?

These gloomy speculations were suddenly ended by a crash in the outer office. It sounded as if ram raiders were going for the petty cash. I dashed out of my room. I was hardly through the door when someone grabbed me by the throat. Before I could do anything my assailant had my arms up my back and was jerking me towards the floor. I just had time to get a glimpse of a terrified Celeste crouching in the corner with her desk tipped up in front of her. Then my descending body met

18

my attacker's ascending knee and the only sensation I had for the next few minutes was pain and sickness. Then everything went dark . . .

When I came round Celeste was putting papers back on her desk, restored to its usual place, and three oversized individuals were standing over me. I goggled at them stupidly for a moment before light dawned. One of them was Charles Carlyle.

'Celeste, get the police,' I managed to wheeze.

'I am the police,' was the classic reply from a man who was by far the oldest of the trio. His head was crowned by a mass of carefully tended grey curls, the coiffeured locks adding a good two inches to his height. He shoved his face right into mine. His breath smelled of whisky, expensive whisky too. Why I should have been able to grasp such a detail at a moment of crisis I don't know, but I did.

'Prove it, Whisky-breath,' I snarled.

He held a warrant card three inches from the end of my nose. Detective Sergeant Tony Hefflin was the name. It rang a bell.

'I see you've heard of me,' he said.

'Nothing good.'

At this the man who'd dished out the physical stuff, a squat individual with the word minder written all over his tightly stretched suit, leaned forward, grabbed my hair and almost jerked my head from my shoulders.

'That'll be enough,' Hefflin said, laying a hand on his sleeve. 'I'm sure Mr Cunane's already got the message.'

'And what might that be?' I gasped.

'Don't be cheeky or you'll get another smack,' the minder growled. He released me with a painful shove. Primitive rage stirred but I kept a grip. This guy would keep for another time.

'We're looking for this gentleman's wife,' Hefflin said in a silky voice, nodding at Carlyle.

'What makes you think he's a gentleman?' I asked. It didn't come out quite as defiantly as it was intended to. I was still gasping for breath.

The minder leaned forward again.

'Careful, Cunane,' Hefflin cautioned. 'I've heard all about

19

your little ways. You were seen loading her into your car. The stewards at Tarn Golf Club got your registration number.'

'Since when has giving an assault victim a lift been police business?'

'Abduction's police business.'

'So's violent assault! Carlyle's a dab hand at that. I could hardly leave the woman lying face down in the mud or hand her over when he started flashing his shotgun.'

Hefflin turned to Carlyle and raised his eyebrows slightly. Perhaps he hadn't been told the reason for my Sir Galahad routine. The minder grabbed me by the shoulders and hauled me to my feet without strain. Presumably he was going to give me another dose of correction but Hefflin stopped him.

'That's enough of that, Olley,' he snapped. 'I told you that I don't need any rough stuff to throw a scare into a no-hoper like Cunane.'

The shaven-headed monolith turned to Hefflin and narrowed his eyes as if weighing up whether it was worth his while to give Hefflin a smack. He looked like a pit bull terrier that had partially assumed human form. The colouring was identical: dark stubble on head and chin, dead white skin with contrasting pink at the mouth, eyes and ears.

'That's all right, Lou,' Carlyle intervened. 'Wait outside, I'll be fine.'

'If you're sure, Mr Carlyle,' the minder muttered doubtfully.

'I'm sure,' Carlyle said.

Lou Olley was so broad across the shoulders that he had to go sideways through the office door into the street. He stood in front of the entrance with his back to us.

'Sorry about that, Cunane,' Carlyle said with a snide grin at Hefflin. 'Lou sometimes takes an exaggerated view of the threats I face.'

'That's OK. Smash up my office, terrify my secretary and knock me unconscious any time you like. Happy to oblige the gentry.'

'Cut that out, Cunane,' Hefflin said. 'You've got some questions to answer. Why were you in that car park if you weren't there to snatch Mrs Carlyle?'

'None of your business.'

'It's my business if some rival of Mr Carlyle has paid you to pressure him.'

'I don't do things like that.'

'Pull the other one, Cunane. What's a notorious Manchester private detective doing at the Tarn Pro-Am Tournament? You were there to cause trouble.'

'So private detectives aren't allowed to like golf?'

'Why were you there? Did Marti arrange it with you?'

'Marti who?'

Hefflin stepped back and looked at me speculatively. His withered features and bouffant hair had a sinister aspect, no doubt intentionally. Then he walked into my private office and riffled through the papers on my desk. He picked up the telephone notepad and examined it closely, holding it obliquely to the light. I felt a sharp stab of panic until I remembered that I hadn't written down a word about the Insull Perriss job, not even his name. Hefflin's inspection was brief but thorough.

'I don't think he knows anything,' he said to Carlyle when he came out. Just who was this Carlyle who had policemen to run his errands and what were they worried about me knowing? I felt as if I was in danger of getting my delicate bits caught in the moving parts of a very large machine.

Carlyle shoved his face up to mine. It added emphasis if not intimacy. I could see the individual black hairs in his nose. There was a scorched red look to his nostrils that meant only one thing.

I shoved him back.

He didn't like it. The furrows on his brow became more furrowed. He straightened his suit and appeared to be thinking. Then he grinned at me. I call it a grin but I imagine a hyena that's just spotted dinner goes through similar facial contortions. He'd finally remembered how to act like a tough guy.

'Listen, bum fluff,' he said. With his public school elocution it sounded like a grotesque joke.

'*Bam flaff,* what's that?' I mimicked.

He didn't like that either. All the loose flesh on his face

21

seemed to gather into one big crease.

'You're nothing to me – got that?' he said in strained tones. 'You shoved your face in where it wasn't wanted.'

'No, I didn't. You were making an arsehole of yourself. Somebody had to do something.'

He tried to grab my shirt front but I pushed him away again. He was a big man but he didn't seem well co-ordinated. Perhaps there'd been too much of the white powder. His dark eyes were glistening.

'If you don't tell me where my wife is right now, I'll . . .'

'Get your steroidal maniac in to sort me, will you? I'm trembling. You listen to me, *bam flaff*! I've no idea where your wife is, but she's well rid of you.'

'I'll pay you well,' he said, switching tack and pulling out a well stuffed wallet. 'She might be in danger.'

'The only danger that woman was in, was from you,' I said pushing his hand away. 'Listen, Sergeant, why don't you ask round at the old club house? Your playmate here was about to knock nine bells out of his lady when . . .'

'You put your oar in,' Hefflin said with a cynical smile on his face. 'You listen, Cunane. I *have* asked around in Tarn, and if you think anyone there is going to corroborate the word of a tuppenny ha'penny private detective against a respected citizen like Mr Carlyle you couldn't be more wrong.'

'I should have known better than to think it, but you might like to enquire with your traffic colleagues about an accident at the M56 Tarn exit caused by a lunatic in a Porsche.'

For a second I thought I saw a faint trace of a blush on Carlyle's waxy features. It may have been a trick of the light. Anyway, he pulled a wad of fifty pound notes out of his wallet and tried to give me some. I pushed him away again.

'Come away, Mr Carlyle, your charity's wasted on him,' Hefflin advised. 'He's pig-headed.'

'Yeah, Sergeant Porker, you'd know about that,' I growled.

Hefflin shrugged, my words water off a duck's back. Laying a hand on his client's shoulder, he started to lead him out, but before he reached the door Carlyle had second thoughts. He turned and laid a couple of notes on Celeste's desk.

'Sorry for the inconvenience, miss,' he muttered.

I strode over, picked up the notes and flung them into the street after him. As a gesture it wasn't very effective. You can't throw paper money with much force. The notes fluttered to the pavement. Carlyle and Hefflin didn't even look round. Lou Olley favoured me with a look of contempt and then fell into step behind his master. I intended my next move to be a scornful turn of the heel and a quick stalk to the inner room to lick my wounds, but I was pushed to one side by Celeste who knelt down to pick up the cash.

'If you can afford to throw money in the street, I can't,' she said, folding the notes into her purse.

At the exact moment that my attackers rounded the corner the unmistakable shape of a breathless and red-faced Clyde Harrow appeared on the other side of the street. The sun gleamed on his bald head as he turned to clock my departing visitors and the same bright light illuminated a crafty and eager expression on his round face. He stepped towards the kerb as if to follow the trio but then thought better of it. Spotting me, he raised his arm and sprinted towards me, achieving a surprising speed for a man of his bulk. I stumbled inside and tried to put the latch on.

5

'Cunane! Cunane, let me in,' Harrow bleated, pounding the glass door of Pimpernel Investigations with his pudgy fists.

'Why? Will you huff and puff and blow my house down?' I mocked.

'You called me,' he shouted and then slammed his shoulder against the door. Physical strength isn't really Clyde's scene but the sheer bulk of the man set the whole front of the building shuddering.

As he poised himself for another charge I considered the situation. 'Things can only get worse,' I thought as I studied the determined expression on the fat man's face. As usual he was clad in garish TV celeb clothes; this time a bright yellow jacket with a clashing red tie. He looked more like a beef-burger vendor than a serious newsmonger, but there was nothing comical about the way he was shaping to ram my door.

'Cunane, you summoned me. Let me in,' he blustered.

'If you've smashed the lock you can pay for it,' I said, slowly opening the door.

'Where is she?' he demanded, pushing past me and opening the door of the inner office.

'It wasn't Mrs Carlyle. It was someone with the initials MK,' I happily informed him.

'MK, MK? That is Mrs Carlyle, Marti King that was. Where is she? Wasn't Carlyle himself here a moment ago? Have you tamely handed the woman over before I've had a chance to interview her?'

'I haven't handed anyone over. She's gone.'

'Dunderhead! I told you to hang onto her.'

'She's gone. End of story! Off you go, Clyde.'

24

'Not so fast, my young friend. I get the glimmerings of a news item there.'

'You're mad. Please go.'

'Not until you tell me why you handed Marti over. Did the usual thirty pieces of silver change hands?'

'I didn't betray anyone. She'd gone before her husband arrived.'

'And her departure had nothing to do with her spouse's arrival? Do you expect me to believe that? How did Charles Carlyle know where to come if you didn't tell him?'

'It may have something to do with the fact that one of the men you saw with him was a policeman who traced my registration number. The other was Carlyle's minder.'

'A policeman? Who?'

'Detective Sergeant Tony Hefflin.'

'Him! Why, the man's already under investigation for corruption. I knew there was a story here but you've blown it by letting the woman go.'

'Can you get this into that fat head of yours? She went of her own accord. Look, you must know I wouldn't sell someone out.'

He studied me closely with those intelligent eyes of his.

'There *is* a story here. I can smell it. I can almost touch it,' he said. 'Damn you, Cunane. Or should I say Pimpernel?'

'Why don't you come through into my room and then we can talk this through?' I suggested.

Harrow looked round the office with a disdainful expression on his chubby features. I began to feel guilty that he'd been cheated out of a story.

Celeste caught his eye. 'Shall I bring coffee?' she asked.

'Coffee!' Clyde boomed as if she'd suggested rat poison. 'The young master will have to come up with a better story and a better drink if he's going to mollify me.'

With that he swaggered into my inner room and parked his considerable frame in the most comfortable chair, my chair.

'What's been going on here?' he demanded, pointing to the papers scattered all over the desk and floor.

'Just like you, Mr Hefflin and Mr Olley were anxious to find out more about my non-existent involvement with Mrs

Carlyle. They didn't try blackmail. Their methods were more direct.'

'Hmmph! Olley, you say – he's a jumped up night-club bouncer with ideas above his station. Believe me, Pimpo-boy, if Hefflin and Olley were here together then you *are* involved.'

I groaned and poured a couple of glasses of Bell's whisky.

'A pedestrian choice, but that's to be expected,' Clyde said sniffily when he saw the label. 'I suppose it's the best you've got.' He took a long pull at his glass and then fished out his mobile and stood down the camera crew that was on its way. Listening to this, I took a drink from my own glass and began to feel better at once.

'I don't know how often I've told those lazy sods to be ready at a moment's notice,' Clyde confided. 'Confrontation, that's what I wanted. The stuff of television. Ah, if only I could have had a crew here while you and Olley and Hefflin were battling it out over the recumbent form of the lovely Marti.'

'Clyde, it wasn't like that,' I muttered, but I might as well have saved my breath.

'It wasn't? With a little judicious editing it could have been,' he sighed. 'Anyway, it's no good you saying you aren't involved. You must have had speech if not full congress with Mrs Carlyle, or how else could you have known that her initials were MK?'

'She left me a note, stupid.'

'Stupid am I, Pimpo-boy? A look-see, if you please.'

'No, why should I?' I snapped angrily.

'Because, dear boy, if you don't I shall persuade my producer to run a little piece about cowboy private detectives running wild. Remember the footage we have of you brawling outside the Crown Court? You could enjoy a brief moment of national fame, or will it be infamy?'

'They were insurance fraudsters angry that I'd uncovered their scam. You promised to scrap that material. The lawyers . . .'

'Ah, the lawyers, Dave. The very devil, aren't they? What was it Jack Cade said? "First thing we do, let's kill all the lawyers." That was during the Peasant's Revolt, as I expect someone of your ilk would know. Yes, we promised *your*

26

lawyers that we wouldn't show that stuff, but *our* lawyers insisted that we hang onto it.'

'You don't care about anything or anybody, do you?' I said, handing over the scrap of paper Marti had left.

'Care? Why, you puppy with your calf-licked hair, I care. I care for Clyde Harrow. I care for my six ex-wives. I care for the fruits of my loins, too numerous to enumerate. I care for my ever adoring public always eager for my latest story . . .'

'You care all right! You care about getting some dirt about the Carlyles that you can use to fix your fat arse even more firmly in the saddle down at that TV company you infest.'

'Why, Dave!' he roared in mock surprise. 'Now you're talking like a real man and not like a day-old kitten mewling for its mother.'

He snatched up the note and read it and then reread it.

'David, my dear, dear lad, most rare pimpernel,' he said in reverential tones, 'I think we have the makings of a major news item here.' His eyes were gleaming like fog lamps. 'Suppose we were to offer you a considerable fee, or more realistically, an inducement such as destruction of all recorded material we have on you, would you be willing to pose as a killer as Marti suggests?'

I reached for the whisky again. As was normal in a Clyde Harrow interview, things were not going according to plan, at least not to my plan.

'Clyde,' I said, trying to frame my words with utmost care. 'You know and I know that the remark about me being a killer was intended as a joke. Mrs Carlyle may have misheard something, some little hyperbolic remark that Janine hurled at me in the course of an argument.'

'Hyperbolic remark! I like that, Dave. It's good coming from you, definitely A-minus! I can see that you're improving under my tuition, but it's so interesting that you should mention that fragrant scribe, Ms White. I was wondering what part she played in all these events.'

'Janine played no part at all, Clyde, and don't look at me like that.'

His fat features were folded into a libidinous grin. I hated the thought of him mentally licking his lips over Janine.

27

'I shall look how I please, young master. Janine White's a wonderful, wonderful woman who deserves only the very best out of life.' A seraphic smile played on his face and his eyes went up into his head.

'I know what you're thinking,' I spluttered angrily.

'All this and telepathic too!' Clyde taunted. My toes itched for contact with his rear end but I struggled for restraint.

'I know that there's currently a vacancy in your marital bed.'

'Ah! Dave, now you're almost coming close to sarcasm. More of this and my ears will start to burn.'

'Tell me about the Carlyles,' I said desperately. 'That was why I was insane enough to phone you in the first place.'

'Capitalist raptors! What more can I say? They have more business interests than a pig has rashers. Surely you've heard of the rugby league team they own. The patriarch, Brandon Carlyle, is on the main board at Alhambra TV and if ever there was an unacceptable face of the market economy, he is it!'

'Rugby league – you mean the Pendlebury Piledrivers?'

'The same. Dear, rich Brandon bought them in a rare fit of generosity, or more precisely when he thought rugby league was going to run at a profit. Since then he's put so little money into the club that they're facing relegation. They don't even have a single Aussie in their line-up. The word is that Brandon hopes to show a profit by selling their ground to a supermarket chain. That would be typical of his lust for lucre. I suffer from it every day in my work.'

'But where does Charles fit in? And Marti?'

'Questions, questions. Are you too lazy to do your own research? I know I'm supposed to be the one who finds things out on behalf of the public, but that's another of the things that Brandon Carlyle wants to put a stop to . . .'

'He wants to shut you down?'

'He does indeed, the insufferable ape! If he had his way the local news would be a mere slogan-trading session wedged between jingles advertising his companies. This upstart former ale-pourer and tavern keeper's son fondly imagines that he and his pack of bespoke-tailored marketing freaks

28

know how to run a TV company. With that viper, if you're not gaining you're failing.'

'Ale-pourer? Tavern keeper's son?'

'He was brought up in a pub.'

'And that debars him from running a TV company?'

'So sorry, Pimpo-boy! I forgot your own lowly origins. All Brandon Carlyle possesses is the ability to juggle the figures on a balance sheet so that they come out in his favour, and he's not even very bright at that. He employs a veritable posse of hangers-onto get all the sums right.'

'All right, so he's a schmuck, but what about the son?'

'That weak-willed brat!'

'He didn't look very weak willed when I saw him.'

'Charles is the eldest of five sons and of the bunch he is the one I prefer, which isn't saying that I like him. The other four are positively pre-human, almost cannibalistic, in their taste for the flesh of anyone who dares to raise cultural issues. There are five daughters too – Brandon likes to do things on a grand scale. Philistines, the lot of them!'

'Clyde, this is very interesting, but why isn't all this stuff more widely known?'

'Dear lad, your innocence warms my withered old heart. Who do you think controls the news media?'

'Oh.'

'The facts are known among the cognoscenti such as myself, but Brandon has always shown a feline grace when it comes to avoiding publicity. He has his cats'-paws to do his bidding. Few of his misdeeds are given a public airing. The rugby team is an uncharacteristic failure.'

'So why was Charles Carlyle battering his wife in a public place?'

'Why indeed? Why do you imagine that I came running to this hovel if not to find that out? I intended to use the material to crack open the carapace of lies that the Carlyle family have surrounded themselves with.'

'In the public interest or the Clyde Harrow interest?'

'How are they separate?'

'Right, but there must be a reason for the battering and then the crazy car chase. Carlyle must have got Hefflin and Olley on the job almost as soon as the missus managed to escape from him.'

'That, dear boy, is precisely what I came round here to find out. Just as Samson used the jawbone of a donkey to slay a thousand Philistines I intended to use you to put a spoke in Brandon Carlyle's wheel.'

'Thanks very much, Clyde. But while you're comparing yourself with Samson, don't forget what happened to him when he met Delilah.'

'Believe me, young man, I have already lost my locks in the service of my art but I will gladly immolate myself beneath the pillars of a temple if that is the price of victory over the Carlyle empire.'

6

In the following weeks the fat man's crack about me being too lazy to do my own research bored its way through my defences like a teredo worm gnawing at a ship's timbers. Expansion of the firm meant that I was spending more of my time directing the operations of others than at the coal face. So, I made an effort to find out what I could about the 'Carlyle Empire'. It turned out that Clyde was exaggerating as usual. I spent several mind-numbing sessions in the Central Reference Library scanning the microfilmed financial pages. There were occasional mentions of Brandon Carlyle and his part in various boardroom battles and takeovers, but I could find nothing that was either creditable or discreditable – certainly nothing that would warrant slaying with the jawbone of a donkey or even a hostile profile in the press. A union leader moaned that Carlyle had put more men on the dole queue than Margaret Thatcher, but that was about it as far as criticism went. The only current stuff about the mogul concerned his involvement with the Pendlebury Piledrivers, which was exciting the sports writers, but then rugby league is very much a minority interest.

There was some information on Tony Hefflin, however. Shortly after his visit to me he was retired from the Force on health grounds – while under investigation.

That was it. I left it there, buried but not forgotten.

It all came back to me one Saturday evening when I was in a Manchester restaurant with my parents and Janine.

We were in a small French place just off Albert Square adjacent to Bootle Street police HQ, Paddy's old stamping ground.

31

'It was a hard world in those days . . .'

'We have moved on since the Middle Ages, you know,' Janine countered, looking up from her langoustines and squaring her jaw at the old copper. 'Half the convictions were secured by phoney evidence with a nudge and a funny handshake for the judge.'

Paddy laughed. 'Ninety-nine point nine per cent of the blackguards we nailed richly deserved it.'

My mother, Eileen, hastened to keep the peace. 'Do you mind not talking shop?'

'Yes, love,' Paddy said obediently.

Just then the calm of the restaurant was shattered by a penetrating noise. It was that unmistakable, eldritch laugh that I'd heard at Tarn – the loud jollity followed by the noisy blocked drain. Startled diners lowered knives and forks and scanned the room for the source. The sudden avalanche of sound had come from a table in the corner, which seated three women. One, with her back to me, had red hair.

'Some people,' Janine muttered, whether at the laughter or at Paddy's remark wasn't clear. She looked over at the three in the corner but made no further comment. She obviously didn't recognise the female she'd last seen sprawled over the sofa in my private office. I did. It was definitely Marti. I felt a certain interest – it's not every day that you rescue someone. I couldn't help glancing over.

A few moments later, though, I was concentrating on a piece of camembert when the laugher laid her hand on my shoulder.

'Excuse me,' she said, 'but I couldn't go without speaking. You're the man who helped me that day at Tarn, aren't you? The detective agency? It wasn't one of my better days.'

I turned and looked up into startlingly green eyes, memory coming into sharp focus. She smiled warmly at me. There wasn't the faintest trace of embarrassment.

'That's right,' I said hastily, trying to push my chair back and stand up.

Before I could move she swiftly bent forward and kissed me on the cheek.

'Thanks for everything. You were wonderful. My husband

32

and his family have everyone at Tarn trained to look the other way when they kick over the traces.'

Then she was gone, leaving only a faint trace of expensive perfume to tell anyone that she'd ever been there.

'What was that about?' Janine demanded emphatically, as I awkwardly reseated myself.

'You know. I told you . . . the woman at Tarn that day you had the quarrel with your editor over advocating mass chemical castration.'

'That floozy! And you still don't know who she is. I'll ask the waiter.'

'That won't be necessary,' Paddy said. 'I know exactly who she is. In fact I can tell you a good part of her life story.'

Looking at Janine's angry face I decided that a show of ignorance was the best card to play.

'Go on then,' Janine urged.

'You're not involved with the woman in any way, are you, David?' Paddy asked with his usual full-bored bluntness. Here we were, happy family together, and he was asking me if I was having it off with another woman. With a family like mine who needs enemies?

'I've been through all this with Janine. The only time I've ever laid eyes on her was when I saved her from a flop into the mud at Tarn Golf Club. The only thing I didn't tell you, Janine, was that when I arrived back at the office that afternoon she'd gone but the grieving husband came looking for her, with a copper and a minder in tow.'

'That sounds about right for the Carlyles,' Paddy murmured. 'They never let go of any of their possessions without a struggle.'

'Carlyles?' Janine echoed. 'Not *the* Carlyles? The Cheshire bigwigs?'

'The same,' Paddy growled, 'and you'd both be well advised to steer clear of the lot of them.'

'Tell all!' she ordered.

'She's Vince King's kid.'

Janine and I must have looked blank.

'Vince King, you know – the safe-cracker and murderer.'

Still nothing registered with either of us.

33

'Such is fame,' Paddy said in exasperation. 'King was one of the worst villains we ever had on this patch. Mind you, he operated all over the country. It didn't matter where it was, if a skilful safe-cracking went down, his name was always at the top of the list of five or six possibles. Most of the early petermen were Geordies who learned how to handle gelignite in the pits. King learned in the army, but he came from a crime family. Nobody's ever worked out exactly how he pulled off some of the jobs he was involved in, but there was nothing he couldn't open.'

At this point Paddy exhaled through clenched teeth as if reliving a painful experience.

'Don't say any more,' Eileen counselled. 'You know it's bad for your blood pressure.'

'Oh, to hell with that. These two will only ferret it out anyway. King's career came to an abrupt end when he was found unconscious outside a GPO facility down by the old Pomona Docks in Salford. There were two corpses inside the building, in the security vault: one his accomplice, Musgrave, and the other a policeman, Detective Constable Fred Fullalove. Naturally King swore blind that he'd been fitted up. Don't they all? It was true that he hadn't used violence before, but there was his military experience to tell against him.'

'What military experience?' Janine asked, almost in a whisper.

'He'd been in the SAS, although back in those days the regiment wasn't so widely known as it is now. At the trial the prosecution was able to establish that he'd had extensive military experience, and that helped to tip the balance against him.'

'Were you involved in the case?' I asked.

'Not that particular one – it was in Salford, and I was head of CID here in the city of Manchester itself. Mick Jones, the man who arrested King, had worked for me . . .'

'Stop it!' Eileen said firmly. 'I'm not going through all that again . . . sleepless nights and bad-tempered days.'

'Sorry,' Janine said, 'am I missing something?'

'What you're missing is that Mick Jones was certainly the most bent copper to serve in Manchester. He was the original so-called "one bad apple in the barrel",' Eileen said sharply, putting her arm round Paddy. 'Though if you ask me there were some barrels that only had one good apple. My dear silly husband here almost worked himself into an early grave trying to convict Jones, and what was the result? The high-ups let Jones slip off to Marbella to enjoy his pension and his ill-gotten gains. He'd never have managed it without help from friends in high places.'

'You don't know that,' Paddy said.

'I know that every time you got in sight of finding the evidence people were tipped off and warned to keep their mouths shut. Why, I had Archie Sinclair practically weeping in frustration all over my kitchen, and you know how tight-lipped he is.'

'Sinclair? The current Assistant Chief Constable?' Janine asked, opening her eyes wide.

My parents nodded but didn't speak. They both seemed to feel that they'd said too much.

'Oh, you can't clam up now,' Janine moaned, but they did.

It was five minutes later when he was sipping a glass of brandy that Paddy opened up again.

'When King was locked up it turned out that he had a common-law wife – a hard-faced German piece she was – and a kid. That was her who was just drooling over David; the kid, that is. I'm not quite sure of all the details but this child, Marti, ended up in a children's home when the mother cleared off back to Germany. Over the next few years Marti's name cropped up in missing person reports when she absconded from the home in search of her mother. She spent a lot of time in Germany, but the German police shipped her back here every time they found her. In the end she landed up in a semi-secure facility near Leeds that made Dotheboys Hall look like a holiday camp. Her own mother turned her in. She didn't want the bother and Marti hadn't got German nationality, you see. Then something odd happened. Marti was fostered by one of the wealthiest families in Cheshire, the Carlyles. No one could work out just why old Brandon Carlyle should have gone to the trouble. I was keen to investigate but I was promoted at about that time and it was out of my hands then.'

'So that's how this ex-con's daughter married into the Carlyle family,' Janine said.

'Not ex-con – King's still inside.'

'But he must have done twenty years by now.'

'He has, and he'll do more as long as there's a Police Federation.'

'This is good stuff!' Janine exclaimed. 'Dave! Why didn't you tell me that What's-his-name Carlyle was brawling with his wife in a public car park? I might have got a decent diary piece out of it.'

'It's all very sad, Janine,' my mother said. 'That girl's had enough trouble in her life without you dragging her name through the press.'

'Oh, it's stale news by now. But still, Dave . . .'

'Your memory's very selective, Janine. You didn't believe me at the time.'

'Oh, f . . . er . . . fiddlesticks . . . I'd have believed you if you'd told me it was one of the Carlyle family involved.'

'You didn't let me get that far, Janine. He told me his name, bold as brass – Charles Carlyle. It was as if he was entitled to knock women about in public places.'

'Charlie – Brandon's eldest son and heir,' Paddy commented.

'How come you know so much about the Carlyles?'

'You don't make as much money as Brandon Carlyle without some questions being asked. His father ran a small pub in Ancoats, and a right thieves' kitchen it was too. There have always been questions about just how Brandon managed to lay his hands on enough capital to get started in business.'

'The way you say that tells me that you think you know,' I said.

'Him and his father, Ted, ran one of the biggest fencing operations in Manchester and Salford. It was a joke. Only about two or three barrels of beer were delivered to that pub every week, but father and son were loaded. They were more careful than some, they salted their money away, and of course there was nothing in writing and no phone conversations. When Ted died Brandon went legitimate . . .'

'And what is his business?' Janine demanded.

36

'You read the financial papers, don't you? He's into just about everything now, but back in the sixties when I ran the ruler over him once or twice he was the big name in one-armed bandits in pubs. There was more than a little difficulty with rival outfits – vans mysteriously burnt out, shotguns going off in the night – but Brandon was too slippery a customer to ever have his collar felt, though I dare say he should have had. Any road up, he went off to New York and founded the Carlyle Corporation. He spent years taking over American companies and selling off the profitable bits, and then he came back here and is still at it.'

'He doesn't have anything to do with that golf club out at Tarn, does he?'

'Hold on, Dave. I honestly don't know what he owns, but you should steer clear of him and his family. I don't think he's overflowing with goodwill towards me and he'd enjoy doing a nasty to you. Anyway, lad, we didn't come here to talk about the Carlyles. I heard quite enough about them when I was in the job – always just within the law they were, and with an army of lawyers ready if any bold plod raised an eyebrow in their direction.'

I looked at Paddy. He'd obviously had his fingers burned at one time or another by Brandon Carlyle. His expression was an invitation to change the subject, so we did.

Janine returned to the topic on the way home. 'You had it off with that Marti, didn't you, Dave?'

I almost swerved the car onto the pavement.

'How many more times do I have to tell you that the woman was paralytic drunk?'

'Not so paralytic that she couldn't skip out of your office.'

'Look, Janine, do you think I'm suffering from some kind of medical condition? Satyriasis, isn't it? I don't have to have sexual intercourse with every woman I meet.'

'Oh, don't you?'

'No!' I snapped.

A spell of heavy breathing and silence followed this exchange. Deansgate was clogged with slow-moving traffic and I had plenty of time to think of something to say. As usual it was the wrong thing.

'Janine, you know you're the only woman I'm interested in . . .'

'Oh, for Christ's sake, shut up! You sound like some pathetic pimply teenager. Have you been watching *Neighbours*? No. I think the dialogue's better in that.'

More heavy breathing followed as I struggled to swallow the insult.

'Your eyes were all over the woman when she came to our table,' Janine said after a while.

'I'm sorry, I can't help the way I look at people.'

'Not *people*, just big-bosomed women in expensive clothes.'

'I didn't even notice her bosom . . .'

'You should have done, she practically stuck it in your face. Your eyes were out on stalks.'

'. . . or her clothes, I was going to say.'

After that we drove in silence to Thornleigh Court. I hung around by the entrance to my flat while Janine dealt with the baby-sitter – a local teenager who came complete with baggy-trousered boyfriend.

When they'd gone I put my head round the door to ask Janine if she wanted a coffee.

'How can I leave the children? You'd better come in, you big slob, unless you prefer to sulk.'

'I don't lust after every female I meet,' I said later when we were in bed.

'No, I suppose not,' Janine agreed. 'It just seems that way.'

'It doesn't! There's nothing wrong with your bosom. I'm perfectly satisfied with it.'

'Thanks a bunch!' she said. 'Pig!' Then she tried and failed to push me out of bed. The funny thing was, the more I protested a lack of interest in Marti King and her anatomy the stronger my feelings became.

7

The front door communicator buzzed at about one-thirty p.m. that Sunday. I was alone in my own flat. Janine had taken Jenny and Lloyd off to a do-it-yourself session at the Whitworth Art Gallery and I was occupying myself with a casual browse through the Sunday papers. I took my time answering the buzzer on which my impatient caller was now attempting to play a tune.

'Are you ready to be gripped in the arms of Morpheus, Cunane?' the unmistakable voice of Clyde Harrow squeaked through the small speaker.

'No, I don't take morphine, Clyde,' I replied, 'but maybe I'll start if you're visiting.'

'Morpheus, son of Hypnos, the god of dreams! Rouse yourself, man! I've come to bear you away to his fabled shrine in Old Trafford.'

I pressed the button to open the door and a few moments later the fat form of Clyde, looking more absurd than ever in tight-fitting Manchester United supporter's kit, was sprawled over the sofa in my living room. I was surprised to see the obese comedian. This was his first ever unsolicited visit.

'No camera team, I swear it!' he said jovially. 'A purely social call.'

'Oh,' I muttered.

'I came to apologise for my recent verbal excesses.'

'How unlike you,' I murmured.

'Laconic as ever, Dave,' he said benevolently. 'I love it.'

'Has Brandon Carlyle fired you then?'

'No, far from it. I'm told that I'm a highly valued asset of his organisation. Such a valued gem indeed that I'm to be freed from the daily news grind and given my own weekly feature slot.'

'Kicked upstairs?'

'Tantamount to that. Accountant's mentality, of course . . . They inform me that the expense of keeping a crew on stand-by for me isn't justified when there's ample material in archives to supply background coverage. But my dear lad, I didn't call to impose my problems on you.'

'No, I'm sure that would be the last thing you'd do.'

'Ouch!' he groaned, playfully smacking his own face. 'Come now, David, a sneer ill becomes your open countenance.'

'What did you come for then?'

'I am the possessor of two tickets for my company's box at Old Trafford. The lads are up for the cup and kick-off is at four. What do you say?'

What do you say? Anything but yes would require acres of explanation. I soon found myself seated alongside Clyde and forty other men in a box suspended above the emerald turf simulating an enthusiasm I didn't feel. I noted that Clyde was one of the few among the TV executives to sport the full supporter's rig. I wondered if they regarded Clyde as a sort of court fool, complete with cap and bells.

'This is how I started out, you know,' he informed me.

'What? Getting yourself measured up for a straitjacket?'

'No, you fool! I was a match commentator. They liked my vivid turn of phrase so much that they gave me my own programme.'

'I'm glad somebody likes it.'

Just watching Clyde was exhausting, and by half-time I was more than ready for the refreshments. When full-time arrived with the home team in front I found that, despite myself, I shared the general euphoria.

There was no rush to leave and soon I was propping up the bar next to Clyde. We both needed support.

'Well now,' he said happily.

'Yes,' I agreed.

'Have you made any progress in finding out what was going on between Charlie and Marti Carlyle?'

40

'No, and I haven't tried,' I said, lurching back to earth with a bump.

'Far be it from me to chide you for neglect of duty, old lad, but if a beautiful woman had thrust herself into my lap like that and then her husband and his bravos came to threaten me I'd make it my business to seek that woman out.'

'I saw Marti last night.'

'Did you?' he gasped, seizing the lapels of my jacket in his enthusiasm.

'What's this about, Clyde?' I growled, brushing him off. 'I only met her by chance in a restaurant.'

'She is interested in you, then?'

'No, no. Get that idea out of your head.'

Clyde looked so downcast that I almost felt a spasm of sympathy for him – almost, but not quite.

'I need ammunition to fight back with,' he moaned. 'I was hoping that you might provide it.'

'I'm sure you were, Clyde,' I said harshly.

'You don't understand, do you? One little chink in that man's armour and I'll reveal him to the world as the criminal he is. Publicity is the one thing these corrupt bosses fear.'

There was a space round us. Clyde wasn't exactly keeping his voice down.

'I did do some research into Brandon Carlyle's so-called empire,' I said.

'And?'

'There's nothing to suggest that he's different from any other rich businessman trying to get richer.'

'But then there wouldn't be, would there?' he said sadly. 'Financial journalists know which side their bread's buttered on and, at best, they only have crumbs of information.'

'What's so terrible about this guy, apart from the fact that you don't like him?'

'What indeed? He seems to be able to blackmail the most unlikely people.'

'He isn't blackmailing me. You're overwrought, Clyde,' I said smugly.

I decided it was time to leave. I walked home, determined to leave Clyde Harrow and his troubles behind me.

8

Despite Clyde's gloomy prognostications I heard nothing more about the Carlyle family over the next few weeks, which suited me perfectly – though I couldn't resist a little background reading on the Vince King case. Just to satisfy my curiosity. Otherwise my life on the emotional white-knuckle ride with Janine skidded along its appointed track until the end of summer when we took a break from each other.

That is, she took a break from me.

Ever the noble character, I stayed in Manchester, happy as an early Christian martyr given a preview of the instruments being laid out for his torture. I was still beavering away at the business, trying to keep the balance sheet of Pimpernel Investigations looking healthy. Janine and the kids departed for points south . . . London, not the Costas. Her mum, she of the cockney whine – *Dive K'nine*, that's what she calls me – wanted her daughter in Twickenham with her for two weeks, and her daughter wanted to be there. No place for *Dive*, especially as Janine carefully informed me that she would be investigating career opportunities on the London papers.

So it was a slightly resentful individual who met Marti King when she entered the offices of Pimpernel Investigations for the second time.

Now it was one of those mornings at the fag end of summer when nothing seems to be happening. You make believe the fine weather is going to go on for ever but you know it's all an illusion. Nasty damp winter is just lying in wait. Work was more a matter of ticking days off the calendar than strenuous effort. Commercial activity had slowed to a crawl. Most of my contacts were sunning themselves on Spanish beaches. So there I was, the Knight of the Sorrowful Countenance, seated in the office wearing my second best blue suit and trying to think of something to fill my day. A rumbling stomach was telling me that lunchtime was near but that was the only sound to be heard at Pimpernel Investigations. I was in the front office trying to summon enough energy to walk to a sandwich bar while idly watching the public pass along the street.

I saw and recognised Marti as soon as she turned the corner. She was walking briskly, with enough attractive curves on display to drive a geometry teacher mad. I had ample time to lock the outer door and retreat into the back office before she saw me, but I didn't, so all that followed was my own fault. Perhaps I *am* a sex maniac. I tell myself that I'm interested in people and that Marti's story was what interested me. At any rate when she opened the door of Pimpernel Investigations and came in I welcomed her with a smile which she repaid with compound interest.

'Is this another of your days for rescuing damsels in distress?' she asked.

'Depends. You're not pissed again, are you?' I liked her bold front.

'A master of the delicate touch!' she said with a grimace. 'I hadn't had *that* much to drink that day you saw me at Tarn. I hadn't eaten for two days and then a couple of brandies on an empty stomach and that row with Charlie, it was enough to make anyone pass out.'

'You call that a row, do you? It looked more like a stand-up and drag-down fight from where I was.'

'Charlie loves the starring role but I didn't come to talk about him. We're having a trial separation. I just called round to see if you'd like to do me a little favour.'

'As I say, it depends. Favours I do at weekends. I'm plying for hire now.'

'I won't be able to pay you anything,' she said quickly. 'Not now.'

She flicked me a cute little smile; cute and little enough to steal the show at any beautiful baby contest. I couldn't hold the strict expression on my face. She must have read me like a book. I could have kicked myself. Rule seventeen in the

Private Detectives Handbook is to give nothing away when discussing fees. Now the pretty lady told me she couldn't pay. Still, she was dressed in a designer outfit which couldn't have left her with much change from two grand, a little number consisting of a three-quarter-length coat in a colour she later informed me was ink, over a white dress with navy flowers.

'Very cute,' I commented.

'Things aren't what they seem,' she continued hurriedly and her confidence seemed to sag a little. 'Charlie is supposed to have undertaken all kinds of financial arrangements but I haven't seen a bean since we separated and now the credit cards have gone kaput.' She focused those cool green eyes on me, two pools of pale emerald quite deep enough for a private detective to drown in.

I've always been soft in the head when it comes to hard luck stories. This one was getting right to the spot.

'What is it you wanted?' I asked, expecting her to touch me for cash.

'You're my last hope really. I know it's cheeky but you did give me that lift from Tarn and that's what put the idea in my head.'

She gave me that appealing look again.

'Go on then . . .'

'My father, he's in prison.'

'I know.'

'Been checking up, have you? Or was it that old gargoyle of a copper you were with? I can spot a bluebottle a mile off.'

'That bluebottle happens to be my father.'

'Oh!' she murmured. Her face fell.

'None of us gets to choose our parents,' I said.

'It's not that, it's just with you being private I thought you wouldn't be connected to the police.'

'I'm not. My dad was a policeman. He could just as well have been a bus driver.'

'Do you think so? Well, I'm prepared to overlook it if you are.'

'Cheek!'

'No, there are some good families that have a copper related. What I came to ask is, would you give me a lift to the

44

prison? He's in Armley Jail, Leeds, at the moment.'

Again my features let me down. Astonishment must have flickered briefly.

'You weren't doing anything when I came except fanning the breeze. I saw you. It would be another chance for you to get out of Manchester again.'

'That's considerate of you. I wasn't in Tarn that day on the off-chance you needed a lift, you know. I was working.'

'Are you working now?'

'Actually, no . . .'

'So what's stopping you? We can be there in an hour, and you'll be back behind your desk by four.'

'I don't want to seem harsh, but what's wrong with public transport?'

'I told you, I've no dosh. Charlie's cut me off without a bean.'

'Surely . . .'

'No, you don't understand. I bet you've never had anyone from your family in prison. If I don't turn up . . .'

'But how were you hoping to get there?'

'I had a car but Charlie sent that Lou Olley round to collect it. I got a lift into Manchester and then I thought you might be able to help.'

'I can lend you some money.'

'That's no good. I'll never get to Leeds in time now. When they've got someone down to see them they bring them into the visiting room. He'll have to sit there waiting for me to come and I won't be there.'

'What about a taxi?'

'Have you any idea how much that would cost? It would be cheaper to take me yourself.'

'It might be and then again a paying customer might walk in here at any moment.'

We both looked out of the window when I said this. The only person walking down the street at that moment was a sad-faced itinerant hauling a tattered bundle on his back like one of Napoleon's soldiers on the retreat from Moscow. He was trailing an equally miserable-looking whippet along behind him.

'OK, I'll grant you there's not much chance of a paying customer,' I laughed, 'but if I take you to Leeds, that's it. I'll take you there and wait outside the prison but then it's straight back here.'

Marti beamed like a small child who's been told that Christmas is coming twice this year.

I looked at Marti and she looked at me. Paddy had warned me to steer clear of the Carlyles but Marti wasn't a Carlyle now, was she? I was out from behind the desk and in the street locking the office door behind us without another word. We set off to collect my car. Taking Marti to Leeds was just something to fill in a blank day, but there was definitely a buzz when I drove out of the multi-storey and saw her waiting on the pavement. Her looks would have made a gay carnival king abdicate.

I was cruising towards Huddersfield at a steady eighty when Marti revealed the next part of her plan.

'You wouldn't consider coming in with me?' she asked.

'No, how could I? My name won't be on the visitors' list.'

'Well, actually . . .'

'What?' I demanded, swerving and almost ending up on the hard shoulder.

'There is a way.'

'You must be joking!'

'No, I told you a little porky before. I didn't just want a lift. I wanted you.'

'A likely tale!' I said, blowing her a kiss.

'No, not like that, I mean as a detective. I want you to get my dad out.'

'Escape?'

'Find evidence about the fit-up. Every time he comes up for parole the Police Federation lobby the Home Secretary, but now McMahon's the Home Secretary it's the best chance he'll ever have. McMahon was his brief at the trial and appeal. He'll have to listen if we can find a single scrap of evidence.'

'Do you turn to a policeman's son to help a convicted cop-killer?'

'I've heard about you. I think you could help my father . . . Oh, it's all gone wrong. If Charlie hadn't been such a pig I'd have hired you, but he's so spiteful. He left me without money on purpose.'

'I don't suppose he thought it might stop you buying booze.'

'I'm not a lush. I told you, that morning was down to drinking on an empty stomach.'

'Or maybe it was all a fine piece of acting.'

'What are you saying?' she said indignantly. Her face matched her flaming hair. 'That I was part of a plan to entrap you? Don't flatter yourself.'

At that moment we flashed past a sign announcing the next turn-off in two miles.

'You'd better come up with some answers quickly or you'll be walking the rest of the way,' I threatened. The trouble with me is that I can never keep up a threat for long, especially with a beautiful woman. She turned those big, appealing green eyes on me. I swerved slightly off the lane.

'Keep your eyes on the road,' she shouted.

'Switch off the sex appeal then.'

'Don't flatter yourself, you big, ugly . . .'

I slowed down to get into the inside lane as her voice trailed off into silence. Then she began talking quickly, almost gabbling.

'What I told you about my father being desperate is true. He's in there for something he didn't do but because he was a career criminal no one will believe him. I got in touch with the solicitor who handled his original trial, Morton Devereaux-Almond. He wrote back saying that he'd always had doubts about Dad's conviction. I persuaded him to come and see Dad, even though he's retired now, but then two weeks ago he backed out. I was frightened to tell Dad. You don't know him, he's so determined. He'd do anything.'

'My heart bleeds. He's inside for two murders.'

'But he never did those! I thought that if I got you this far you could say your name was Devereaux-Almond and come in with me.'

'Oh, great! So you don't just expect me to go prison visiting. I've got to impersonate someone else to do it.'

'They never ask for proof of identity.'

47

We passed the intersection, still going slowly. Swarms of white vans passed us, then Dutch lorries heading for the ferries at Hull.

'Does this mean you're coming?' Marti asked shyly.

'It means I'm thinking. You seriously imagine I'll bluff my way into a prison as this Morton Devereaux-Almond?'

It must have been my day for devilment because there was something about her crazy idea that was appealing. I suppose the truth is that I was bored. Bored with business, bored with the long, empty summer days.

'It's easy.'

'Suppose they check documents?'

'Oh, they never do. Dad's only a category C prisoner now and there's usually a queue a mile long. All we'll have to do is go to the office and sign in like everyone else. Please . . .'

'Suppose they decide I look a bit iffy and order a strip search? I don't fancy some greasy warder shining a light up my nether regions.'

She laughed. The roof stayed on the car.

'You don't look iffy. If anything you're overdressed for visiting.'

'And you're not?'

'I like to give Dad a boost. He says the idea that I'm doing well is all that keeps him sane.'

'Yes, but he might throw a wobbler. He'll know I'm not this Devereaux-Almond.'

'Don't worry, I'll whisper to him who you are. He's too quick to give anything away.'

'Like father, like daughter,' I muttered, accelerating into the overtaking lane.

Marti's guess of an hour to reach Armley Jail was an underestimate. The fast overtaking lane was crowded past Bradford, but, having negotiated something called the Armley Gyratory, we were outside the grim Victorian prison by two. We parked the car as close as we could get and joined others making their way to the Bastille.

I got that old sliding sensation in the pit of my stomach again, just like a man starting a solo journey down the Cresta Run on a baking tray. I love it. I love the sensation of setting off and not knowing where, when, or if I'll ever arrive.

'This doesn't mean that I'm going to spend the next few months investigating his case,' I cautioned as we passed under the gateway.

'Go on, you're a fair man. All I ask is that you listen to what Dad has to say. You saved me that day at Tarn, it's the least you can do.'

'I don't quite follow your logic there,' I said. 'I'm only going to listen, mind you.'

Things didn't dovetail as neatly as Marti expected. We were almost at the end of the queue which gave me plenty of time to study the many warning notices. Impersonation of an authorised visitor was listed as an indictable offence right up there with drug smuggling. It was too late to draw back; processing began. Everyone was searched, bags handed in, and gifts sealed for later checking, but there were no strip searches. Male hands were marked with ultra-violet fluid. When we finally reached the office I handed in the visiting order in the name of Devereaux-Almond.

The officer looked at it, checked off the name and then slapped another form in front of me.

'You've not filled in what relation you are to King,' he said grumpily. An overweight baldy of about fifty-seven, coasting towards retirement, he kept shuffling uneasily on his stool. Piles, I guessed unsympathetically. His shiny, near-translucent skin was dead white except for a multitude of blackheads. I stared at him, perplexed. Long explanations would only land me deeper in the mire.

'Partner,' Marti said urgently, 'Morton's my partner.'

'In for a penny, in for a pound,' I whispered when I scribbled the lying word into the relevant box and handed the paper back to the surly screw. He ran narrow, suspicious little eyes over it as if fearing that the paper would turn into a clenched fist and punch him in the mouth, and then led us forward. Without another word he waved us into the queue waiting to be led through the prison. We inched ahead with the throng. Neither of us spoke for a while.

'Dave?' Marti said eventually. 'You don't mind if I call you

Dave, do you? It is your name, isn't it? I heard that friend of yours.'

'It's all right by me.'

'I wanted to ask you something personal.'

'Fire away.'

'Is there something wrong with me? You don't seem to want to look at me directly.'

'What?' I was confused. I felt as embarrassed as a teenager caught poring over a girlie mag by an anxious parent.

'Yes, I've noticed that you glance at my eyes and then away. Is there something on my suit? Pigeon dropping or something?' She looked down at her front and brushed her fingers over her breasts.

I drew a deep breath. I knew what the answer was but I didn't like to say anything. Thanks to Janine's words my eyes must have been avoiding Marti's physical charms.

Marti threw her head back and laughed, and what a laugh. That terrible gargling sound reverberated off walls that had absorbed ten thousand screams, sighs and moans of despair, but nothing as weird as this. It sounded oddly defiant.

'I'm sorry,' she said when her clatter had stopped echoing around the dismal corridors. Women running the WRVS booth craned their heads out of their stall to see the cause of the disturbance. I was surprised that an emergency medical team didn't arrive to offer assistance. She laid a hand on my arm. 'I'm sorry. It's just that you look like a startled fawn . . .'

'God Almighty . . .' I muttered under my breath. Marti knew how to pick a quarrel.

'It's your partner, isn't it? Janine? I've read her stuff in the paper. She's terribly down on men. A real ballbreaker, I should guess.'

'You guess wrong.'

'Listen, she's got nothing to worry about. After marriage to Charlie Carlyle, any other man . . . Well, let's just say that train, the libido express, pulled out and left me on the platform and it'll be a hell of a while before there's another connection.'

'Kind of you to set me straight, but giving you a lift to Leeds wasn't intended as a proposal of marriage.'

'Now you're sulking.'

50

'I'm not.'

'Oh, really?' she said coyly. 'I hope I haven't upset you. I know how easily hurt some of you big boys are. Poor Charlie! I could put him off his Quaker Oats for weeks with the wrong word.'

'I bet you could, but I'm not Charlie.'

'No. 'Course you aren't. I should think it needs something really heavy duty to put a dent in your ego.' Then she started laughing again. 'I could get to like you, you know.'

'I'll wait in the car if you prefer,' I offered.

'Don't be such a lemon, Dave! A single girl's got to get her fun somewhere.'

I was about to tell her that I could now see why Charlie had been trying so hard to alter her appearance at Tarn Golf Club but I didn't get the opportunity. Another glum warder clinked his keys, opened the door of the visitors' room and beckoned us forward.

'I'm sorry, Dave,' Marti said, linking my arm, 'but being in this place makes me feel giddy. You have to have a laugh or you'd start tearing your hair out.'

'Forget it,' I mumbled. For me the effect was deadening.

9

The room was crowded. A dull roar rose as the away team greeted the boarders. Dozens of tables with attached chairs were occupied by earnest little groups all talking fifty to the dozen like a bookmakers' convention. A lot of the prisoners seemed to be in their early twenties, or even younger. Mums and dads and teenage girlfriends were haranguing shaven-headed youths. Older, sadder women clutching infants were talking to their imprisoned mates, poring over photos of absent pals.

'He's over there,' Marti whispered, gripping my arm tightly.

You certainly couldn't miss King. He was years older than almost everyone else, but he was different in another way. He was calmly scanning the room, completely at his ease, a distinguished figure, aristocratic even. Only the Day-Glo bib he was wearing marked him as a prisoner, and on him it looked like a badge of rank. We picked our way through the crowded room towards him and he spotted us when we were halfway there.

I don't know what it was, exactly, but as we went through that assembly of disappointed people I felt my spirits lifting. I wasn't about to burst into song, but after the gloomy wait in the corridor outside and the po-faced screws it was a relief to find that the man we'd come to see was a human being and not a monster. At least to outward appearances he was.

A slight person, he rose to meet us. His hair was grey, artfully combed from the side to conceal an almost bald scalp. His expression was as benign as a Japanese Buddha. The eyes gazing out from the rather pinched face were completely inscrutable. The nose was sharp and prominent, his chin less so – firm, finely modelled, but not a major feature. His lips were thin, close pressed and anaemic, but smiling now. He didn't look much like Marti except for those luminous, intent eyes. They were the same shade of green as hers. For the rest I'd have to say there was something meticulous about him, an air of control. His green cord trousers were neatly pressed, brown leather shoes polished; the feet tiny and dainty as a young girl's. Unlike most of the others he was wearing a shirt, a cotton check. Had he been dressed in an expensive suit, you could have taken this former safe-cracker for a scientist, a professor of quantum mechanics or maybe a surgeon. His hands were very well cared for: no self-administered tattoos for Vince King, no layer of grime under the nails.

Taking his eyes off Marti, he shot me a keen look, neither friendly nor unfriendly, but knowing. I might have been there to spring him for all he knew, but he gave no sign.

'Marti!' he said warmly, kissing her. 'I can tell you're coming a mile off. That laugh, it's not getting any better, is it?'

Marti responded by giving a demonstration of her vocal gymnastics. Heads turned in our direction.

King hugged Marti and patted her as if checking that she was real. The noise she was generating gradually died away. I could see her lips moving as she whispered an explanation. I thought I caught the word 'partner'. Eventually Marti broke away and sat down.

Turning to me, King shook my hand, or rather he tried to crush it. For a small man he was strong. As he tried to squeeze the blood out of my fingers, I countered with a crusher of my own.

'Lovely!' he said, pulling his hand free and shaking his fingers in the air. 'Marti, it looks like you might have got yourself a real man at last. I don't know who the hell you are, mate, but you're no solicitor. Shaking hands with one of them is like trying to milk a dead cow.'

'Dad, don't get the wrong idea. Dave is only doing me a favour by bringing me here.'

'Go on!' he said, slapping my shoulder like a buyer in a cattle auction. 'You could go further and fare worse than this chap now you're shot of Carlyle. You're not wed or anything, are you, lad?'

I shrugged my shoulders to signify nothing in particular and sat down under the vigilant gaze of two officers and any number of CCTV cameras.

'Christ!' King continued. 'You're not quite as broad across the shoulders as the Millennium Dome, but you're not far off. Gordon Bennett! With shoulders like yours I could have ripped them safes out and worked on them at home.'

'Dad, you're embarrassing Dave. I hardly know him.'

'She likes big hunks, you know,' King bantered.

'Leave it, Dad. Dave's easily upset.'

'He doesn't look it! This lad knows how to take a bit of fun. That Charlie Carlyle's a real lamp-post of a fella. The trouble is someone forgot to switch his bloody light on.'

'Charlie's not thick!'

'He must be if he wants to give my little girl the bum's rush.'

'Dad, I'm not here to talk about me and Charlie. We've got our differences but to be fair the fault's not all on one side.'

'Hark at the High Court judge,' he said to me with a chuckle. He smiled at me, giving me the chance to inspect all his teeth. They were clean, white and even. The smile didn't make him any easier to read. His eyes remained as blank as an unmarked grave.

'If you'd let me get a word in edgeways, I was going to tell you that Dave's a detective. The reason I brought him here is to listen to your story. He might be able to help you.'

King was now listening to Marti with a curious intensity.

'Detective,' he snarled. 'He's not a bloody copper, is he?'

'He's private, Dad . . .'

'What if I was a copper?' I said. King was in here for two cold-blooded murders, not vandalising a bus shelter.

'You wouldn't be worth a bucket of warm spit, would you?' King hissed. 'That's what.' All trace of geniality had gone.

'Simmer down,' Marti insisted. 'I can't stand all this aggro, Dad. You said they were giving you something to help you with these rages.'

'Tranquillisers, that shit. They can shove their chemical coshes . . .'

'All right, Dad. I get the message. Dave Cunane's a *private* detective. I trust him.'

54

'Trust him? The only copper I'd trust is a dead one and then I'd want to dig him up and drive a stake through his heart to be sure.'

'Dad,' Marti pleaded. 'For God's sake, Dave isn't a copper. His father was but Dave's not and never has been. He's willing to listen to what you have to say.'

'Cunane, did you say?' King asked in a perceptibly less aggressive voice. 'There was a Cunane on the Manchester police.'

'My father,' I said. 'And if . . .'

'OK, OK,' King said, raising the palms of his hands in a pacific gesture. 'I suppose the bastards have a job to do. I tell you what, though, the scumbag who put me in here, that Jones . . . that peevish rat . . . he was as bent as a nine-bob note.'

'You being the world expert on police corruption,' I snapped.

He gave me a crooked leer. 'Perhaps I am. Has your old fella filled you in about *Detective* Inspector Jones?'

'No,' I growled.

If his sneer got any cleverer it would be sitting for A levels.

'Handed in his truncheon, has he, your old fella? Gone to the great cop-shop in the sky?'

'No, he hasn't. My father sweated blood trying to prove that Jones was bent. The fact that he failed tells me something.'

'What are you saying?'

'If they didn't find anything against Jones, maybe he was as straight as you're twisted.'

King started grinding his teeth. For a moment I thought he was going to have a stroke. Then he recovered. The cheeky grin came back.

'Feisty bastard, i'nt he?' he muttered, turning to Marti.

Marti looked at me. 'It's your own fault, Dad, you shouldn't have provoked him,' she said wearily. 'Can't you see the problem I have, Dave? He's like this with everyone who could help. You know what he told the probation officer?'

'Oh, forget that wimp,' King said in an undertone. 'I've slopped out better shit than him.'

'Typical,' Marti sniffed. 'He told the man that he'd accept parole when the Home Secretary sent him a letter of apology for the way he'd been treated. So the prison governor won't even forward an application to the Parole Board.'

'I don't want parole. I want justice. I was innocent. Jones fitted me up.'

The three of us sat in silence for a moment. The babble of conversation all around passed us by. I was the first to speak.

'Look, there have been fit-ups before but who's going to believe that Jones shot two men, one of them a copper?'

'And who else was it, if not him? Me, that never did anyone in me life? We were just starting to shift the gear. I went round a corner and bingo! Out like a bleeding light. Someone coshed me, and not with PP9s in a sock either. It was an expert who used a proper persuader. Hardly left a mark. Then what? I come round. Dennis and this copper are dead. The alarms are ringing like the bells of hell and the filth are all over me like eczema.'

'You must have had someone else helping you.'

'No, it was just the one.'

'They said DC Fullalove must have found you and you shot him.'

'They said – they never explained what Fullalove was doing there on his own.'

'You shot him and then you struggled with Musgrave, who knocked you out before you shot him.'

'Yeah, and then a million quid's worth of registered mail just walked while I was on the floor?'

'They said it was a case of thieves falling out.'

'Bloody fit-up, that's what it was. Someone removed a whole load of registered mail while I was lying unconscious.'

'That still doesn't put Jones in the frame.'

'Who else but him? Everybody knew he was bent. What did he say about finding me? He'd received an anonymous tip-off. Ha! Where do you think I got my information from? Him. He pulled the double cross and fitted me up.'

'So you're saying your inside information came from him?' King looked at Marti now.

'It wasn't directly from Jones. He told someone else who told me.'

'And who was that?'

56

'I'm no grass. If I'd given one name they'd have squeezed me for every name I knew.'

'So you prefer to stay in here for the rest of your life,' Marti said bitterly.

'Yes,' King said. 'I know it was Jones. Prove that and then you'll find out the rest. I swear on Marti's life that it must have been that bastard who killed Dennis and the copper. Knocked me out and shot the pair of them. I never even went into the room where they were killed. Quick in and out, me. I was noted for it. You don't dawdle in a high security vault.'

'So Jones shot them,' I said slowly. 'I see. A detective inspector shot two men dead, nicked the money and no one suspected a thing.'

'Exactly.'

'You had a trial. Why did none of this come out then?'

King shut up for a moment. His guard was down. He stretched his hand across the table to Marti before speaking.

'I had my reasons for keeping shtoom about bloody Jones at that time, didn't I? But I never admitted the killings and I never will. Marti, love, I've told you before. It's a waste of time trying to get me out of here. I'm not going until they admit that I was fitted up and that's never going to happen.'

'Oh Dad,' she pleaded. 'Other people have grassed.'

'Not real people – just scum.'

'You'd be free. You could come and live with me.'

'Inside or out, I'll never be free until they show that it was Jones fitted me up. Hey, Mr Detective Cunane! A sudden panic, that's what the learned friends said it was. Tell me this, do you think I'd have needed a shooter to deal with one lone copper twenty odd years ago?'

'You don't look so hard,' I murmured.

'Hard enough to have kept my head above water in prison for twenty odd years.'

'That doesn't mean you have to spend the rest of your life here,' Marti insisted.

'Get used to it, love; you mean well, but I'll die in here and to hell with the lot of them.'

'Dave, say something to him.'

57

'What can I say? He's right. If he thinks he was fitted up why should he admit that he did the killings?'

King looked at me and laughed out loud. It wasn't Marti's hair-raising cackle, but a plain, honest laugh. 'Are you sure you aren't a Yorkshireman, son? They're plain spoken in this nick, I'll tell you. Plain as a kick in the lats, some of them. Or is it that you like the thought of me rotting away? Most of the filth love that.'

'I've nothing against you. Maybe you killed those men or maybe it all went down as you say.'

'It did.'

I looked at him. The eyes were just as inscrutable as before, the expression as determined. I could have hit him, he was so smug and self-satisfied in his proclaimed innocence.

As Marti had no doubt calculated, I felt a powerful urge to prove or disprove what he was saying. Stupid, but that's me.

'Help me prove it then,' I said, fatal words.

'Why should I bother? You said your old man couldn't come up with anything against Jones and he had all the resources of the Old Bill behind him.'

'Yes, but some of his colleagues weren't too helpful . . . you know what I mean.'

'Who should know better? I knew exactly what the market value of a policeman's co-operation was at one time. Why do you think they're all so happy to leave me in here for a crime I didn't commit? The bastards never stood a chance of getting me for the ones I did do.'

'It was a long time ago. People might be willing to talk now,' I suggested.

'Leave it, son. The geezers I'm up against don't let things drop. They've got too much to lose. Get on with your life. Marti's a lovely girl, she deserves better than that puff Carlyle. Maybe you're the one, I don't know.'

With that he turned away, conversation over. He was only down for an hour with us, and I was glad that he hadn't requested two as he was entitled. It was like a hospital visit where you pass over the bunch of grapes, tell the patient that it's raining outside and then find that you've run out of chat.

Father and daughter talked stiltedly about her childhood for the rest of the hour.

At last a bell rang and we got up to leave. I went out on my own, leaving Marti to bid her father a fond farewell. The bracing air helped to clear my head.

We didn't drive straight back. We stopped at Hartshead Moor Services on the M62. Visiting Vince hadn't upset Marti's appetite. I respectfully watched her devour a Kentucky Fried Chicken meal while I sipped my coffee.

'What was all that about the geezers he's up against?' I asked. 'Does he mean the Police Federation?'

'Dad's always claimed that there was a lot more involved than ever came out at the trial.'

'And we're not permitted to know what it was?'

'I've begged and pleaded with him. You heard what he said.'

'There's not much chance of getting him out until he tells us the full story. Even if I believed that Jones killed those two men I'd have to know a lot more about what was behind it all. Why would a copper kill just to send Vince down for life? They had him at the scene of a robbery, and homicide's quite a step up from adding a couple of extra lines to a suspect's statement.'

'You're saying that because your father was a policeman.'

'Not *all* coppers are bent.'

'So you don't think he's innocent?'

'I expect most of the men in that room would say that they're innocent.'

'I know Dad was a thief but he never would have shot anyone. Cool and collected, he's noted for it.'

'He didn't exactly come over as the world's greatest pacifist, did he? I don't know what he's capable of.'

'Why would he have denied it all these years?'

'I don't know. Some people won't admit things even to themselves.'

'Wonderful, pop psychology! You're saying that he's been "in denial" for more than fifteen years? Dave, I came to you because I thought you were intelligent . . .'

'And here's me thinking it was my good looks.'

59

'Stop it! You must know now that Dad's not like that. Being inside all this time hasn't curdled him. Whatever you think, I'll never believe he did it.'

'But you're his daughter. I'm not related. And talking of relatives, what happened to your mother? She wasn't convinced enough to stick around, was she?'

'Sticking around is not my mother's forte,' she said. Her expression became closed, and I didn't push it.

10

It was a week before I heard from Marti again.

'Have you still got a totally closed mind or is there something between your ears besides cotton wool?' she asked when I picked up the phone.

'And when did I last stop beating my wife?' I replied. I almost blurted out then that I'd read the reports of her father's trial and appeal but something made me keep my mouth shut.

'Your performance last week was pretty limp considering you're supposed to be the great private eye.'

'You and Vince don't need me, Marti. You need a priest.'

'No, listen, something's come up. I want to show it to you.'

'Why didn't you come round to the office? You found your way here last week.'

'That friend of yours, Janine White, is she around?'

'She's still on holiday, back at the weekend.'

'Oh, well, even so, it might be best if we met somewhere else.'

I got the impression that fear of Janine's frowns was only part of her reason for staying clear of Pimpernel Investigations.

'Just what was it you had in mind?'

'Nothing romantic, if that's the way your mind is going.'

'Marti, just because you've got time on your hands, it doesn't mean I have.'

'I told you, I want to show you something.'

'Is Charlie leaning on you?' I asked.

'No, no, nothing like that. Well, it's just . . . Look, do you know Deansgate?'

'Do I know Deansgate? Does the Pope have a balcony?'

'You know the motorbike shop where they sell Harley-

Davidsons? Right at the end of Deansgate? There's a new little wine bar on the corner of a block just past there. I'll meet you in half an hour.'

I was going to question the benefit of sipping over-priced Beaujolais in such an out-of-the-way spot but she hung up. Then I guessed its remoteness was what made the place attractive. Despite what she said, the heat must be on. I was glad of another excuse to hang the 'Closed' sign up. The weather was warm, but being Manchester there were big clouds sweeping in from the west and it might rain at any time. A walk with Marti at the end of it was just what I needed.

As I hiked away from town along Deansgate, away from the interesting shops selling pianos and pastrami and on past the old railway warehouses and accessory outlets, the afternoon crowds thinned to a trickle. I eyeballed the wine bar Marti had selected for our tryst. Situated at the bend in the road, it guarded Deansgate like a sentry box. I spotted an Asian woman scanning the street from a seat in the window. Then I realised the Asian woman was Marti in a headscarf and sunglasses. I quickened my pace.

She was seated at a table for two and there was a bottle of red plonk in front of her.

'So, why all the mystery?' I asked when I pulled up a chair.

Marti didn't reply. Instead she poured me a glass of wine. 'Sup that, Sherlock,' she commanded.

'You've got the wrong idea about me,' I mumbled as I raised the glass. 'Mastermind of detection I ain't.'

'Oh, don't be so humble. I've heard things about you. They say that some who messed you around didn't live to brag about it.'

I went hot and cold, then the wine went down the wrong side of my throat. I started choking and spluttering and I couldn't stop. Heads turned, conversation stopped and a waiter bustled over, agog to use his Heimlich manoeuvre training. I managed to cram a handkerchief over my mouth and get some air into my lungs before he started bruising me.

'Are you sure you're all right? It wasn't the wine, was it? I'll bring you another bottle,' the hovering waiter, a dark, Spanish-looking youth with black gelled hair and a single earring, said comfortingly. Maybe he was worried that customers choking to death in his window would be bad for trade.

'No, no, I'm fine. It was just one of those things,' I gasped while struggling for breath.

'He likes to bolt his wine down,' Marti added with a laugh, fortunately not one of her seismic efforts.

'That's a bit rough,' I said. 'Who have you been talking to? What have they said about me?'

'I just heard that, well, you know . . . Certain criminals who went up against you . . . let's just say they haven't been answering their correspondence lately.'

I could feel myself starting to choke again.

'I wish I'd never opened my mouth. I wouldn't if I'd known you were going to have a seizure,' Marti said quickly.

I grabbed her wrist.

'Who's been telling you all this rubbish?' I demanded.

Her headscarf slipped, revealing a yellow bruise on her upper left cheek. I let her wrist go.

'Take off the glasses,' I said.

Reluctantly she did. Somebody had given her a beautiful black eye.

'Charlie Carlyle, I presume,' I said, 'and don't bother telling me that you walked into an open door. I've been involved in too many domestics to accept that excuse.'

'It wasn't Charlie. As a matter of fact, it was an accident.'

'So that's why you're hiding in a remote wine bar and wondering if I do knock-off jobs on the side.'

She laughed. This time it was the full throated ear-clatterer, delivered with head well back and chest heaving. Discounting the aural effect, it was quite a spectacle. In Italy a crowd would have gathered round us. This being rainy Manchester, the other imbibers scanned us covertly but made no moves in our direction. I realised then that Marti needed the harsh glare of the Tropics rather than the dull diffuse light of Manchester. If she was a painting, she was a Gauguin not a Rembrandt. She was one of those rare birds which gets blown to these sunless shores by some chance storm.

'Oh Dave! You've got a wonderful imagination. You're

wasted as a private detective. I'm here because I have something to show you and I chose this place because it's one I happen to know. It's handy for the Metro. Here, read this, before you crack up.' She opened her handbag and pulled out a long envelope with a thick wad of paper inside.

'Read it!' she urged. 'I got it yesterday and it might help to convince you that my father's innocent.'

I was unwilling to do as I was bid. Had she really heard a whisper about me or did her speculations date from that day when Janine was sounding off about me being a killer? I had to know.

'I'll read it when you tell me where you heard all this rubbish about me.'

'Listen, forget that. I was just teasing you.' She focused those lovely green eyes on me before she put the dark glasses on again. A man could dive in those cool limpid pools and forget himself, which was exactly what she intended.

'I need to know. If someone's going round saying I'm a killer I want to know who it is.'

'Don't be so touchy. You were quick enough to believe that my dad's a killer.'

'I want to know. Was it Clyde Harrow?'

'Who's he?'

'Clyde Harrow, he's on local TV. You know, with the coloured shirts and all the ex-wives.'

'Never heard of him. I don't watch TV.'

'Don't pretend you just plucked the idea I'm a contract killer out of thin air.'

'I told you. I made it up. Don't be difficult. Read the letter, it's from Dad's solicitor.'

I looked at her for a long time before I opened the envelope. What could I do, short of blacking her other eye? She certainly knew which key to use to wind my clockwork up. I wondered why Charlie had bashed her this time.

'I'll read this but I'm not saying a word until you tell me what you know,' I warned.

It was a long typed letter, produced on a manual typewriter, not a word processor. I read it carefully. It took me ten minutes.

Morton Devereaux-Almond apologised for not going to the prison, then in carefully chosen words he went over the events of Vince's trial. He left the impression that James McMahon, the defence lawyer, had been incompetent. The gist seemed to be that if there were shortcomings in the defence they should be laid at McMahon's door, not his. He implied that McMahon had allowed a material irregularity to pass unchallenged. As McMahon was now Home Secretary, and the third or fourth most important minister in the present government, it was possible to guess that a certain amount of political axe-grinding was going on.

I put the letter down and folded my arms.

'Well?' Marti queried.

I kept my mouth shut.

'Oh, I haven't heard anything. I was kicking off at you because you were so hard on Dad. Remember that day at Tarn when you sorted Charlie? It put the idea in my head that you're a man who doesn't go in for half measures.'

'Like your father,' I said nastily.

'No, not at all. The whole point about Dad is that he was never violent.'

'Except when he trained with the SAS.'

'Don't be ridiculous. Thousands of men have served in the Regiment.'

'Yet according to this Devereaux-Almond,' I said, waving the letter at her, 'that was one of the points that weighed most heavily against him.'

'That was just one of the unfair things. As if every man who's had military training becomes a cold-blooded murderer.'

'The victims were both shot between the eyes with pinpoint accuracy from a considerable distance, implying a trained marksman. Then each was given an additional bullet through the side of the head – the famous "double tap" of the SAS.'

'I should have known better than to confide in you. A proper weather vane, aren't you?' she sniped, snatching the letter out of my fingers.

'Sorry, but it's only what a lawyer would say. How did you really get the black eye?'

She touched her bruised face gently. 'That's a long story. I didn't come to you for help with my personal problems.'

'Are you sure?'

'Certain! What do you think about what Devereaux-Almond says about the trial? Surely there's doubt.'

'I wouldn't like to say,' I murmured. I was still irritated and short of breath.

'You must have some opinion.'

'Must I? Forget about the double tap then. Nobody had heard about that twenty years ago, but it was stupid of the defence to bring your dad's army record up. It allowed the prosecution to claim that the killings were military style.'

'That's what I'm saying. Dad's brief was more anxious to prove the case against than to help him.'

'OK, let's accept that James McMahon MP was incompetent – or at least Devereaux-Almond is prepared to hint that he was, now he's safely retired himself. Unfortunately, that isn't grounds for an appeal. The trial judge is supposed to . . .'

'Judges, ha!'

'Listen, Marti, up to 1996, there were only three grounds for appeal, including material irregularity, but now appeal's allowed if the conviction is considered "unsafe". The court's unlikely to think that your dad's conviction is unsafe without new evidence, and where's that going to come from when he won't even discuss the case?'

'Don't you think I know all that? I've been over it a hundred times.'

'Fair enough. This Devereaux-Almond says that he feels McMahon wasn't very convincing when it came to cross-examining the police.'

'Dad wanted to sack him. McMahon wanted Dad to plead guilty.'

'How old were you when all this was going down?'

'I was eight but I've had to live with it every day since. You don't know what it's like. We were well off one day and then down in the gutter the next. My mother abandoned me when he was found guilty. She just dumped me on social services and shot off back to her relatives in Germany.'

The wine bar didn't boast a squad of gypsy violinists

playing diminuendo chords but I knew when my heart strings were being plucked. As usual, it worked.

'All right,' I said gently. 'McMahon could have done more. He could have challenged the police evidence. They were tipped off about the robbery but Fullalove arrived on his own, and then Jones turned up later. That seems odd. McMahon should have been harder on the forensic evidence, but the trouble is that McMahon went onto higher things. Not many lawyers are going to accept that a man in his position made a total mess of your father's defence.'

'They didn't. Dad was refused leave to appeal. There were insufficient grounds.'

I sighed. I didn't know what else there was for me to do.

'Won't you at least admit that there are grounds for doubts?' she pleaded. 'I hate the thought of Dad dying in that place. He was so active. He used to take me out in the country all the time when I was a child. He'd walk miles with me on his shoulders.'

'There may be some little hook we can hang an appeal on,' I conceded. I wanted to let her down as lightly as possible. 'The courts are more lenient than they were. Do you mind if I make a copy of the letter back at the office? I need to think about it. I can't tell you at a first glance. Maybe I'll show it to a lawyer friend. There might be something, there might be nothing.'

'Do you think there's a chance?'

'It is funny the way the police weren't challenged about finding your father like that. There can't be many criminals who just fall into their laps so easily.'

'Hah! Criminals!' she said with a curl of her lip.

'Marti, Vince admits that he was a professional criminal. Whatever happens he's not going to come up smelling entirely of roses. They'll probably still want to blackball him at Tarn Golf Club.'

'He'll be in good company then, won't he?' she said with a smile. 'I knew you were the right man that day you plucked me out of the mud at that dump.'

'The right man for what, Marti?'

'Well, who knows? What I said before about not having

67

romantic ideas . . . I don't think I'm going to feel like that for the rest of my life.'

'Yet you think I'm a hit man.'

'No, that was just a joke. Believe me.'

'Do you want to come back to the office with me while I photostat this? We can get a taxi and be there in minutes.'

She took her glasses off. There was a faint blush of colour on her face that hadn't been put there by her husband's fist. Perhaps she was remembering her nap on the couch in my office and my partner's interpretation of it.

'No, Dave, I'd better not,' she said quietly. 'I can be on the Metro in five minutes. You look after the letter and I'll be in touch.'

'Where are you staying? I could give you a lift.'

'No, it's better this way,' she said, getting up to go.

'I could follow you, you know.'

'Better not, Dave, you'll only be disappointed. Let's just see how things work out, shall we?'

She leaned forward and blew me a kiss.

I watched her leave as she'd watched me arrive. She moved along the pavement like royalty at a command performance. It was a pity she'd married a wealthy wife beater; she could have made her living on a fashion catwalk. Then I got a grip on myself. What was I doing in the middle of a weekday afternoon ogling a woman I hardly knew with my tongue hanging out like a rottweiler in a butcher's backyard? I swigged the wine in my glass and got up to go.

As I slithered across the highly polished pine floor towards the exit the Spanish-looking waiter raised his eyebrow and shot me a curious look that could have meant anything. It could be that the lad was constructing his own little fantasy about his customers. Whatever his daydream was, I knew that mine was a waste of time.

'Hasta la vista, Manuel,' I said.

'Yo,' he replied, as cool as the ice he was dumping into a champagne bucket.

11

'You're a stupid fool, Dave,' Janine said dismissively. Two weeks in London had sharpened her up even more. I loved the mixture of acid and syrup she ladled out by the bucketful. So did her readers. It was masochism, I suppose. She wouldn't tell me the exact details but I gathered that her editor had upped her salary to help her decide to stay in Manchester.

'Thanks,' I drawled. 'Nice one.'

'For God's sake, the Vince King case was a *cause célèbre*, at least here in Manchester, even if there hasn't been much interest in it in recent years.

'Everyone thought he was guilty, so that makes it so,' I said. We were reading through press cuttings on Vince King and his trial that she'd brought home from the office.

'Dave, as the man said, "It's the evidence, stoopid!" Look at it, there's masses of the stuff. King's prints were on the gun.'

'That was the economy,' I muttered.

'What?'

' "... the economy, stupid," that's what he said. Clinton.'

'Oh,' she sighed in exasperation, ignoring my correction. 'The younger of the two victims, Dennis Musgrave, was only eighteen. He was King's inside man at the GPO facility. He always pulled his jobs with the help of an inside man.'

'Not the actual safe-cracking.'

'Whatever . . . He needed Musgrave to get him into the secure area in the first place. There were so many alarms and safety devices it would have taken him a week to get near the high value safe without Musgrave. Musgrave was married with two children – did I say he was eighteen? Must have been a fast worker. Anyway, Musgrave, the poor prat, had told his wife that they'd soon be moving to a detached house in

Worsley worth forty thousand. Three witnesses claimed they saw Musgrave with King at the Sawyers Arms in Tyldesley where Musgrave lived . . .'

'I have my doubts about that. King was a complete professional. He'd never have been seen with an accomplice before a job. Police all over the country were on the lookout for him. If they'd clocked Musgrave they'd have known exactly where King was going to strike next.'

'Are you saying three witnesses were liars?'

'They might have seen Musgrave with someone in the pub. I just think it couldn't have been King.'

'Why not? Because his daughter's got a bust you could ski down and come-hither eyes?'

'We're back to that, are we? Janine, if you knew how spiteful all that sounds . . .'

'I hope you're not stereotyping me into some category of *spiteful* feminists,' Janine snapped with a cynical laugh. Things had been going well between us since her return. I'd practically been living in her apartment for the three days since I collected her at the station on Saturday. Everything had been sweetness and light until now, Monday evening.

'Dave, you're such an easy mark for a sob story. You need somebody to go out with you and fend off these predatory birds. Marti probably got that bruise when Carlyle threw his wallet at her.'

'They're divorced, or getting divorced.'

'Strange, I'll believe that when I see it in print. There's been nothing so far. That type of woman doesn't cut herself off from her meal ticket on a passing whim.'

'You're probably right,' I admitted. 'But I wish you'd drop all this stuff about Marti. OK, I mean, she is attractive but not as much as you.' I came round the table behind Janine and slipped my hands under her breasts.

'Not now, Dave,' she murmured, twining her fingers in mine as they moved to unfasten her blouse. 'Later. Jenny's reading in the next room.' She turned and gave me a consolation kiss.

I drew a deep breath and went back to my side of the table.

'By the way, has there been any mention of payment for this

investigation?' Janine insisted relentlessly, which I suppose is why she's such a good journalist.

'No, she's got no money.'

'Yet she walks round with the most expensive designer clothes from Selfridges.'

'How do you know it was Selfridges?'

'Because the last time I was at the Trafford Centre I went into Selfridges and priced that suit she had on when she was so elegantly draped over your sofa. Eight hundred and fifty pounds.'

'All right, I'm a fool, I admit it. But I promised to have a look at her father's case and I will, with or without your co-operation.'

'Don't get huffy with me, dear. You need me to see you straight,' Janine said briskly. 'Now, back to the case. What about DC Fred Fullalove? How do you explain him away?'

'King swore that he was never even in the room where Fullalove was killed. It was an annexe away from the safe room.'

'Yet the forensic scientist, Dr Sterling Sameem, testified that fibres on the soles of King's trainers and clothes could only have come from the carpet in that room. Here it is . . . "The chances of there being similar fibres picked up elsewhere are remote because that room was carpeted with a defective batch that was only sold to the Post Office." Face it, Dave. You don't need this. Your firm's doing well, you're on the right side of the police for once. Send the letter back to her and tell her that you've looked into it and you feel there's no chance.'

'I'll think about it,' I said. I was thinking about it. I was thinking about Vince King walking round and round in his cell like a caged tiger. I was thinking about Janine too.

'I'll have to see her,' I said at last. 'And before you ask, it's not because I'm panting after her. I couldn't just snub her in a letter, I'll have to speak to her.'

'You're just old-fashioned, aren't you?' Janine said sarcastically.

'Yes, I am,' I said. 'Which is why I want to settle down with you.'

'Dave, you'll have to give me more time. I can't just plunge into a permanent relationship. The last man I trusted wasn't

71

happy until he'd put an ocean and a continent between us. Now you want to rush off because I disagree with you.'

'No, it's not that. I understand how you feel.'

I turned to make the long trek to my own flat next door. We didn't usually sleep together on weekday nights, though I was often summoned to her flat of a morning by desperate pleas for help to get Jenny and Lloyd ready for school or nursery.

'Look, don't go yet,' Janine said, pulling me back. 'Listen, you can't solve every mystery,' she said seriously. 'It's no good taking the whole world on your back. There are all kinds of things King could do for himself. If he'd make an admission they'd consider him for parole and he could take up his own case, but from what you said he doesn't sound all that anxious to get out.'

I looked at her earnest, grave face. Her eyes were full of intelligence and feeling, but intelligence doesn't always hack it. Like a lot of very clever people, Janine was capable of making elementary mistakes. Or was I the one making the mistake?

I must have continued my movement in the direction of the door because Janine laid a firm hand on my arm.

'This way, stoopid!' she said, leading me to her bedroom. 'Wait while I see if the kids are asleep.'

It didn't require strong-arm tactics to lure me into her bed.

'Where do you think we're heading, Dave?' she asked, as she lay in my arms after we'd made love.

'I don't know. I think the idea that life is leading us somewhere is an illusion.'

'Don't go all deep and philosophical on me. It doesn't suit you,' she said, pinching my shoulder painfully. 'You know what I mean – us.'

'Where do you want us to head? I've told you often enough what I want.'

'I'm never going to be totally dependent on any man again.'

'I rather hoped that *you* were going to keep me . . . and we're not all like Henry Talbot.'

'That bastard!'

There was a period of silence while we both considered Henry's perfidy.

'Listen, I'll probably be staying in the Manchester area for quite a while.'

'Great!' I said, sincerely.

'I thought I might look for a bigger house, somewhere out near Prestbury, Alderley Edge, somewhere where there'd be decent schools for Jenny and Lloyd.'

'Sounds good,' I said cautiously. My thoughts had tended more in the Cheadle or Handforth direction. A shanty right here in Chorlton-cum-Hardy would have been fine by me. Janine's editor must have come up with lots of financial arguments to keep her in Manchester. By the time you reach Alderley Edge the leafy suburbs are so verdant that you're almost in virgin rainforest.

'I thought I might hire a live-in nanny as well. It's unfair to keep expecting you or your parents to step in whenever there's an emergency.'

'Love, you know that's absolutely no problem. We all love the children.'

'Dave, it's no problem for you but it is for me.'

'Oh,' I said, pondering why it was better to pay some dozy teenager to look after the children.

'I mean, we'd still keep in touch. Like at weekends and everything as we do now. There's no one else.'

'I see,' I murmured. My voice was almost a whisper.

'Look, I've tried marriage and that stuff. It doesn't work.'

I said nothing.

'We could go on holiday. I thought the Seychelles sounds great, those long deserted beaches, or we could try Greece or Barbados, wherever you'd prefer.'

I said nothing.

'Dave, you're going to have to face the fact that I'm not the sort of homebody, apple-pie baking, slipper-warming little wifey that you're looking for.'

'Now you're talking nonsense. When have I ever said that I was looking for someone like that?'

'Oh, you imply it often enough.'

'Rubbish! You're imagining things. I think you've every right to make a career for yourself.'

'It might be better if you looked for someone else,' she said, slipping away from my side and moving to the edge of the bed. 'This Marti will be free soon. I should imagine she's very loving and fertile. She probably wants half a dozen kids.'

'I know nothing about Marti. She might already have a dozen kids for all I know.'

'In that case,' she said in a less determined voice, 'perhaps you do need to look for a little homebody. Hanging around with me is doing you no good.'

'And how do you think I'd find one of these homebodies, assuming that they still exist? Advertise? "PI requires simpering homebody as wife, uncritical hero-worshipper and mother of children. Must be able to darn socks and make hot-pot while he's out playing macho-man on the mean streets of Manchester."'

We both laughed at this. I could feel the tension dissipating.

'You're a clinging devil, aren't you, Cunane? I'm not going to get rid of you easily,' she said.

I turned to grab her but she slipped out of bed, naked as she was, and going over to the dressing table began jotting notes on the pad she kept there. Unlike Marti King's, my libido hadn't taken a train ride out of town. Aroused, I slipped over to her and ran my hand down her back.

'Hmmm, lovely,' she purred. 'I see you still need me to take care of you. I was jotting down some notes for an article. You've given me an idea . . . "The Plight of the Traditional Male".'

What followed was certainly traditional enough.

12

Waking up and looking at Janine's face on the pillow was my idea of a good start to the day. Jenny and Lloyd thought so too. They'd joined us some time during the early hours. They were both fast asleep.

Janine woke with a groan. 'Devil,' she said, grinning and kissing me. 'You've worn me out.'

I laughed. 'Stay at home if you like. Take the day off and bake an apple pie.'

'Don't start that again. Dave, you are going to be all right, aren't you? I mean my move and everything? I couldn't stand it if you turned all mushy and whimpery.'

'What, me? I thought I was the original macho-man.'

'Stay that way, please,' she said. 'I couldn't stomach any gush of emotion.'

'When have I ever had any emotions or feelings?' I said, leaping out of bed and getting into my trousers before the children woke up. 'I'm off to work unless you want me to take Lloyd to the nursery.'

'No, as usual I'll just struggle on until I drop,' she said with a sigh.

Before leaving the room I looked back at her and the children. Their two little bodies were jammed up as close as they could get to their mother. Janine smiled at me. Why did everything always have to be so complicated? I shook my head and left. Plenty of men would jump at the chance of the refrigerated relationship Janine was offering.

When I got to my own flat I looked at the clock. It was still incredibly early, not yet seven. I showered and put on my second best tracksuit and went out for a run on the Meadows. I didn't want to be cool, sweaty was more my inclination. It was one of those sharp, bright northern mornings that partly make up for the grim, dark dampness of the winter months. Even so early, things were stirring down by the banks of the Mersey. There were joggers and twitchers and riders all moving along the path beside the swiftly flowing river. Its colour was the usual dull peaty brown this morning, no chemical spillages up in Stockport last night. Traffic was humming along the nearby motorway but at this time in the morning the sound wasn't intrusive. All us early risers like to pretend that we're deep in the countryside.

As I ran I felt a surge of energy and determination. I could take all that Janine threw at me and come back for more. She was right, I am a clinger. I didn't run too far, just enough to work some of the tension out of my system.

I jogged along a winding, narrow lane with a hawthorn hedge on one side and a ditch on the other. A Grand Cherokee jeep came rocketing round the bend towards me. If he was trying to kill a pedestrian he was going the right way about it. He was right in my path. I jumped to the edge of the ditch and waved. His windows were blacked out but he must have seen me. Instead of swerving away, the jeep turned towards me, ploughing right into the ditch and sending up a bow-wave of spray. I dived for my life and jammed myself against a barbed-wire fence. By the time I got the dirty water out of my eyes the jeep was gone, zooming round the next bend.

Joyriders infest the Meadows but they usually come on scramble bikes or old bangers. I decided the incident wasn't worth reporting to the police. I was alive and I still had my life to get on with.

Full rush hour was getting under way when I jogged out of the Meadows and reached Edge Lane. Back at the flat I had another shower, grabbed a bowl of Corn Flakes and put on my grey suit, then joined all the other grey men heading towards the inner city. There was no sign of Janine and her little brood.

When I got to the office Celeste was waiting on the doorstep. 'What's this?' I joked. 'Are you after promotion?'

'How did you guess?' she asked in all seriousness. 'I've enrolled for a course at college. I want to be a legal executive.'

'Does that mean Pimpernel Investigations will be losing you

soon?' I asked, carefully keeping any suspicion of eagerness out of my voice.

'Oh no, Mr Cunane, I'll have to qualify first, but don't worry, I won't need much time off. Just when there are exams and things.'

'Anything I can do to help, just give me a shout,' I said pleasantly. 'You know I need you here.'

My feeling of benevolence towards the world didn't last for long. I sat at my desk and flicked through the morning mail that Celeste brought in. It was the usual stuff except for a begging letter from a psychic in Barrow-in-Furness who offered to solve any case I was involved in.

'File this under "Nutters",' I told Celeste.

Then I sat back. I had an appointment at one-thirty with the claims office of a major insurance company to collect the fee for a fraudulent claim I'd exposed, then the day was my own. I put my feet up on the desk and folded my hands behind my head. By rights this should be an easy, carefree day. Physical stress had been eased by the run along the Mersey, but like the proverbial small cloud on the horizon I couldn't lay aside my unease about Vince King as easily as Janine had suggested. The evidence against him was just too complete. Here was a man who had pulled many spectacular jobs, always without violence, and never leaving a clue. Then it all goes to pot. He kills his accomplice, Musgrave, who wouldn't have been suspected, and a copper; and then he's found unconscious and smothered in forensic evidence linking him to the murder.

Solicitor Devereaux-Almond's letter mentioned procedural errors at the trial, but that didn't take me very far.

There was only one person I could ask whether the whole thing was a set-up: my own father, Paddy. My stomach started tying itself in knots again.

I picked up the phone and informed Paddy that I would be paying a visit.

'Get in touch with me on the mobile if you need me,' I told Celeste. 'I'll be in Bolton.'

'Shall I start timing you for expenses?' she asked, taking out the large diary we used to work my hours on various cases.

It was on the tip of my tongue to say no, but then I

remembered what Janine had said about Marti's expensive clothes, and of course Devereaux-Almond and McMahon had all received their fees for the King case long ago. Why shouldn't I? It would make it easier to explain to Janine.

'Yeah, normal out-of-office expenses,' I said.

They used to say that the fastest way out of Manchester is through the pub door but the road to Bolton is pretty quick. My route took me along the same multi-lane motorway that had recently taken me to Leeds and I thought of Marti and her little deception as I drove over the Barton Bridge with the green Egyptian-Greco-Roman-Byzantine-Michelangelo-Wren, no-influence-spared domes of the Trafford Centre on my right.

Leaving the scented breezes of Trafford behind, I turned off the orbital motorway for the Bolton intersection. There was a gradient all the way, reminding me that, once upon a time, this was the place where the mills met the hills.

I drove past close-packed pie shops and chip shops, curry houses and chapels converted into mosques. Red brick buildings gave way to grey stone ones and then I was out on the empty country road that cuts through a spur of the West Pennine Moors. This route weaves its way across ravaged fells, ancient sites of manufacturing, now reclaimed for reservoirs and farms. The hillsides are pocked with old coal workings and there are clumps of cottages that once housed weavers.

The fold my parents share with a dozen other romantically minded townies consists of six or so cottages strewn along a rutted track which loops steeply down the hillside, meanders for a mile or so, and then rejoins the main road.

The individual who 'farms' this land, Jake Carless, offered me a mixture of grunts and scowls as I crawled past him.

Paddy was at his door. He was rigged out in 'country clothing' of such profound authenticity that it made the two-hundred-year-old stone doorway that framed him look like a cheap stage set. Immensely strong Timberland shoes, massively thick moleskin trousers, a leather jacket and pullover whose combined chunkiness would have made a mediaeval archer wonder whether he needed sharper arrows;

the whole ensemble was intimidating. I felt that if the man within was annihilated, the clothes would go marching right on.

'What's this all about?' he thundered as I got out of the car.

'Vince King. I went to Leeds to see him.'

'Meddling again!' Paddy exploded. His face turned an ominous shade of purple. My mother appeared and looked at him nervously.

'Calm yourself, dear. I'm sure our David has a good reason,' she said soothingly.

'Good reason! Our David be damned! King should rot till he dies. That young copper was only twenty-six.'

'So there wasn't any doubt about the conviction?' I asked eagerly.

'Doubt? There's always doubt about a conviction. Fifty per cent of the time at any trial is spent by highly paid know-all lawyers kicking up the dust and trying to raise doubts.'

'His solicitor, Morton Devereaux-Almond, has written to Marti. He reckons that King's brief, James McMahon, was incompetent . . .'

'Marti? Oh, it's *Marti* now, is it? Daughter of a bloody murderer, last in a line of criminals going back to God knows when? When we had you baptised we should have given you the middle name of "Fickle".'

'And your parents should have called you Blockhead,' I shouted back angrily. I could feel the heat rising to my face like steam from a kettle. 'I'm not allowed to mention a woman's name without you assuming I'm bedding her.'

'And aren't you?' Paddy demanded with a cynical leer.

'David, we're only worried about Janine. We wouldn't like you to split up. You know how fond we are of the children,' my mother interjected with a placatory smile.

'How many times must I tell you that Janine isn't interested in any kind of relationship that you'd recognise as normal,' I spluttered. 'I've offered her marriage, I've offered her co-habitation on any terms she cares to choose, I've even offered to become a human doormat and let her wipe her feet on me every time she comes in the house if that's what pleases her.'

'You must have done something to upset her,' Paddy

79

persisted. 'This time last year she was ready to settle down with you.'

'She was at a low ebb then, but she's riding high now. She doesn't want to be permanently involved with a sleazy private eye. In fact, I doubt if there's a man anywhere who could fill her exacting requirements.'

'Feeling sorry for yourself, are you? Is that why you're consoling yourself with this Marti?'

'I'm not consoling myself with anyone. How many times do I have to tell you? I only got involved because she asked me to check out her father's case. I do have to work for a living, you know.'

This was greeted with withering scorn from the man in the rustic rig. My mother gave me a more sympathetic hearing. 'It is true that some of Janine's articles do seem to be a bit one-sided,' she said tentatively.

'What do you mean, woman?' Paddy grated, unwilling to be argued out of his determined stand.

I laughed in his face. Janine would have eaten him for breakfast but my mother belonged to an older, much more patient breed of females. Nevertheless, I knew there was steel in her backbone. There must have been for her to have put up with Paddy for so long.

'I mean, Paddy *Blockhead* Cunane,' Eileen said coldly, 'that Janine takes a militant position in the sex war and that perhaps what our David is telling us is the truth.'

Paddy looked at Eileen and then he looked at me. He shook his head. 'What the hell!' he muttered. 'I'm going to repair the garage roof.' Eileen tugged his armoured sleeve.

'No, you're not,' she said firmly. 'You're going to stay here and help our David. If he wants to work for Marti King she's as much entitled to his help as anyone. The poor girl's had a hard life, and anyway, you did the garage roof last week.'

Paddy sat down heavily and let out a long sigh.

'Let's hear it,' he said finally.

I must have been doing a spot of heavy breathing myself because Eileen darted out into her kitchen and returned with cups of coffee in the time it took my blood pressure to return to normal.

'You were on the Manchester force when King was convicted,' I said, struggling to keep my voice even. 'Did you hear the faintest whisper that there was anything iffy about it?'

'I don't know what to believe these days,' Paddy said sadly, shaking his head. 'Every time I open the paper there's some case at the Court of Appeal. In those days before PACE a lot depended on the integrity of the officers taking statements, doing interviews. We were trusted then . . . What was it the Lord Chief Justice said when he threw out the Birmingham Six appeal – "wholly incredible" that the police had conspired to make a case against them? I'd have agreed with him. We thought the system was basically straight – but now, who knows?'

'Dad, did Jones fit King up and kill the other copper?'

'I doubt it,' he said, with his chin stuck out like a chest of drawers. 'Mick Jones was more interested in keeping villains out of jail than sending them there.'

'But he must have wanted to get some convictions if only to boost his own credibility. Is there any chance that he, and not King, might have shot those two men?'

'A few years ago anyone suggesting that English coppers went round shooting people would have been certified, but these days? Your guess is as good as mine. I'd have thought it was unlikely, and even now you'd have a job getting the Appeal Court to believe it. This goes a bit further than firming up "verbals". Though, God knows, they'll believe more or less anything else about police corruption.'

'OK,' I agreed. 'Forget that. Just for the sake of argument, let's say that some person or persons unknown did the killings.'

'Oh, aye,' Paddy said sceptically, 'they've done a hell of a lot of crimes recently.'

'It was up to the Crown to prove King guilty, not up to him to prove he was innocent, and King's solicitor seems to be suggesting that they didn't play by the rules at his trial.'

'I see,' Paddy said with a grin, 'the old incompetent defence plea. You do know that they've widened the grounds for appeal against conviction? The verdict's got to be unsafe, and

81

if you can persuade them that King's trial lawyer didn't get the court to look at some piece of evidence they might . . .'

'It's not just that. Devereaux-Almond says an incident occurred in the trial.'

'Go on.'

'During a lunch break towards the end of the trial one of the jurors, a woman, was in a pub near Preston Crown Court. As she was waiting at the bar she overheard McMahon talking to Devereaux-Almond. He was saying that King's only chance was to plead guilty and try to cop a manslaughter sentence because his military training made him act instinctively when attacked. Devereaux-Almond was telling him that there was no chance that King would ever agree to that.'

'So what happened?'

'The juror reported what she'd heard to a court usher. The judge called in McMahon and the Crown prosecutor. Devereaux-Almond expected McMahon to come out saying that the judge had ordered a retrial but he didn't. He said he'd agreed with the judge and the prosecutor that his remarks weren't material and the woman would be instructed to disregard them. The trial went ahead. Devereaux-Almond feels that McMahon was certain King was guilty and that he didn't press the police or the forensic scientist hard enough.'

Paddy pulled a wry face. 'Hmmm . . . nice one, that. Interesting that McMahon went onto become Home Secretary.'

'So what?'

'So, although you don't any longer have to prove that the lawyer was "flagrantly incompetent" you'd have a hard job convincing them McMahon was no good in view of his present job.'

'What about evidence? Devereaux-Almond felt that the forensic scientist, Dr Sameem, was let off very lightly by McMahon.'

'All that means is that McMahon must have felt that Sameem had some other damning evidence that it was better not to draw the jury's attention to. Listen, David, you're on a hiding to nothing digging into a twenty-year-old case. Whatever she's paying you, it isn't enough.'

82

I must have smiled.

'She's not paying you! So forget it, you daft bugger! Anyone who'll do owt for nowt will steal, that's what they used to say round here. Let King get the Criminal Cases Review Commission interested. They're supposed to check up on these hopeless cases.'

'He won't ask them.'

'So why should you bother? Just being contrary and awkward again, aren't you?'

'No I'm not!'

'Oh, yes! You'll do anything to put the police in a bad light.'

'Not at all.'

'What is it then? You want to succeed with Mick Jones where I failed, is that it?'

I shrugged my shoulders and started to leave. The truth was I didn't exactly know why I was getting myself involved with King. The old man might even be right and my motive might be to put one over on him. All I knew was that I'd been asked to help and I couldn't come up with a convincing reason why I shouldn't.

I kissed my mother, made an excuse and left.

13

'Owt for nowt' was how my father put it. 'In for a penny in for a pound' was my own reaction. Once out of the parental cottage and back on the old rambling track I pulled out Morton V. E. Devereaux-Almond's letter. His address was in Rochdale, so I decided to pay him a visit as I was already in the Pennine margins.

I took the long way round the lane to the main road back into Bolton. When I neared the town centre I veered off towards Bury. My journey lay through Fairfield and Jericho and onto Norden, a newish suburb on the northern side of Rochdale.

There was a shiny new top-of-the-range Daimler saloon parked outside the double garage at Devereaux-Almond's detached neo-Georgian red brick house. The house was set in a substantial garden, looking across fields towards a reservoir and the hills beyond. Nice, though my inclinations tend towards the flatter and greener perspectives of North Cheshire. It can be hell in winter up here in the hills, not that climate seemed to bother Almond. His garden was like a lush green oasis, with well-tended lawns and flower beds at the front and a mass of shrubbery and more lawns at the back.

I approached the front door and rang the bell. The porch was flanked by two small brass cannon of the type they use to start yacht races, and I wondered if they were legal under the new fire-arms law. They gave the house a colonial flavour. I wouldn't have been surprised if the door had been opened by a turbaned Indian soldier rather than the faded, bitter-faced elderly woman who did open it.

'Can I see Mr Devereaux-Almond about a matter affecting one of his former clients?' I enquired, enunciating the many vowels in the solicitor's name with particular care. She scowled as if my request was an invitation to become a Jehovah's Witness. I quickly passed her one of my embossed business cards. The doubtful expression didn't lessen as she squinted at it. When she raised the card to her eyes I noted that she wasn't wearing a wedding ring and didn't seem to be quite as richly clad as one might have expected the chatelaine of such a villa to be. She was wearing a white housecoat, more like an overall really, over a faded floral dress.

'Are you police?' she asked with an aggrieved air. 'He's finished with all that now.'

So much for business cards, I thought.

'No, it's about a letter Mr Devereaux-Almond recently wrote to a client of mine. Her name is King but Mr Devereaux-Almond might know her better as Mrs Marti Carlyle.'

The Carlyle name produced a reaction. Her eyes went up into her head and then she studied my card again with a deepening frown on her face. Her hand had never left the door handle and she still appeared to be considering the possibility of slamming the door in my face. Eventually she made her decision.

'I'll see if he's at home,' she said reluctantly. 'You wait here.'

'Outside?'

'You'd better come in,' she muttered, waving me to a chair in the hall with a gesture of such economy that further verbal expression was unnecessary.

The hallway didn't appear to get much use. The furniture was all new, laid out like a showroom. My eye was taken by the one incongruous feature – a large picture of the Sacred Heart of Jesus in a massive dark frame by the entrance of one of the reception rooms. Mandatory for a nineteenth-century nunnery, it was as out of place here as a swear-box in a Royal Marines barracks. I mulled over the incongruity. The other pictures were prints of Lakeland scenes in light-coloured frames. Possibly Mr Devereaux-Almond was a man with a tender concern for his spiritual roots. The Sacred Heart was definitely making a statement about something.

The door through which the grim-looking skivvy/drudge/wife/partner had vanished opened and she popped her head

85

round it. Her washed-out blue eyes studied me appraisingly. I was sure she missed nothing of my thoughts about the religious icon.

'He's transplanting.'

'Oh!'

'In the greenhouse. He'll see you there.'

She led me through the kitchen which was decorated with religious pictures and encouraging proverbs and out by a back door. She motioned towards the greenhouse with the same spare signal she'd used at the front door.

'Thanks,' I muttered.

My impression of Morton V. E. Devereaux-Almond was that he didn't live up to his name. He had the length of body but not the grandeur to be a Devereaux-Almond. A tall beanpole of a man, there was something indecisive about him. He seemed young to have retired. He was holding a small brass watering can in one hand and a trowel in the other and was finding it difficult to decide which to discard as I approached. I held my hand out and made sure the smile on my face was in full working order. The handshake gave him a problem. He havered for a moment and then transferred the can to the hand holding the trowel. Then he put both down, wiped his hands across the front of his multi-pocketed gardener's waistcoat, and shook my hand limply.

'You must excuse me, Mr Cunane. Can't neglect these little beauties,' he said, gesturing at a tray of seedlings. His voice was high-pitched and uneven, putting me in mind of a delicate plant.

'I've come on Marti King's behalf. She wants me to investigate the circumstances of her father's trial to see if there's any chance of getting him out of jail.'

'A difficult task then. Almost an impossible one. He's a stubborn man, King. He could have tried for parole after doing two thirds of his sentence.'

'That's the problem, isn't it? He insists he's innocent of the crime he's doing time for. He also claims that his trial was somehow rigged.'

Devereaux-Almond stepped back as if I'd slapped his face. He puffed his cheeks up and slowly expelled a stream of air.

'Rigged trial, eh? That's off the wall even for King. We don't rig trials in this country. Procedural irregularities, that's all I suggested in the letter.'

'You seemed to be hinting that James McMahon should have insisted on a retrial when that juror overheard those comments he made to you.'

'I never hint at anything,' he said, turning to his seedlings.

'Marti, that is Mrs Carlyle, drew that inference from your letter.'

'Mr McMahon was a very experienced barrister. He took silk early, a brilliant man, one of the leaders of the Northern Bar. He himself suggested raising the issue before the Court of Appeal and they thought that the judge's directions to the jury were entirely proper, so I'm afraid that this is one hare that just won't run.'

'I'm sorry we're at cross purposes. Marti takes your letter as evidence that there were serious errors in her father's trial – not just McMahon, but the judge was at fault for directing the jury to ignore the defence of manslaughter which McMahon introduced even though King was adamant that he never fired at anyone.'

I pulled out a handkerchief and mopped my forehead. The temperature and humidity in the greenhouse were oppressive.

'You'd better come along here,' Devereaux-Almond suggested. 'You look like an England cricketer opening against Sri Lanka in the monsoon season.' He led me out to a garden seat under a cherry tree.

He must have caught the interrogative glint in my eye because he went on: 'My wife died some years ago. Bernadette, her elder sister, acts as my housekeeper. I hope she didn't give you her usual frosty treatment on the doorstep. She takes a rather protective attitude towards my privacy.'

I smiled politely, refraining from pointing out that he obviously needed someone to look after him. His waistcoat was wrongly buttoned up and he was wearing odd socks.

'No, what happened at the trial was this. Mr McMahon thought King's best chance was to plead guilty to involuntary manslaughter – that he shot the victims when they attacked

87

him and that his reaction was instinctive and the result of intensive military training. King wouldn't hear of it, but James McMahon wanted to keep it as a line of last defence. You know it often happens in these cases that the accused sees how well the prosecution is going and then changes his mind about the plea. Of course King was too stubborn to do that despite the overwhelming evidence.'

'According to King the evidence wasn't overwhelming.'

'Naturally, but, be that as it may, Mr McMahon's well-intentioned efforts to bring out King's excellent military record backfired. The Crown was able to plant the idea in the jury's mind that King was a cold-blooded killer despite never having been involved in violence in his previous criminal career.'

'I thought a brief was supposed to accept the client's instructions – as relayed through you, of course.'

Devereaux-Almond's expression darkened.

'Oh dear,' he piped, his voice rising to a squeak. 'I wish I'd never written that letter now, but Mrs Carlyle seemed so desperate when she phoned. I'm afraid I was too kind. I just wanted to reiterate that McMahon, as he himself admitted, may have mishandled the defence. You know it's one possible line of approach to the Appeal Court, especially since the Criminal Appeals Act 1995.'

I sat for a moment listening to the birds singing and trying to work out what to ask next. Devereaux-Almond beamed at me in a vague, unfocused way.

'How's the cricket going?' he asked. 'I went out to Australia for the last Test series.'

'Sorry, I didn't have the radio on in the car.'

'It's your office location,' he said, tapping my business card which I'd given him. 'Just down the road from Old Trafford. You must have lots of opportunities to slip off there for an afternoon. I'd have loved that, but I was stuck up here in Rochdale up to my eyes in conveyancing and wills.'

'I don't get much time to watch cricket.'

'Pity,' he said.

Light finally dawned on the thought that had been stumbling about in the shadows of my mind.

'Can I ask you a question, Mr Devereaux-Almond? How did you come to represent Vince King? Did he choose you, or did someone ask you to act for him? You weren't the duty solicitor, after all, and King was arrested in Salford.'

Devereaux-Almond started fiddling with the zippers on his waistcoat.

'I don't see the relevance of these questions,' he said slowly.

'Would you mind telling me how many murder cases you've been involved in? I'm only trying to follow the same line of enquiry you suggested about Mr McMahon.'

Devereaux-Almond abruptly jumped up from the garden seat and began striding around the lawn, his fingers fidgeting with one zip after another. I know a certain amount of eccentricity is considered amusing in legal circles, but Morton V. E. Devereaux-Almond was expanding the envelope. My sessions of gazing out of the office window have made me a connoisseur of walks. Ludicrous was the only word for Morton's walking action. Watching it induced nausea. His legs were completely uncoordinated with his arms. It was as if his brain had to send a conscious signal for each movement and he'd somehow got his wires scrambled.

Faith in his abilities would be the only reason to choose him as your defence solicitor, abilities that weren't very evident so far.

'I'm afraid there's no further point to these enquiries,' he said after a few minutes of pacing. 'If you see King tell him he'd be well advised to show repentance if he doesn't want to spend the remainder of his life behind bars.'

'You can hardly expect him to repent if he is innocent.'

'Rubbish! The world and his wife knows that he killed those two men, and now if you don't mind . . .'

'I don't care much for Vince King myself, Mr Devereaux-Almond,' I said evenly, 'but his daughter does, and somebody seems to have bowled him a googly somewhere along the line.'

Devereaux-Almond's lips puckered with distaste and he drummed his fingers against his forehead as if keying a message to his brain. 'It seems that the awkward Mr King has found a remarkably suitable representative in you, Mr

Cunane,' he said, enunciating clearly and slowly as for an idiot. 'Let me assure you that the man's defence was conducted as well as it possibly could have been, and if you think there's money to be gleaned by smearing his defence counsel and myself, go ahead. Your efforts will take you precisely nowhere.'

'But your efforts have taken you somewhere, haven't they?' I said cheekily.

'If you mean to imply that I didn't do my best for King, or that there was some kind of murky conspiracy involved in his conviction, that's a damned lie.'

'You still haven't told me how much experience you have in murder cases.'

'Get out of my garden, you squalid little man,' he yelped. On cue, the sister-in-law appeared at the kitchen door like a square leg umpire. I accepted my dismissal.

14

No sooner had I pulled out onto the main road back through Rochdale than my mobile rang. I pulled onto the verge to answer it, expecting it to be Celeste with an urgent summons back to the real world of debt collection, fake insurance claims and no time to watch cricket matches.

It was Marti.

'Dave, can I see you again?' she asked.

'Sure, but why? Has something come up?'

'You might say that, but I'd rather talk to you face to face.'

'OK, where?' I asked agreeably. After the interviews with Paddy and Almond my feelings towards Marti had softened. If she'd asked me to come to Leeds again I'd have agreed. That's the way my mind works, I do things by opposites.

'You sound pleased with yourself,' she said.

'No more than usual. Bigheadsville, Oklahoma; that's where I live, baby.'

'Hey! Less of the baby, big boy! Bring that solicitor's letter with you. I'll see you at that wine bar where we met before at about two.'

'No you won't,' I told her. 'I've got an interview with the Northern Mutual Insurance Company then. They pay for my services with coin of the realm.'

'You don't mind twisting your knife in the wound, do you? I've said I'll pay you when I can.'

'It's not like that at all, chuck. I'm on your case now. I just hate a client to get ideas above her station.'

'What? Have you found something?'

'My office at four,' I said.

I was back in Manchester in time to grab a sandwich at the

office and then scuttle over to the head office of the Northern Mutual Insurance Company. They hang out in a shiny modern office block in the commercial centre of town. Northern Mutual are a tight-fisted bunch, but they've put the butter on my bread for the last few months. I'm not entirely happy about working for them because at times they seem too anxious to snatch the crust out of some poor widow's mouth, but with the false claim business becoming a major industry they provide work for characters such as myself. I have to make some compromises to survive. In this case the trade-off between honour and starvation involved working with Ernie Cunliffe, senior claims executive at Northern Mutual.

It was a case of old school tie in reverse, or that's what I tell myself. I sat next to Ernie for five years at school and a pretty obnoxious creep he was then. Sly farts and peevish titters were what he specialised in. Time hadn't improved him. Ernie, who came from a rough part of Salford and whose father worked in one of the few remaining coal mines, left our Alma Mater at sixteen and went into insurance. I stayed on for sixth form and university entrance. Isn't education wonderful? Anyway, despite sharing a classroom we inhabited different worlds then and I saw little of Cunliffe after he left until he emerged as a purchaser of my services.

Ernie's one of those people who never miss a chance to remind the less fortunate how well he's done in the world. A real high flyer, he is. I mean, OK, if you think driving the latest BMW and having a big house in Wilmslow with pillars by the front door is what life's all about then Ernie has something to shout about. Employing me as a lowly claims investigator seems to give him a buzz. I wasn't snobbish at school, or I don't think I was, at least not intentionally. But I suspect that there's a little worm of resentment gnawing away somewhere under the Cunliffe cranium.

That's another thing. Ernie Cunliffe is almost completely bald on top, his shiny dome crowned with a few pale wisps combed up from the side like snow drifting off Mont Blanc. Every time we meet he asks if I dye my hair.

I like to respond by combing my fingers through my shaggy locks to prove that I'm not wearing a toupee or a wig. These fancies were weaving their way through my thoughts as I waited to be ushered into Cunliffe's superb minimalist, ultra high-tech Scandinavian office on the top floor of the NM building, itself a nightmare of Toytown architecture. A dream or a nightmare of blond wood and bare boards, every time I visit the important Ernie they've redecorated. There's always some new touch. This time it was a tiny spotlight on a long stem, carefully beaming a soft, pinkish light to bring the best out of Ernie's waxy green complexion. He saw me giving the room and himself the once-over as I went in. He was wearing a standard flavour-of-the-month charcoal-grey suit.

'Don't look down your long nose at me,' Cunliffe told me when I handed over the video showing that the claimant, a council worker called Carl Russell who said that his lumbar vertebrae had been bruised so badly that he was permanently crippled, was well enough to play football on the close where he lived. I got the long lens sequence through the fence of a nearby cemetery after three days' observation. The cemetery backed onto the small estate where Russell had a flat and he must have felt safe enough from prying eyes in there. The job hadn't been cheap. I had to bring in two part-timers disguised as gardeners to maintain the surveillance.

'Oh no,' I said hastily. 'I don't think anyone should get more than he's entitled to.'

'Why the long face then?'

'I was just wondering if you ever investigate employers as thoroughly as you do these little creeps. I mean, the guy was crushed when a skip fell on him and it was his firm's fault.'

'It's up to the Health and Safety people to sue, Dave. You know that. I'm going to throw the book at this bugger. Fraudulent claims are going through the roof. We'll have him jailed.'

'Is that necessary? I mean, you can see in the video . . . he was moving awkwardly.'

'Still an old softie, aren't you?' As Cunliffe lifted up his hands to tick off his points like a teacher hectoring a backward child, I noticed that he was wearing a new signet ring on the little finger of his left hand. There was a beautiful brown and yellow tiger's eye cabochon set in it. 'One. Russell has fooled the medical establishment. Two. He's fooled his employer. Three. He's gone round in a wheelchair for a full year, all in the hope of collecting from his employer's liability insurance. However, he's not going to. Move back six squares and go to jail, that's him.'

'So Russell does time for fraud. Some fat cat employer has an accountant showing him how to evade tax, and if he kills someone in his factory he gets a thousand pound fine.'

'All right, Dave, if your conscience is too tender for this work . . .'

'I didn't say that.'

'Look, this guy thought he could rip us off for half a million or more. We're not talking charitable donations here.'

'You're right,' I assured him. Looking into Cunliffe's cold grey eyes I didn't need any reminder that the Northern Mutual had nothing to do with charity.

'Fine, your cheque will be in the post tonight and I'll send you the file on another interesting mobility problem that's come up. They're all the rage at the moment.'

'Thanks, Ernie,' I said sincerely, smiling until my face hurt.

I left the insurance building a few minutes later after the usual detailed account of how well his children were doing at their private school, of how nicely the new BMW cornered and how good his golf handicap was. The thin wisps of hair on Ernie's head glowed like a halo in the glare from the spotlight.

I walked along Market Street. I couldn't help noticing how many men of my own age and above there were. Mooching around aimlessly, most of them, with a half stunned look on their faces. Their clothing was anything but prosperous – faded blue jeans, dirty trainers and tatty T-shirts that looked as if they'd seen service mopping the floors of Oxfam shops. Wealth was trickling down to the masses all right. At this rate it would have to go on trickling for another millennium before some of these people got a decent bite at the cherry.

I strolled through St Ann's Square with its better dressed people and younger, more hopeful faces and headed for my office. Soon I turned the corner into the narrow street where the headquarters, indeed only quarters, of Pimpernel Investigations stand.

Flashing ambulance lights strobed out from the pavement in front of my office. My jaw dropped open with a click. Two paramedics were kneeling over the prone figure of a man. They were working frantically to staunch blood which was dripping off the pavement into the gutter. A little ring of spectators was being held back by a PC. I joined them. Even at this distance there was something familiar about the man on the ground.

As I got closer the paramedics started hauling the injured man into the back of their ambulance. I got a glimpse of his face. It was Lou Olley, the minder who'd accompanied Charlie Carlyle that day in the spring. The crew had fitted him up with an oxygen mask but it didn't take a PhD in pathology to see that he was as dead as a mackerel. His arms flopped limply off the stretcher.

A female PC began to block access with police tapes strung between lamp-posts.

'I've got to get through, my office is down there,' I explained. My heart was beating so strenuously I was sure she would hear it.

'Sorry, you can't pass. You'll have to go round,' she insisted.

At that moment a white van arrived and more uniformed police piled out into the narrow street. Simultaneously, the ambulance started pulling away in the opposite direction. The young woman officer hurried away to report and another fresh-faced copper, this time an Asian lad aged about twenty, replaced her.

'Listen,' I said, lifting the tape and nodding towards the retreating WPC, 'she told me I could nip through. My office is only over there.'

The young copper looked at me, looked at the office and then at his superiors who were in conversation on the other side of the van, and let me through. I dashed to the door of Pimpernel Investigations. It was locked. There was a note, 'Back in five minutes', taped on the inside of the glass door. I looked down the street past the van where crowds were observing from the Deansgate direction. Celeste was among them. She waved excitedly. I abandoned the office and made my way past the blood-stained gutter on the opposite side of the street.

'Did you see it?' Celeste asked excitedly. 'They're saying it was a shooting.'

'He must have been run over or something,' I murmured hopefully.

'No, there's a man over there who saw the whole thing,' she said, pointing to an elderly white-haired man in a Barbour jacket who was giving his name and address to a uniformed sergeant.

'And where were you, miss?' I asked gently. I was grateful that she'd seen nothing, particularly that she hadn't identified Olley.

'You expect the mail to be posted, don't you?' she countered smoothly. It was true there was a letter box just round the corner. There was also a travel agency where Celeste's sister worked. In the circumstances I decided to let things rest. She'd probably been round the corner most of the time I was away.

'Right. What are they saying?' If there was gossip Celeste would have learned every detail by now, but before she could speak another contingent of police arrived and began pushing us all back towards Deansgate. We shuffled along obediently, and Celeste filled me in.

'I heard that man telling the copper that someone came up behind the guy that was shot. They were on a mountain bike and had a mask on. Shot the dude four times. God! I wish I'd been here,' she said fervently. 'I could have been a witness. It must have been cool.'

The mad pounding sensation returned to my chest. Where the hell was Marti King? I looked at my watch. It was two minutes after four.

'Celeste, stick to being a legal executive, will you? It's a lot safer.' By this time we'd been pushed all the way back along Deansgate. The crowd spilled over into the roadway. Cars started sounding their horns.

'Are you all right, boss?' Celeste asked.

'I'm fine. It's just that I was expecting a client at four. I'd hate to think she got mixed up in this.'

'No, that's OK. It was Ms King, wasn't it? She phoned to say that she wouldn't be able to make the appointment. She'll be at the Renaissance till five if you still want to meet her.'

96

It took me exactly two minutes to traverse Deansgate as far as the Renaissance Hotel. I didn't know what I expected to find – Marti King putting a notch on her shooter, perhaps. I certainly wasn't analysing the social implications of local dress standards as I ran down the traffic-clogged street.

I found her in the bar – where else?

15

'Are you the lady's husband?' the owl-faced barman called over as I approached Marti.

Speaking to her seemed more important than correcting him.

Marti was sitting, or rather slumping, over a low table. I tried to rouse her. She was completely zonked out. There wasn't a flicker from her eyes when I tried to wake her.

'She said she was expecting you, and honestly, sir, if I'd known she was going to get like this I wouldn't have let her stay.' He sounded anxious, even scared.

'How long has she been here?'

'Since two.'

'And she's not been out at all?'

'Of course not,' he said indignantly. 'You don't think I'd let her go out in this state? She was well plastered when she came in. She tried to buy drink with her gold card, Mr Carlyle. I let her have a couple of small brandies because I didn't want her making a scene.'

'Two small brandies?'

'Well, maybe more . . . I tell you, she was well away when she came in.'

His name tag said he was Clifford, and he screwed up his eyes and studied my face intently as if to memorise it. There was a pair of glasses tucked in the top pocket of his jacket.

They say your whole life flashes before you when you drown, and I started to drown the instant I heard that Lou Olley had been shot. I visualised all the times I'd been interrogated and worse over matters that had nothing to do with me – but I did have something to do with Lou Olley. I did have something to do with Marti, his boss's wife. It couldn't be

98

long before the plods decided that I must know why Lovely Lou was ventilated. I could hardly blame them. It was done on my doorstep. Why? Why? Why?

When the barman misidentified me it was like being thrown a lifeline. The last thing I needed was someone saying, 'Oh, yes, that detective where there was the shooting? He was with Mrs Carlyle at the hotel.' Ordinary citizens don't think like this, but they don't get pulled in as often as I do. The barman must have read the expressions of fear and relief chasing across my face as gratitude at his concern. I decided to go along with it.

'What do I owe you, Clifford?' I asked, taking out a twenty.

'I kept a tab,' he said, turning to his till.

I added another twenty after a glance at the tab.

'Keep the change,' I muttered.

Clifford beamed his appreciation and looked at me expectantly. I looked back at him. What was I going to do next? Getting out fast seemed like a good idea. I half turned towards the revolving door. As I did I saw that the manager and the hotel porter were poised at the exit of the bar. Turning on my heel and making a dash for it wasn't an option.

'I'll keep an eye on her if you want to bring your car up,' Clifford suggested.

My mind was racing. I was trying to visualise Janine's reaction if I arrived at Thornleigh Court with Marti slung over my shoulder. She'd be at home now after collecting Jenny and Lloyd. Leaving Marti to her own devices never crossed my mind.

'I don't like moving her,' I said hesitantly. 'I know it's a nuisance, but do you think I could get a room here, either for the night or until she feels better?'

Clifford lifted the bar flap and dashed up the steps for a whispered consultation with his boss and the porter. After a moment all three approached me.

'There's no problem at all, Mr Carlyle,' the manager said smoothly. 'If you'll just come up and sign the register, Clifford and the porter here will get Mrs Carlyle upstairs. We're always happy to oblige a member of the Carlyle family.'

I followed him to the desk and the receptionist passed a

registration slip. Signing my name, I got as far as the letter C and then hesitated. 'Tell me, has Mrs Carlyle been here before?' I asked cautiously.

'Yes once, about a month ago. She got in a bit of a state and your father sent his chauffeur to collect her in the Rolls-Royce.'

'Oh, that was it,' I said completing the Carlyle signature with a confident scrawl. 'If I need a doctor . . . Mrs Carlyle's unwell . . .'

'Don't worry, sir, we know how to be discreet.'

I got proof of that when I turned round. Clifford and the porter were already hustling Marti off towards a service lift. There were hotel guests dotted about the entrance area but I don't think they got a glimpse of Marti's disposal. The sunken bar and dining area was in semi-darkness.

I followed them and when we arrived at room 111 on the first floor the two men carefully deposited Marti on the bed. They both hovered by the door for a moment. One of the problems of impersonating Charlie Carlyle was that the man was noted for his well-stuffed wallet. I fished out my own emaciated pouch and put a tenner in each man's hand.

'Look, I'm really grateful,' I said diffidently, 'and the fewer people who know about this the happier I shall be.'

'Don't worry,' Clifford said. 'You can count on us. Would you like me to get them to send up some black coffee?'

'Yes,' I said, as Marti gave a stifled groan from the bed. 'That sounds like a very good idea, but leave it for an hour or so. I'd like to let her sleep this off before I try to wake her.' Then I remembered why I was here. The image of Lou Olley lying in a pool of his own blood was seared into my brain. I felt a shiver go up my spine.

I went over to Marti. She was lying awkwardly with her head propped against a pillow. I tried to make her more comfortable. I began to unbutton the expensive soft chamois leather jacket she was wearing. Her breath carried the sweet rich smell of brandy. I dropped the jacket on the floor and made her comfortable on the bed. She slept soundly.

I sat in the chair beside her. The room was filled with the faint hum of distant machinery and there was little air circulating in that hermetically sealed space. My own eyes began to feel heavy. I loosened my tie and slipped my feet out of my shoes, and before I knew it I had drowsed off.

When I woke I looked round at Marti, and her eyes popped open in a disconcerting return to consciousness, reminding me of her behaviour the first time I'd met her. I looked into those green orbs and as before it struck me that there was no expression there. The way she snapped back into wakefulness was chilling. She was like an automaton returning to full awareness at the flick of a switch.

'Oh, it's you,' she muttered without any trace of slurred speech. Her faint German accent was slightly more pro- nounced, but that was the only sign that she'd been on a drinking spree. She looked round the room and took in her surroundings. 'You know this is all your fault?' she said with a wave at the standardised furnishings. 'If you'd come to the wine bar at two like I originally asked I'd have been on a train by now.'

'What are you on about?' I asked.

'I've finally left Charlie.'

'You and Charlie must have had the longest ongoing break- up in history,' I joked.

'You've no idea how difficult it is to get away from the Carlyle family with a whole skin. What they have, they hold on to.'

'Do you know what happened outside my office?'

'Why should I? Thanks to you I've been in this dump all afternoon.'

'Lou Olley was shot dead by someone on a bike.'

Those two cool splinters of jade that had been intently focused on me now shifted to the ceiling as she took in the news. There was no shock, no intake of breath, no wailing and no hair-pulling; just a long pause while she considered the news.

'You think I had something to do with it?'

'Did you?'

'How could you even ask?'

'I have to ask. You were supposed to meet me at four; Charlie Carlyle's minder gets bumped off outside my office at five to. There's got to be a connection.'

101

'What connection?' she challenged. 'I was supposed to meet you at two, not four, and was planning to be on a train by three. There must have been a long queue of people who had it in for that pig Olley. He was the family collector, the one who kept an eye on the businesses that weren't quite so legal.'

'So it was coincidence that he was near my office shortly before you were due to arrive?'

'I wasn't due to arrive. I phoned your secretary and told her to tell you that I'd be here.'

'I didn't get the message until after the shooting.'

'So what? Do you think I arranged it all?' Getting unsteadily to her feet, Marti headed towards the door – probably making for the little bar in the entrance passage, but at that moment a maid arrived with a steaming coffee pot and Marti slumped into a chair. The maid put the coffee down without a word and paused to ask a question.

'Yes?' I said, wearily searching for my wallet.

'The lady's luggage, it's downstairs, sir. Will you be wanting it?'

I nodded.

When she'd gone I poured us both a cup of coffee. We drank in silence. A couple of minutes later two brand new Louis Vuitton suitcases were deposited in the room.

'Sobering me up, eh?' Marti eventually muttered with a grin.

'Sobering you up?' I gasped. 'I wish I knew your trick. You spend the afternoon pouring brandy down your neck but it seems to have less effect on you than lemonade.'

'That's just me,' she said proudly. 'Good metabolism. I'll live to be ninety.'

She swallowed the last of her coffee and I poured her another cup. 'I must get to London,' she said. 'I can't get away from Charlie in Manchester. He has too many contacts.'

'Listen, Marti, I don't care if you live to be a hundred and twenty and I don't care where you want to go, but I do want some answers,' I said fretfully. 'Why were you so keen to meet me this afternoon? Were you trying to fit me up or were you arranging for me to get the same treatment Olley got?'

'Dave!' she said with a laugh. 'You'll have me in stitches. As if I would want to harm you or anyone.'

'Why did you want to see me?'

I had news of my own for her but it seemed better to suss out why hubby's minder had got his jolts just before our rendezvous.

'Could you lend me the money to make a fresh start?'

'*What!*'

'I need cash. I'll pay you back.'

'And how much are you after?'

'A couple of thousand would do, just until I establish myself in London. You'll get it all back.'

'You've got a great sense of humour.'

'No, I'm just being practical. I'll need to get my own place and you know they ask for a deposit. There'll be no trouble in repaying you. Charlie's got to come through with what he owes me.'

I was undecided.

'Come on, Mr Detective, don't tell me you haven't got some salted away. If you really want to piss Charlie off, help me now. He'll come out in lumps when I don't come running home to him.'

I smiled at this not unpleasant idea. I had to admire her cheek. A second ago I was all set for a heavy question and answer session and now I was worrying about my bank balance. I made a motion of the shoulders that was halfway between a non-committal shrug and a shudder. Marti must have taken my movement as a refusal because she carried on arguing her case.

'I'll find a good job in London. Paul Longstreet will see that I'm all right.'

'*The* Paul Longstreet, the one with the clubs?'

'Yes, he's an old friend of Dad's, but if you'll lend me the money I won't be completely dependent on him while he fixes me up with something.'

'But doesn't he have all these lap dancers and such like? Is that what you're thinking of doing?'

'Oh, Dave,' her head went back as the laughter pealed out at ear-shattering volume, 'you think I'm a stripper?' I could see her head going back for another full-blooded chortle and I grabbed her.

103

'Haven't you got any volume control on that guffaw of yours?'

'People have been asking that since I was two years old, but I can't help it. You think I want to take my clothes off for greasy businessmen and that they would pay to look at me? Dave, that's the most flattering thing I've heard in weeks.'

Laughing again, she stood up and began fumbling for the zip at the back of her dress.

'You want to see me strut my stuff?'

'In the circumstances I'd rather postpone that pleasure indefinitely.'

'Ach! The awkward girlfriend! Dave, you deserve better.' She finally managed to locate the zip and in a second her dress, a navy and silver silk creation, was fluttering down to join her jacket on the floor. The lingerie revealed, which definitely wasn't from Damart, left little to the imagination. 'Ha! I can see I've embarrassed the great detective. Dave Cunane, you're blushing.'

'I am not!' I protested. There was a reaction that reminded me that I was still alive but I wasn't about to discuss it with her. 'Get yourself covered before someone comes in. I've registered in the name of Charlie Carlyle. How will I explain this if he shows up?'

'Oooh, naughty Dave! I wonder why you did that? But that makes it all right. Husbands and wives are allowed to look at each other,' she said, looping her hands behind her back to slip off her bra. I stood up.

'No, don't go.' She laughed again. 'I only want a shower.' She skipped across the carpet to the bathroom, at the same time flipping her bra off and tossing it over her shoulder at me. 'If you think your girlfriend wouldn't mind, you can come in and scrub my back for me. I can feel that train with my libido on arriving back in the station.'

I took this as a joke because the next thing she did was to shut the bathroom door and lock it. As soon as I heard the lock snap into place I plucked my mobile out of an inside pocket and phoned Janine.

'Dave, what's happening?' she said immediately. 'The police have been round here looking for you.'

'I wish I knew what was happening myself. What did they say?'

'They want to interview you in connection with an incident outside your office. I don't think they wanted to arrest you but one of them was all for kicking the door of your flat in. They might have done if I hadn't told them I was Press.'

'You should have let them try. That's a steel reinforced door.'

'Don't change the subject. What's going on? It's that Marti woman, isn't it?'

'Why do you say that?'

'Because the Carlyle Corporation has put out a statement denying that the man who was shot in the street practically at your front door was an employee of theirs, that's why.'

'Oh, denial. That figures.'

'It doesn't take a genius to put two and . . .'

'. . . make five,' I interjected. 'Listen, trust me, Marti isn't involved in that way and neither am I, but she could be in trouble. Do me a favour, go into my flat and look in the bottom of the freezer. You'll find a bag of frozen peas with some money in it.'

'Money? How thrilling, my partner has his assets frozen,' she said sarcastically.

'No, it's just a little hot money that I was chilling out for a rainy day.'

'Funny! And what am I supposed to do next?'

'Do you think you could find your way to the railway station in Stockport? Meet me there in an hour or so?'

'I don't see why I can't catch the train at Piccadilly like anyone else,' Marti grumbled as the taxi that was trundling us along Didsbury Road towards Stockport halted at traffic lights.

'Because if the police or your husband's friends are looking for you or me they're much more likely to be at Piccadilly than at Stockport.'

'If you're so careful why don't you drive me down to London yourself?'

'Marti, I do have a life here apart from sorting out your affairs.'

105

She was quiet for a while after that, deliberately turning her face away from me. I tried to work out what had been going on but I couldn't come up with answers that made sense.

Was it all coincidence? Hope said yes. Common sense said no. If the killer had been stalking Olley, my street would have done as well as anywhere. It was relatively quiet. Still, shootings aren't everyday events, are they? A contract killer would have wanted to go over the ground before doing the job. Escape's always priority number one for such people.

So the killer must have known where to come looking for Olley, and that could only mean – what? There were a thousand possibilities, but the one that wouldn't leave my mind was that Marti knew Olley was following her and that she told someone and arranged the whole thing, or – what? – Or my phone could be bugged . . . Or Olley told someone where he was going, someone who wanted him out of the way. Or someone was using Marti as a Judas goat, staked out to trap a tiger – Except she wasn't in the trap at the crucial moment. She was draped over a table in the bar of the Renaissance, which would be hard to beat as an alibi.

The thoughts went round and round, and eventually I cleared my throat to ask her again.

'You think I was responsible for Lou Olley's death, don't you?' she said before I could open my mouth.

'I don't know what to think.'

'Suspect, then?'

'If it was a coincidence it was very convenient that you were in the Renaissance instead of my office.'

'That looks bad, doesn't it?'

I kept my mouth shut.

'Dave, when you told me Olley was dead I know I was supposed to go into hysterics, howling and pretending that I was totally shocked, but I'm not like that. I've had all the shocks knocked out of me. When other kids were opening their Christmas presents I was being chased round Hamburg by the German border police. When normal girls were trying on their first party frocks I was breaking out of children's homes. By the time I was fifteen I'd been arrested, beaten and bullied more often than I can remember. I don't react like Ms

106

Average Brit. I learned early on that bad things happen if you let anyone know what you're feeling.'

'Marti, I'm not your judge. I'm going to help you to get to London . . .'

'But you'd like to think that I'm innocent, wouldn't you? That would help you to sleep easy in your bed with that hard-faced bitch who's got her claws into you?'

'There's no need for that.'

'Come with me, Dave.'

'You know I can't.'

'You're getting middle aged, aren't you?'

'So, I'm supposed to come over like some silly teenager when a beautiful woman makes herself available, am I?'

She laughed, not the full banana. It was just a little chuckle by her standards, but I could see the taxi driver watching us in his mirror.

'At least you think I'm beautiful.'

'You knew that already, didn't you?'

She laughed again. 'I really do fancy you, you know, Dave. We could make a good team. OK, I knew that Lou Olley was on my trail, that's why I wanted your help, but I didn't know that he was going to be killed. That was nothing to do with me, I swear. I don't know who arranged it, but I can't say I'm surprised. Lou lived very close to the edge.'

'Are you involved in something?'

'The only things I'm involved in are getting away from Charlie Carlyle and trying to help my fool of a father.'

I sat quietly for a while. I decided that it didn't matter whether I believed her or not. I was still going to help her. It was up to the police to sort out the Olley killing. The taxi trundled down the hill towards the viaducts and steep valleys of Stockport.

'Did you find anything to help my dad?' she asked eventually. 'You said you were on the case.'

'Yeah, I was. Has he considered applying to the Criminal Cases Review Commission?'

'Oh them! Of course he has. They said there was no new evidence and that the trial was properly conducted.'

I handed her Devereaux-Almond's letter.

'This guy is a genuine copper-plated bastard. He was no more use to your father than he would have been defending himself – less, probably.'

'You saw him?'

'This morning, and I think you can take it that he's now retracted all his reservations about your father's trial.'

'Oh, thanks a lot. Devereaux-Almond is the only person who expressed even the slightest interest in proving that Dad was wrongly convicted, and now his nose is out of joint.'

'You don't get it. He never should have been defending your father in the first place. I asked him how many murder cases he'd handled and he went off like a rocket. I can't understand how your father ended up with him.'

'What do you mean?' she asked.

'I was going to check out just why the double-barrelled berk was chosen as Vince's solicitor when Olley turned up dead on my doorstep . . .'

'. . . and I turned up drunk, is that it? Just drop it, Dave. I don't want you sticking your nose in with Devereaux-Almond.'

She fished in her bag for a moment and came up with a scrap of paper on which she scribbled a number.

'You'll be able to reach me at this number for the next couple of days, that is if you change your mind about stopping with Ms Frigid of Fleet Street.'

I took the paper and tucked it in my wallet.

I didn't say anything. There didn't seem to be too much to say. The taxi jerked and jolted its way through Stockport and deposited us at the railway station. Janine waved to us from the steps. She was shepherding Lloyd and Jenny and looked in no mood for long-winded explanations of which I'd prepared several during the journey. Her face was set into a pleasant, concerned smile resembling an accidental, oddly shaped spill of concrete.

'Here,' Janine said curtly, thrusting the plastic wallet containing my secret cash reserve into my hands. 'I'll be in the car over there.' She dashed off without a second glance, but the children were looking over their shoulders as she towed them to her battered Fiesta.

'Looks like Madam will be requiring a detailed statement,' Marti said. I could see she was shaping for a laugh.

'Don't,' I snapped. She reined herself in. I gave her £2000 in twenty pound notes. She watched me count it from the bundle. When I finished counting I was left with a hundred pounds in my hand.

'I hope this isn't going to leave you short,' Marti said.

'I'll be all right,' I muttered.

'In that case you might as well let me have the lot. I'll pay you back as soon as I can,' she said, giving me that cheeky smile of hers. She held her hand out and I gave her the remainder of my frozen reserve.

'Listen, if you don't get in touch I'll phone as soon as I get somewhere and give you my address.'

'No, Marti, that might not be a good idea. What I don't know I can't tell.'

'Mr Supercautious!' she said, giving a mild version of the clattering laugh. 'Do you think we're spies or something?'

'Hadn't you better get your ticket?'

'You want to rush away and rebuild your bridges with Ms White, don't you? Come here first.'

Obedient as ever I leaned towards her and she gave me a very energetic kiss. When I eventually managed to unclinch myself she uncorked the clarion laugh at top volume. All over the station people stopped doing what they had been doing and looked. I slunk away as rapidly as I could.

'Am I allowed to know what's going on?' Janine asked frostily when we'd got back to Chorlton and she'd managed to get Jenny and Lloyd squared away for the night.

'There's nothing going on,' I said disingenuously. 'Nothing you need to know.'

'Maybe I don't need to know, but I'm going to know. That man Olley was somehow mixed up with Marti King, wasn't he?'

'I neither know nor care if he was.'

'Yet you part with your life savings to help her get away.'

'I was going to ask you about that. There was well over five grand in that freezer . . .'

109

'You're lucky someone looks after you. I pocketed it. I might let you have it back if you answer my questions.'

'This isn't what they mean by chequebook journalism, is it? You're supposed to bribe me with the paper's money, not my own.'

'Dave, you need to get your story straight. Those coppers who came round seemed very certain that you were involved in the Olley killing right up to the tidemark round your mucky little neck.'

When I told her everything I knew she was disappointed. There was no story in it for her, at least nothing that could be printed without the Carlyle family getting in touch with their lawyers.

'What were you doing with all that money anyway, Dave?' she asked when I'd finished my inconsequential tale.

'Am I going to get it back?' I enquired. The money was part of what I'd received for various delicate transactions I'd been involved in – not money laundering or anything like that. Insull Perriss had paid me cash for collecting the material his blackmailers had on him. I was providing a public service really.

'You're sure you're not a hit man, Dave?' Janine asked as she delved into her bag.

'The only person I've ever felt tempted to hit is you,' I told her. 'If you hadn't blurted out all that stuff in the office that day about me killing people Marti King would have forgotten all about me by now.'

'I don't think so, Dave. You're not a very forgettable person.'

'Why don't you keep the money and use it towards the deposit on your new luxury pad in the Cheshire stockbroker belt?'

Janine passed me the wad as if it was burning her hand.

Paddy's phone call came just as I was on the point of sleep.

'Were you involved in that shooting today?' he asked in a barely audible voice.

'No.'

'Stay clear of the Carlyles. Brandon's a crook and a clever

one. I don't know how he did it, but he had the "one good tickle" all these career criminals pray for and he's been careful ever since. There's no knowing what he might do if someone starts poking around in his murky past.'

'Right, Dad, I'm not involved any more,' I said, comforted by his concern.

Before sleep claimed me again I wondered what he wasn't telling me. It was King's past I'd been prying into. What was the connection with Brandon Carlyle?

16

It was ten a.m. the next day before I got a visit from the constabulary.

Celeste showed DCI Cullen and a detective sergeant into my office. I held out my wrists for the cuffs as they trooped in.

Brendan Cullen was dressed in his usual high fashion 'Man at C&A' grey suit. He was the image of a smartly turned out policeman to anyone but a raving clothes snob like me. I looked again: there was a certain fullness, a sleekness about him that I put down to increased prosperity since his last promotion. I've always regarded Bren as a friend but with the understanding that he puts duty above personal matters. What I like about him is his unworldliness. His attitude to dress is an example of this. He could afford made-to-measure suits but I know he has a puritanical contempt for such indulgences. As long as his clothes are clean and new that should be enough. The fact that no off-the-peg suit will ever match his long body, short legs and expanding waistline is neither here nor there, a frippery undeserving of consideration. I've told him to wear sports jackets and slacks but no, a suit goes with the rank, so suit it must be.

The detective sergeant, who was called Munro, more than made up for Cullen's advance in the avoirdupois department. Lean to the point of emaciation, Munro was also a paragon of contemporary fashion. He was clad in a hideous brown suit with a four button jacket. His hair was close shaven and dyed yellow, not blond. Only a floppy blue cap with a bell on the end was needed to complete the picture of Big Ears and Noddy.

'What's this? My day for tailoring advice?' I quipped.

'Always joking, aren't you, Dave? One of these days I will

come in here and slap the cuffs on you.'

'What's stopping you? A murder five yards from my door, so it must be down to me. Isn't that the principle you lads operate on?'

'As it happens, it isn't. We know you knew Lou Olley and we know he knew his way to this office.'

'Let me guess . . . ex-detective sergeant Sticky Fingers Hefflin?'

'Correct.'

'I expect he told you that I was nursing a grudge because Olley beat me up?'

'He did have some suggestions on those lines,' Cullen agreed.

'The woman, sir . . .' Munro interjected.

'All right, sergeant, I'm coming to her,' Cullen muttered, waving his hand as if brushing away a troublesome insect.

'Yes, Dave,' he continued, 'it looks as if you've made another friend for life in Mr Hefflin.'

'I'm glad he doesn't like me. I can't stand corrupt coppers.'

Munro glared at me angrily. Cullen swung round and gave him one of the lazy grins that are his trademark.

'Now come on, sergeant, simmer down. Dave belongs to the irregular branch of our profession. He loves to wind us *real* detectives up, don't you, Dave?'

I shrugged my shoulders at the backhanded testimonial.

'Our ex-colleague was most anxious to implicate you, almost as keen as he was to prove that he had no involvement himself. Fortunately for you, the late Mr Olley had his snout in so many different troughs that people with a better motive for offing him than you are coming out of the woodwork like rats at a barn shoot. A very nasty gentleman was Mr Olley. The current word is that he didn't like paying his gambling debts. He was into an equally unsavoury customer for over a hundred thou.'

'So you've not brought the rubber truncheons? I'm told that someone was all for smashing in the door of my flat last night.'

Munro looked uncomfortable.

'This is informal, Dave, but you know and I know what effect the name Cunane has in certain quarters at Bootle Street.

113

As far as they're concerned you're Dishonest Dave with a capital D.'

'But you know different, Bren . . . er, Mr Cullen.'

'I called round to let you know that you needn't flee the country just yet.'

'I appreciate that.'

Cullen exchanged a glance with Munro. I twigged what was going on. This was intended as a lesson for the junior copper, a variation on the good cop, bad cop routine. Cullen was showing Munro that a spoonful of sugar could produce better results than a sackful of arsenic.

'You can help me, though.'

'Oh, yes,' I said warily.

'You aren't involved with Charlie Carlyle's wife, are you? Professionally or otherwise.'

'What do you mean by involved?'

'Come on, Dave. We both know your lustful nature.'

'Bloody cheek!'

'Are you giving her one on the side?'

'No.'

'If not,' he said slowly, looking me in the eyes, 'stay clear. Light the blue touch paper and retire ten paces is very good advice with that one.

'You're twisted, you know that?'

'It's the job, Dave. It's a long time since either of us was an altar boy. Where is she?'

'Who?'

'The only person who can tell us if her husband had any involvement in the hit on Olley. Don't pretend you don't know her.'

I could feel the waters closing over my head.

'Mrs Carlyle wanted me to prove that her father, Vince King, wasn't guilty of the murders for which he's serving life imprisonment.'

'Hah! Any progress so far?'

'Some, but as my enquiries don't come cheap and Mrs Carlyle is short of the necessary I've had to put that operation on a care and maintenance basis.'

'Dave, you're a barrel of laughs. We both know you run a

114

one man and his dog operation, yet here you are going on like Richard Branson.'

'I hire people in when I need them, including a good number of ex-coppers.'

'OK, you're the Businessman of the Year, but what about Mrs Carlyle?'

'I've told you what I'm doing for her and that's the limit of my involvement with her.'

'So she didn't try to score off a big soft lump like you for a bit of sympathy? Dave, don't forget I know you. According to Hefflin, you saved Marti that day at Tarn Golf Club. What would be more natural than for her to turn to you if she needed a bit of protection?'

'I'm running a legitimate business here and you're taking up my time . . .'

'You know where Marti is. Tell me and you'll not hear another word about all this.'

'What sort of business do you think I'd have if I went round giving information about my clients? I have no idea where Marti King is now but if she's got away from Charlie then good luck to her.'

'Perhaps a day in the cells at Bootle Street might persuade you to change your mind.'

'I don't know where she is.'

I got the full benefit of the Cullen grin after this. I didn't know which way he was going to jump. He had nothing on me and he knew it, but when has that ever stopped the police harassing me? Cullen wasn't stupid. He knew I was hiding something. He turned from me to his sergeant.

'Step outside for a moment, will you, sergeant?' he instructed Munro, who obeyed with a sulky frown.

'Where did you get the kid?' I asked as the door closed. 'On a Job Seeker's allowance, is he?'

'Joke if you want but the laugh will be on you if you're covering for that woman and she turns out to be a killer. Friend or no friend, I'll do you as an accessory.'

'I don't know where she is.'

'OK, Dave, you're not telling, but just don't get the idea into your head that you can stick your long nose into this. I'd hate to see you stretched out on a slab like Lou Olley. He was another clever guy with a lot of jokes.'

'He wasn't joking when I made his acquaintance.'

'No, and he isn't now. I've been at the PM this morning. Someone put two in his head and two in his body – special point two-two ammo, hollow point, Stinger bullets. This is premier league crime, Dave. Stay well clear.'

'Right, guv!' I said in a cockney accent.

Cullen stood up, shaking his head. At the door he turned round, anxious to have the last word. 'Dave, are you really making some progress in getting Vince King out?'

'Yes,' I said bravely.

'Well, if I was in charge of a massive detective machine like you I'd suspend operations until I knew exactly why Lou Olley was slotted.'

He favoured me with another of his enigmatic grins. This time I felt a shiver as if someone was walking over my grave.

17

When they'd gone Celeste came in.

'Do you want me to spray air freshener in here?' she asked.

'Why?'

'Oh, they stink, that lot. If you could bottle their odour you could market it as Human Repellent.'

'I had no idea you felt so strongly about the Blues.'

'I can't stick them. My brother's got a BMW and they're always stopping him just because he's black.'

'Celeste, if you want a career as a legal executive you're going to have to get used to them. They're not all bad. The one with the suit that looks like a sleeping bag, DCI Cullen; he's all right.'

'If you say so, Mr Cunane,' Celeste replied, scepticism dripping from every syllable.

I looked at her. This was the second time in recent days that I'd found myself defending the police. What was happening to me? I shook my head.

'Any business coming our way?' I enquired. My question was far from casual. As I'd boasted to Cullen, I had a number of casual employees, all of whom knew how to charge for their services.

Neither the cheque nor the promised file from Northern Mutual had arrived. No doubt Ernie Cunliffe was demonstrating just who was top of the class these days. I made a mental note that I wouldn't phone his office and give him the opportunity for a little gratuitous fun. One of the advantages of being at ground-floor level on a busy street in Central Manchester is that I get a fair number of casual callers. Some of them think that I'm a branch of the Citizen's Advice service but others have problems that I can help to solve. If I stuck to the casual callers I might make enough to just about pay the rent and live on air. I told myself that I had to look on their problems, impossible to resolve though most of them were, as the price I paid for independence from the likes of Ernie Cunliffe.

'Yes, there's a lady waiting for you. She looks like a real saddo.'

'Wheel her in,' I commanded. 'Oh, and Celeste, if she's not out in ten minutes you might like to pop your head round the door and ask if I want coffee. Then if she's biting the carpet you can wrestle her out into the street.'

'Yes, boss,' she said scornfully.

After that the day went ahead briskly, if not very profitably.

The lady Celeste brought in was a tall, painfully thin and anxious woman of about forty with a *café-au-lait* complexion. She was clad in a long raincoat of identical colour to herself that reached almost to the ground and she said she wanted me to help her feed the pigeons in the park. They say pet-lovers begin to resemble the object of their affections. This lady's nervy, jerky manner seemed to confirm that.

Mrs Griffiths had prominent, watery blue eyes. Too much iodine or something, I guessed.

Her problem was simple. Every morning she went into her local park to feed the birds. All I had to do was turn up and walk into the park with her to shield her from the attentions of a fanatical pigeon hater who was threatening to ram the bird food down her throat. As the park was local and the time early I agreed.

A second-hand book dealer I know always tells me that he's had a 'slow week' when I try to offload some of my surplus reading matter on him. It looked like being a fast day at Pimpernel Investigations, because no sooner had Mrs Griffiths departed than Celeste showed in the next customer.

When he came in I thought someone was pulling a wind-up. We've all heard of Elvis lookalikes; the elderly man who shuffled in now was a Harry H. Corbett lookalike. He was clutching a trilby in his hand and sported a head of dense black hair. Far from receding with age, the man's hairline appeared to be advancing down his forehead like a coal tip on

118

the slide. Bushy black eyebrows, long sideboards and heavy black plastic framed glasses completed the impression of a man in disguise.

I looked at him for a moment before speaking. I wondered if I was expected to guess who he really was. But no, he was a bona fide customer.

His problem was that he'd lost his wife . . . Not a bereavement, he'd just mislaid her.

It took some coaxing to get to the facts. He had a curious way of speaking. Every other sentence he uttered was a question spoken softly in a pronounced Yiddish accent that life in Manchester hadn't erased. The sentences were punctuated with significant hand gestures.

Mr Levy told his tale with an air of world-weary sadness. He was wearing a well-cut green three-piece worsted suit complete with gold watch chain and was shod in a pair of those expensive handmade brown leather brogues that are supposed to be the trademark of the English land-owning classes. An exotic touch was supplied by the silver-handled cane he carried.

It turned out that Mr Levy was not in fact a country landowner but a gentleman of the turf.

'You've heard of Pearl,' he said with quiet pride. 'That was me. Started from a little shop much smaller than this office.'

'Weren't they taken over by . . .'

'I sold out five years ago. You know how many betting shops I had? Thirty-nine!'

I don't know whether I was more flattered or surprised. Whatever else he was, Mr Levy must be a millionaire many times over. I decided to drag the conversation back to the matter in hand: 'And now your wife's gone missing?' I said.

'Blunt, businesslike . . . I like this,' Levy said in a deep, rumbling voice. He didn't seem to be overwrought about the disappearance of Mrs Levy.

'Er . . . when did you know she'd gone?' I asked.

'Two months ago, end of June. We married in April.' He made a chopping motion with his right hand into his left palm.

'So let's get this straight. You were married approximately

four months ago and then two months after the wedding Mrs Levy went AWOL?'

He nodded gravely.

'Have you made any effort to trace her?'

Levy smiled and then shrugged as if I'd asked for the combination of his personal safe.

'Mr Cunane, anyone ever call you names, eh?' he said, illustrating his difficulty with expansive open-handed gestures. 'Some of my friends have names for men who can't keep their wives in order. Not very nice names, not names that I should wish someone to call me. At first I thought . . . maybe another man. It happens, yes? So I waited for her to get in touch. Anyone would, right? Then I found that she'd gone home to her mother. Only me, do I have the mother's address? No. So what do I do? I come here.'

'I see.'

'It's like every day is holiday when you marry a young wife, isn't it?' he asked.

I nodded, waiting for him to go on, but he paused courteously for my comment.

'Just how young is your wife?' I asked awkwardly.

Now my potential client's head started rocking while his right hand gyrated at the same tempo as if he was conducting the Hallé Orchestra through a slow movement. A faintly rueful smile played on his lips as he spoke. 'Is twenty-five too young? Asking too much, eh?'

'From you or her, Mr Levy?'

'Yes, that's the question. Yes, her or me, eh?'

'So your wife is twenty-five?'

'She could be about that, yes. I think so.'

'Is she or isn't she?'

An expressive shrug was the only answer I got.

Mr Levy's elliptical remarks set off a warning bell. Once I traced a 'missing wife' only to find that she was a stalker's prey. What sort of husband doesn't know his wife's age?

My suspicion communicated itself to Mr Levy because he leaned across the desk with the gravity of a man making a final plea to his bank manager. 'She's not Jewish, you see,' he insisted. 'I made a mistake by marrying out, not that I'm prejudiced. Waste of time, isn't it? Life's too short.' He then placed a large brown envelope on the desk and signalled me to open it.

'How do you mean?'

'Angelina couldn't cope with life in a new country.'

'I see,' I muttered. Not that I did see. I was busy looking through the documentation he'd provided. Angelina was certainly his wife. He'd brought the marriage certificate and wedding photos to prove it. Angelina was a Filipino woman, a mail order bride.

I looked at him quizzically.

'Three years ago,' he said, 'a friend told me I should go on a cruise to the east. Fine and dandy, I'm not getting any younger, am I? So I go with him. We get to Thailand and suddenly it's raining young women, all eager for a bit of fun. I mean, old as I am, I still have feelings, yes? At first I thought they were just being friendly. Hah! I haven't had any operations to put that department into retirement, have I? All is hunky-dory, we get back to England and there are certain consequences . . . I can tell you this – you're a man of the world aren't you, Mr Cunane?'

I nodded, trying to guess what was coming next and keep the smile off my face.

'Hah!' he laughed, banging his cane on the floor. 'I go to the clinic for treatment and I say to the doctor, I bet you don't have many men of my age coming here for this. Well, laugh, the doctor's in stitches! Doctor Mac-What's-it, he says, you're not the oldest. We had a guy of ninety in last week. Gonorr what-you-call-it, same as you. You old geezers go on the cruises, I know all about you . . . He's a good sort, that doctor, knows how to put a man in an embarrassing position at his ease. He's like you, Mr Cunane, nothing can shock him.

'So I go again the next year and this time I take precautions but still I have to visit that same doctor again. You know, this time it is embarrassing. He thinks I don't learn by my mistakes. So this year when my friend comes round I say, let's try somewhere different this time. We go to Bangkok but for the food and massage only. The ship sails to Manila and there we get off. We meet not just the girls but their whole families,

121

lovely people – mother, father, brothers, sisters, uncles, aunts, grandparents . . .'

The silver knob of Levy's cane rose and fell as he registered each degree of his lady-friends' kindred with a rap on the floor.

'So the next thing I know we're all talking about marriage and I find that, old as I am, I'm engaged.'

'Did any money actually change hands?' I asked.

'Hah! The cynic!' Levy said, tossing his head back. He put a finger to the side of his nose. 'I did pay for her air fare, clothes, trousseau and expenses, and if it seemed to run a bit expensive who's to say it shouldn't? Those people haven't got much.'

'I see,' I muttered.

'You can see she came with good references, even one from her parish priest. I took her to Ireland with me . . . the racing . . . I don't know, maybe it was being in a Catholic country again made her homesick.'

After half an hour of him lobbing my verbal volleys back to me as I tried to probe the circumstances it emerged that Mr Levy suspected that his wife might have saved up her spending money and flown off to Manila – there were charges for air tickets on her credit card statement – and would I like to go and fetch her back?

'Now, Mr Levy, it's not like changing your library books. I can't just go over there and pick her up off the shelf.'

Mr Levy took a chequebook from an inside pocket and with elaborate slowness opened it, then took out a gold-capped fountain pen, unscrewed the top, and poised the nib above the paper. He looked at me expectantly.

'Name a figure,' he commanded. 'You might be out of the country two weeks, say three weeks. You could do the job in a couple of days and the extra time will be a bonus for you, yes?'

I got the impression that this wasn't the first time or even the hundredth time Mr Levy had got a result by waving his chequebook at someone. There was a glint in his eye as he tried to coax compliance out of me. Was I supposed to drool with greed?

That little glint in his eye made my decision easy. 'Sorry, but I'd be taking your money for nothing. I can trace your wife in

Manila without leaving this office. I can get a private detective over there to find her and ask her to get in touch.'

'You go yourself and I'll pay. That's the best way, isn't it?'

'No, Mr Levy, it isn't. We aren't even sure that Angelina's still in the Philippines. Did she have any friends in England?'

'Married two months, we were. No time for friends, was there?'

'I don't know. Did she go out? Did she meet people?'

'I told you. I gave her a wonderful home. Everything delivered from catalogues. No need for her to go out, was there?'

'What about your relatives? Was there one of them she might have been interested in?'

'Do I have relatives now? Do I look like a man with relatives?' He sounded quite offended.

'She must have met someone . . . the milkman, the gardener?'

He shook his head resolutely. I could feel Mr Levy's two brown eyes boring through to the back of my skull.

'Did she phone the Philippines often?' I asked after an interval.

Levy shook his head impatiently.

'Enough questions,' he said and then flashed his pen over the chequebook again. 'I pay you, you find her.'

'It's not that simple,' I argued, fully aware that to Mr Levy it apparently was that simple. You press the right buttons and a guy gets on the plane to Manila in pursuit of errant wife – simple.

'What's the matter with you?' he asked, rapping the side of his head with his index finger. 'You want to let a paying customer walk out?'

'No, I'll take a normal advance to get someone else to trace your wife in the Philippines, a local man. That will be much cheaper for you. I'll just charge a handling fee.'

I scribbled a figure on a scrap of paper and pushed it to him. He shook his head and then made out the cheque.

'You'll never get rich looking free horses in the mouth, Mr Cunane.'

'True, but maybe I won't get my teeth kicked in so often this way,' I muttered to myself when he'd gone. I studied the picture of Angelina that he'd left on my desk. Her head was tilted back. Even teeth were displayed in a warm smile and a lock of hair tumbled across her forehead. Her features were as regular as a child's drawing and about as appealing. If this was what Mr Levy wanted in a wife, how did he fill her requirements? That was easy. He was rich and gullible.

So why had the wheel come off the wagon?

Some private investigators of my acquaintance would have bitten Levy's hand off right up to the armpit. What could I have asked for – £10,000, £20,000? Perhaps even more to deliver Angelina to England, willing or unwilling. A real shark would entice Angelina back by offering to split the take with her. She wasn't unattractive. Yes, a forward lad would work his wiles on the lovely Angelina and use her to squeeze poor, rich Mr Levy like a lemon, or do something even more sinister. After all, as his wife, Angelina stood to inherit Levy's worldly goods. The possibilities were endless.

Mr Levy must have been a shrewd operator at one time, but now here he was walking into the office of a private investigator he didn't know from Adam and throwing his chequebook around. Possibly the shock of Angelina's departure had knocked him off his gimbals, though he certainly didn't look grief-stricken. I scratched my head and tried to work it out. I told myself there must be a catch in it somewhere. Levy didn't seem to be in the grip of Alzheimer's, but you never can tell.

I spent much of the rest of the day on the phone and fax machine. I phoned the home number of a private detective I knew in Sydney. It was one o'clock in the morning there as he immediately informed me.

'Jeez, I dunno, mate. You pommy bastards. Don't you work normal hours?' he grated in an exaggerated Strine accent.

'Cut the crap, mate,' I said. Tommy Braithwaite had emigrated from Manchester only three years previously. 'You're always saying you want to keep in touch with your roots.'

'Yeah, well cobber, Dave, me old bludger, what's this Sheila worth to me?'

I named a figure and after some addition for unsocial hours he promised to phone back, which he did half an hour later.

Braithwaite gave me the number of a reliable man in Manila who was used as a stringer by the agency for which he worked. It was 1.40 a.m. in Manila when I spoke to the Filipino detective. He made no fuss about the time but quickly robbed me of the illusion that all Filipinos speak fluent English with an American accent. His language was Spanglish with quite a lot of other words thrown in. After half an hour of linguistic gymnastics and much debate about fees he agreed to track down the homesick runaway and persuade her to get in touch with her old man.

My day's labour wasn't concluded. At around four Celeste showed in a hard-eyed young woman in leather trousers with silver rings through her eyebrows, a Miss Greenidge. I sensed a certain aggressive streak in Miss Greenidge's makeup as she bounced up to my desk and plonked herself in front of me. She fronted at me boldly as if challenging me to turn her down. Celeste watched me too.

'Coffee for two, Celeste,' I said before turning to the client.

Would I care to help her gather evidence for a sexual harassment case against her former boss? She had the money to pay me. A legacy had recently come her way.

I would. Employment tribunals represent an expanding field for the upcoming private investigator.

Georgia Greenidge poured out her story. The confusingly named George Gammage, her supervisor at a credit card company, wanted to have his wicked way with her. She had made it very clear that she did not welcome Gammage's attentions. Now he'd fired her and she wanted to do the business on him.

I scrawled the words *Greenidge, Gammages, Damages* on my notepad, a limerick already struggling to be born at the back of my mind.

The euphoniously named boss had tried his luck with most of the other girls in the office, always threatening to reward failure to co-operate with dismissal. I studied Georgia's features as she spoke. There was something legendary about her – the Greek legend about the three sisters who share a

125

single eye and a single tooth. That wasn't fair, but she was on the ugly side of plain without having the sort of face that makes young children cry out in fright. You could say she was strong featured. As these un-correct thoughts popped up unbidden, like poisonous mushrooms on a dewy green lawn, I struggled to suppress them.

Plain or ugly, Georgia was entitled to help. All I had to do was to contact nine other women who'd recently left the office and find out if they were prepared to make statements against Gammage. The man was obviously a menace, a man of no restraint if he was prepared to resort to blackmail to impose himself on poor Miss Greenidge. Clearly, he had Georgia on his mind.

When she'd gone I jotted the names Greenidge/Gammage on top of a file and then wondered idly if it was the potential for alliteration that attracted Gammage. I decided not.

These thoughts were still buzzing round my head when I joined the stream of traffic leaving Manchester along with all the other sex-hungry office workers, disappointed husbands and pet-lovers.

18

'Dave, you look like an actor who's just been told that he's not getting the star part he was promised.'

'I don't know what you mean.'

'Yes, you do. You were hoping that Cullen would arrest you and give you the reason you needed to get involved with the Carlyles.'

I'd made the mistake of telling Janine about my exciting morning. Being told that she knew me better than I knew myself was mildly annoying but I didn't feel like starting a quarrel.

'Not at all,' I claimed. 'The only thing I'm devoted to now is the steady accumulation of capital, a healthy bank balance, and the prospect of being able to convince the woman I love to relax her defences long enough for me to get close to her.'

'But which woman is it that you love?' she asked.

'You know very well.'

'Let's just try to get through the next few months without any more crisis calls to deliver cash to indigent rich women at Stockport Station and then we'll see how things are working out.'

'Yes, that's all I want,' I said lamely. 'Let's get on with our lives.'

'Yes. Listen, Dave, you need to keep your nose right out of that designing little tramp's business. Our crime editor on the paper reckons that the police are putting Olley's murder down to family squabbles among the Carlyles, so your new lady friend is probably involved right up to her false eyelashes.'

'Oh!'

As often when perplexed I retreated to my kitchen. I'd been spending so much time in Janine's flat that my own kitchen was showing signs of neglect. There was brown carbonised grease on the oven racks. Working slowly, I rubbed each metal bar down until the gleaming steel underneath was completely revealed. Then I noticed dirt or grease in the narrow cracks where the glass of the oven door fitted into the frame. It took me the best part of an hour of dedicated labour before the last trace was removed. By then I was beginning to feel hungry.

I cooked a large portion of pasta with mozzarella and tomato and stolidly munched my way through it. As digestion eventually took hold ruffled feathers folded back into place. I was as comatose as a recently fed crocodile by the time the phone rang.

It seemed to be ringing with an unnaturally penetrating noise. As my hand went down to the receiver an expectant voice at the back of my brain seemed to say 'Marti?'

'Cunane?' a disappointingly deep male voice enquired.

'Yes,' I grated, finding the word right at the back of my throat.

'I've got to see you, it's urgent.'

My caller obviously expected me to know who he was but for the life of me I couldn't place him. My brain seemed to be clogged with glue.

'Why now?' I asked, playing for time. 'Can't you see me at the office tomorrow?'

'Smart idea,' the voice commented sarcastically. 'The police still have tapes up round the spot where they hope to prove I arranged for Lou Olley to be killed. I'll look well walking into your office past a parade of CID men.'

The penny dropped. It was Charlie Carlyle. I tried to get my brain into gear.

'You could come round,' I suggested tentatively.

'They've been asking me all day long if I'm involved with you in some way. The last thing I want is to come round to your dump.'

His sweet-natured comment restored normal service to my cortical processes.

'Where would you suggest that's grand enough for you? A suite at the Midland?'

'I'm sorry,' he said in exactly that tone which conveys lack of sorrow. 'That came out wrong. I'm stressed. Listen, I must speak to you about Marti. It's life and death really.'

'That urgent?' I muttered.

'Cunane, I know I offered you cash in hand last time we met and you threw it back in my face but I'm really begging you now. Name your own price; anything, a job, some action, anything you want. I need to see you.'

What was going on here? He was trying to put me in the frame for the Olley killing.

'Oh, yeah, Charlie boy,' I drawled. 'I turn up for a meet and you finger me to the fuzz as the stage manager of Lou Olley's final scene?'

'Don't be so dramatic, Cunane. No one thinks you arranged Olley's death, but I know you had something to do with my wife's sudden exit. I'm desperate to see her again.'

'Why?'

'Turn up and find out if you haven't lost your bottle.'

'And why should I do that? Last time we met you had a bent copper and your minder with you. I may be stupid but I don't intend to repeat that experience.'

'That was a total mistake, Olley's fault. I swear on my mother's grave that I'll be on my own.'

I was quiet for a moment. If I'd received a tenner every time I'd heard some scumbag swearing on his mother's grave I'd have been able to retire years ago and motherhood would have gone out of fashion. But caution was at war with curiosity and it was finding itself outgunned.

In the end I arranged to meet Carlyle in the car park of a hotel near the airport about halfway between his home and my dump. Janine had suggested that I was seeking a starring role in events which were none of my concern yet here was Charlie Carlyle, *the* Charlie Carlyle, demanding to meet me.

The rough-spoken world was shrouded in darkness when I got out of the flat. It was foggy with an early autumnal mist.

I drove carefully down the M56 to the turn-off for the airport and then on past the second runway to where the Swiss Village Hotel nestled in a valley close to the ravaged woods of Styal. I stopped on the road outside the hotel and went ahead

129

on foot. The intermittent roaring from the runway apart, it was a quiet night.

Sure enough, there was a Rolls-Royce sitting in isolation at the far corner of the almost empty car park. I couldn't see anyone moving about but that proved nothing. Carlyle could have a hundred men concealed. When I retraced my steps to my own car I had the feeling that in every sense I'd come too far to turn back. I'd helped Marti and inadvertently Charlie. To the police I was already culpable. Self-preservation dictated that I try to find out more.

As soon as I pulled into the car park Carlyle flashed the lights of his Roller at me. I slipped the Mondeo into a space next to him and wound down my window. There was an answering buzz as his electric window slid open.

'Cunane! Get in, man! I'm not sitting here shouting across at you,' he said. Even in the dim lighting of the car park Carlyle's red face seemed to be glowing from an unhealthy source of internal heat.

I shook my head.

'You get in here, big boy. Last time we met you had muscle with you.'

He gave a sour look at this reminder and reluctantly abandoned the padded leather and mahogany luxury of his car. You can't really slam the door of a Rolls-Royce but Charlie did his best. The door shut with a heavy clunk, and he joined me. Suddenly the Mondeo felt crowded. There was a smell of new leather from the jacket he was wearing. The man who sat next to me now was very different from the aggressive maniac of our first encounter and also from the would-be hard man who'd come looking for Marti at my office. All the stiffness had gone out of him. He slumped into the car seat like an outsized sack of spuds.

'What gives, Chief?' I said.

'Was it you with Marti at the Renaissance yesterday?' he asked nervously.

There didn't seem to be any point in denying it so I nodded my head.

'Thank God,' he gasped fervently.

'How did you find out?'

130

'The manager phoned to remind me that I hadn't paid for the room my wife and I had used.'

'Oh,' I murmured.

'Crafty bugger, aren't you?'

'Have you told the police I was impersonating you?'

'Like hell I have. Where's Marti now?'

'Why?'

'She's not with you, at your flat in Chorlton, I mean?'

'No.'

'No, I didn't think she would be.'

'What does that mean?' I retorted. 'Don't you think my squalid little home would be good enough for her?'

'Cunane, we seem to have got off on the wrong foot. Can we rewind things back to the beginning and start over?'

'You trying to bash Marti's head in was the foot we got off on, mate; and then you having me slapped round my own office by Olley and that tame policeman of yours.'

'It's no good me apologising for what Olley did but what you saw at Tarn that day wasn't quite as it seemed.' There was a bashful grin on his face.

I suppose it was the curiosity that had brought me so far that kept me sitting there waiting to hear what the poor little rich boy had to say.

'You're a cheeky devil, aren't you, Cunane? Signing that register in my name . . . but your sheer brass neck has saved me some awkward questions.'

'Oh, yes? Were you busy making sure Olley's gambling days were over?'

Charlie-Boy clenched his fists and ground his teeth in anger. I tensed myself to hit him back if he went into rage-overload.

'Of course I wasn't,' he eventually bleated. 'Do I look like the sort of person who does that sort of thing?'

'If you want sympathy from me you've come to the wrong shop,' I told him.

'Answer me,' he insisted angrily. 'Do I look like the sort of person who gets involved like that?'

'Don't come fishing for compliments from me. I saw the bruise you put on Marti's face.'

'What are you on about? I told you, I've never hit her.'

131

'Oh yes?'

'Get out of this bloody heap of scrap metal and we'll sort this out once and for all,' he snarled. 'You need a good smacking and you're going to get it.' His hand clawed along the door searching, but failing, to find the handle.

'Fine by me,' I said. 'I'd just love to see what you're like when you haven't got a shotgun or a minder with you.' This produced no reply apart from a lot of very heavy breathing. He struggled to master his temper and stopped trying to open the door.

'I didn't come here for this,' he muttered eventually. 'What the hell are you, Cunane? Some sort of antediluvian Communist? I thought you were a businessman.'

I made no response to his plea for capitalist solidarity. He sounded pathetically sorry for himself.

'I was involved in some very delicate negotiations at the time Olley was stupid enough to get himself killed. The people I was with are not the sort you can ask for an alibi.'

'Oh, I see, criminals. What were they, Turkish drug dealers?'

He laughed, and he laughed, and he laughed. Tears started streaking down his fleshy face. He took out a handkerchief and began dabbing it at that big red dial of his. I didn't feel exactly gratified to be the source of so much mirth but I wasn't in any doubt that he was amused. I told myself that his change of mood was down to relief that we weren't trying to punch each other's lights out.

'Christ! Cunane, it's true what they say about you,' he wheezed eventually.

'What?'

'That you've got a vivid imagination, that's what. Listen, man, there are occasions in business when it's not a good idea to make it public knowledge who you're talking to – take-overs, mergers, that sort of thing. Believe me, when there's big money involved I'm not about to put much faith in the confidentiality of the constabulary.'

'So when did you decide that it was time for Olley to cash his chips?'

'I'm telling you that I had nothing to do with Olley.'

132

'Do you ever stop lying?'

'You're just like the police, aren't you?' he said. 'Do you ever believe what anyone tells you?'

'Convince me then.'

'The firm had to let Olley go. You saw what he was like. He couldn't make the transition from being Mr Heavy-about-Town to being a . . . oh, hell! . . . a business associate. He hasn't worked for us in months. I think I just about managed to convince the police of that, but they want to see Marti to confirm that I haven't any motive for killing the thick-necked yob. Her disappearing like this, it's a damned nuisance.'

'Oh dear,' I muttered. 'What a shame.'

'I'm not going to insult you again by offering you chicken feed. Name your figure, man, but I need to know where Marti is.'

'Sorry, no can do.'

'What is it with you? I am her husband.'

'Yes, and you just happen to like using her as your sparring partner.'

'That again! You may not believe me but I've never actually struck her with my fist.'

'Chuck it, Charlie. I've seen her with a black eye. She was terrified of you.'

'Did she say it was me gave her the black eye? No! Or me that she was terrified of? No!' There was something in his voice that rang true. Charlie wasn't a clever enough liar to keep faking all that indignation. There was no doubting what I'd seen at Tarn, though. Charlie-Boy liked to use his strength, if not his fists, on women.

'I'm not denying that Marti and I have had our problems but if you guessed for a million years you'd never come up with the reason, not even with your imagination.'

'So what was the reason?'

'None of your business,' he snapped. Then he paused for a moment. 'Let's just say that Marti is more ambitious for me than I am for myself.'

'How cryptic,' I sneered.

'You'd never believe me if I told you the full story.'

'Try me.'

133

'Some other time. Believe me, all that's urgent now is that you tell me where Marti is. I know she trusts you. She must have told you where she was going.'

All kinds of thoughts went through my mind. By letting the Renaissance alibi stand, I was already an accessory after the fact as far as the law was concerned.

'Why were the police so certain it was you at the Renaissance?' I asked. 'Surely they asked the staff for a description.'

'You were wearing a blue suit, I was wearing a blue suit. You're tall, I'm tall. You've got a ruddy complexion, so have I,' he explained.

'Speak for yourself,' I said. 'You've got a face the colour of a boiled lobster.'

'No more than you have,' he replied evenly. 'The proof of the pudding's in the eating – your general description fitted me well enough to satisfy them.'

Talking gave me a little time to think. Strengthening Charlie's alibi might just give Marti the weapon she needed in her matrimonial battle with him.

'Get out of the car then,' I ordered. 'I'll have to phone her and find out if she's willing to talk.'

'Thanks, Cunane,' he sighed. 'You won't regret this.'

'I don't want anything you've got on offer. Try to buy me again and the deal's off.'

'For Christ's sake, man, just cut out the dramatics and phone her.' Having said his piece Charlie hopped out of the car with surprising agility for such a large man. He stood by the Rolls and lit a cigarette. I looked at his face as he held the lighter up.

He leaned back into my car .

'Listen, mate, I'll do you a good turn – have nothing to do with my dear father-in-law, Vince King. My old fellow might get seriously peevish if you do.'

'Oh, thanks for the advice, old boy,' I murmured in a cut-glass accent. There was something about Charlie that brought out the unwashed proletarian in me. Even so, I took out my mobile and phoned the number Marti had given me.

'Who is this?' a flat Yorkshire voice demanded. I guessed

134

that I was speaking to Paul Longstreet, the popular mogul of the lap dancing world.

'Dave Cunane, I want to speak to Marti King,' I snapped.

'Are you the new man in her life, cocker?'

'No, I just want to speak to her. Is she there or not?'

'OK, don't get your knickers in a twist, lover boy. I'll see if she wants to chat.'

I could hear the flesh peddler bawling Marti's name. I cringed. I should never have let her go. It was a large house because he went on shouting for some time before the phone was picked up.

'Dave, is that you? When are you coming down?'

'I'm not. I've got dear old Charlie here. He wants to talk to you.'

'You bastard!' she shouted. 'You've told him where I am.'

'No, I haven't. He wants you to give him an alibi over the Lou Olley killing. The police seem to think that it might have been a crime of passion.'

There was silence for a moment and then the familiar mad laugh rang out. Even on a phone it sounded like Concorde crashing the sound barrier. At last she calmed down enough to speak: 'Put him on, Dave. This could well be the most expensive telephone call in the history of the Carlyle family.'

Next morning I was up bright and early and on the road before seven. I jogged along Edge Lane towards the little park where the pigeon lover awaited. I spotted her at some distance. She was clutching a large white plastic carrier bag. We were on converging courses for the park gate and she was through it before I was. Unseen by Mrs Griffiths, another figure emerged from behind a tree. A stockily built woman, struggling to carry a yellow plastic bucket, she headed for the same corner of the field that my customer was making for. Hoping to reach the collision point before she did, I accelerated.

'You mad bitch!' the woman suddenly shrieked. 'You won't be told, will you? Those birds come and roost on my roof. Go and feed the shitty things in front of your own bloody hovel!' The aggressor looked about fifty, with greying hair and a very

135

determined expression on her face. She swung the bucket back, preparatory to giving Mrs Griffiths an early bath.

'No, don't do that,' I said in my most reasonable voice.

'And what bloody business is it of yours?' the avenging fury demanded.

'He's here to see you don't get up to any mischief,' Mrs Griffiths crowed in triumph.

The ice-cold water hit me full in the face. I gasped and involuntarily took a step forward.

'Don't you dare to raise your hand to me,' my assailant screamed. 'I only did that to teach you a lesson.'

Mrs Griffiths gave me a beatific smile and then turned back to her pigeons.

19

The early morning action invigorated me. I got into the office before Celeste. Her resolution to show mustard keenness hadn't lasted. I left the mail for her to sort and retreated to my inner sanctum. I was in an excited mood: apprehensive but not frightened. How long would it take Cullen to match up the description from the Renaissance Hotel with the real Charlie Carlyle? Surely he couldn't be deceived for much longer. I looked up old cases in the files. I tidied my desk. I repositioned the furniture slightly. I found it hard to stop looking at my watch. It crossed my mind to write out instructions for Celeste in the event of my incarceration. The part-timers would all have to be paid.

The time crept slowly up to nine o'clock and then on. No DCI Cullen, no Sergeant Munro. At twenty past nine the front door rattled and I almost jumped out of my skin, but it was only Celeste.

'Sorry I'm late. Alarm clock didn't go off,' she explained. 'I'll make it up tonight.'

I nodded.

'Are you all right, Mr Cunane?' she enquired. 'You look as if you're expecting something.'

'Really?' I said, genuinely surprised that I was so transparent.

I told her about my dawn encounter with the pro- and anti-pigeon forces.

'Are you expecting the Press or something? It's just that your office looks much tidier than usual.'

It crossed my mind that Celeste was much more perceptive than I'd given her credit for.

'You know this legal executive course you're on?' I asked.

She tried to hide a guilty frown.

'They haven't been on to you, have they?' she said. 'I didn't go last night. It was my cousin's eighteenth birthday, I couldn't not be there.'

'So that's why the alarm didn't go off?' I muttered.

She shrugged apologetically.

'No, it's not your college, Celeste. I was wondering if as well as being a legal executive you'd like to take more part in the actual work of the firm. You know, go out on jobs. Most of it's terribly boring – sitting in the car for hours waiting for someone to come out on the street so you can put legal papers in his hand. Routine things like that.'

'Are you joking me?' she asked earnestly. Her eyes were the size of saucers. She let out a long slow breath.

'No,' I said.

'You know, to be honest, I've been waiting for a chance like this for months. I think I could really do well at detective work. That's why I signed on for the college course. I was beginning to give up hope.'

'You must keep on going to college,' I said solicitously. 'That will give you lots of options for the future.'

'I got five GCSEs, you know. I've always wanted to be a detective but I knew I could never join the police.'

'The first thing you'll have to learn, Celeste, is to keep on the right side of them.'

'Like you do, boss,' she commented with a hearty laugh. 'I saw you send that young copper out with a flea in his ear. He didn't know where to put himself when he came into my room, the little Muppet.'

'Celeste, that was a thirty-two-year-old detective sergeant.'

'They'd hand him his balls on a plate, round where I live.'

'Ugh!' I muttered.

'You knew that Olley, didn't you? The one that got himself killed? He threw my desk over and mashed you up that day, didn't he?'

'Yes,' I said, wondering what was coming next.

'I won't mention anything to the police about that . . . I mean, he was asking for trouble.'

'Celeste, I haven't offered you promotion to shut you up.'

'No?' she asked, her eyes gleaming.

'No, the police know all about that incident. For the record I had nothing to do with the death of Lou Olley.'

'I wouldn't care if you had,' she said defiantly.

'Well, I didn't, and the only reason I'm offering you a new start is because it'll be good for the business.'

'OK,' she said. I could see she was unconvinced. She gave me a beaming smile. 'You went to Armley Jail with that Marti King, didn't you?'

'How the hell . . .'

'My older sister's boyfriend's in there. She saw you. He gets on well with Vince King. Lennie, that is, the boyfriend.'

'Small world,' I muttered angrily. I wondered what other secrets were about to be laid bare.

'It is. Lennie says that she hasn't visited Vince since she got married and now she's suddenly started all this about getting him out. I mean, he's not any more innocent now than he was five years ago, is he?'

'No,' I agreed.

'If he is innocent, that is.'

'So what does Lennie say?'

'Vince thinks it's because she wants him to take care of Charlie Carlyle and his dad. He reckons it's all because she wants a divorce, but the only way Brandon Carlyle will ever let her leave the Carlyle family is in a pine box.'

'What?' I gasped. Suddenly Celeste had my complete attention.

'Yes, if her old man's running loose it'll give the Carlyles something to think about. He really hates the Carlyles does Vince.'

'Why?'

'I don't know. He won't tell Lennie anything about that. He says it's better if he doesn't know.'

'Any more revelations?'

'No, that's your lot, boss.'

I hadn't anything to say to that, so Celeste smiled warmly and said, 'I'll just go and sort through the morning mail.'

The chat with Celeste really churned me up. I sat at my desk struggling for calm. After a few minutes I managed to convince myself that Charlie hadn't wanted Marti's address so he could kill her. He'd only spoken to her on the phone anyway. Then I experienced another sudden stab of anxiety. Suppose Cullen was playing a waiting game? Suppose he was having me watched? I got up suddenly and walked through to the front office.

'Just going down the street,' I told my new assistant investigator.

I walked up to Albert Square. There was no sign of any interest in my movements. Perhaps I was becoming paranoid. I made my way back to the office.

'Fax, just come in from Manila,' Celeste announced.

It was from the agency I'd contacted. Angelina Maria Theresa Levy, formerly Angelina Maria Theresa Corazon, had left Manila via Singapore on a flight arriving Manchester on 28 August. So when Mr Levy was hiring me to go to the Philippines his wife had already been back in England for over two weeks. I decided that a personal visit was in order. Meanwhile, Celeste was watching me with an unhealthy eagerness. I was already beginning to understand how Victor Frankenstein felt that night in Ingolstadt when his creation smiled right back at him for the first time.

'Oh yes, Celeste. Now if Mr Levy's wife's back in England she's probably working somewhere local. I'd like you to phone agencies that employ Filipino staff as domestics, waitresses, etcetera and see if they've got an Angelina Maria Theresa Corazon on their books. Some of these people can be sticky about giving out names, so be creative, say you know her and would like to employ her again . . . Use your imagination.'

Celeste looked up at me as if I'd just handed her an Oscar. The phone was already in her hand. I made a rapid departure.

Mr Levy lived out at Bowdon. I took the long route through Sale and Altrincham rather than the motorway. I needed time to think. There were still aspects of this assignment that puzzled me.

His house was larger than I expected. An Edwardian building with a double bay front, it was built in the style of Norman Shaw. The original bold bare walls were now partly

140

covered in ivy and the leaded windows were small and horizontal. Steep pitched roofs with tall chimneys gave the building an imposing character. Somehow it looked too grand to be a private residence – it could have served as the headquarters of some secret government department. A jungle of dark vegetation, rhododendrons and pines, provided a suitable backdrop and gave the building an air of isolation and complete privacy. I wondered what had gone through Angelina Corazon's mind when she was ushered into this building to become the wife of a man she barely knew.

At the doorstep I searched in vain for a bell. There was an impressive bronze lion's head with a massive knocker looped through its maw. I struck a couple of heavy blows against the door. The sound hardly had time to reverberate through the house before someone was shifting bolts and turning locks on the other side.

'Oh, it's you,' Mr Levy said disappointedly. 'It could have been my lucky day, yes? Angelina might have come back.' He reluctantly opened the door and allowed me into the entrance hall. The first thing I noticed was a faint aroma of fresh paint but otherwise it was like stepping into a museum. Facing me, a splendid panelled staircase in light oak was hung with expensive looking pictures. Above the stair landing and looming down over the entrance hall there was a life-size portrait of a woman clad in a long, bilious green gown. Even in full daylight the picture was illuminated by a pair of spotlights. The female portrayed wasn't Angelina Corazon but a sharp-featured, dark-haired European woman. The artist may have been under instruction to highlight the pearl necklace the woman wore. It certainly blazed out against the dull green background. I took the subject to be Levy's mother, because there was a strong family resemblance, especially in the eyes and hair.

Art Nouveau chairs lined the hallway like guardsmen on parade.

'School of Glasgow, aren't they?' Mr Levy commented impassively. 'If you're going to do something you might as well do it properly. The chairs are genuine C. R. Mackintosh originals.'

He looked at me expectantly.

141

'Charles Rennie Mackintosh,' I responded, like a contestant in a knowledge quiz.

His eyes lit up. 'Not for sitting on, are they?'

'I won't sit on them,' I assured him.

'Coming in, or just talking?' he asked pointedly.

'I'd like to do both,' I muttered.

Levy led me past the staircase along a corridor that penetrated into the depths of the house. As I walked behind him I studied his jet-black hair minutely. There was no sign that it was dyed, but then Levy could afford the services of an expert hairdresser. Very likely someone called every couple of days to give him a rinse. He led me into a modern kitchen dominated by an immense Aga range. It was unpleasantly warm. Here again the furnishings were elaborate although modern: heavy oak, with innumerable variations on the theme of cupboards. On one wall there was a large framed colour photograph of the same woman who dominated the hall. It looked old and the woman looked younger, in her late twenties. She was wearing pearls again, just a single strand this time. Her dark eyes were an almost luminous shade of brown.

'German fittings,' Levy said sadly, with the air of someone making polite conversation. 'They do the best kitchens. I've put the best of everything in this house – I've had people up from the Whitworth Gallery.'

'I'm not surprised,' I said.

'We consulted them about the Edwardian decor. I wanted everything right.'

'It's very impressive.'

'Yes, I've had people round from television wanting to use the house as a period location but I couldn't allow that. Too many might get the wrong idea, yes? Crooks, riffraff and such, eh?'

'Dangerous times we live in,' I murmured. Levy seemed to be in a world of his own.

'Most people would say that, wouldn't they? Look after your possessions, that's what you must do, yes?'

'Everyone should be prudent.'

'You joke me, Mr Cunane?'

'No, no. Not at all,' I said. 'Why should you make things easy for them?' I realised that I was slipping into Mr Levy's own mode of speech.

'For all the place is worth to me now I'd make them a present of it. I'd help them to load my stuff on their van.'

'You mustn't think like that.'

'Sit down, Mr Cunane, make yourself at home. Would you like a coffee or something stronger?' He gestured towards a cupboard which was crammed with bottles of whisky. They were arranged in alphabetical order like books in a library. 'I collect them,' he explained. 'I've got over a hundred different kinds of single malt in the house at the moment. Have a glass, I can see you're tempted. I so rarely have anyone here to drink with, it'll be a treat for me.'

'It's a bit early.'

'A conventional type, are you? No, I think not. Go on, have a glass with me.' He reached down a bottle from an Islay distillery that I'd never heard of.

'Have you seen one like this?'

'No.'

'This is a rare one,' he said, beaming with pleasure. 'I have to send off for it. They say the Queen Mother likes it.'

He stroked the bottle proudly and held it up to the light.

I laughed. 'I may not be conventional but with all due respect to royalty I find that lifting my arm at half ten in the morning isn't a good start for the rest of the day.'

'Go on, Mr Cunane. Those who drink beer will think beer, and those who drink rare whisky will think fine thoughts, yes?'

'Put like that, how can I refuse?'

'You are the wise man of Manchester, aren't you, Mr Cunane?' he said as he poured out two healthy shots of the pale, peaty coloured liquid. 'Charge me for the whole day if you like. I know you've something unpleasant to tell me. I'd rather buffer myself before I get the bad news.'

'It's not necessarily bad news,' I said.

I estimated that the heavy cut-glass tumbler he pushed towards me cost the equivalent of my disposable income for a week.

143

'You can put tap water in that if you want, or even Canada Dry,' he invited. 'I'm not a purist.'

I sipped the neat whisky. He smiled at me in apparent pleasure and then took a gulp out of his own glass. Leaning back, he balanced the drink in two hands above his watch chain like an alderman at a civic reception. A solid seeming figure, wearing a dark three-piece suit today, there was nevertheless something desperate about Mr Levy. His formal clothing – suit, crisp white shirt, tie with Windsor knot, diamond cufflinks, polished black shoes – it was all too much. The man looked like a theatrical knight whose dresser has just turned him out for a Royal Command performance.

'Are you on your way somewhere?' I asked.

'No, I stay in. Angelina might call.'

'I see.'

The explanation struck me as false. He'd waited two months before doing anything about Angelina's disappearance and now he was scared to go out in case she turned up?

When he seemed about as settled as he was going to get I told him that Angelina was back in England and probably in the Manchester area. He didn't take the news well. First, he blew his nose on a large coloured silk handkerchief, then he wiped his eyes, and finally, to my embarrassment, he began to sob openly. Weeping elderly men are not part of the culture that I've been raised in.

Awkwardly, I went round the table and put my arm on his heaving shoulders. He shook silently for a moment or two and then drew away. Not knowing quite where to put myself, I sat down again. Like a small seismic disturbance the shoulder-heaving grief subsided quickly and Levy poured more whisky into our glasses.

'You think I'm a fool, don't you? An old man chasing a young woman who only wanted a marriage certificate and a passport.'

'We don't know what her motives were. Perhaps there was some difficulty and she found it hard to explain it to you.'

Removing his glasses he wiped the tears away and focused his eyes on me. No longer magnified by his heavy spectacles, his eyes looked small and artificial, like the dark glass buttons on a teddy bear's face. He gazed at me steadily. The room was quiet apart from the whine of distant engines.

'My assistant is trying to trace her through employment agencies. Did Angelina have any kind of qualifications or special interests? Is she a nurse or a nanny or something?'

He shook his head. 'What's the use of tracing her? She obviously doesn't want anything to do with me.'

'You don't know that. Anyway, if you're going to separate you'll need to know where she is so you can serve whatever legal papers may be required.'

'That's a bit direct, Mr Cunane, but you're right. You think I've been a complete fool, don't you?'

'Of course not.'

'Oh, come. Young men think old men are fools. Old men know that young men are.'

I was getting slightly tired of this. Levy had more wise sayings than a box of Christmas crackers. I decided to bring things to a head.

'Can I search Angelina's room, her cupboards and so on?'

He nodded.

In my experience this is always the crucial moment, a fork in the road. The deserted party can refuse. He or she can cling to illusions . . . the lover, friend, wife, husband is going to be back at any moment. Or they don't do that. They avail themselves of my services. They trace the missing person and settle for whatever they can get.

Now we were down to business the tears dried up. Levy's round little face became hard. All the self-pity had melted away like snow in spring sunshine.

'There's no easy way to put this, Mr Levy, but has she ripped you off for much money?'

'Only a few thousand. This isn't about money, Mr Cunane.'

'No, I didn't think it was.'

'I stopped her credit cards when she disappeared in Ireland. Now don't say anything, Mr Cunane. It wasn't meanness. I thought if someone had taken her – against her will, say – well, they'd have to let her go if she had no cash.'

'Makes sense,' I said, trying to wipe any surprise off my face. I pinched myself. Was this the same man whose

145

recklessness had worried me? 'Where is her room then?'

'Our bedroom . . . Top of the stairs on the right,' he said without further explanation.

I walked up the stairs past the full-length portrait and into the master bedroom.

But for one feature it could have been a display in the Victoria and Albert museum. The solitary jarring note was a modern king-sized four-poster bed. It was one of those high-tech Swedish affairs with all kinds of gadgets for raising and lowering.

For the rest, a beautiful plaster ceiling, superb period drapes, a chaise longue, armchairs, more C. R. Mackintosh upright seats, Art Nouveau lamp stands, a Tiffany shade on the main room light, many rare-looking pieces of porcelain, all created the illusion of a room at the turn of the century.

Larger pieces of furniture were in the same shade of light oak as the stairwell, as was the floor where it wasn't covered by oriental rugs. It was like looking at a shiny page in an auctioneer's catalogue. I wasn't qualified to say if it was all genuine but it looked more authentic than I felt. The right-hand bedside table was cluttered – books, glasses, indigestion pills – but the other table was bare. I knelt down and checked under the bed. There was nothing there to suggest that the bride from Manila had ever lived here, not a shoe or a casually discarded bra or anything.

I checked all the drawers and they were equally unrewarding. On the dressing table there was a heavy silver Art Nouveau picture frame. It didn't contain a picture of Angelina, though. The same pearl-bedecked woman who hung in the hall and the kitchen peered out narrowly across old Levy's nuptial couch. It was creepy really. Levy must be fixated on her. I turned to the massive wardrobes. These were to scale with the room, each big enough to provide emergency housing for a family of five. The right-hand one was crammed with Levy's suits and jackets and shoes. In the left the sole garment was a long white jacket and dress. A faded spray of flowers was still pinned to the jacket lapel.

I stood in the middle of the room trying to emote. Nothing came. A woman had lived here for two months, packed up

146

everything and cleared off leaving no more trace than a casual visitor stopping overnight in a hotel. For a moment I was gripped by suspicion. Was I going to make a grisly discovery at the bottom of the garden? No, that was impossible. I knew Angelina was alive. If this was some cunning deception and Levy had done away with his mail order bride, would he draw attention by involving me?

I walked back to the kitchen.

'Come through,' Levy invited, opening a side door. It led to a dining room with place settings for twelve and then into a large drawing room dominated by a pair of French windows opening onto a lawn. There were more pictures and more expensive furniture. The walls were masterpieces of decorative art in themselves. I don't know how much repro Edwardian hand-blocked wallpaper costs but there was surely enough on these walls to pay my office rent for a year. As my eyes tracked round the room I spotted two more pictures of the lady with the pearls. This time she was in pole position over the fireplace and on one of the walls.

Levy walked over to the elaborate carved mantel and took down a photo of Angelina in the white costume with the spray of flowers that hung in the wardrobe upstairs.

'Lovely, isn't she?' he asked but my eye was taken by something else. As he removed the photo another was revealed behind it, of Marti King and Charlie Carlyle. Marti was in a wedding dress and Carlyle in a grey morning suit. I felt hot and cold at the same time. Wonderful! An associate of the Carlyles is slotted, practically on my doorstep, and the very next day this weird geezer who just happens to have one of Marti and Charlie's wedding snaps on his mantelpiece drops by and tries to persuade me to take a two- or three-week break in the Philippines. What was going on?

I turned towards Levy suddenly, violence not very far from my mind.

'I wanted that for my Angelina,' Levy commented before I could speak, mistaking my interest in the wedding photo.

'Oh, what?' I snarled. I could hardly pull my eyes away from the picture of a young, smiling Marti.

'The wedding dress. Elizabeth Emanuel. Cost old Brandon

147

a bomb but he wanted the best of everything for his son's wedding. I would have done the same for Angelina, but we got married in the registry office and she preferred a suit.'

'Oh, right,' I muttered. His comment flummoxed me. Levy was making no effort to disguise his knowledge of the Carlyle family. Either the man was a superbly gifted actor or his connection with the clan was fortuitous. I was still deeply suspicious.

'She's beautiful, isn't she, my Angelina?' Levy asked. He mistook my preoccupation for interest in his bride.

'Very, very,' I assured him.

'I'll get you a copy of this photo, yes? It's better than the one you had before. You can fax it to your office.'

Levy busied himself for a moment with extracting a copy of the photo from a large album and then he went to a fax machine in the corner of the room.

'I keep in touch with my broker on this,' he explained.

I gave him the number of my own fax machine and he despatched the picture of Angelina to Celeste.

'So you know Brandon Carlyle,' I said eventually when he'd finished fussing with the machine.

'You say you know the Carlyle family? I only mentioned Brandon's first name,' he retorted sharply.

'No, it's just that Marti Carlyle is a sort of client and I met Charlie last night.'

'Hmmm,' Levy murmured, looking at me speculatively. He lifted the heavy black spectacles off his nose and looked at me again. 'The Carlyle family don't encourage their acquaintances to indulge in loose talk about them.'

Whether it was the Queen Mother's preferred malt whisky or just simple bad temper I don't know, but I felt a surge of anger at his reproof. My face was burning.

'Funny you should say that, Mr Levy,' I rapped back coldly. 'A copper told me practically the same thing just the other day but Charlie is all in favour of me talking about him – to the right people, of course.'

Levy replaced his specs and exclaimed, 'What is this? I have annoyed you?'

'Sorry, it's not your fault. I'll leave before I say something I'll regret and get started on tracking down Angelina.'

'No,' Levy said firmly. 'Sit down, Mr Cunane. I have few
enough visitors that I can afford to send one of them off in a
temper. Something is going on involving my old business
partner Brandon Carlyle and his family and I want to know
what it is.'

Determination more than made up for Mr Levy's small size
and age. He backed me towards a large armchair and almost
before I knew it I was sitting opposite him with another glass
of malt in my hand.

'Look, you must know I can't tell you anything
confidential,' I muttered. 'Would you like me to go blabbing
the details about Angelina all over Manchester?'

'If it brought her back to me I might not mind.'

I sipped the whisky and said nothing.

He stared down at the misty liquid in his own glass. 'Marti
is a troubled spirit. I like her and I wouldn't want any harm to
come to her,' he said cautiously.

'Harm!' I exploded. 'What harm? Not like Lou Olley, I
hope?'

'So, you are mixed up in that?' he said with a triumphant
smile. 'I read that the killing occurred in the same street your
business is in.'

'Pure coincidence,' I snapped, and then felt bitterly annoyed
that he'd somehow turned the tables on me. He was the one
who should have been explaining his connection with the
Carlyle family.

'Don't tell a bookmaker about coincidence. I've lived by the
laws of chance all my life. I'm only alive thanks to a lucky
chance.'

'Really?'

'Yes, I was one of the last Jewish children to get out of Berlin
before the war broke out in 1939. My parents were not so
lucky.'

'Oh.'

'My sister and I were fostered with a family in Cheetham
Hill. She was all the family I had.' He gestured towards the
portrait over the mantelpiece that dominated the room. The
woman's eyes seemed to be staring right through me. 'She was
all in all to me, was my Leah.' He took his handkerchief out

again and wiped a tear from his eye. 'But you don't want to hear about a boring old fool like me, do you?'

'That's your sister?'

'Of course. The pearl necklaces are in every painting. The only things from our family that we were able to bring with us from Germany were some pearls. Leah sold them to get me the money to start in business. I promised her that I'd replace them and every time I bought her some pearls we had her picture painted, or her photograph taken.'

'Her presence is rather dominating.'

Levy looked at me shrewdly. 'You are a wise young man. You are going to ask me what Angelina made of all this.'

I wasn't but he was going to tell me.

'I owe everything to Leah. She died nearly three years ago . . . liver cancer. I was so lonely when she'd gone. This house was her idea really. She was older than me and she remembered our grandparents' home back in Berlin. Leah hoped that by making everything as real as it was back in those days she could live in her happy memories. You must understand I couldn't change anything. That would be treachery to Leah.'

It did cross my mind to wonder how his Filipino bride had enjoyed living in a house so obviously full of ghosts but I held my tongue. Mr Levy took a strong pull of his whisky and then held the glass out for me to fill.

'So you know all about Lou Olley?' he asked slyly.

'I know nothing.'

'That was a bad business. I told Brandon that the man had no restraint but he brought him into the firm just to tease Charlie. Brandon is always trying to make his sons into tough men, but what's to gain? They are what they are. I've told him to leave them alone but he won't. Brandon thinks he's like Abraham in the Bible – founding a tribe. Pshaw! What a mensch! What that man's got in his trousers, he'd have populated Cheshire with his offspring by now if his wife could have stuck it, poor woman.'

'Look, I'd better be going now,' I interjected.

'Stay. I've told you. You charge me double time for today,' he ordered with a rather twisted smile on his face. 'Here, you're not drinking with me. I take offence.' He snatched the

150

bottle and filled my glass practically to the brim.

'I was the numbers man for Brandon. In his business you couldn't keep books. I kept it all in my head for years. He'd say, "Sam, I want you to get this down." He'd hand me a sheet of paper with some figures on and I'd remember them. It's a trick I have but it's made me a wealthy man, and for what? You like the house?'

'Yes, of course.'

'It's a prison to me. You find my Angelina and I'll tell you more than anyone else knows about Brandon Carlyle. In fact, I know more about Brandon than he knows himself.'

'Listen, Mr Levy, have you ever heard of a solicitor called Morton V. E. Devereaux-Almond?' I asked. I don't know what prompted me to ask the question but it was connected with seeing that photo of Marti and Charlie nestling at the back of Levy's mantel.

Levy shook his head. 'This is about Vince King, no?' he said.

'Devereaux-Almond,' I insisted. The drink made my voice sound harsh.

'There are some things that are too ugly to know about. You don't want them in your mind. That's what plagued my poor Leah all her life, thinking about what happened to our parents. Hatred eats you up worse than cancer,' he said with a sigh.

'I see,' I snapped, surprised by my own vehemence. 'So we should forget all the bad things that happen and let the people who did them get away with it. Is that it?'

'You are a young man, yes, Mr Cunane, but you'll need to be a brave one, and brave though you may be I don't think you'll want to pay the price that may be demanded for prying into the affairs of Brandon Carlyle.'

'What price? This was all a set-up, wasn't it? Finding Angelina? You wanted me in the Philippines because something's going down here in Manchester.'

'So suspicious even! You remind me of Leah. Nothing's going down. Believe me. I would be the first to know. Brandon was as upset about the murder of this Olley creature as Olley's own mother was.'

As he said this Levy gave a chuckle. It sounded sinister.

'I say "mother" but then I wonder?' he continued. He laced

151

his fingers across his chest and tucked his thumbs under his shirt collar. 'Do creatures like Lou Olley have mothers or are they specially bred for crime in some dark cellar?'

'You might know the answer to that,' I muttered.

Levy gave me a very odd look. Fatalistic you could call it, or perhaps sorrowful.

'Ah, Mr Cunane, I see you already know too much or maybe not enough,' he said enigmatically. 'Find my Angelina.'

20

It was three in the afternoon before a taxi deposited me at the end of the little street where the pulsating headquarters of Pimpernel Investigations stands. My head was still spinning from Mr Levy's whisky when I lurched up to the front door.

'Long liquid lunch, Dave?' Clyde Harrow asked with a knowing smile. He was wearing a plaid jacket that was a strain on the eyes.

'Breakfast, as well as lunch,' Celeste commented saucily from behind her desk.

Clyde gave her a wolfish look as if she was news on the hoof.

'What are you here for?' I asked nastily.

'You, Dave,' he said cheekily. 'You're the man in the news at the moment. I came for an interview.'

'I don't do interviews for less than three hundred pounds.' I might have asked for a million for all the effect this ploy produced.

I noted the ominous way Clyde was waving his mobile like a loaded gun. No doubt he was hinting that he could have a camera crew with us in minutes. I gloomily recalled previous 'No comment' interviews. With Clyde's ilk, a denial is as good as an admission of guilt.

'I know nothing about the Olley killing,' I pleaded desperately.

'I know that, Dave,' he agreed.

I dared to snatch a breath. Harrow flourished his mobile with a condescending gesture. 'I'm sure you're an expert on the local gangland scene, but the Old Bill have got the Olley case sewn up tighter than a nun's knickers. The whole shebang's on tape apparently.' He walked over to the window and pointed to a video camera mounted high above the back entrance to a jeweller's shop. 'Yes, dear lad, they're talking about an early arrest, and these street killings are stale news in any case.'

'I don't expect Lou Olley was quite so blasé about it.'

'The public have seen enough of them. Olley was no one in particular. A small-time club bouncer. No, what's sexy at the moment is animals, and from what I hear you're involved in them right up to the top of your fancy red braces.'

'I don't wear red braces.'

The taste of Sam Levy's Islay malt hung in the back of my throat like a bad dream. Another minute of this and the office would start going round and round in front of me.

'Shame on you!' Harrow scoffed. 'I should have thought that they're obligatory for a rising businessman like you.'

'What are you on about?' I growled. The man was like a nasty, snapping little dog and he needed to be put back in his kennel.

'Pigeons, you fool. Pigeons.'

I looked at Harrow and then at Celeste. They grinned at my bewilderment and exchanged glances. I could feel the ground shift under my feet. Who was running Pimpernel Investigations these days?

'You'd better come into the private office then,' I mumbled.

'Not for three hundred,' Harrow said with a smile.

'Count this one as a freebie,' I told him. 'Celeste, bring us some coffee,' I ordered. She needed to be reminded of her status.

'I've found out where you-know-who is,' she said proudly.

'Later.'

'Yes, boss. Black and beautiful, is that what you want, eh? Like me?'

'Yes, Celeste, like you; black, beautiful and silent.'

She pursed her lips and bustled over to the coffee machine.

Putting Clyde Harrow in his place wasn't quite so easy. I spent the best part of an hour trying to persuade him that the Chorlton pigeon war, as he insisted on calling it, was a non-event. Mrs Griffiths belonged to an animal defence group which had put him on to the story.

154

All the time that Harrow was speaking I was racking my weary wits with the question of why a murder in the centre of Manchester was no longer news. I was no wiser when he left. He'd suggested various little stratagems to me – that I recruit a band of helpers to confront the anti-pigeon forces; that I retaliate in kind with a hosepipe – all intended to give him a 'fun' story of three minutes' duration.

When he'd gone Celeste came in.

'I take it you're not pleased with me, Dave,' she said boldly.

'I'm not unhappy, Celeste. You'll learn.'

She favoured me with a broad smile.

'I found Angelina . . . she's working for a catering firm out at the airport. Shall we go and pick her up?'

'Dilemmas, dilemmas,' I said quietly. I told her about the shrine to Saint Leah that Mr Levy had created in Bowdon and my doubts about where Angelina fitted into it all.

'You mean we might not tell him where she is?'

I nodded.

'But he's a client. It's up to him what he does with the information,' my nineteen-year-old assistant argued sensibly.

'You're right,' I agreed. 'But it's just that you need to learn from day one that there is sensitive information in the private detective business and . . .'

'We've got to make sure that there's no comeback before we start handing the stuff out?' she said, completing my thought.

'Something like that. I think we need to just sit on the news for a day or two until we've sussed out exactly what's going on. He's waited for two months. A day or two longer won't hurt him.'

Sam Levy had told me to bill him for a whole day. That was only fair because the rest of that day wasn't much use to me. I took a taxi home and then had a long, very hot bath in an attempt to sweat the excess alcohol out of my blood.

I needed time to think.

My new mountain bike has more springs on it than a tart's mattress but I usually manage to work up a sweat on it. When I reached the Meadows it was one of those clear, calm evenings we occasionally get when dusk seems to creep on so

155

imperceptibly that twilight might last forever. Dark clouds were moving slowly against a very deep blue evening sky. The lengthening shadows suited my mood.

I pedalled along the Mersey bank taking the upstream route towards Northenden. The river rushed past, the dark waters in a hurry for their union with the Irish Sea at Liverpool Bay. What was I in a hurry for? My life had no direction. Here I was tearing along a narrow path, pounding the light alloy pedals, flicking through the Shimano gears, and for what? I tried to shake the mood of depression that a morning of whisky drinking had brought on. Why was I down? I had a job, a good life by most standards. But it didn't seem to be quite enough. I tried to take my mind off my problems by concentrating on the puzzle Mr Samuel Levy represented.

I rode on to the point where Palatine Road crosses the river.

I was approaching the bridge when they emerged. Like magic, five youths suddenly appeared in front of me; two were black, one mixed race and two white. I knew I was in for bother when I saw that three of them had the hoods of their anoraks up. The biggest and tallest of them grabbed my handlebars. I'd already slowed, so he didn't jerk me off the bike as he'd intended.

'Hey, let us have a ride on your bike, mate,' the hooded youth bawled, holding on to the bars firmly. His gang laughed. The equation was so simple: five against one; my property was about to become their property.

It wasn't the ringleader's lucky day. My bleak mood and the adrenaline surge made me nasty. I swung both my feet up and over the bike and into Hoody's chest, a spectacular move by any standard. I was surprised at my own agility. The hooded youth was taken completely off his guard. He shot away backwards, off the path and down the steep bank into the dark swirling waters below. It wasn't deep enough to drown him unfortunately, as the immediate volley of curses proved, but he'd have trouble climbing back up the steep embankment.

As the other four, all big lads more like eighteen- or nineteen-year-olds than school kids, surged forward I whipped the stubby little bike pump up from its fixture.

'Come on,' I snarled. 'I can't take you all but I'll mark one of

156

you.' The ferocity sounded convincing even to me and it certainly was to them. These things are ninety per cent bluff. They counted on numbers. I was relying on a rush of blood to the head. It was as if the ground under their feet had turned to treacle. The forward charge slowed to a stop. No one wanted to be the first to come into contact with the pump. In the gloom against the dark bridge it must have looked like a club.

'Cream the fucking bastard,' the bedraggled leader screamed from below. They looked down at him and then at me. 'Christ, I'm drowning,' he shrieked as the river stones suddenly slipped under him.

'Come on, brave lads,' I taunted.

They backed off. One of them started pretending that helping his friend in the water was more important than kicking my face in. The others suddenly became observers.

I was on the bike and racing towards Chorlton before they had time to change their minds. Oaths and stones were hurled but none of the would-be muggers chanced his arm directly. As for me, I made the return trip to Chorlton Meadows in record time.

I got back to my flat and had a shower, and I was towelling myself down when I heard a familiar but unexpected knock on the door. I slipped on a dressing gown and let Janine in.

'You're looking pleased with yourself,' she said grumpily.

'And why shouldn't I?' I demanded.

'Are you on something, Dave?' she muttered sarcastically. 'You've got a wild look in your eyes. Come round for a drink. I'm going stir crazy next door.'

'What's up?'

'Oh, you wouldn't understand,' she said in a disgruntled voice. 'You think all women should be good little mothers sitting with their infants twenty-four hours a day, darning their man's socks when they're not passing out the Band-Aids.'

She came close and I gave her a hug. She responded. I slipped my hand down towards her derrière.

'No, not tonight, Dave. You know the rule,' she scolded. 'Weekends only.'

I removed the offending appendage but not before giving a gentle nip.

157

'What's brought all this on?' I asked sympathetically.

'Dave,' she said firmly, 'you know I'm not going to unburden myself on the subject of the hardships of motherhood so don't even ask. Come round for a coffee and a chat. I'll go mad if I watch another TV programme about single glamorous females having it off all over New York.'

I laughed and followed her as she turned to the door.

'Oh, no you don't,' she warned. 'I know you, get some clothes on. I'll leave the door off the latch.'

A moment later I was sitting fully clothed in her lounge. There was coffee on the table in front of us.

'This is jolly and domestic,' I said.

'Yes, isn't it?' Janine replied bleakly.

I laughed.

'What's got into you tonight?' she asked. 'I don't know whether I prefer you like this or all stormy and angst ridden.'

'Take me as you find me,' I invited.

'I'd rather not.'

'Janine, you know that murder in the street outside my office?'

'Of course.'

'Do you think it's un-newsworthy? I mean, if you had any info on it do you think your editor would run it on the front page or would he say this is boring and pop it at the bottom of a column on page twenty-nine?'

'You're up to something, aren't you?' she asked eagerly, all her ennui suddenly cast aside. 'Tell me what you know.'

'Nothing, it's just that a TV journalist was at the office today and he said the Olley killing was hardly even a story. No interest to him.'

'Come on, Dave, stop being devious. You know something.'

'I know that Clyde Harrow works for the Carlyle Corporation.'

'I don't,' she spluttered.

'If I was talking to Janine the lover I might be tempted to say something but I'm talking to Janine the journalist now and I can't say anything.'

'Can't you just pretend that they're both the same woman?' she said in a husky voice.

'It's not the weekend, dear,' I pointed out.

She raised her right eyebrow by less than one millimetre.

A few minutes later we were in her bed. She had her arms round me.

'You're so uncomplicated, Dave. Are you sure you want me?'

'You know the answer to that.'

Afterwards Janine propped herself on one elbow and looked down at me seriously.

'Listen, I didn't just knock on your door tonight because I was desperate for adult company. Henry's been in touch.'

'That bastard! What does he want? Money?'

'Worse, he wants to see the children. He's moving back to England. He's got a job here in Manchester.'

'So he didn't make it in Hollywood?'

'Dave, you're not listening. This isn't just about him. He wants to pick up the pieces . . . between him and me, I mean.'

'Oh.'

'What do you mean, "Oh?"'

'I don't know.'

'He says he needs us.'

'Oh.'

'Stop that!'

'What am I supposed to say? We just make love and then you announce that your ex-husband is back on the scene. What do you want me to do? I've always made my feelings clear.'

'I suppose you have, but you could say something like you'll bash his head in if he shows up.'

'Oh, yes, and be told that I've got regressive tendencies.'

'I expect I've asked for that, but do you honestly think I could go back to him? He's been shacked up with a succession of brainless bimbos for the last two and a half years and now he wants to exercise his paternal rights.'

'Janine, you'll have to see your solicitor and decide what to do.'

'I liked it better when you were ready to threaten violence at the drop of a hat.'

'You've trained me out of that.'

159

We lay in silence for a long while.

'I'll put the frighteners on him if you want,' I said at last.

'Tell me about Olley,' Janine replied.

'OK,' I drawled. I knew when to change the subject before things got too heavy. I told her about the curious Sam Levy.

'You don't know that he isn't really just after this Angelina,' she said.

'So he sends me on a three-week holiday to the Philippines?'

'I don't buy this idea of Carlyle wanting you out of town just because someone might decide that you were at the Renaissance and not him. If the police were going to do that they'd have done it already. No, if the Carlyles are trying to get you out of the country it's because you know something and they don't want you blurting it out in that uncomfortable way you have.'

'Me blurting things out! That's rich.'

'Really. You must be aware of something that they don't want disclosed. Think, you big bozo! What is it? Did Vince King tell you something?'

I did think, but nothing came except sleep.

21

Dawn patrol at the park was more exciting than I'd bargained for. The anti-pigeon brigade was fully mobilised. A gaggle of determined-looking women were waiting for Mrs Griffiths as she approached the park gate.

I positioned myself in front of the nervous bird lover.

'That's him! That's the bastard that threatened me,' a voice screeched. It was the woman who believed in early morning baths.

'Stand aside, please,' I said. 'This is a public park and we're entitled to go in.'

'You're not, you hired thug! We're not going to let those filthy flying rats be fed,' the fanatic gabbled. Then she folded her arms and stood directly in front of me. 'Just try what you did yesterday and see what you get,' she trilled in a high-pitched voice. Her sheeplike cohorts baaed their support. The urban guerrilla then plucked out a small package which she hurled at me with all her strength. I skipped to one side and the paper bag burst in the road revealing its disgusting contents.

I turned to Mrs Griffiths and led her away.

'But I've got to feed my birds. They depend on me,' she said pathetically. She was as desperate for the martyr's flames as her antagonist.

'We'll try the other gate,' I said, leading her along the pavement at the side of the park. As we went more missiles followed. One burst in an overhanging chestnut tree and I was splashed by the filthy contents. Jeers of glee rang in my ears. Nevertheless Mrs Griffiths fed the birds.

'Morning, ba-aass,' Celeste drawled. She was already at her desk when I arrived. 'Are you sending me out on the job today?'

'Good lord, Celeste, I was on a job before seven this morning. Let me in the door before you start demanding orders.'

'Sor – ree,' she pouted. 'Pardon me for breathing.'

'I didn't mean it like that,' I said hastily. 'I've had a rough start to the day.' I told her about the bird feeding incident. 'And if that leech Clyde Harrow oozes into here I don't want you to give him the time of day. I wouldn't be surprised if he hadn't put those women up to that little stunt.'

'You mean like . . . faking the whole thing?' she asked, wide-eyed.

'It's possible. Just be on your guard.'

'I'll smack his silly face.'

'No!' I said quickly. 'Just be non-committal. Say nothing that he can quote back at you.'

Celeste looked as if I'd taken the shine off her day but I relented. 'All right,' I said. 'This is what you do. First assignment. When does Angelina Corazon start work at the airport?'

'She works the two till ten shift.'

'OK, get yourself down there by one-thirty. Take the photos with you and check that you've got the right woman and then tell her that her husband wants her back.'

'I don't know, boss. Is that ethical? I mean if Mr Levy's paying us? Shouldn't we tell him where she is first?'

'We'll tell him tomorrow. I just want Angelina to have a chance to make a getaway.'

'You mean so that we'll be able to screw more money out of the old guy?' she asked. 'Like by finding her again?' She was genuinely perplexed, but I wasn't about to tell her that Levy was probably playing some twisted game on behalf of the Carlyle family.

'No, after we give him the news tomorrow that's it. We send in our bill.'

Celeste shook her head. 'There's something you're not telling me,' she said astutely.

'That could be,' I agreed, 'and talking of bills, has anything come in from Northern Mutual?'

She riffled through the envelopes on her desk. 'Nothing

162

here from them. Miserable gits, aren't they, these insurance companies,' she commented.

'No, not them, just a certain Ernie Cunliffe who's decided to sit on our bill to teach me a lesson.'

I went into my inner office, more to confirm my status as the management of Pimpernel Investigations than because I had anything special to do there.

Celeste came in with the mail and a cup of coffee twenty minutes later. She was beginning to understand that I need a few minutes in the office on my own to acclimatise myself for the day's strife. I sipped the coffee.

'Thanks, Celeste. I'm going to be on the Greenidge/ Gammage case for the rest of the morning.'

'Are you sure you don't want me to put someone else on to that? Joe Mulrany phoned to ask if we had anything for him.' Mulrany was a retired policeman who was augmenting his pension with occasional work for my and other agencies.

'No, I have to keep my hand in.'

'Mulrany was moaning about his daughter's university fees!'

'Oh, hell! Give him the job then, but make sure he knows he's on an hourly rate and that I want a blow by blow account of every interview.'

'OK, boss,' Celeste said, heading for the phone.

I felt a twinge of regret. Investigating the likes of George Gammage was the sort of thing that brought you into contact with ordinary people, something that had been in short supply lately.

22

Celeste's solo mission to Angelina Corazon was not a success. The woman gave her the brushoff.

'The horrible racist bitch! She isn't even good-looking,' Celeste fumed. 'She hit me in the face as soon as I mentioned Levy's name.'

'What makes you think she's racist?'

'There were half a dozen of them – those Filipinos! All jabbering and pointing and laughing. I hadn't a chance to explain that I hadn't come to cart her off back to her old man. She just went mad, lashing out. Look at my lip. I'll swear she's bust it.'

'I'll get you some ice,' I said, going to the fridge. 'This calls for a bonus. Levy didn't say that his beloved was violent.'

'Bonus! I never thought I was going to get my face smashed in,' Celeste muttered tearfully. 'And she might be his beloved but he isn't hers. You should have seen her face when I told her I was from him.'

'I should have, but you wanted a solo mission. Don't get too upset. This is what it's like. Half the time total boredom, the other half nursing bruises. You have to face it. We find people who don't want to be found and they get violent.'

'There was no need for it.'

'That's the beauty of on-the-job training.'

'Oh, I get it! You sent me there to put me off. Man's work, is it?'

'Not at all! How did I know how Angelina would react? We'll do some overtime if you're still keen. We can pick her up again when she comes out of work and trail her to where she's living and try to interview her when she's in a more receptive frame of mind.'

164

'You mean spend Friday night tracking this bitch?' Celeste asked in amazement. 'I don't know. I usually go out.'

'Whatever, but I want this Levy business sorted. I don't want it dragging on into next week.'

In the end Celeste did come back to the airport with me and from there we trailed Angelina to a house in Levenshulme. I decided not to risk a direct confrontation. I dropped Celeste off at her home in Ayers Road and then took myself off to my lonely bed.

23

When I got to the office that Saturday morning it was a fine autumn day, clear skies and bright sunshine breaking through layers of mist. There wasn't much traffic going into town at nine a.m. and I was looking forward to a couple of uninterrupted hours while I worked out what to do about Sam Levy.

I had a decision to make. Levy had more or less promised more information about the Carlyles and their link with Devereaux-Almond in exchange for Angelina's address. I had the address now. It hadn't been particularly hard to find. The question was: should I use it to try and get the inside story about Vince King and his wonky solicitor out of the old man?

I busied myself with sorting the mail while I thought it out.

Marti was in London starting a new life. Vince King would probably be freed in a few more years. My business was thriving. The only cloud on my personal horizon was the imminent showdown with Henry Talbot. No, the more I thought about it the more certain I became that I didn't want to hear any more about the Carlyle family and their doings. I was in deep enough as it was.

I picked up the phone and dialled Levy's number. He answered immediately.

'Oh, it's you.'

'Yes, I've got Angelina's address for you. She's living in Levenshulme.'

I dictated the address.

'Is there a man in the picture?'

'No, we don't think so. She's sharing an apartment with a number of other Filipino women who work out at the airport.'

'This is bad. I'd have preferred it if there was someone else, but to be rejected just so she can peel potatoes in some kitchen . . . it's a blow.'

I paused for a moment. He didn't sound very tragic. How did he know that Angelina was working in catering? I hadn't told him . . . She could have been doing anything.

'Mr Cunane, I must see you. I have much to talk about and it's not something I can discuss over the phone. You know . . . that other matter you mentioned . . . Devereaux-Almond – I could fill you in about him.'

'Actually, Mr Levy, I'm more or less putting that in cold storage until Ms King makes her requirements known to me.'

'Oh no, it doesn't work like that, Mr Cunane. Once you've started you can't draw back. If it had been anyone else that had started prying into these matters things could have been allowed to rest, but because it's you . . . You don't understand there are life and death matters involved.'

'Come on, Mr Levy. That's a bit dramatic, isn't it? I may have a slight reputation in Manchester but I'm hardly in the Sherlock Holmes class.'

'Stupid man! Be quiet! I'm not trying to flatter you. It is because you are your father's son that certain people won't sleep easy in their beds until they know just which way you are going to jump.'

'I don't follow you.'

'No, you don't, but you are prepared to blunder about in matters which have already cost more than one life.'

'This whole thing with Angelina was a scam, wasn't it?'

'I don't know what you mean but I must see you and talk to you.'

'I don't think so. I'll put my bill in the post and I'd welcome an early settlement.'

'Cunane, listen . . .'

'No, you listen. As far as I'm concerned my business with you is now finished.'

'Are you at your office? I can come down there.'

'I am, but why don't you go and see your wife instead? If you come down here you'll only find a locked door.'

I put the phone down. It rang almost immediately but I didn't answer.

After a few minutes of listening to it ring over and over I went into the outer office and made myself a cup of coffee. Then I got a book on divorce and started reading that with my feet on the desk. It didn't take long to discover that Henry Talbot stood little chance of gaining anything more than limited access to his children.

I read for about an hour. I could have left the office but I was prepared to entertain Sam Levy if he did come banging on the door, so I hung on. At about eleven there was a muffled banging on the street door. I went through to the outer office expecting to see him in his three-piece suit at the door.

It wasn't him. The three-piece suit was there but the filling was different. My caller was ex-Detective Sergeant Tony Hefflin. As soon as I appeared a sick smile passed over his face. He stopped banging and fished something out of his jacket pocket. It was a thick wad of notes. He held it up and riffled through it, smiling and gesturing that the money could be mine.

I watched his performance for a moment. This was a man I could take a serious dislike to. His clowning was attracting attention from passers-by. I opened the door unsure of whether I was going to thump him or invite him in.

'You've got a nerve coming here,' I snarled.

By way of reply he held the wad of twenties under my nose.

'Sniff that . . . lovely, eh? It could be yours, sunshine,' he sneered.

'Oh, and what have I got to do? Gun someone down in the street?'

'Don't give yourself airs, Cunane. I've heard you're not above a spot of evidence bending when it suits.' He pushed past me into the office.

I could feel my cheeks burning and I lifted my fist to give him a smack but he anticipated me by grabbing my wrist.

'Guilty conscience, eh? You soft wassock! Cut out the tough guy act before I break your arm.'

I shoved him clear and tried to regain self-control. I had a very strong urge to muss up his perfectly set bouffant locks.

'Get out of here,' I yelled, 'and keep your money in your

168

pocket. You don't have a warrant card now and I don't have to listen to you.'

He laughed and flashed me an irritating smile.

'If I was still in the job I'd have sorted you long before now, Mr Fancy Pants Private Detective.'

'You're not, though, are you? So buzz off.'

'Mr Carlyle wants to see you. I brought these along as persuaders,' he said, waving the notes again.

'Tell Charlie to get stuffed.'

'It's Mr Brandon Carlyle, not Charlie.'

'Same difference. Has Sam Levy been on to him?'

For the first time since he'd arrived the sneer left Hefflin's face. He looked puzzled.

'You're way off beam if you think Brandon Carlyle is the same as Charlie . . . Chalk and cheese, those two, and as for Sam Levy I don't know what you're talking about. I only came to politely invite you for a word with Mr Carlyle Senior. I wanted to bring along a couple of assistants to make sure you came but he insisted that I offer financial compensation instead.'

'Keep the money, Goldilocks. You're a joke and so is your boss. Tell him all he has to do to talk to me is pick up a phone.'

I pushed him towards the door.

'Ignoring Mr Carlyle is a big mistake, Cunane. You'll regret this.'

I shoved him out of the office and locked the door. He stared in at me for a moment, eyes as cold as a fish, and then took a mobile out of his pocket and turned away.

The phone started ringing as soon as I reached my inner office.

'Bugger off, Carlyle,' I said as soon as I picked it up.

'You're a very hasty young man, Mr Cunane,' a smooth voice replied, 'just like my own boy, Charlie. It was about him that I wanted to talk to you.'

'What about him?'

'About the interesting fact that my son appears to be able to bi-locate.'

'Bi-locate? What are you on about?'

'Come, come, Mr Cunane. I understand that you received a

169

Catholic education. Surely you remember that bi-location is one of . . .'

'Yeah, I know – the ability to be in two places at the same time.'

'Yes, apparently my son has that remarkable ability so I suppose that makes me God Almighty,' he said with a chuckle. His attempt at humour sounded nasty. The silky quality of the voice was unpleasant too, like the hissing of a burst water pipe.

'I've already said all I have to say about that to Charlie himself. There's no point in this conversation.'

'Come to see me, Mr Cunane, I insist. Hefflin is waiting outside your office. He has the limo with him.'

'No, I won't.'

'Very well, my next call is to a policeman named Cullen. He will be very interested to learn that you gave Charlie an alibi for the Olley shooting.'

'You'd drop your own son in it?'

'Like a shot, Mr Cunane. Like a shot. I'm an honest citizen with a position to uphold.'

24

I know that the Duke of Westminster has a big spread in South Cheshire but for sheer ostentation Brandon Carlyle's place took some beating. You had to pass a pig farm to get there. Carlyle's residence was called Moat House Farm after one of the many moated farms in that part of Cheshire but in its new form had been christened 'South Pork' by the local wags. Everything about it was new and shiny, and the only items lacking were the price tags. The entrance from the main road was big enough for half a dozen five-axle artics to park in with room to spare and was surrounded with red brick walls topped with spiked railings extending to the horizon in both directions. Black and gold wrought-iron gates whirred open when Hefflin touched a switch.

'You want to watch that lip of yours when we get in here, Cunane,' he commented sourly.

'Oh, aye?'

'Yes, someone might bust it for you.'

'Are you offering?'

'God! You are behind the door, son. Mr Carlyle has his own rugby league team. There's always a few lads down here enjoying the country air.'

'The Pendlebury Piledrivers? I hear they couldn't blow the skin off a cold rice pudding. Facing relegation, aren't they?'

'Listen, dickhead, I'm only telling you this because your dad was in the job. Some of those lads are fanatically loyal to Mr Carlyle. He pays them and feeds them and, believe me, if he tells them to give you a pasting you'll be the one facing relegation.'

'I am impressed.'

Once inside it was like Disneyland without the giant

rodents. Clumps of white plastic statuary dotted the grounds here and there, mostly of classical goddesses more voluptuous than any Greek of the pre-silicone era could have imagined. There were 'features': paved areas, trickling water, arbours, bays. All set in velvet green lawns against clashing yellow and red flower beds.

Now I saw the full extent of Brandon Carlyle's power. Only a man with the influence to frighten planning officers out of their wits could have got away with such an eyesore.

As we approached the sprawling red brick structure the impression of unlimited wealth carelessly spent increased. We entered a courtyard faced by the blank doors of garages along one side, only they weren't blank. Each door had a small concrete 'water feature' fixed in the middle of it. It could have been the show room of some demented supplier of grotesque garden equipment. Detail extended as far as giant plastic butterflies and insects stuck on the walls. Opposite the garages, across a small lawn complete with fountain, there was another sprawling building which reminded me of a sports hall or gym. As we got out of the car I saw that that was exactly what it was. The low, dark shapes of American fitness machines were visible through the windows and further back there was an extensive pool.

The mansion itself had enough pillars to make the likes of Ernie Cunliffe green with envy. Six lofty Corinthian columns as high as the three-storey house supported a Greek style portico complete with carved pediment of gods battling centaurs.

'Seen enough, have you?' a suave grey-haired man with a deep tan asked as he stepped out from behind one of the pillars. Brandon Carlyle looked younger than I'd expected. Dark, intelligent eyes studied me from a fleshy face. He had a large, bulbous nose and even now, at midday, looked as if he needed a shave. The impression was of firmness masking an underlying brutality, more like a soldier who's risen from the ranks than a born member of the officer class.

'A fine house, eh?' he continued.

'It's certainly an eyeful,' I said cautiously.

'Yes, I'm proud of it,' he replied and held out his hand to be shaken. 'Brandon Carlyle, Mr Cunane. I must say that I'm interested to make your acquaintance.' His accent was aggressively Mancunian.

'I'm sorry to say that the feeling isn't mutual, Mr Carlyle,' I said, ignoring his hand.

'Oh, so you're one of them fancy folk who tries to make a virtue out of pig ignorance, are you, Cunane?' he asked, making an effort to keep the smile on his face. 'We know how to deal with people like you round here.' He turned to Hefflin who had taken position one step behind him like a gun dog. 'Present company excepted, Tony, but it's nice to have my prejudices confirmed. Stupidity and ignorance, it's got to be bred in the bone with some of these coppers – a self-selected bunch of thickies.'

'Like your rugby team, then?'

'Team's doing fine.'

'Is it? Two good runs in the cup in the last five years and bottom of the table for the rest of the time?' I sneered. This touched a raw nerve. Carlyle's face seemed to lose some of its tan.

He put his hand on my face and slapped my cheek slightly.

'Hey, young Cunane, you're forgetting something.'

'What?'

'Your fucking father was always mob-handed when he came to see me but you aren't.'

'So what?' I replied, patting the thick wallet in my inside jacket pocket. 'How do you know I'm not carrying a gun?'

Carlyle's face lost its remaining trace of tan as he stepped back smartly and tried to put the pillar between himself and me. 'Hefflin, you bloody idiot,' he snarled in fright. 'I should have known better than to trust a copper, ex or otherwise.'

'He's pulling your leg, Mr Carlyle,' Hefflin assured him and jerked my jacket open to reveal the pacific state of my chest.

'Very funny, Cunane,' Carlyle said, keeping his distance. 'Your father was just the same. Full of stupid tricks. It's nice to see he's passed something on to you besides stupidity.'

'OK then, if that's all you wanted to say I'll be off,' I said, turning. Hefflin laid a hand on my chest. I shoved him away.

'Right! I warned you, Cunane,' he said, waving his hand

173

frantically. Five hard-looking no-necks stepped out of the gym. The Piledrivers' back row. They might not have stopped many opposing teams this season but there were enough of them to intimidate me.

'Which ones have piles and which ones can drive?' I asked.

'Shut your stupid face,' Hefflin said. I could see he was on edge. His bouffant hair was positively quivering. 'Another word and they'll take you apart.'

'That lot? A team from the Blind School would run rings round them.'

'All right, Mr Cunane,' Brandon Carlyle said pleasantly. 'You've made your point. You're a big tough boy and you don't scare easily. We're all duly impressed. All I want is a few words in your shell-like.'

'Good, well keep it brief and I'll be on my way.'

'Not so fast, young man. There's no need for any unpleasantness . . . yet. Let me show you some of my toys. They cost enough. Have you ever seen a fountain like this?' He took an electronic device out of the pocket of his grey jacket and pointed it at the fountain. A jet of water shot sixty feet into the air and coloured lights came on.

'As a matter of fact I have,' I said. 'It's like a theme park. Is that where you got your ideas?'

'Eeeh, aren't you sharp? Proper comic turn. Mind you don't cut yourself, won't you?'

'Glad you like the routine.'

'You'd better come in. All I wanted was to show you that my house is full of the latest electronic gadgets. There's nothing to touch it in this country. The fittings were done by the same people who did Bill Gates' house in Seattle.'

'I'm impressed.'

Eyeing me narrowly, he turned and walked into the house. The doors opened automatically just like a shop. I didn't need a signal to follow. Out of the corner of my eye I saw the heavy squad closing up on me. The entrance atrium lived up to expectations. I almost stepped into a sunken pool full of fat carp swimming sluggishly in the glow of coloured lights. Flat screen monitors lined the walls displaying a sickening and constantly changing array of Old Master pictures. I could feel

174

my stomach heaving. The only item in the whole huge room that couldn't have been manufactured yesterday was an antique ice-cream cart, the sort with two handles that they used to push through the streets. Lettering on the side, in faded paint, spelled the word 'Colonna'.

Carlyle mistook my thoughtful expression.

'I see from the way my interior décor turns your nose up that you're a snob, young Cunane,' Brandon hissed, 'exactly like your dad. It didn't take much to put that long snout of his out of joint. Tell me, are you interested in architecture, stately homes and other such rubbish?'

'Yes,' I admitted.

'A connoisseur, eh?'

I shrugged.

'I'll bet you're in the National Trust, aren't you?'

'I am.'

'How did I guess?' he sneered. 'Back in the eighteenth century, what do you think raggedy-arsed bastards like yourself and your dad made of places like Chatsworth or Ickworth House? I bet they turned their snotty noses up. Now it's all fodder for your bloody heritage industry.'

'Crap! There's such a thing as excess . . .'

'Excess be damned, this place is making an impression on you and that's what it's for. I'm not one of them mealy-mouthed, whispering dicks who apologises when some arty puff mentions bad taste. Christ Almighty! If a water cascade a mile long was good enough for the First Fucking Duke of Bloody Devonshire when he laid out his spread, why shouldn't I do as I please without asking some lardy-arsed committee? Unlike these Dukes I came by my wealth by my own efforts.'

'Well done, your grace,' I said, tugging my forelock mockingly. 'Now you've fried all the chips on your shoulder perhaps you'd like to tell me why I've been dragged out here?'

'Cheeky bugger!'

'Not at all. I'd no idea you were so desperate for company. I heard that you like your privacy.'

'Oh, you have, have you? Been hearing a lot of things you shouldn't. You're one of those pricks who's walking round

175

with your tongue hanging out waiting for any lying little bit if gossip you can use against people who've made something of themselves. You and all the other tight-arsed little bollocks who won't let a man enjoy what he's earned. I'm telling you, this country's going down the pan until it starts letting people really use the wealth they've created.'

'You poor old rich thing,' I sympathised, 'what you have to put up with.'

'All right, Mr Bloody Private Detective Cunane, that's enough of your bullshit for today,' he snapped.

We were now standing on a polished marble floor in front of a quadrangle of huge white airport-lounge-style sofas. There was a glass dome above us. I didn't know whether Carlyle expected me to sit down, do a clog dance or kneel and pray at his shrine. From my point of view this was one of those interviews best conducted while standing. I scanned the area for a quick escape route. The heavies were blocking the doorway through which we'd entered. There were other doors, but no doubt Brandon could control them with his electronic zapper. By now I wouldn't have been surprised if he'd touched a button to reveal a tank full of hungry crocodiles. It would have been in character. As intended, I was impressed but I wasn't going to let him know that.

'I didn't start it,' I said. 'It was you who told me that I've inherited my father's stupidity.'

'Well, I'm not a stupid father. I want to hear from you exactly what you've been playing at with my son Charles.'

'Ask him.'

'I have and he comes up with some cock and bull story of you providing him with an alibi for the time Lou Olley was killed.'

'If that's what he's told you, who am I to contradict?' I asked. I looked at the heavy bronze candlesticks on a nearby table and wondered what would happen if I grabbed one as a weapon.

'Tell Mr Carlyle a straight story, you crooked bastard,' Hefflin yelped.

'Or what?'

'Did you help Charlie to kill Lou Olley?' Brandon demanded.

176

'I would have thought you knew all about that,' I muttered.

'Meaning what? That I arranged a murder that could bring discredit on my whole family? Talk sense, Cunane.'

'It certainly had nothing to do with me . . .'

'But it was right outside your office.'

'So? It's a public street.'

'Are you fucking my son's wife?'

'No.'

'What are you messing around with her for then?'

'She wants me to prove that her father was wrongly imprisoned.'

'Bloody lying bastard!' Brandon shrieked and then launched himself at me. It was totally unexpected. He landed a couple of ineffectual punches on my face before I fended him off. Hefflin grabbed him and two of the rugby players had me by the shoulders before I could do more.

Brandon retreated to a corner of the room wheezing away like a broken down steam engine. His lips were flecked with foam. Hefflin fussed round him like a mother hen and after a moment Brandon took out a tiny pill box and slipped something under his tongue. My earlier guess about his age was wrong. He was on the wrong side of three score and ten. As I beamed my defiance across at him I felt something trickling down my upper lip. I licked it and tasted blood. The savage old trout had burst my nose. I took out a handkerchief and dabbed the offending area. This evidence of his prowess pleased Carlyle. He came over and the flanking heavies gripped my wrists as if expecting me to try to assault the old villain.

'Not so tough as you make out, are you?' he sneered triumphantly.

'Is this the point where your flat-footed rugby team hold me while you hit me in the face?' I asked.

'Oh, hell! Come over here, you young fool,' he said with a complete change of tone. 'You can go,' he said to the muscle squad. 'And you as well, Tony. I expect I can talk to Cunane without having to be guarded like the Crown Jewels.'

'Are you sure, Mr Carlyle?' Hefflin ventured.

'Go!' Brandon ordered with a flick of his hand.

177

Hefflin went. I followed Brandon and sat on one of the oversized sofas opposite him.

'I know this place is all a bit over the top,' he said quietly. 'It was one of my late wife's projects but since she died I can't quite seem to get it completely right. I've nothing against the National Trust. We were in it when she were alive.'

'Oh.'

'Listen, lad,' he said conversationally. 'Sometimes I think I was never happier than when I were a boy living in two rooms above a poky little pub in Ancoats. All cotton mills in those days, it was. 'Course it's gone now, that; and if you think this is an architectural nightmare you should see what they replaced those streets with.'

'I do see it, every day.'

'Of course you do, lad. I forget. Trouble with having money is it takes you away from your roots. That's why I'm fond of my team . . . fonder of it than I am of this place, any road. I keep having it redecorated and they always rip me off. Perhaps if you're so bloody strong on good taste you can take it on next time.'

'Thanks for the offer but interior decorating isn't really my scene,' I said with a laugh.

'Tell me the truth. Do you think my Charlie was involved in killing Olley?'

'I honestly don't think he's got it in him,' I said.

'No. I can't make my mind up whether to be happy or sad about that, but I suppose you're right.'

'Great.'

'You're not trying to blackmail him or anything, are you? No, I shouldn't ask. You're a chip off the old block. Right bastard your old man was, but not a bent one.'

'Gee, thanks for the testimonial,' I said, getting up.

'I'm not done yet,' the patriarch snapped, 'sit down!'

I sat.

'My Charlie might be a bit of a fool to himself, but what about his wife? She's a designing little piece with brains enough for both of them. Did she have anything to do with Olley's death?'

'No more than your son did,' I said.

178

He looked at me for a long time.

'I wish I could be so sure,' he said. 'Now she was bred in the right stable for that sort of thing. You want to stay well clear of Vince King. He's poison, that man, absolute poison.'

'What's all this about, Mr Carlyle?' I asked, trying to switch on the charm. My smile probably came out like a sneer but Carlyle responded.

'Do you know much history?'

I shrugged.

'The Roman Emperors, people like that . . . it was when they got older that their problems began. Who's going to succeed? Who's going to get the money? There can only be one bum on the top chair at the Carlyle Corporation.'

'Really?' I said.

'Don't be snide. It's true. I've no idea what Charlie was up to, or if he had Olley topped, but it makes me nervous. They're frightened I might take my money offshore and put it in a perpetual trust so that they can't get their hands on it.'

'Who's scared?'

'My sons and their wives – especially the wives. Charlie is the most loyal, but that wife of his! I regret ever taking her into my home. This is how kindness is repaid. She's trying to get that father of hers out so he can pay back some imagined score. He's insane. You must realise that.'

'Vince King didn't strike me as insane.'

'So you know him?'

I looked at Carlyle intently. He stared back, silently challenging me to go on. His eyes were very dark and very mobile, ageless, full of cunning. There was a lot he could tell me but this wasn't the time. I was tempted nevertheless . . .

'King swears he's innocent, yet he let the police and the law railroad him. I wonder why that was?' I said.

Brandon continued to give me the hard eye.

'Maybe you haven't inherited so much stupidity as I thought. If you've a scrap of intelligence you'll stay out of that business and let it sort itself out,' he said quietly.

I tried to stand up again but he laid a hand on my sleeve to restrain me.

'There's another thing too. I've got enemies. I accept that.

179

That fat slap-head Clyde Harrow is one. Don't think I haven't heard that he's going round town looking for dirt about me and my family. Just wait until his contract is up for renewal. He'll sing a different tune then. It'll be tears and "Yes, Mr Carlyle. No, Mr Carlyle. Three bags full, Mr Carlyle," then. We'll have to see how far it'll get him and I don't mind if you tell him that.'

'Fine,' I muttered, 'that's no skin off my nose.'

'What I say next might cause an abrasion. You've been pestering Sam Levy for information about me.'

'I've done no such thing,' I said angrily.

'Leave Sam alone,' Brandon thundered. 'He's mad with jealousy and rage. He's insane.'

'What, another old friend of yours?'

'Stop pestering him.'

'I haven't pestered anyone.'

'Oh, haven't you? You've been going round flapping your ear hoping to pick up dirt which you can relay to Harrow.'

'I haven't,' I said hotly.

'The trouble with Sam is that, unlike that toad Harrow, he really does know one or two things which are to my disadvantage. Sam's not been normal since his sister passed away. Unhinged, he is. Broods on his troubles, like. I've tried to help but there's nothing I can do.'

'Was it your idea of helping to provide him with a mail order bride?'

'Christ! Do you think that was me?' he cackled. 'Sam's older than me. Why, I'd have had half a dozen myself if they were any good. No, I stick to vitamin pills and gingko biloba.'

'I've not tried to pump any information out of him, nor have I spoken to Harrow about him.'

'Right, well keep it that way and here's an honest threat for you . . .'

'What?'

'If Sam Levy knows where the bodies are buried, so do I.'

'What are you on about?'

'I'm on about this, you young smart-arse. I know approximately where and when two well-known Manchester criminals disappeared and I know why two children were born to a certain infertile couple in Tarn. I wonder how keen you are to see that story in the papers or on the Clyde Harrow show? Have I to say more?'

It's strange. Working among the morally challenged elements of Manchester's citizenry has given me a certain familiarity with being threatened. At least, I thought it had, but then until I met Brandon Carlyle I'd never been threatened by an expert before.

I'm not really sure how I got away from his hideous mansion in South Cheshire. I've a vague memory of the head creep Hefflin holding a car door open for me and then the next time I can remember anything I was back at home in my flat staring at a blank wall.

25

'Dave! Dave!' Janine shouted through the letter box. 'What's the matter with you? Open up.'

Her cries became more and more anguished until eventually they penetrated the deep mood of gloom I'd wrapped myself in since leaving Brandon Carlyle. I couldn't shake off the certainty that there was only one person other than Dee Elsworth that I'd ever trusted with the story of what had happened to those two would-be killers and that person was Janine White.

'Have you been taking something? You look dreadful,' she said when I opened the door. 'Why did you put the bars on the door?'

'Perhaps I wanted privacy.'

'What?' she asked uncomprehendingly. 'Dave, are you ill? Shall I get a doctor?'

'There's nothing wrong with me that a change of company won't cure,' I said bitterly.

'You're not yourself. Listen, I was thinking of us going away for a few days at half-term. I mean, all of us together as if we were a family. I know you'd like that.'

I was going to reply but Jenny and Lloyd came in.

'Ooh, are we all going away?' Jenny chanted. 'Can we go to the seaside?'

'Dave's not well, love. Take Lloyd back to the flat and put the telly on.'

'Where shall we go? There's a girl in my class called Michelle O'Dell who says Blackpool's common but Miss Seagrave told her she was stuck up.'

'I don't think we'll be going to Blackpool, darling. Perhaps we could find somewhere quiet and peaceful in Wales,' Janine

182

said. 'What do you think, Dave?'

'Would Miss Seagrave approve of somewhere quiet in Wales?' I asked Jenny.

Jenny looked at me with eyes as big as saucers. 'She's always telling us to be quiet but I'll ask her,' she said after pondering the idea. Then she thought for another moment. 'Miss Seagrave says there's lots of things you can do in Blackpool if the weather's bad,' she said, and then she took her brother by the hand and left us to ourselves.

'Are you all right, Dave? You look as if you've had a funny turn,' Janine commented with unusual solicitude.

'You could say that but I'll get over it,' I told her.

'Who's upset you? It's not me, is it?'

'No, sometimes things happen that can get on top of you. I'll be all right in a while,' I assured her.

'It's just that something's come up and I need your help.'

'Oh, yes,' I said vaguely.

'Henry's calling round tomorrow.'

'Oh, is he?'

'You might show some response,' she said angrily.

'OK, I'm responding. What did you want . . . a car bomb? A fall off a high building? You name it . . .'

'If that's how fucking seriously you take this . . .'

'What do you want me to do?'

'Forget it! I'll try for a baby-sitter despite the short notice.'

'What do you want me to do?'

Janine put her hands on her hips and looked at me as if the situation was all my fault. I could see she was on the point of tears.

'What's got into you, Dave? I was . . .' She bit her lip.

'We all have our off-days and this is mine,' I muttered, awkwardly putting my arms round her.

'I don't want the children to be here when he arrives. Jenny still talks about Henry a lot but Lloyd's forgotten all about him. He's no right to barge back into our lives demanding to see them.'

'No right,' I agreed, 'except that he is their father.'

'You've been more of a father to them in the last year than he ever was.'

'Maybe, but you've made it very clear that I shouldn't get too close.'

'Oh shit, Dave! Is that what this is all about? Are you throwing a moody because I won't let you get proprietorial and stick the banns up?'

'It's nothing to do with that . . . well, not directly.'

Janine pushed herself free from me. Tears had been replaced by anger and frustration.

'Oh fuck! Fuck! Fuck!' She stamped over to the drinks cupboard and poured herself a stiff whisky.

'Hmmph! I suppose you're going to say this is all down to me,' she shouted, having knocked back her drink.

'I'm going to say that if you don't stop swearing Jenny will be bringing a note home from Miss Seagrave.'

She laughed and then swung a mock punch at me. I ducked and pushed her back.

'Cunane, you're a sly bastard, aren't you? How am I ever going to get free of you?' She started laughing helplessly and collapsed on the sofa.

I poured myself a drink. I decided that now was not the time to tell her about Brandon Carlyle's threat.

'Seriously, Janine, what do you want me to do? Short of assassination, that is?' I said, when I'd seated myself next to her.

'I thought you might take the children out tomorrow. It would be better if they aren't around. I'll try to work something out with Henry. The solicitor says he has the right to see them but I want to make it clear to him that he can't just drop in at any old time.'

'That's fine, it'll be my pleasure,' I said.

'Do you want to come round tonight?' she asked. 'I missed you last night.'

'Sorry, something's come up. I won't be able to make it.'

'Not sulking, are you, big boy?'

'There's something I need to get right in my head first, Janine. I'd be no use to you anyway.'

'Ooh, such modesty. I know where I can get Viagra. There's a man in the office . . .'

'That's not the problem,' I snapped.

'Tell me then.'

'Something's surfaced from the past. I need time on my own.'

'I don't know . . . you men with your pasts. I didn't tell you yesterday but I had a phone call from Clyde Harrow. He wants me to go out with him.'

'What?'

'There's some TV awards thing. He wants me to go with him. He is pretty high up in TV,' she said coquettishly.

'He's so high, he's started stinking.'

'Don't be jealous now. A girl has to make the most of her chances.'

'You'd better be careful. Clyde's like you. He has strong views about marriage.'

'Oh?'

'Yes, he can't get enough of it. He's been married six times and now he's looking for the seventh Mrs Harrow.'

'You can't be serious.'

'I am and Clyde is. Why should a man who can't stop at number one stop at number six? You could be the seventh Mrs Harrow.'

'That's definitely one harrowing experience I want to avoid. I told him I'd have to think about going with him.'

'Think long and hard. Clyde's methods of seduction are strenuous. He's not above a spot of blackmail.'

'Like you?'

'Oh for God's sake! Clyde's a one-off.'

'Is he the one who's ruffled your feathers?'

'Is he hell!' I growled. 'It would take more than an old ham like him to do that.'

Looking at Janine's concerned expression helped me to make up my mind. If Brandon didn't want me to see Levy, then I would see him.

'Dave, you look better already,' Janine said with a laugh. 'The colour's come back into your face.'

'Great,' I said gloomily.

'If I can't lure you to my bed I'll have to love you and leave you,' Janine announced. 'I must go, the children will be fighting. Eleven tomorrow? And Dave, you've got the key if you change your mind.'

185

'OK,' I murmured. I could do without the fussing.

When she'd gone I brought the bottle over from the cupboard and poured myself another drink. I put a Leadbelly album on the CD player. I lay on the sofa for a long while watching the evening draw in. Gradually a chill, empty feeling began to creep over me. I shook myself and poured more whisky into the tumbler, but it did no good. There were no answers at the bottom of the glass. I felt as if I stood on the edge of a precipice. After a while, still lying flat on my back, I picked the whisky bottle up by its neck and held it above my face. It was more than half empty. I knew that if I had another drink it would all go downhill from then on.

'Damn Brandon Carlyle!' I thought.

I put the bottle down and lay there thinking for a long while, then I struggled to my feet, made myself a cup of coffee and had a shower and dressed. The heat put me in a better humour with myself.

Then I phoned Sam Levy.

'I knew you had sense,' he said.

'That puts you in a class on your very own,' I replied.

There was a pause while he thought about that, then, 'The self-depreciating humour, yes? Nobody has that like us English.'

'It's self-deprecating, Mr Levy.'

'Yes, so you call me in the evening to correct my grammar?'

'Yes, I mean no. I called to tell you that I paid a visit to your old friend Brandon Carlyle today. He didn't seem very happy about your mental status.'

'I should worry what Brandon thinks about me? For this you call me? I think you called because you're curious to find out more about Miss Marti and her papa. That's the bone you want to chew, no?'

'No, I mean yes. Hell, I'm so confused between you and Brandon I don't know what I mean. Did you get in touch with Angelina?'

'Don't change the subject, Mr Cunane. Brandon leaned on you, yes?'

'How did you know?'

'Any meeting with Brandon is no joke. Self-depreciating, he

186

isn't. He likes to send people away with a flea in their ointment.'

'He succeeded this time.'

'And now you want to put something in his medicine? Am I right or am I wrong?'

'No! Listen, he has some dirt on me . . . not dirt really, just something that's better forgotten . . .'

'Mucky stuff, dirt.'

'I don't care about me, but there are other people involved who might get hurt.'

'If you play with tar, some sticks on your fingers.'

'Spare me the philosophy, Mr Levy. I just thought that if I understood what's at the bottom of all this I might be able to see my way out of this mess.'

'God forgive me! I should tell you to move to another town but I won't waste my breath. I know what sort you are. You'd better come round and we'll talk. Maybe I can get some sense into your head.'

26

It took the best part of half an hour to get to Sam Levy's house. I'd thought it was isolated before but now, approaching it in the dark, it seemed to be crying out for attention from the criminal fraternity.

'You ought to get some security lights and alarms and better locks,' I said when Levy opened the door.

'I told you already. If they want to rob me they can take the lot and welcome.'

'No, really,' I insisted. 'You can't see the house from the road with all those trees and bushes. You ought to do something.'

'You want to come and live with me now, you're so worried?'

I must have looked aggrieved at this because he laughed and led me into the kitchen. The kitchen table was laid with a meal for two. There were even candles.

'Are you expecting someone?' I asked.

'What are you? A ghost? Indulge me, Mr Cunane. I satisfy your curiosity as far as I can and you share a meal with me. Don't worry, the food's not poisoned.'

I tried to smile but it came out more like a grimace.

'I'm joking you, Mr Cunane,' he said. 'The depreciation's too much for you, eh? Sit down. By the looks of you, you need feeding.'

There was nothing I could say that would stop him. Soon he was ladling a rich-smelling stew onto a plate in front of me. I gave it a half-hearted poke with my fork.

'You want to know what it is?' he asked with a laugh. 'You guessed it's not pork, eh?'

'It's not that,' I said hastily. 'It's just that I don't usually eat this late.'

'Faddy eater, eh? Eat, then sleep. Let your digestion work while you rest. That's what I say. Best topside beef, brandy, red wine, onions and herbs in that. No bacon though. Simmer slowly and eat it late. I always cook too much. Superstition, yes! I think if I have the food someone will come and join me, and now they have.'

'Mr Levy, I'm sorry about Angelina. I can go with you if you want to try for a personal reconciliation.'

'No, no, you were wise about that. Best to let her make her own mind up. Besides, the boats will still be sailing to Thailand and Manila next year, eh? Perhaps this time I'll find a Jewish Philippine girl.'

The rich aroma was doing its work and I tucked in despite myself. Levy poured out a beaker of red wine. 'Drink,' he ordered. 'I cooked the meat in this.' I looked at the bottle: Musigny AC. I'm no wine buff but I knew enough to know that it was very expensive.

'Extravagant, eh?' Levy conceded, 'but what else should I cook *boeuf bourguignonne* in but the best burgundy wine?'

'You certainly know how to look after yourself,' I agreed.

There was silence while we ate. I felt some of the tension drain away.

'I know how to look after myself, but you're too polite to say what you're thinking,' he said eventually. 'If I live so well why has my wife left me? That's the question, eh? What's wrong with a rich old cocker that he can't hang on to a wife from a country that has too much population and too few dollars? You think Angelina leaving me was all a trick laid on for your benefit, don't you?'

'Mr Levy, if I could understand women I don't think I'd be in the trouble I'm in now,' I said. 'I don't know why Angelina left. Why don't you ask her? I know I'd like to ask Marti King what her game is.'

'Hah! I like this. Direct, no messing.'

'That's me,' I agreed.

'Marti, I can help you with, but first tell me what Brandon's been doing.'

I related the whole story, Dee, Janine, Marti, the visit to Vince, Celeste's comments, everything.

When I finished Levy shook his head. He pushed the dishes away and gave a long sigh. I waited expectantly with a hundred questions to fire at him.

'David,' he said. 'Can I call you David?'

I shrugged.

'You did something for me. You found Angelina . . . you could have ripped me off but you didn't. I owe you something. I know you suspect that my coming to you was part of some deep laid plot but it wasn't. I had no idea that you were involved with Marti.'

'Bit of a coincidence,' I muttered, studying his benevolent expression for a sign that he was lying. He was so genial that it was hard to be sceptical.

'Yes, but that's all it was. These things happen. I was a bookmaker, I should know.'

'All right, so tell me why my taking an interest in Vince King has got Brandon Carlyle in such a lather?'

'I can't. Trust me. If I told you what's worrying Brandon there are people who'd snuff you out like that candle just to be sure that you didn't share your knowledge with anyone.'

'Brandon . . .'

'No, not him. Your little chat with Brandon must have reassured him or you wouldn't be here now. There are other people who have an interest in seeing that Vince King stays locked up.'

'You promised if I found Angelina . . .'

'I promised to tell you about Devereaux-Almond and I will. He was . . . well, let's say he has a gift. With me it was numbers, with him it was pieces of paper. He knows how to create a screen of words and paper round matters which a man like Brandon has to keep hidden.'

'So he helped Brandon ensure that Vince King was found guilty?'

'No, no. Can't you understand? The last thing a man like my former partner would want is to be tied up in something like that. All he did was to encourage Devereaux-Almond to handle King's affairs. It was like entering a yearling in a race for three-year-olds. With the brief advised by Almond, a man who knew everything there was to know about shell

190

companies but nothing about crime or juries, King was bound to take a fall. There was no need to fix anything, the legal system fixed him. King was a fool. He knew how important Devereaux-Almond was to Brandon and he must have thought they'd see him right. He gambled and he lost.'

'But he didn't do the murders?'

'Murders, schmurders! Who knows? Who cares?' Levy asked with a dismissive gesture. 'Vince King did plenty of crime. He's where he ought to be, believe me.'

'Maybe I'd be happier if there were some other prominent citizens doing time along with him.'

Levy laughed at this.

'You mean me, yes? More self-depreciation?'

I shook my head.

'David, I've told you enough already. You must drop any interest in King now. Stop being noble, yes? He's a dangerous man to know, particularly for you. Marti was naughty to get you mixed up in this. She must have known who your father was.'

'What's that got to do with anything?'

'I've said enough.'

'You haven't.'

'Enjoy the food and forget you ever heard Vince King's name. He's forgotten now and he should stay forgotten. Listen, I'll give you a bonus for finding Angelina so promptly. You take your young lady and her children away for a long holiday. When you come back all this will have blown over and Brandon won't have any interest in you. Yes, that's a promise.'

I tried to coax more information out of him but it was like banging my head against a brick wall. I gave up and we talked about his holidays in Thailand and his house. I enjoyed the meal, which was delicious, and he was flattered when I told him so. We finished the wine. Eventually I left.

'You really ought to get this place secured,' I said again as I stood in the hallway.

'Listen, David, the professional criminals know who I am,' he said with a chuckle. 'They know that if they messed with me they'd go home with their heads in a sling.'

'What, do you practise karate or something?'

He chuckled at this thought.

'David, how do you think a bookmaker collects awkward debts? I may be retired but I still know the right buttons to press if I want something done. Why, that little punk Lou Olley started out working for me.'

'There are always amateurs.'

'Yes, there are always amateurs to consider and sometimes one gets lucky, eh? But a bookmaker knows how to take a loss. If he's any good he takes the occasional lucky amateur in his stride. What he has to look out for is the well-organised pro who's decided to take a risk.'

As I drove back to Chorlton I felt easier in my mind, but for all his geniality and the touches of pathos there was just a hint of something sinister about Sam Levy. Was it chance that he called on me after Olley was killed? Some chance.

Back at Thornleigh Court everything was as calm as a megalithic tomb. Even the air seemed still.

I took Janine's key and let myself into next door in my stocking feet.

'Dave, is that you?' she called.

I made no reply. Opening the door of her bedroom I shed my jeans and shirt and slipped in beside her. The warmth of her body was like fire, and I held on to her as if she was my one contact with reality.

27

Although it was Sunday morning the trading at the Trafford Centre was relentless. Droves of drugged-looking people gawped at the endless succession of shop fronts. I'd gone there with Jenny and Lloyd on a whim. There were all kinds of ways I could have entertained them for the day. I could have gone to my parents if I hadn't felt peevish about my last reception there. I could have gone to Chester Zoo but that would have been too painful. The whole situation there was too much for me: sad caged animals staring out at sad, divorced and legally restricted dads giving their separated offspring a permitted airing. At least, that was the fancy I'd had when I'd last trailed Jenny and Lloyd round there. There was a rival attraction I could have chosen, the Blue Planet Aquarium, but I'd seen enough of sharks and cold fish to last a lifetime. So the Trafford Centre it was. Before setting out I fixed the rack onto the car and put my bike on it.

I had a plan at the back of my mind.

First, we took an early lunch at the Rainforest. Artificial animals I could stand. Lloyd watched the gorillas vibrating as he munched his way through the unusual menu. That took us the best part of two hours.

Next we went into a bike shop and I bought Jenny and Lloyd a bike each, by no means the cheapest ones either. I bought them helmets and knee pads and elbow pads. I bought them cycling clothes. I bought them locks and I bought them gloves. I bought first aid kits, repair kits and route maps. I bought racks to mount the whole ensemble on my car and then spent half an hour in the car park getting everything squared away.

The kids were bubbling with enthusiasm. I almost had to tie

Lloyd up to stop him trying out his stabilisers round the busy ten-thousand-space car park. Finally, we set off for Dunham Massey. Brandon Carlyle's words were echoing in my head as we entered the National Trust property. Time had turned the bricks here to a pleasing dark rust shade though I doubted that they'd ever been that precise raw red favoured by Brandon. The immemorial oaks and the restrained architecture did something for my bruised spirit but they weren't the objects of the exercise. We pedalled past the house, turned right at the water mill and went down to the tow path along the old canal.

We cycled for some miles before I made a discovery – you can take young children so far and then they flake out. We ate our sandwiches and rested and set off back. We didn't get far. Lloyd came to a dead stop. He was falling asleep over the handlebars. I took him off his bike, and having tied it on top of my own, put him over my shoulder and walked. Jenny struggled along beside me on her own bike, needing constant encouragement and many stops. It took us hours to get back to the car park at Dunham Massey. We were almost the last to leave before it shut.

It was quite dark when I got the pair to their mother's door, still in their cycling gear.

'Oh, Dave!' Janine gasped. 'What have you done to them? I've been frantic.'

'We went for a little bike ride.'

'It was great, Mum,' Jenny, who had revived slightly, confirmed.

'Look at them, they're covered in mud.'

'It'll wash off,' I muttered.

Janine started peeling the children's clothes off. 'Where've they got all these things from? I asked you to look after them for a couple of hours, not re-equip them from the skin out.'

'Dave bought us new bikes,' Jenny said. 'Mine's nicer than the one Michelle O'Dell's got.'

'Oh, really,' Janine murmured. 'Does Dave know that Michelle's daddy owns a chain of car salesrooms?' She shot me a fierce look.

'And we got the helmets and the pads and the shorts and we had a meal at the Rainforest and a picnic by the canal bank and

194

Dave carried Lloyd all the way back and the man at the car park was waiting to lock up when we got there,' Jenny recounted breathlessly. 'Miss Seagrave says we should write a diary about interesting things that happen and I'm going to write it all down and do a picture of Dave carrying Lloyd . . .'

Janine lapsed into an ominous silence. She led the children into the bathroom and I departed for my own flat. It was about an hour later that my phone rang.

'Are you there, Hercules? You'd better come round and explain, hadn't you?'

I went meekly enough.

'Do you mind telling me what your idea was?' Janine demanded

'No idea, I just thought I'd like a bike ride and I could hardly fit the pair of them on my handlebars.'

'This is some obscure way of getting back at me over Henry, isn't it?'

'No, and how did you get on with him?'

'Don't try to change the subject. I want to know why you suddenly decided to spend hundreds of pounds on my children. Is this your way of telling me that we're breaking up?'

'No, and since when are we into "my children"? I thought we were moving towards saying they're our children.'

'They're my children, not yours,' Janine snarled, her expression as fierce as any she-wolf defending her cubs.

'Why shouldn't I spend my money on them? We're supposed to be partners, aren't we? Do I have to ask your permission every time I buy them an ice cream?'

'A couple of brand-new bikes and all the trimmings are hardly the same as ice cream. You're trying to make some kind of statement, aren't you?'

'Janine, you're twisted. I don't analyse every action for significance as minutely as you do. I wanted to take them for a ride and I bought them the gear and we went. Full stop, end of story.'

'There's more to it than that. You've never had a sudden rush of blood to your head like this before and you still haven't told me why you threw a wobbler yesterday.'

'I didn't throw a wobbler, and maybe I want to be generous to your children because I won't ever get the opportunity to be generous to my own.'

'I've never said I wouldn't like another child,' she said angrily, 'but if you're expecting white weddings, bridesmaids and all that crap, you can stuff it.'

'You misunderstand me. I don't mean . . . I've already got two children and someone's put them in danger.'

'What are you on about?' she said hotly.

'Dee Elsworth. I'm the father of her twin sons . . .'

'The banker's wife who gave you the Lowry . . .' She started laughing. 'Oh, Dave, this is too much. What was it? What did they call it? A stud fee?'

'It was nothing like that, but you'd never understand. Brandon Carlyle has threatened to expose Dee and to have her garden dug up where those two men who tried to kill me and rape her are buried. Someone's opened her big mouth about something that was supposed to be secret.'

'I see! You think I've told someone what you told me. How dare you!'

'Well, haven't you? It could hardly have been Dee.'

'This is so nice. This is lovely. Dave Cunane's big secret is out in the open, so naturally it must be me who told the world? There must be a thousand ways Carlyle could have discovered your guilty secret.'

'It's not a guilty secret. I've done nothing to be ashamed of and if he didn't learn about it through you, how did he learn it?'

By way of reply Janine picked up a plate one of the children had left in the room and hurled it at the wall. Then she stormed off into the bathroom and I heard the sound of running water.

'Bloody men!' she swore when she came back. 'One of those animatronic apes at the Rainforest Café that Lloyd was burbling about has more sensitivity than either you or Henry Talbot put together. I've never mentioned your feeble little adventure to another soul, not even my mother . . .'

'All right! All right!' I shouted, jumping to my feet. 'Men are bloody useless! Of course we are. It's our nature. Someone like you could never make a mistake, could you, Janine? Of course, you're not the one who shouted that I was a killer in Marti King's hearing that day at my office. That couldn't have been you, could it?'

'So that's it? That's the charge? That's what all this face-pulling and lip-curling is about?' she said, giving a pretty fair impression of incredulity. 'I plead guilty and proud of it. If you'd wanted to keep your shady past that secret you should never have said a word to me in the first place. How was I to know that poor little rich Marti was earwigging?'

'I may have a shady past but now I've got to live with your big gob, haven't I? And while we're being so graphic about each other's faults, why don't you admit that you're as neurotic as hell? If you think I set out to buy your children's affection you're crazy. I'd never do that. I'd never need to.'

The confrontation had brought us face to face. Whatever Janine believed, I'm not a man who lets his fists do the talking for him, but I'd said plenty and I didn't trust myself to go on. I turned and started towards the door.

'Taking your bat and ball home because I won't play by your rules, are you, Dave?' Janine asked quietly. 'Don't go. I haven't finished with you yet. We've got to fix up about this holiday. Half-term starts next week and I want Jenny to be able to tell the Blessed Miss Seagrave what her arrangements are.'

I stayed where I was, breathing heavily. To say I was flabbergasted at her change of tack was incorrect. I don't think I had any flabber left to be gasted.

'Don't shout again, you'll waken the children,' Janine warned.

'Smashing perfectly good plates is OK, I suppose?' I commented mildly.

'Christ, Dave,' she said with a smile. 'You've got them both so tired they'll sleep till doomsday. I don't know how Miss Seagrave will cope if Jenny's late for school. She's the register monitor.'

I smiled.

'Come here, stud,' she said.

28

I thought the weekend had been heavy but it wasn't until I was arrested on Monday morning that the roof really fell in.

I suppose it was considerate of the Cheshire Constabulary to send plainclothesmen round to my office rather than the traditional Black Maria to Thornleigh Court, and they did say that I was only going to be assisting them in their enquiries, but nevertheless they hauled me off to Wilmslow police station. It amounted to arrest. Being grilled by the police these days is like slamming into a rubber wall. They're all so polite. 'Assisting' or being compelled, I came to a full stop and was left under no illusion that I could get up and walk out.

Not that I wanted to. I wanted answers about the brutal murder of Sam Levy just as much as they did.

Sam had been found on Sunday evening by the hairdresser who called every week to cut and tint his hair. The old man was lashed to a chair and had been brutally beaten. Death appeared to be due to heart failure or sheer terror. The house was ransacked from top to bottom. To the police it looked like a burglary that had gone wrong – that was until they found my fingerprints in several rooms. Then their busy minds set to work on other scenarios.

I spent most of an exhausting day fending off their questions. There was enough information on offer to divert their suspicions. Angelina of course was right up there with me as a prime suspect, and apparently she'd pulled another disappearing stunt which made her slightly more favourite than me. As the afternoon wore on, though, I detected a shift in emphasis away from myself and Angelina ... Had Mr Levy ever expressed any fears of burglary? Had he revealed to me that he kept considerable amounts of money on the premises?

I told them about Leah's pearls. It was safe enough to assume that they were somewhere in the house. Other visitors must have been as able to guess that as I was.

The questions went on relentlessly. What did I know about the sex cruises to Thailand and the Philippines that Mr Levy had started taking soon after his sister's death? Had he mentioned any unsavoury characters trying to blackmail him? Had I tried to blackmail him? Who were the people who had arranged his marriage? What money had changed hands? What had happened on the honeymoon trip round the Irish race courses? Did I know of any Irish extortionists who might have learned of Mr Levy's wealth?

I gave out what I knew and gleaned what I could.

It was late in the afternoon before they let me go. There had been a similar murder of a wealthy recluse in South Cheshire three months previously. A Liverpool gang was suspected. Why, I don't know, except that it's an article of faith among the Cheshire police that the worst crimes on their patch are down to Liverpudlians. The Carlyle name was never mentioned. Nothing was said about the Olley murder. So I felt under no obligation to volunteer information about either. In the light of Brandon Carlyle's threat, doing so might have compromised Dee Elsworth, her children and myself – compromised us more fatally and permanently than a spot of embarrassment at some article in a Sunday paper could have done.

All the way back to Chorlton I tried to argue myself into believing the Liverpool gang hypothesis. I tried and I failed. There were just too many coincidences piling up one on top of the other. Olley just happened to have been killed outside my door at a time when Marti was supposed to be paying me a visit. The very next day Sam Levy, friend of the Carlyles, chose to send me on a convenient trip east of Suez to retrieve his wife. Worst of all, Sam had managed to get himself killed after starting to tell me all about the murky dealings of the Carlyle family.

Janine was standing at the open door of my flat when I got back to Thornleigh Court. The phone was ringing in the room behind her.

'It's been like this all afternoon,' she said breathlessly.

199

'Like what?' I said irritably.

'The police left your door open when they carted some of your clothes away.'

'That's all right, I gave them the key to get in. The clothes will be back as soon as they establish that they're not covered in Sam Levy's blood.'

'That old man? They think you killed him?' she asked in astonishment.

'No. It's what the police call "eliminating a suspect from their enquiries". Naturally when they find my fingerprints in someone's house the first thing they think is that a sleazy private eye like me would be bound to knock off one of his clients.'

'Stupid pigs!' she said surprisingly. I was warmed by the idea that someone was on my side.

'So what else has happened?'

'That phone, it's been driving me mad. It keeps on ringing but when I answer it whoever's on the other end puts it down.'

'One-four-seven-one?'

'Number withheld.'

The phone was still ringing. I picked it up. 'Hello?'

'Cunane, ring this number from a public call box,' Tony Hefflin ordered before rattling off a number and then disconnecting.

'Carlyle,' I told Janine.

I made the call from the street.

'What have you told them?' were Brandon Carlyle's first words.

'What should I have told them?' I said angrily. 'Ask your tame bent copper. If I'd said anything you'd have police cars parked all over your lovely flower beds by now.'

'I know what you're thinking, Mr Cunane,' Brandon said. All the breezy self-confidence had vanished from his voice.

'I'll bet you do,' I muttered.

'I had nothing to do with Sam's death. You've got to believe me. I'm sorry I threatened you but I can't have folk scrabbling round for muck. I thought you were going to exploit Sam's little weakness to dig up some dirt.'

'So there's dirt to be dug?'

200

'Not like you think. I've been in business for forty years. There's bound to be something that interested parties like that toe-rag Harrow could use to smear me.'

'I wouldn't say anything, would I? Not with you threatening to expose my own lurid past.'

'Look, I'll level with you, Cunane. That was a bluff. Tony Hefflin told me that there'd been an investigation to find if you'd had anything to do with that pair disappearing, and the kids . . . well, I happen to know that Harold Elsworth is infertile. He booked into a clinic that I have an interest in. So if she didn't have the kids by you she had them by someone else.'

I felt myself going hot and cold. So Harold Elsworth knew that he couldn't be the father of Dee's children . . . My throat was too dry to speak but I needn't have worried. Brandon Carlyle had enough to say for both of us. 'Honestly, Cunane, I'm grateful to you. I'd feel happier if you'd let me show my gratitude in a tangible way.'

'You'd feel happier if you could pay me off, then you'd think I was in your pocket.'

'If you can tell me what the hell's wrong with money changing hands I'll buy you a bloody brass clock,' he blathered. 'What do you think makes the world go round? And it's not as if we don't owe you. First our Charlie, and now me.'

I hung up. I felt as if I was suffocating. Was there anything this appalling family didn't know about? I loosened my tie and hurried across the road to the flats. A brand-new four-wheel drive was parked close to the entrance. It didn't belong to any of the residents, but I found out soon enough who the owner was.

'David, my old son, returned to us like the prodigal from his husks among the cities of the Plain,' the plummy voice of Clyde Harrow boomed as soon as I went into Janine's flat. She and the two children were seated and looking at the roly-poly TV personality with the fixed gaze of rabbits waiting for a cobra to strike.

'Uh, Dave, you know Clyde,' Janine muttered awkwardly.

'To know him is not to love him,' I said grimly.

201

'Ah now, young master, don't be harsh. I was in danger of becoming half in love with easeful Death until I bethought myself of this good lady. Believe me I had no idea that you and she were *en famille*, as it were, when I invited her to accompany me to the annual award show. I merely called this evening to see if she cares to respond affirmatively to my humble invitation. There's just the faintest ghost of a chance that I may be in the running for an award myself, and one feels so gauche if one hasn't a lovely lady at one's side on these occasions.'

Janine and I exchanged a glance. Her expression was unreadable.

'Ah, well . . . erm, Clyde,' she said blushing. I looked in astonishment. I'd never really seen Janine blush before.

'Go, Janine,' I said when I found where I'd left my tongue in my cheek. 'You might get a good story out of it. I'll look after the children.'

'Am I to take it that these splendid children, these delights come among us trailing clouds of glory, are the products of your union?'

'Clyde, I won't be able to come. It'll mean a night in London,' Janine interjected. I could hardly cope with the surprise that she hadn't blown Clyde out already, so I kept my mouth shut.

'But the young master has given his connubial consent and you have it on the word of a Harrow that there will be nothing untoward.' Clyde gazed at Janine with a rapt expression on his clownish face. I couldn't have trusted him less.

'What do you think, Dave?' Janine said eagerly.

'Go,' I gasped, not wanting to be the dog in the manger at their love-fest.

This was all the invitation Clyde needed to expand and fill all available space. I must say that for once I was almost grateful to him. While I listened to his practised patter as he simultaneously entertained the children, chatted up Janine and did his best to flatter me, I didn't have to give attention to the thought that lay like a heavy stone across the back of my skull – that the death of Sam Levy was my responsibility. On a rational level I knew it wasn't. I told myself that it could have been an aggravated burglary as the police suspected, but guilt cut into me like a knife. I could have done something. I should have done something.

The spell Clyde cast was eventually broken by Lloyd. 'Mummy, I'm hungry,' he piped up from the corner of the floor where he was lying on his stomach playing with his small collection of toy cars. 'When are we going to have our tea?'

'Aha! The voice of reality, youth is not to be denied . . . had we but world enough and time . . . but I will arise and go now,' Clyde said.

'No, stay and eat with us, I'll put something on,' Janine volunteered. Not for the first time that evening I goggled at her. The culinary arts were not the area of Janine's greatest expertise. Pizza and chips or fish fingers taxed her. I can't say I rushed to second her invitation. As we were in Janine's living room I supposed it wasn't my place to do that anyway.

Clyde stood up and patted his stomach.

'To be truthful, dear lady, I can feel my own gastric juices beginning to whimper for a revictualling. I see from the expression of dismay on the face of your love-sick swain here, that any call on you to feed my appetite will cause domestic problems . . .'

'No, stay, Clyde,' I countered. 'I'm sure between our two larders we can find enough to satisfy even such a demanding appetite as yours.'

'Mummy, I'm hungry,' Lloyd reminded.

'Yes, so am I,' Jenny agreed. 'But why has Mr Harrow said that Dave's a sick swine? Miss Seagrave says that calling names leads to fights.'

'Clyde didn't mean that he doesn't like Dave. He said swain, not swine,' Janine explained.

'What's a swain then?' Jenny persisted.

'A rustic lover,' boomed Clyde.

'Oh. But I still want something to eat.'

'In that case may I suggest a takeaway meal?' Clyde said. 'Please allow me to supply it. I know an excellent Chinese establishment nearby which will be happy to deliver all our requirements.'

It seemed churlish to quibble, and the next few minutes

were spent in listing and ordering. Clyde went out to phone in the narrow hallway and when he returned told us he'd ordered a Chinese feast. We made small talk for twenty minutes and then a hamper full of goodies arrived. I stayed in my seat while Janine bustled off to find plates and utensils but Clyde took me to one side. He carefully positioned himself so that I was screened from Janine's view.

'Ah, dear lad, a temporary embarrassment,' he said, smiling warmly.

'What?'

'By oversight I've come without my wallet. Could you oblige me with the necessary? I will repay you almost instantaneously.'

I paid the delivery man. It turned out that Clyde had ordered enough for eight adults, but that was no problem because he ate as if he hadn't seen food for days. He chewed his way remorselessly through packet after packet of prawn balls, cashew nuts, fried rice and duck's wings, chattering all the while. The two children watched in awe and timidly nibbled their portion while Janine and I struggled to keep up with him. Food disappeared with amazing rapidity, paper and foil cartons piling up in a heap.

'A true feast,' Clyde remarked, 'demands an appropriate beverage.'

'China tea?' I suggested.

'Ha!' Clyde sneered. 'Ever the humorist, dear boy.'

I went next door to plunder my wine rack. I brought back three bottles, intending to allow him to select one but he had all three open in the time it takes to turn a corkscrew. I made no protest. The food and alcohol were just what I needed to blunt my own guilt about Sam, but a little voice was whispering that Clyde Harrow never did anything without a purpose. I allowed myself to wonder what he was up to.

Janine eventually departed to give Lloyd his bath. Jenny went into her bedroom to start her homework and Clyde and I were left to peer at each other over the remains of our feast.

'You don't seem to be at the top of your form,' Clyde commented. 'Don't you like Chinese food?'

'Well enough, especially when I'm paying for it.'

'I told you, that was an oversight which I shall presently correct, but surely your downcast looks aren't due to the attention that I've paid to she who walks in beauty like the night . . .'

'Can the quotes, Harrow!' I snapped. 'I'm up to here with poetry. Tell me what you've really come creeping round for.'

Moving his hand down from his brow to his chin, Clyde wiped the supercilious grin off his wide features and replaced it with a serious frown. 'Alas, I was beginning to hope that I'd finally penetrated the wall of hostility you surround yourself with.'

'Cut the crap and get on with it,' I urged.

'My situation is getting a little desperate on all fronts.'

'What's your problem?' I asked.

'No problem apart from a shortage of inside information.'

'And why should you think that I'm in a position to supply that?'

'But you are, old lad. Don't deny it. My contacts tell me that you've spent the day discussing the gruesome demise of Brandon Carlyle's best friend. There must be some trifling nub of fact, some irritant, that I can use to the great man's detriment.'

'Clyde, you're crazy,' I said with a sigh. It may have been the alcohol that made me lose my caution but I found myself relaying Brandon's comments about Clyde's employment prospects and his later strenuous denial of any part in the death of Sam Levy. The truth was, I was past caring.

'I can tell you that the police are almost certain that the killing was part of a bungled attempt at robbery,' he said when I'd finished.

'Or was made to look like it,' I corrected.

'Hmmm, as you say. A sword thrust through the arras, eh? "O what a rash and bloody deed is this!" *Hamlet*, act three, scene four, old lad . . . But where does it leave me? If I was to drop a casual hint that Carlyle's connected the only consequences would be a call from his libel lawyer speedily followed by security men to escort me off the premises of Alhambra TV. You must find out more.'

'I've found out plenty.'

205

'Such as what?'

'You know the Pendlebury Piledrivers fans have held demonstrations because they've lost so many games?'

'Of course, rugby league isn't my game, but I saw to it that there was full coverage of that.'

'Did you know that one reason why the squad are so feeble is that they all work part-time as body guards for Chairman Brandon?'

'There you are,' Clyde said excitedly. 'You must find out more of these illuminating details. Research! Research!'

'How, though?'

'Pursue the leads you have. This all started when the luscious Marti threw herself into your lap.'

'In case it's escaped your notice, I have a business to run. I can't just hare off after any clue that appears on the horizon.'

'So, don't. Take your time. Softly, softly catchee monkee, but in the meantime I need yet more assistance from you.'

'That's all I exist to do, Clyde, provide you with help.'

'Sarcasm mars your natural frankness, David. I should avoid it. What I need from you is help with this story about the pigeon war.'

'You've got to be joking.'

'No, I need to come up with unusual and humorous local material. I see you as the source of a potentially endless supply.'

'Thanks.'

'Let me make my farewells to the fragrant Janine and I'll fill you in on the details,' he said, getting up with surprising agility for a fat man who'd just consumed the best part of two bottles of wine and five normal-sized Chinese meals. 'Come down to the car while I explain, unless you'd like to come on with me for some further sustenance. This Chinese muck isn't very filling.'

29

I'll never know how Clyde did it, but when I arrived at the little park with Mrs Griffiths in tow the crowds were already gathering. It was all set out like a well-rehearsed play. Two hostile bands faced each other, leaving a narrow gap on the pavement. It was into this gap that I led Mrs Griffiths. I'd ensured my own anonymity by wearing a ski mask. Sadly I could see from the way that Mrs Griffiths flung her bag of food on the ground that her heart wasn't in the work any longer. She was no fighter.

'We can come back when there aren't people about,' I said encouragingly.

'No, it's not the same as when it was just me and the pigeons. I'm taking a holiday with the money that Mr Harrow's given me.'

'But what about the birds?' I asked. The whole flock had settled in front of us. The yells and screams from the street weren't putting them off breakfast.

'Oh, there are others,' Mrs Griffiths said vaguely, waving in the direction of the bird lovers.

I shook my head in disappointment and led her out of the park. I could see Clyde in the distance with two camera crews. A young man with a minicam jostled his way into the foreground.

'That's him!' the anti leader shrieked as I pushed forward trying to shelter my client. 'Get the bastard.' This was the signal for the two sides to clash. Opposing forces surged forward but I nimbly withdrew Mrs Griffiths and bustled her off down a side street.

When we were safe I looked back. The entrance to the park was blocked by a struggling mass of humanity. There were perhaps a hundred people there, and to my satisfaction the anti leader was being rolled on the ground with her skirt over her head. Through the din I could hear the voice of Clyde Harrow bellowing directions to his crews. As the police dramatically swept into view the birds took off en masse, flying low over the seething crowd. It was a terrific shot and I hoped Clyde got it.

Celeste was already installed when I reached the office.

'Still feeling tolerant towards the Dibbles then, Mr Cunane?' she asked, referring to my visit to the nick yesterday. 'Do you want me to get in touch with my cousin the solicitor about false arrest?'

'Celeste, friction with the fuzz is the last thing we need in this job,' I explained patiently. 'They didn't actually arrest and charge me. I was helping with enquiries.'

'You're too easy going, boss. You should demand damages.'

'As you're so desperate to get in touch with a solicitor I'd like you to ring Mr Devereaux-Almond in Rochdale. Don't let on that you're connected with me. Say you're phoning from a tax office in . . . Preston, yes, that's it, Preston. You can't trace any details of tax being paid for fees that Almond received for a case sixteen years ago. Be as difficult as you can and make it clear that you're considering prosecution if he doesn't come up with some answers.'

'But what exactly do you want to know?' she asked.

'I want to know who paid him to represent Vince King.'

It wouldn't do any harm to pull the solicitor's chain. He was my only lead now.

'And send Mrs Griffiths a bill. Be creative. Send a copy of it to Clyde Harrow.'

'Oh, and this came,' she said, handing me a cheque. It was from Ernie Cunliffe.

'Goody,' I replied, retreating to my inner office to consider my next step before Celeste started asking further questions. The truth was I didn't know the answers. I didn't know where I was going or what I was doing. I looked at the cheque. The numbers were comforting. Cunliffe had actually added a bonus. I decided a phone call was in order. Surprisingly my call went straight through without the usual opportunity to listen to the complete works of Vivaldi.

'Thanks for the payment . . .' was as far as I got before dear old school pal Ernie was all over me.

'Dave! I'm really, really sorry about the delay but one of our major shareholders raised concerns about employing you, mate. Major snafu. Red faces all round down here, I can tell you, with yours truly the reddest of the bunch . . .'

'What are you talking about? Who is this major share holder?'

'It's an institution, not a person, and it wouldn't mean anything to you if I told you, but there's no trouble now. In fact, they're all smiling like pigs in muck when Pimpernel Investigations is mentioned. Head Office is very pleased with your work. We want you to be our lead investigator for the North West region. It means a hell of a lot of work coming your way. I'll fax you the details unless you'd like to come round. I could see you right now if you like.'

'Fax them, Ernie, mate,' I said quickly. Ernie's sea-green features were too much for me at that time of day.

I came back to reality with a bump when the intercom buzzed and Celeste announced that she couldn't get through to Mr Deverell-Rimbury.

'Devereaux-Almond, or even plain Almond as in nuts from trees.'

'Sorry, Mr C, but he's not there. Someone who says she's his sister says he's gone away . . .'

'Sister-in-law, name of Bernadette.'

'Whatever . . . but he's not there and she says she doesn't care about his unpaid taxes – gave me a right earful . . .'

'Celeste!' I yelled.

She appeared at the door a moment later.

'Initiative, girl, initiative! If he really isn't there we want to know where Devereaux-Almond is now. Put the fear of God into this woman.'

'And how am I supposed to do that?' she said, putting her hands on her hips. 'I'm sure she suspects me already.'

'Phone her again and tell her that you're reporting Devereaux-Almond to the Law Society for suspected

209

corruption. I want that double-barrelled git on the phone in five minutes or else I want to know his present whereabouts.'

'Pardon me for breathing, I'm sure, but why is all this so urgent? What's it in connection with?'

'Vince King!'

Celeste gave me a strange look, but she made no further objections.

'Boss, shall I send the posse round to her if the Law Society doesn't work? They'll get the news out of her in jig time.'

'Let's hope that's not necessary.'

Later I phoned George Gammage. It had turned out that he hadn't been harrassing Georgia at all. He was just a nervous little man after a date. I'd set him straight on the ways of difficult women. I was hoping that Marti might have an account at the credit card company where he worked. She did – and it didn't take much pressure to encourage him to send me copies of her recent statements.

30

I intended spending the afternoon studying Ernie Cunliffe's fax and musing about wealth creation. I would need extra employees, cash, vans and surveillance equipment. The prospect of wealth made me uneasy.

There was only one cure that I knew . . . spending money.

I sauntered into King Street, went into the first men's clothes shop I came to and bought myself an expensive cashmere jacket.

'I've got some messages for you,' Celeste announced when I blew back into the office, 'but there's someone to see you.' She grimaced and nodded her head at my inner sanctum.

DCI Brendan Cullen was sitting in my chair with his feet up on the desk.

'Hey, Brennie baby, I've only to whistle and that girl out there will come in and hurl you into the street by the scruff of your neck,' I told him, only half in jest.

'Yes, she looks a tough cookie and I gathered that the constabulary aren't flavour of the month with her,' he said dryly. His features were set like a soldier's on a bronze war memorial.

'I'm working to convert her,' I assured him.

'I wish to God that was all you were doing, Dave. I'm shocked by your attitude . . .'

'What do you mean?'

'I mean that since you started digging and delving into the affairs of Marti King and her father two citizens have been sent on one-way rides to the cemetery.'

'That's totally unfair and you know it.'

'Do I? Listen, Davie boy. We're roping the Olley and the Levy killings together. There's a combined GMP/Cheshire

211

squad investigating and I'm in joint command. We're calling it Operation Calverley. So far the common factors in both cases are that the victim was financially involved with the Carlyle family and both were acquainted with a certain Manchester private investigator.'

'Hold on, Sam Levy . . . '

'Was brutally murdered and guess who was the last person he met?'

I slumped onto the sofa. 'So?' I muttered.

'You know a lot more than you're prepared to admit, but do you know how Levy met his death?'

'I was told that he was tied up and beaten, and the shock led to heart failure . . .'

'That's what was put out for public consumption but actually the poor old guy was virtually dismembered before he died. There was blood over the walls in every room in the house. He was dragged from room to room probably to get him to tell something. And it wasn't his sister's pearls the attacker was after, either. They were still in an open shoebox under the stairs.'

'Angelina . . .'

'Has gone missing too, but her movements on Sunday afternoon are well accounted for.'

'As are mine.'

'Yes, as are yours,' he said reflectively.

'I expect her Filipino friends would give her an alibi . . .'

'No, she was in church acting as godmother at a baptism ceremony. The priest, who doesn't know her personally, has identified her and her signature's on the baptismal register.'

'So the main suspects are in the clear?'

'No, Dave, there's a world of suspects out there. I didn't tell you that your friend Mr Levy was seriously connected with crime.'

'What?'

'He had a great affection for jewellery shops, did Sam. He served time in Borstal in 1945 for doing a jeweller's in St Ann's Square. He was arrested after another job in 1948. The guy driving his getaway car piled it into a lamp-post on Cheetham Hill Road . . . One man got away, took all the stuff with him too, but Sam and two others were nabbed.'

'And?'

'What do you think Sam did when they got him to the nick? He only head-butted the desk sergeant. Of course, they punched his liver and lights out for him, that was par for the course for resisting arrest in those days. So they put him up on the ID parade next day and he was all covered in bandages and plasters. The jeweller couldn't have identified him if Sam had been his own son. He was a smart lad was Sam.'

'If you don't mind getting beaten up, that is.'

'He didn't. His mates were IDed. The pair of them got five years' penal servitude and the cat. An assistant at the jeweller's was clobbered pretty badly.'

'The mates, one of them wouldn't happen to have been Carlyle or King?'

Bren gave me a crooked smile. 'No. Carlyle would have been old enough, but King was still in short pants.'

'So what happened then?'

'We never got Sam for anything. We think he set up as a fence with Brandon Carlyle's old man. Used his loot to finance a chain of bookies when gaming was legalised.'

'What are you saying? What's my involvement supposed to be?'

'Dave, I'm saying what I said to you before. You're stirring up muck at the bottom of a very murky pool. There are a lot of people who don't like that. Don't be surprised if they try to stop you.'

'That's rubbish! If you believe the Carlyles are involved why hasn't the old man or Charlie been pulled in?'

'Good question, Dave. I was hoping you might tell me the answer to that.'

Cullen fixed me with that oh-so-sincere look of his. I responded by telling him about my most recent dealings with Brandon Carlyle.

'Nice to know Brandon denies everything,' he said when I finished.

'Don't take my word for it,' I said hotly. 'Drag him in and give him the third degree. That's what you do to me.'

'Oh, listen who's feeling sorry for himself. But sincerely,

213

Dave, I would drag Brandon in if I could get authorisation but apparently he's a no-go area where criminal investigation's concerned. You've heard of the "Teflon Don"? The Yanks eventually jailed him with the RICO law, but this old sod of ours is inviolate. Your father was the last copper to tangle with him and that was back in the Dark Ages. There seem to be orders from on high that he's not to be interfered with.'

'Meaning what?'

'The blocks go on when his name comes up and they come from someone above chief constable level. I know that from Archie Sinclair.'

'And do you know why?'

'There's only one reason I can think of why no one's allowed to get near him. It's not drugs or any kind of ongoing investigation either. It's got to be something to do with national security.'

I laughed out loud.

'Now I've heard everything!' I mocked. 'He's the chairman of a rugby league club, not the head of MI5. I've heard of paranoia but this beats all.'

'Go on, laugh. It's incredible, but how do you think he gets away with it? Precisely because no one can believe it.'

'You're barking, mate!'

'I tell you, I've gone through the records.'

'Just what are you saying, Bren? Financial corruption? Political pressure? The funny handshake brigade? What?'

'I can't tell you. All I know is that Carlyle's got some sort of protection from on high.'

'OK, for the sake of argument I accept what you're saying, but what's it got to do with me?'

'Just this. For some obscure reason Brandon Carlyle seems to be interested in you. If you find anything I want to be the first to know. I can't be doing with all this secrecy.'

I laughed again.

'Now what's so funny?'

'You are. You've got two police forces behind you but I'm expected to solve your problems.'

'You should be flattered.'

214

'Not me, guv!' I said, standing up and ushering him towards the door.

'You've changed, mate. I think I liked you better when you were a no-hoper.'

'Fine, Bren! It's OK for you to get promoted and fart about in your C&A suits but I should still be going round with holes in my shoes. It doesn't work like that.'

'Spare me the angst, Dave. Just remember what happened to Lou Olley.'

I didn't feel too pleased with myself when Brendan walked off into the street without another word or a backward glance.

'Penny for them, Mr Cunane?' Celeste said.

I looked at her, grateful for the interruption to an unpleasant train of thought.

'What are you thinking about?'

'Nothing of life or death importance, I hope,' I said.

'Listen, you don't need to have these dirty police booger-men walking in here whenever they please. My cousin Marvin's a solicitor and he says they've no right . . . '

'Celeste, DCI Cullen is one of my oldest friends, or at least I thought he was.'

This produced a look of total incomprehension from Celeste. 'Hmmm, it's your funeral,' she commented. 'Anyway, I've been making some progress with that Deverell-Rimbury . . . I mean Almond, whatever. He's buggered off from Rochdale. Bernadette says he's got a boat at Fleetwood where he sometimes stays, a fifty-foot cruising yacht called *Spirit of the Hills*.'

'Did she say when he went?'

'Yes, she's quite upset about it. Last week, two men called at the house. Normally they don't see a soul for months. Dev what's-his-name was very angry with the first man and then right after the second came, he packed up and cleared off. I tried to get more out of her but that was all she knew. He comes and goes without telling her.'

My mouth must have dropped open because Celeste gave me a very odd look. 'Are you all right, Mr Cunane? Have I done the wrong thing?'

'No, you haven't, but maybe I have. Listen, Celeste, phone

215

Harry Sirpells . . .' She grabbed her pad and pencil like a model of secretarial efficiency. 'He's a PI out in Rochdale. Ask him to discreetly check out Morton V. E. Devereaux-Almond's background. I particularly want details about how he got rich, but stress to Harry that I don't want any waves, and make sure you get the name right this time.'

'Do you think Almond had Vince King's loot?'

'Not that, at least I don't think so.'

'How shall I ask Harry Sirpells to prioritise this?'

'What?' I asked, looking at her blankly. She'd swallowed a business manual since I promised promotion. 'Oh, yeah, it's urgent enough, or at least I think it is,' I muttered.

I turned to retreat to my room, almost overcome by the flood of information that my instruction to Celeste to show initiative had unleashed.

'Wait! There's more,' she protested. 'This came,' she said, handing me a heavily taped up envelope marked Confidential in deeply scored characters. 'A messenger dropped it in. Then Clyde Harrow phoned. He wants you to meet him at after six in that pub near Quay Street where all the soap stars go. I've to phone his PA if you can't make it.'

'Sound!' I said ironically. Celeste beamed in pleasure.

'And Mr Cunliffe wants you to phone him about the new cases. There are more in the pipeline. And Ms White called to see if you could pick the kids up.'

'Right, well I'll be working on the business plan if you haven't got anything else for me.'

I opened my desk drawer and fished about for a paper knife. The confidential letter contained the credit rating and recent statements of Marti King. She had enough left on her plastic to buy Pimpernel Investigations several times over. I'd been had for a mug.

I tried to work out why. There were no transactions from the day Marti had left for London. She must have feared that Charlie or Brandon would track her movements from the card.

I phoned Janine on her mobile.

'What did I tell you?' she asked triumphantly when I broke the news.

'She's not going to get away with it,' I said indignantly.

'Forget her, Dave, but don't forget Jenny and Lloyd . . . there's fish fingers in the freezer. I must go, I'm in a conference.' She hung up.

For once, domestic obligations had lost their charm. What I felt like was going to London and getting Marti by the scruff of her pretty neck. I phoned Paul Longstreet.

'Who is this?' he whined. 'This is supposed to be my private line.' In the background I could hear female laughter. It didn't take much imagination to work out how the Lord of the Lapdance liked to spend his afternoons.

'Cunane.'

'Who? Oh, Marti's Mank lover boy.'

'Where is she?'

'Got a monk on, have you, Manky man? Listen, chum, I'm not your bloody telephone exchange. I'm sick of this. I've had nothing but phone calls and visits from heavies demanding to know where she is.'

'Heavies?'

'Yes, refined ones. I had a couple round here last week looking for her and I told them what I'm telling you now. I don't know where Marti's taken her pretty little ass, and I wouldn't tell if I did, but I don't. OK?'

'No, I mean, wait.'

'Pining, are you? She left a message for you. I couldn't make head nor tail of it. She said if you were to enquire after her I was to tell you that there'll be a letter waiting for you at a certain wine bar. I don't know what's up with first-class mail.'

'Thanks,' I muttered.

It didn't take me many minutes to find that no letter had yet arrived at the wine bar on Deansgate.

31

When I reached Clyde's plasticated drinking parlour at seven he was already enthroned in his corner with his usual gang of sycophants. A chubby, rosy-cheeked young woman with an incipient double chin was perched next to him on the bench seat. She was practically in his lap and enjoying the sensation to judge by the expression on her round face.

Beyond, there was a circle of members of the public studiously pretending they didn't know who Clyde was, but nonetheless sitting with ears expectantly cocked for one of his witticisms.

'Up the whites!' he bellowed when he spotted me.

'Stow it, Clyde!' I said half-heartedly.

'Here, old lad, I saved you a drink,' he said, thrusting a lukewarm pint at me. 'Your spot was great. We've already had a big reaction. E-mails galore. People are demanding to know who the masked pigeon defender is. I shouldn't be surprised if the animal rights people don't come through with some big commission for you.'

To my horror this introduction produced a ripple of applause from the public.

'Clyde!' I spluttered. 'You promised to keep my name secret.'

'Ha ha!' he cackled. He stroked the denim-swathed behind of the moon-faced young woman. She gave him a tolerant smile. 'Come out of your cloister, brother, and admit the truth. You want publicity as much as the next man.'

'Nothing of the sort,' I said indignantly. 'I only came down here to make sure that you keep my name out of any publicity about that nonsense this morning.'

'Dave, you can't hide anything from me or from the Argus-eyed gaze of my reportorial associates.'

'Clyde, you're going to need somewhere to hide if I hear

218

that you've broken a promise you made only yesterday.'

'Oooh! Hark at you!' he mocked. 'Threats are what I thrive on. My silence will remain golden if you can rake up some juicy scandal about someone we both know and loathe.'

I looked at him stupidly.

'Good, that's settled then,' he said briskly. 'Now to matters mundane. Brother David, I've left my wallet in the car. Would you oblige me by settling at the bar for myself and Lauren?'

He inclined his head towards the door and disentangled himself from the young woman. Puppy-like, she made as if to follow her master.

'Lauren, my love,' he said, favouring her with a rancid grin, 'I must confer alone with Brother David someplace hence.' Then, when I'd paid his bill, he linked my arm and frog-marched me towards the car park. Behind the pub there were some deserted trestle tables on a patio looking out towards the canal basin. Despite the chill wind, we settled on either side of one of these. As I looked around I noted that there were pigeons everywhere.

Clyde followed my glance. 'Ah, the winged rodents, Dave, or should I say your feathered friends?'

'Shut up, Clyde!' I snapped. He rolled his eyes derisively.

'Honestly, Dave, I can fix you up with Lauren if you're tiring of Janine,' he said. 'Athletic lass, she is; firm-fleshed and clear-eyed.'

'Clyde, I didn't come here to get fixed up with one of your cast-offs.'

'Lauren's definitely available, if slightly shop-soiled,' he murmured with a sigh.

'Great! So I collect your returned empties now.'

'Now, share and share alike. You know me. I haven't forgotten that my outing with the fragrant Janine is coming up soon.'

'Make sure you don't forget your manners.'

'Why, is Janine likely to allow me to? Do tell.'

'I came to tell you that there's to be no encore of this morning's fun.'

'But that was excellent material. I can't just abandon such a dramatic tale in mid-story.'

219

'You can and you will.'

'What have you to offer in return?'

'Nothing much,' I conceded.

'Fine then, brother, you can expect to see your name . . .'

'No,' I said desperately. 'There is something. Marti King . . . she's up to some villainy.'

'Such as?'

'You know she wants me to get her father out of clink?'

He nodded.

'It isn't just down to family feeling. After all, he's been in since she was eight.'

'Do tell.'

'Vince King's got something on Brandon, some dirty little secret.'

'But . . .'

'There's no but about it. The solicitor at King's trial was specially chosen for incompetence and Sam Levy said as much, then he gets killed. Big coincidence, eh?'

For the first time in my acquaintance Clyde seemed to be lost for words.

'What do you think?' I asked.

He shook his head.

'When you've been divorced as often as I have you know that incompetent solicitors are two a penny. The prosecution had a strong case against King, and Levy was killed by a thief.'

'There's also the fact that straight after I questioned Almond, King's solicitor, he did a bunk.'

'Maybe you just have that effect on people, Dave. No, if you could show that Brandon Carlyle abused Marti as a child that would suit my purposes very well.'

'Abused? Are you crazy?'

'Not at all. I think it fits the facts better than some nebulous plot that you'll never prove in a million years. All you need is a statement from Ms King that Brandon abused her after he took her from the children's home and my troubles will be over.'

I suddenly felt very hot and uncomfortable. Clyde's 'solution' of my little puzzle certainly would suit him very well. The only problem was I knew it wasn't true. Victims of child abuse go through life with terrible mental scars. From what I knew of Marti King she didn't come into that category.

'Where might Ms King be now?' Clyde asked with an innocent smile on his face.

'I've no idea,' I said quickly.

'Dave, you're not a very convincing liar. Did I tell you that my producer thinks there might be mileage in a search for the Masked Pigeon Protector?'

'You bastard, Clyde!'

Clyde found this very funny. He bent double laughing. ' "Why bastard? Wherefore base?" ' he snorted theatrically. ' "When my dimensions are as well compact, my mind as generous, and my shape as true as honest madam's issue?" *King Lear*, act one, scene two, old lad.'

'There's nothing compact about you, you fat old fraud,' I snarled. 'And as for generous . . .'

'Listen, my legitimate friend. I want the location of the delectable Ms King and I want it pronto.'

'There's no way Marti was abused. If you knew her . . .'

'Dave, if you'd been in the news manufacturing industry as long as I have you'd know that facts are as pliable as the elastic in a whore's knickers. Let me once meet Marti and I'll spin such a story from what she says that Brandon Carlyle will be out of the TV business before his breakfast porridge has time to cool.'

'Get stuffed, Clyde!'

'Such discourtesy!'

'I haven't a clue where Marti is.'

'I'll give you a week and then we'll roll over that stone you've been lurking under and see what the light reveals.'

'I've nothing to hide.'

'Oh ho! Naïve lad, when I've finished with you you'll be lucky to get a billet as a school crossing patrolman.'

'You really are a bastard, you know,' I said with feeling.

'Now gods stand up for bastards!' he said with a crazy laugh. 'Don't think too badly of me. I'm hanging on by my fingernails at Alhambra. They fear that if they cast me off I might slide over to a rival channel. Colour and laughs and vulgarity, that's what I bring to the drab lives of you little people.'

'Bugger off!' I said, getting up and walking away.

32

After the session with Clyde, getting Janine to agree to take the promised half-term break at Blackpool was child's play. The closeness of the resort to Fleetwood was an added attraction: combining a seaside holiday with winkling out the elusive Devereaux-Almond should be easy.

'How's Miss Seagrave?' I asked Jenny when I collected her from her ballet class the next evening.

'She's hurt her foot climbing.'

'Oh poor woman!' I sympathised. 'Does that mean you haven't got a teacher?'

'No, Miss has her leg in plaster, and she's got this stick. Michelle O'Dell said she'd get done for assault if she hit us with it but Miss Seagrave just laughed.'

'Sensible woman, sounds like she's got the patience of Job.'

'Who's Job?'

'This man who had a lot of troubles.'

'What sort of troubles?'

'Oh, horrible ones. He came out in boils for one thing.'

Jenny thought about that for a moment and looked at me meaningfully, but she had too much of her mother in her to pursue any obvious comparisons.

'Weather's not too good,' I said. 'Do you like walking in the rain?'

This produced a look of horror.

'That's what you do in Wales. You know, where we're going this weekend,' I explained.

Again there was a significant pause for thought.

'Do we have to walk?' she asked.

'We could go on the bikes, I suppose, if I got you rain capes

222

and a bike for your mum, but that's what you do in Wales. Walk about a lot, look at the views.'

Later that evening I joined Janine for a drink.

'Dave,' she said, in her 'special request' voice. 'There's a little snag about the weekend trip. You know I was going to borrow that cottage in Llanberis?'

'Yes, terrific,' I said heartily. 'It'll be great. I'll be able to go jogging for miles.'

'There's just a teensy-weensy problem. Jenny's got it into her head that she'll be bored. You know there's nothing worse than trying to entertain her when she's bored.'

'Gotcha!' I said agreeably.

'Look, would you mind awfully if we went to Blackpool instead? It has the seal of approval from the sainted Miss Seagrave and Jenny's set on it.'

'I don't know. Blackpool isn't everyone's cup of tea. Too proletarian.'

'Dave! You're coming, no argument.'

'I hear what you say. I suppose there's always the sea breezes.'

She looked at me uncertainly and then changed the subject.

'You know Jenny's really extraordinary at times. Some of the things she says. She's had her head stuck in an encyclopaedia and then she started demanding that I get her a bible, of all things. I think I'll have a word with Miss Seagrave. I don't want her turning my child into some sort of religious fundamentalist.'

'I suppose we could fix the kid up with the collected works of Germaine Greer as an antidote,' I said laconically.

'Go on, laugh, as usual. But I'm serious.'

'So am I, love,' I said.

The mention of love diverted us to other things and it was after one a.m. before I got back to my own flat.

The flat looked as if it had been bombed. Every single item had been taken from where it lived and dumped in the middle of the room. I couldn't believe my eyes. The steel door was intact. I went through to the kitchen. The window had been forced and there was a footprint in the kitchen sink, but we were on the fourth floor. I looked out of the window expecting to see a body spread-eagled on the concrete below, but there was nothing. The waste pipe from the kitchen and bathroom ran close to the kitchen window and must have supplied the intruder with his access, but whoever he was, he was good.

'God! You don't think it's bloody Miss Seagrave, do you?' Janine asked when summoned. 'She goes mountaineering.'

'No, she's got a bad leg,' I replied automatically. I was stunned. Breaking and entering was the last thing I'd expected. With a front door like the entrance to Fort Knox I often neglected to set the alarm.

Janine looked at me with narrowed eyes. 'How do you know about Miss Seagrave?' she demanded.

'Don't worry. I haven't been trying to get off with her. Jenny told me.'

'Are you going to get the police?' she asked. 'I can't believe all this was going on while we were next door.' Every room had been rummaged through and whoever did it wasn't some junky looking for easy cash. The drawers had been systematically emptied from the bottom up, furniture pulled away from the walls, even the mattresses turned over.

'I don't know. I don't think I want the boys in blue poking round here again.'

'You gave them your key last week. It might have been them.'

'So why did they shin up the drainpipe?'

'Or perhaps it's that Brandon Carlyle.'

'I don't think burglary's his style.'

'Who then?'

I shrugged. I tried to put my best face on things. I went to the freezer. That had been done over too, but my frozen assets were intact. Janine had started putting cushions back on the sofa.

'Leave it,' I said. I couldn't face having all my useless pieces of memorabilia gone through again, even by someone as close to me as Janine.

'Come next door,' she suggested. 'I don't want to sleep on my own after this.'

Before following her, I set the alarm.

There are burglars by the hundred in South Manchester but

224

I'd only heard of one who'd leave cash lying around. The same one who'd left Leah Levy's pearls.

Janine greeted me at the door of her bedroom with two tumblers of whisky in her hands. I almost snatched mine off her. The harsh taste in the back of my throat was a comfort.

'This is serious, isn't it?'

I nodded.

'You're in the shit again, aren't you? It's something to do with that Marti, isn't it?'

'We don't know that,' I insisted. 'I'm expanding the business. There could be any number of people whose noses are of joint.'

'Dave, be serious! Are you saying some rival detective agency has turned over your place for spite?'

'Not spite, information. They might want to know why Northern Mutual are so keen to favour me . . . it could be blackmail . . . anything.'

'But Dave . . .'

'It's possible. They'd have access to the expertise.'

'I hope to God it is a rival business. I don't think I could survive another experience like last time. I was in intensive care for almost a month.'

'That was because you didn't listen to my advice. You've got me with you now and we don't know that whoever did this even knows your name.' The words sounded unconvincing even as I said them.

They say there aren't many atheists in foxholes, and whatever Janine White's feelings about me and the whole male sex were, she took a very firm grip on my arm before settling down to an uneasy sleep.

33

No one's indispensable, they say. I wasn't. If I'd had more prescience I'd have seen all the signs on that Thursday morning after my flat was done over.

Celeste was already installed at her desk with the phone pressed to her ear when I arrived.

Organising the expanded Pimpernel Investigations operation had been simpler than I expected. There were plenty of experienced former police wishing to supplement their pensions with a little surveillance work.

All I had to do was to recruit them as self-employed and pay them when I got paid. The hard part was providing the vans, the video cameras, the phones and the other surveillance gear.

Managerial skill came in keeping my investigators' noses to the grindstone. All my ex-coppers knew a hundred different ways to skive. It was hard to blame them.

I should have got an inkling of how Celeste was coping when I overheard her talking to one team on an estate in Salford – men who'd worked for me before, not part of the Northern Mutual intake: 'Listen, if you don't stay where you are I can't be responsible for you getting home in one piece,' she said.

'Trouble?' I asked.

'Oh, nothing,' she said quickly.

'Right,' I said vaguely. I should have twigged then that I was the one Celeste was threatening them with, but I didn't. The truth was that my mind wasn't on the job. I was thinking about burglars.

'What we need is someone calling them every few minutes to check that they're on station and get reports,' Celeste observed.

'Yes, but who and from where?'

'We've got that storeroom at the back. That's big enough for a table and a switchboard or even more,' she said eagerly. 'Or we could put up a partition in your office and then we could advertise, perhaps for two people, then there'd always be someone free for an emergency.'

'The storeroom sounds like a good idea.'

Celeste flashed her perfect teeth at me.

'Then I'd have more time out here to sell the firm and get us more clients,' she said.

'Yes,' I agreed before turning towards my own secluded desk. I intended to think bitter thoughts about Clyde Harrow but Celeste hadn't finished.

'Another idea is that we could use the Internet and laptop computers,' she said. 'We could get these cameras and make them download pictures of themselves actually doing the job. I mean, why should we pay them for doing nothing? It isn't as if they're still in the fuzz.'

'Oh, come on, Celeste.'

'No, Mr Cunane, why should we pay them to sleep?'

Celeste was right about us needing more staff, but where was all the extra work coming from? I only knew one businessman powerful enough to cause such a sudden change, but if Brandon Carlyle thought he had me bought and paid for, he'd have to think again. I told myself it might not be him.

'You're a hard woman,' I said to Celeste with a laugh and departed.

I couldn't help noticing that my office was large. It wouldn't be difficult to put another couple of desks in and leave plenty of room to spare. My reverie was interrupted by a loud knocking on the door, which was then flung open by an Afro-Caribbean youth who was struggling to carry two very large boxes of A4 paper.

'Where do you want these?' he gasped.

I nodded towards a vacant corner and he dumped them there just as another youth came in the door carrying a similar burden. I recognised the contents of my storeroom. I staggered to the door. A third burdened youth was making his way forward.

227

'Isn't it good?' Celeste asked. 'I got them from this youth scheme in Hulme. They're going to do out the storeroom.'

'Oh, that was quick,' I gulped.

I returned to my desk watching out of the corner of my eye as the entire contents of the storeroom were piled into my office. Shortly after boxes stopped coming in, hammering and banging commenced.

'What's that?' I demanded, putting my head round the door.

'Oh, they're just running extra power cables in there,' Celeste explained.

'Is all this coming out of your wages?' I asked.

'You did say to use the storeroom so I just got on with it,' she said.

I nodded and retreated to my den. By lunch time BT engineers had installed the phone lines.

'So what are we doing about the extra staff?' I asked.

'I know some people,' she said tentatively.

I remembered the story of Sam Levy and Angelina's relatives.

'No, I think if you phone an agency you might get some people down here today,' I suggested.

'Who'd be in charge of them, like?' she asked intently.

'I would,' I said. 'This place is too small for an office manager, but I might think of giving someone a bonus for showing the new girls the ropes.'

She smiled.

I went back to my planning and worrying. I looked at the books stacked on top of the filing cabinets. Something seemed wrong. They were in a different order than when I'd left them. I asked Celeste: she hadn't moved them. I got that horrible sinking feeling that had hit me last night. I wanted to be sick. Instead I phoned a friend, Mark Ross, an expert on alarms and passive security.

Ross was round in half an hour.

'Yeah, I'm afraid your alarms have been by-passed, Dave, and it was an expert who did it,' he said, replacing the cover on the circuit box. 'I can repair it for now but if you want to be secure you need to get the alarms reinstalled, otherwise whoever did this can walk in here anytime he chooses. This is what you get for moving into the big-time.'

'What have I got in here that would be worth anyone's trouble?' I asked.

'I don't know, Dave, but you appear to have insect infestation as well.'

He laughed when I pulled a face.

'Electronic insects, Dave. There were two bugs in your room. Expensive little beggars too, state of the art they are. Do you mind if I keep them? It'll save you the call-out fee.'

When he'd gone I tried to make sense of what had been going on. Sam Levy had been tortured, presumably to make him reveal something. My flat and now my office had been thoroughly searched, but what for?

The only certainty was that all this madness started when I began poking around in the affairs of Vince King. Marti must be the one with the answers.

I left the office to check out the wine bar again. If Marti had been expecting that my mail would be searched that might explain her odd method of correspondence. It only took me ten minutes to stride along to the end of Deansgate.

'Ah, Mr Cunane,' the waiter I'd christened Manuel said, in broadest Mancunian, 'that letter you've been waiting for, it's come.'

I snatched it out of his hand.

All it contained was a blank sheet of note paper with a flimsy piece of Rizla paper folded inside. There was a North London address pencilled on the tissue, but no telephone number. I screwed the paper into a tiny ball, walked out of the bar and crossed the road. I stood on the bridge over the canal basin. Why did this always happen to me? I looked down at the scummy, oil-stained waters below. Dark and impenetrable, they were. I flicked the paper into the air and watched it land on the dirty surface. It floated for a moment and then sank.

If I was going to keep my head above the murky waters then I needed some answers.

Celeste met me with a disapproving frown when I got back to the office.

229

'Two girls have come from the agency,' she said. 'I've started them on the phones but there's not enough work for them yet.'

'Fine!' I barked. 'You're in charge for now.' I dashed into my room and slammed the door.

'Pops!' I said as soon as he picked up the phone.

'Don't call me that,' came the familiar waspish tones, 'I'm not a bleeding Yankee.'

'Are you OK, no trouble or anything?'

'No trouble, unless you call stopping Jake Carless fly-tipping trouble.'

My sigh of relief must have been audible.

'You've landed us in it again, haven't you? You stupid . . .'

'Don't say that!' I begged. 'The last old timer who told me I was stupid has ended up dead.'

'Who?'

'Sam Levy.'

'So you have got your nose in that? I heard a whisper.'

'Dad, do you know any reason . . . Is there any way someone might think that you'd passed some information on to me that might cause serious embarrassment . . .'

'Who's been talking?' There was an unfamiliar note of anxiety in his voice.

'No one, it's just something Levy said – that it was because I'm your son that somebody might be upset.'

'Bloody old lady, that's what Levy was. He should have kept his mouth shut.'

'Tell me what you know. What's the connection? What am I missing that everyone else seems to know about?'

There was a very long pause. So long, that I began to wonder if he was still on the line.

'I can't tell you anything,' he muttered eventually. 'You're not in the Force. Anything I know is official.'

'Dad, are you listening? This is your son here?'

'I can't say anything . . . official secrets.' His voice sank to a whisper.

I came close to pleading with him after that but he wouldn't open up. All he said was that he'd take Mum on an early holiday. He wouldn't tell me where. When he rang off I held the phone in my hand for a moment and looked at it in horror. How could I tell if it was bugged? I couldn't.

My next call was to Janine.

'The holiday,' I said, 'something's come up.'

'It's about last night, isn't it? If you've put my children in danger . . .'

'No one's in danger . . . just precautions, that's all. Listen, I'll not be back till very late. Maybe not till tomorrow morning.'

'But your flat, when are you sorting that?'

'Something's come up, something I've got to see to. I don't think you're in any danger or I wouldn't go.'

'Dave, you'd better be right. I couldn't go through any of that again.'

34

It wasn't until I was on the M6 stuck in a three-lane traffic jam outside Birmingham that I began to relax. Jammed in the stream, there was nothing I could do now except be patient. I didn't know exactly what I was going to do when I got to the address in Finchley. Marti might not even be there. I let my mind go blank, not difficult in the circumstances.

When I found myself grinding my way along the North Circular Road, I became fully alert again. It was dark; rain was streaming down, visibility was poor. The roads were crowded. I reached the address Marti had supplied only to find that there was no parking space within a quarter of a mile. I drove up and down the crowded streets. Finchley reminded me strongly of the crumbling South Manchester suburbs. Rotting window frames and sagging bays, houses painted every colour of the rainbow, it was all familiar.

I finally managed to park near Finchley Central tube station. My clothes were soaking before I'd walked for five minutes. I got lost several times, which was just as well, because anyone following me would be hopelessly confused.

When Marti opened the door it was clear that our thoughts were travelling in the same direction.

'Is there anyone following you?' she said, looking out into the sheeting rain beyond. Then she almost snatched my arm off, pulling me inside and tugging me along the hall and into her ground-floor flat.

'I knew you'd come when you got the address,' she crowed. 'Couldn't keep away, could you?' She let go my arm only to wrap herself round every other part of me. She kissed me with every sign of genuine passion.

'Whoa!' I said pushing her off. 'I've not come here for the

sake of your lovely green eyes.'

'Jade eyes,' she corrected. 'I prefer jade.'

'Do you? I'd prefer some answers to a few questions.'

'You've not come all this way just to collect a few quid off me, have you?' she demanded.

'Why do you think I've come?' I asked. I looked at her closely. She seemed to have shrunk in size if that was possible. She wasn't wearing very much, a thin blue silk dressing gown over a negligée.

'You know how to embarrass a girl, don't you?' she said coyly. 'I've thought of you every day since Stockport Station.'

'Yes, that was interesting, wasn't it? Me handing over two grand to a woman who could have bought and sold me.'

'Don't be so bourgeois, Dave. A girl's entitled to see if a fella can come up with the readies if needed.'

'Is that what you do now? Are you on the game?'

For reply she smacked me across the face, hard. I flared up, my muscles stiffened for action, but then I remembered how we met – when Charlie Carlyle was testing his strength. I took a step back.

'That was a shitty thing to say,' she gasped. She slumped into an armchair.

'Was it? Perhaps you'd like to explain why you needed my money when you were wadded?'

She reached over to the table and took a cigarette from a pack.

'I'm off the sauce,' she said brightly as she lit up. 'I haven't had a drink since Manchester.'

'That long?'

'Don't be snide. You're still in Ms Ironpants' good books, aren't you? I thought she might have dropped you judging by the speed you got here. I posted the letter yesterday and it's only eleven p.m. now.'

'This isn't about me, Marti, it's about you.'

'Don't be such a boy scout, Dave. You can have your money back tomorrow if that's all that's interesting you.'

'It's not all that's interesting me. For one thing, why did you have to contact me through the wine bar? What's going on?'

'You wouldn't understand.'

'Try me.'

'Dave, you're so straight and squeaky clean it makes my eyes sore just looking at you. I suppose that's why I fancy you . . . attraction of opposites, but you haven't got a clue about what really devious people get up to.'

'You're such an expert at back-handed compliments, aren't you? But I'm not going until you tell me what's going on.'

'Sit down,' she said with a pout. 'Looking up at you's making my eyes water.'

'I've got all night.'

'Are you sure? Does Ms Ironpants know where you are? Will she turn up with the kiddies like she did last time?'

'Forget Janine and tell me what you've been up to.'

'If you must stand over me, make us some coffee.'

'You've got some irritating little ways,' I said when I'd made the coffee. My cheek still stung.

'You're no angel yourself. You led me on, you and your fancy suits. That day you took me to Leeds your tongue was almost hanging out.'

'Rubbish!' I said, glaring at her. Why did all my conversations with women have to get down to the hormonal level?

'Don't say you weren't interested in me. You looked like a starving bloodhound slavering over a raw steak, and why did you go up against Charlie if you didn't fancy me?'

I had no answer for that. If I'd said that I'd have stopped Charlie even if she'd looked like a hag from hell she wouldn't have believed me. I hoped it was true.

We stared at each other. It looked like game, set and match to Miss King.

'Look at you! You idiot,' she said eventually. 'There are clouds of steam rising up from you. Get those wet clothes off before you pass out on the carpet.'

'I won't pass out.'

Total immersion in icy rain, followed by the swampy heat of this room and my disappointment at failure were having an effect, but that was none of Marti's business. I could dry out on the long journey home.

'Don't be such a schoolboy,' she sniggered. 'I'll get you something to put on if you're afraid of me seeing your lovely bod.' She got up and went into the bedroom which was just round the corner of the L-shaped room, and after rummaging through a very large closet stuffed to bursting with clothes fetched out a long coat. Whatever else she'd left in the North she hadn't parted company with her wardrobe. There were a lot more clothes there than she'd had when I saw her last.

She flung the coat at me.

I threw it back.

'Put it on! You can either take your clothes off and let me dry them, or you can get yourself off to Manchester now. Suit yourself!'

'I don't need anything from you except an explanation of what's been going on. You know exactly why Olley and Sam Levy were murdered.'

'Sam Levy!' she gasped. The colour drained out of her face. 'Oh, God, no.'

I stepped over to her. The pupils of her eyes were dilated. She was in shock all right. I grabbed her and led her back to the chair. She started to cry.

'Not Sam! We never should have started this. Damn Charlie to hell!'

'Started what?' I said eagerly. All thoughts about wet clothes evaporated.

'You're a bastard just like all the rest,' she snarled. 'You want me to talk, don't you? But Sam didn't deserve to be killed.'

'I never said he did.'

'What happened?'

I was stung by her attitude. She didn't deserve the sanitised version.

'He was tortured to death on Sunday morning for some piece of information or some object. They dragged him through every room in his house so it's likely his killers thought he had something hidden. There was blood all over the place and nothing was taken.'

She put her head in her hands and wept bitterly. Brilliant actress or distressed woman? I wasn't sure which. My instinct said that she was genuine, but then I'd been wrong before.

'It started as a game really,' she said eventually. 'Charlie's

235

family's the pits, the absolute pits. His brothers make the Addams family look like a Mastermind panel, and their wives! Sweet Jesus, they look like corpses that embalmers have despaired of. Bungalow Billy's wife's had her face lifted so often she looks like a starved cat. Her eyebrows are almost at the back of her neck.'

'Who's Bungalow Billy?'

'The second son after Charlie. Brandon likes to stir up rivalry between him and Charlie, but Billy's so thick . . . he still needs help tying his shoelaces. That's why they call him the Bungalow.'

'Nothing upstairs?'

'Yes. I suppose you think all this is funny, but living with them's a nightmare. Every time you meet one of the wives they run through a little list. "Have you got this? Have you got that? Have you been here? Have you been there?" But most of all it's about husbands. "When did Charlie speak to Brandon last? Did Brandon ask him this? Did bloody Lord God Almighty Brandon Carlyle ask him that?" If you want to know why I turned to drink you just need to spend an hour or two with them.'

'I see,' I muttered. 'You don't like your in-laws.'

'Stop it, this isn't a joke! Poor old Sam, he was the nicest of all Brandon's sneaky friends.'

'Sorry.'

'Of course it's him who's to blame.'

'Who? Brandon? He killed Sam?'

'No! How would I know who killed Sam? No, I mean that Brandon's to blame for that family. Without him they'd all have sunk to their natural levels, dossing about in some filthy council flat and scratching their beer guts wondering where their next pint was coming from. All that man knows is how to put one penny on top of another one. That's all he thinks about from morning till night.'

'You married into them.'

'I had to.'

'Did Brandon abuse you as a child?'

'What do you mean, abuse?'

'Sexual abuse.'

236

She started laughing hysterically.

'Sexual abuse? Brandon? Are you insane? I've just told you, all Brandon thinks about is making more money. Unfortunately he's a genius at that. I expect he charged his poor wife for sex. The only thing he thinks women are for is making babies. That was another reason why things got unpleasant.'

'I don't understand.'

'No you don't, do you? Listen, Charlie is the best of that bunch but that's not saying much, God help me. He's lazy but he does have a brain of sorts inside his fat head – unlike you, Cunane.'

'Thanks.'

'Can't you understand what I'm saying? Brandon's over seventy. All his kids except Charlie are total der-brains. Spassers, the lot of them, except Charlie. When Brandon goes they'll all be back in the gutter in five years. Most of his businesses aren't even legal, and the ones that are, are just for recycling funny money. What you see of the Carlyle Corporation is just the tip of the iceberg, and there are a lot more like Lou Olley working for Brandon. Oh, yes, they'll think possession's nine tenths of the law once Brandon goes. I can see everything going down the tubes. I told Brandon that it was time he let Charlie take a greater part in running things. At first the old miser seemed quite pleased but then Charlie got a bit above himself . . .'

'You mean you got a bit above yourself, don't you? Is that what it was about that day in the car park?'

'Aren't you sharp?'

'What were you trying to do, get Charlie to put him in an old folk's home?'

'Old folk's home!' she shrieked. 'The only way to make Brandon quit is with a bullet in his head.'

35

Marti clapped her hand over her mouth. She looked vulnerable and silly and sweet and she cried and I put my arm round her and five minutes later I was in bed with her. There's really no good way of wrapping it up. With some men it's booze, with others it's gambling, but show me a pretty face, a few tears and . . .

It was Marti who brought things back to the subject of Brandon and Charlie.

'Dave, we should have done this as soon as we met,' she said, which was fairly heart-warming, I suppose. She was on her side stroking my shoulder and I was admiring the view. I knew she was a liar and possibly a murderess, but I was in a state where moralising about my own or anyone else's behaviour was redundant.

'I wanted you that first day. You really swept me off my feet. I woke up on your sofa and I was trying to work out what I had to do to attract your attention and make you do what rescuers of damsels in distress are always supposed to when I heard your dragon-lady shouting the odds outside the room.'

'Lay off Janine,' I murmured.

'Did you really kill someone?'

'Did you?'

'That's quick of you, isn't it?' she said, giving my shoulder a painful nip. 'I haven't killed anyone yet, but it's not for want of trying. Oh, Charlie's such a wimp! If he'd had anything about him he'd have had the old geezer certified years ago and then packed his brothers off somewhere where they could drink themselves to death without anyone objecting, but he won't act. He won't do anything without me there to push him. He wants the end but he won't supply the means.'

I nestled back in the pillows and cradled my head in my arms.

'So just what was your little plan to get rid of Brandon?' I asked.

'Aren't you the sly one?' she whispered. 'Can't you think of something more interesting to do than trying to worm that out of me? I can.'

'Listen, honey bun, whoever killed Sam Levy was searching for something – and he seems to have me down as the next on his list. My flat and my office have been broken into and searched. The rather strange solicitor who acted for your father did a bunk almost immediately after I paid him a visit. I need to know what's happening. It concerns Brandon, but how I don't know.'

'Root of all evil, isn't it?' she said, snuggling up alongside me and busying her hands at various little tasks. 'Money, I mean. Brandon Carlyle has a secret and it's a big one. He was quite small-time but then he suddenly rocketed into international finance, Mr Big-time Brandon Carlyle. Damn him!'

Without any warning she sank her teeth into my shoulder. I yelped with pain.

'No gain without pain, Dave,' she gloated as she pinioned me by the shoulders. 'Not like my father-in-law.'

'Get off!' I groaned feebly, suddenly realising why the female black-widow spider is so deadly.

'It's all in his photo albums . . . There he is . . . posing outside some local alehouse . . . with a bunch of tearaways . . . Mr Small-time Villain . . . Then you turn over the page . . . and he's in Wall Street, USA . . . rubbing shoulders with billionaires . . . Where did he get the money? . . . Not from Manchester, that much I do know . . . My dad's involved . . . Get him out of prison . . . He'll tell you the whole story.'

In the tiny part of my brain that was still capable of rational thought I realised that I was losing the plot. Mata Hari coaxed military information out of her victims after she made love to them. Marti, on the other hand, was holding a one-sided conversation as she turned my body into a human trampoline. Her words became louder and her voice hoarser as she reached a crescendo. After letting out a piercing yell she rolled off me. I hoped the neighbours were deaf.

Her unconventional method of relating a story left us both exhausted. We lay together in silence now, a silence that was anything but companionable. I was working out how to extricate myself. Finding out who was responsible for my troubles in Manchester suddenly seemed a lot less important than escaping from the trouble I was in now.

'I'll bet it's not like this in Ms Ironpants' bed,' Marti said eventually.

'Dead right!' I snapped.

'She's a frigid mare, isn't she?'

'Leave her alone,' I ordered, remembering loyalty too late.

'I'll bet you're like an old married couple,' she said with a laugh. 'Stale as last week's cheese.'

'No, we're not.'

'She's a man hater.'

'Better than a man eater!'

'Ha, ha! Still got your sense of humour then.' She threw her head back and let the laughter rip, the full, throbbing ear-splitter. I lay back helplessly, expecting to hear police sirens echoing the din as they raced through the rain towards us.

'You're mad!' I exclaimed.

'Dave, I'm not letting you go,' she said possessively. 'Stay here with me. Charlie's persuaded Brandon to come up with some money for me and that's partly thanks to you. I can set you up in a business or we could go abroad. I speak German, you know. We've got the whole EU.'

'No,' I croaked.

'Yes,' she retorted. 'You'll stay. I can give you everything you want.'

'You can't,' I mumbled.

'Is it kids? We can have kids of our own,' she insisted huskily.

Then she laced the fingers of her right hand into the fingers of my left and put me into a painful wrist lock. I don't think she intended it as a joke. I looked at the bedside table for a lamp or something I could belt her over the head with. There was nothing apart from an overflowing ashtray.

'Is this something your dad taught you?' I gasped through gritted teeth.

As suddenly as she'd put on the hold she released me. I let out a sigh of relief and massaged feeling back into my fingers. Marti leaned out of bed and lit a cigarette.

'Don't say you're a wimp, Dave. I've had enough of that with Charlie.'

'I don't know what you're expecting, but I don't normally need to use my karate skills when I'm in bed, nor do I need a blood transfusion.'

'Oh, diddums!' she said, blowing smoke in my face. She was so ridiculous that I almost had to laugh. The smile was a mistake – she was on me again like a tigress. I was ready this time, though, and I managed to elbow her off.

'I thought you had stamina, Dave,' she protested, retrieving her cigarette from the ashtray. 'Don't you want to make love?'

'Yeah, make love not war, but I wasn't expecting to do three rounds with a tag wrestling team.'

'Oh, poor Dave,' she said, kissing me. 'We haven't done three rounds yet. Stay a bit longer and I'll tell you how we tried to do Brandon in.'

'Tell me now and we'll see what happens afterwards,' I said. Desire for knowledge was a long way stronger than desire for anything else, but I hadn't bargained on Marti's little wiles. She started stroking and teasing and touching and kissing and giggling.

'Love first, talk after,' she chanted over and over.

'You sound like the pigs in *Animal Farm*,' I complained. 'Four legs good, two legs bad.'

'But four legs is good, Dave,' she giggled.

'I don't know about Brandon, but you've nearly done me in, you mad bugger,' I muttered, rolling her onto her back.

'Liar!' she said triumphantly. 'I knew you had true grit.'

Afterwards we talked. I was totally drained, almost too tired to work my jaw muscles. Marti seemed to have gained new strength. I tried to keep her talking.

'Do you know what I wanted Charlie to do?' Marti confided. 'I wanted him to arrange for Brandon to have an accident with one of those computerised gadgets he's always

241

playing with. Really neat, that would have been. But of course Brandon has so many CCTV cameras that he spotted the big ape trying to alter the timer on the door controls. That was just before you saw us having our little disagreement at Tarn Golf Club.'

'So that's what that was about,' I said.

'Then I did something a bit silly.'

'What, you?'

'Yes, I started visiting my dad in prison. I knew it would annoy Brandon. He's always discouraged me from having contact with Vince.'

'You and me both.'

'I don't know exactly how I found out, but as a child I sort of absorbed the idea that Vince was very bad news. Brandon used to freeze whenever I mentioned him. I only twigged that he was scared stiff of Vince when I grew up. Anyway, I thought if I started visiting the old man again, even encouraging him to get himself out of prison, it might make Brandon want to retire to somewhere nice and warm like Australia.'

'So what effect did this have?'

'Brandon exploded. I've never seen him so angry. Charlie wouldn't back me up. That was when I decided to leave him. I know it's naughty, but I thought if Brandon's so frightened of Vince then maybe I can get my share of the pie by really getting Vince out. That's when I thought of you.'

'Thanks a bunch.'

'I'd heard Brandon rave about your father from time to time. You were there. It all seemed to click into place.'

'How nice for you.'

'Anyway, it worked. Brandon had been all for cutting Charlie and me off without a penny after the stunt with the door controls but after I went to Armley Jail with you he changed his tune. He came over all soft and agreeable then.'

'Why?'

'Who can say? There must be money involved. That's the first love of his life. I know my dad knew Brandon before he went inside. I can remember both Brandon and Sam Levy from when I was a very small child. Uncle Sam, that's what I used to call Levy. It was a big joke to them. "Do a dance for Uncle Sam," they'd say or, "Tell Uncle Sam how much money your dad's got," and then they'd both start laughing.'

'I see where you get your sense of humour.'

'Sam practically lived with Brandon. They'd go in this room together and lock the door for hours. Brandon would come out and he'd sing silly little ditties . . . "Sam, Sam, the memory man, boil his head in a frying pan," is one I remember.'

'Whatever it was Sam remembered, his memory must have failed him at the end,' I said grimly. 'He couldn't tell his killers what they wanted to know.'

'Brandon would never have done any harm to Sam. Are you certain it wasn't just a robbery that went wrong?'

'Leah's pearls were left untouched in an open box. What sort of thief ignores that kind of loot?'

'She was a bit of a pain, was Leah. Always scowling, found life a bit hard, she did. She treated Uncle Sam as though he was her son. I used to think he was.'

'Get back to Vince and Brandon,' I suggested.

'It's funny. When they put Dad away I suddenly went from being a child surrounded by friendly adults to someone who had no one. It was as if I'd got leprosy or something.'

'How do you mean?'

'They didn't want to know me. My mother, Brandon, Sam, Leah, all my father's friends; they all went out of my life. You can't imagine what that's like.'

'No, I suppose I can't.'

'I went wild.'

'You still are.'

'The last time I ran away from the children's home in Leeds the social workers took me to see Vince in prison. Nice of them, wasn't it? Real confidence building. I thought they were going to lock me up in the cell with him. Anyway, Dad said he'd phone somebody and get me fixed up.'

'And did he?'

'The very next day Brandon Carlyle turned up with a brace of lawyers. That long streak from Rochdale, Almond, was there.'

'He calls himself Devereaux-Almond now.'

'That was after he got the yacht and joined the golf club.

243

Anyway, Brandon took me away. I was never out of sight of a member of the family for months after that. I don't know how it happened but I calmed down and I've been with them ever since, one way or another.'

'Clyde Harrow wants me to get you to say that Brandon sexually abused you as a child.'

'Clyde Harrow as in game shows and TV comic news? What's it got to do with him?'

'He wants to discredit Brandon.'

'And you've been discussing me with him?'

'Not really, he's blackmailing me.'

'But he knows enough to suggest that Brandon was having sex with me. You can tell him that I'd rather cut the old sod's throat with a rusty razor than accuse him of that. He's puritanical, is Brandon. The only woman he ever showed a spark of interest in was his wife, Seraphina.'

'Seraphina?' I repeat. 'Sounds Italian.'

'She was. Italian by way of a fruit and veg shop in Ancoats. Her family used to organise the Italian processions in Manchester. Seraphina was always talking about those days and teasing Brandon – he's of Italian extraction too. Carlyle's not the original family name.'

'Oh,' I muttered.

'Brandon took it hard when Seraphina died. The stubborn old devil should have handed over the reins then. Not that he gave Seraphina an easy life, with all those kids – five boys and five girls, and she lost some too, but she had a really big heart. They all bicker and fight now but there was love there when we were kids. Seraphina was the only real mother I've ever known. My own doesn't want to know me.'

Suddenly Marti's mood seemed to change. She turned to me.

'You want me for myself, don't you, Dave?' she asked. From the quaver in her voice I sensed that tears weren't far away. Hard as nails on the outside, Marti was still as vulnerable as that child who'd been abandoned.

'Of course I do,' I said. I took her in my arms. She was warm but the bed suddenly felt cold and slick against my skin.

244

'Hold me for a while,' she said. 'I expect you think I'm just a sex maniac.'

'No, I don't,' I protested hollowly. I felt rotten.

'You're the only man I've ever slept with apart from Charlie.'

I didn't know what to say. Guilt was battering at me like the monsoon rain rattling against our window. It sounded more like the tropics than London.

'You haven't just come here so that you can use me, have you?' she asked.

'I don't want to use you, Marti. I don't want to use anyone. I admit that I want to find out what's going on and that I came to ask you questions, but I didn't come here expecting to . . .'

'Lay me, that's what the lads say, isn't it?'

'Yes, but I'm not a lad.'

'You're a good-looking guy, Dave. I expect you get lots of offers.'

'No, I'm . . . ' I said, then shut up when I realised what I was going to say.

'You're attached to Ironpants and her children. You're already spoken for, aren't you?'

'I wouldn't quite put it like that. Janine values her independence.'

'She's a fool. I'd change places with her in a second, but I'm not going to get the chance, am I?'

Again I didn't know what to say, so I didn't say anything.

'At least you're honest, Dave,' she said with a sniff, 'but this man Harrow, he sounds like a pig. I'd hate to think that all this evening means to you is the chance to do his dirty work for him.'

'It's not like that,' I said hastily. 'I'm sorry, Marti, I told Clyde his idea was stupid but he wants to pull Brandon down. He's obsessed. The man eats, sleeps and dreams with thoughts of taking over Brandon's spot at Alhambra TV.'

'Don't we all,' she sighed, 'but not like that. The business would lose millions. How's he blackmailing you? Those killings you did, I suppose?'

'No, will you get that idea out of your head? Was it you who told Brandon about that?'

245

'I may have mentioned it. He was getting heavy with Charlie and me about the hit on Lou Olley. I had to say something. He's really worried about you. Your father's the only copper who's ever given him a fright. He thinks you're out to get him.'

'And when did you discuss all this?'

'When we met to work out the divorce settlement. Thanks to you I had a few cards in my hand. Brandon believes that Charlie was involved with the hit, but I know he wasn't.'

'Because you arranged it?'

'Wouldn't you like to know?' she laughed. 'No, seriously, it wasn't me. I'd like people to think I'm capable but it wasn't me.' I felt the gloom lifting as Marti recovered her sense of humour.

'Then who was it?'

'I don't know. The main thing is that Brandon thinks it was Charlie and he's willing to pay me plenty to back up Charlie's alibi if necessary. I've already had the first instalment.'

I lifted her chin up and looked straight into those green eyes. How could I know if she was telling the truth? I was tempted to believe her. Marti didn't give a damn. If she'd killed Olley, she'd have admitted it.

'You haven't told me why this Harrow is blackmailing you.'

'Forget him. It's just this media madness. If you must know, he's threatening to make me a figure of fun on his TV channel. It'll wreck any chance I have of turning my business into a success.'

'I don't know that it would,' she replied slowly, 'but I can stop it if you like. A call to Brandon and Alhambra will reschedule Clyde Harrow and his funnies to four in the morning. But maybe you're right. Some of these media people never give up once they get their knife into someone. Some of them think they're the King of Italy, the Queen of England and the Pope rolled into one big salami, as Seraphina used to say.'

'There is no King of Italy now.'

'I hate change,' she said with a laugh. 'If only we could stay here for ever,' and then she sighed again and kissed me.

'We'd get a bit cramped,' I retorted. 'I can't make you out. You want to get rid of Brandon yet you're still in touch and everything.'

'Brandon's successful,' she said with her eyes glittering. 'He's got money and power and influence. They all last a lot longer than love, cara mia.' To emphasise her remark she pinched the lobe of my ear.

'Ouch!' I spluttered.

'All I've ever wanted is for Brandon to move over and let Charlie have some room at the top, but he won't budge.'

'How sweet of you. You've already said that a bullet in the head is the only way to get rid of him and that Charlie's tried to arrange an accident for him.'

'Don't be thick, Dave. I don't want to kill Brandon. That would wreck the business. I want him to gradually hand things over to Charlie and me . . .'

'Particularly to you.'

'What's so wrong with that? The idea of him having an accident with the door was that he'd have to let Charlie run things for a while. It's just a matter of financial realities. If Brandon pops his clogs tonight the Carlyle Corporation is finished, but if he doesn't hand over soon it'll collapse anyway. He's not the man he was.'

'So it's all a power struggle between you and Brandon. Don't you care who gets hurt? What about Sam Levy?'

'Yes, what about him?' she echoed.

'You say I'm thick, and I probably am, but can't you under-stand? Somebody else has decided to join in your little game, somebody even less scrupulous than you and Brandon, and I'm not the only one they're interested in. According to your sleazy pal Paul Longstreet . . .'

'Don't be such a prude!' she snapped. 'You've never even met Paul.'

'Will you shut up? According to Longstreet, a couple of heavies were at his place asking for you.'

'When?'

'Today, I mean yesterday afternoon. They must be the same people who did over my place in Manchester. They're looking for something. They think we've got it and they're not too fussy about how they find it.'

Marti sat up. She didn't say a word. Then she got out of bed

247

and began getting dressed. Her movements were quick but there was no sign of panic.

'Now what?' I asked.

'You should have told me that the instant you arrived,' she said. 'Why do you think I didn't trust the mail or the phone?' She looked at her watch. 'We could have been well clear by now.'

'Clear of what? You know something, don't you?'

'Dave, all I know is, we've got to get away. Now, this minute. Don't you understand? If they followed you they could be here any time.'

36

Marti went over to the window and gently moved the curtain to peek out into the street. Relinquishing our sweat-soaked sheets, I stood behind her. It was still raining heavily. The sodium lamps gleamed over pools of water in the streets.

'They're there,' she gasped. 'Look, two of them.' She grabbed my hand and pulled me until my eyes were on the same level as hers. 'Fifth car along on the right. Can't you see them?'

Sure enough, a white van about a thirty yards away was occupied. Water was streaming down the windscreen but behind it two blurred white blobs were visible. The street lights behind the car silhouetted them. They were facing in our direction.

'We've got to get out. They might come to kill us,' she said quickly. She drew the curtain back into place. 'Don't just stand there admiring yourself,' she snarled. 'Work out some way for us to escape!'

I was already pulling my clothes on. Marti dashed over to her closet and hauled down two even larger cases than she'd had at the Renaissance in Manchester and began frantically cramming her designer clothes into them. I opened the flat door to reconnoitre the hallway. Further along the corridor was the door to another ground-floor flat, and a stairway led up to the first-floor flat.

'Do you know the people in the other flats?' I asked when I came back.

'I've only been here a few days,' she grunted as she struggled with the suitcases. 'Dave, it's your last chance now. Leave Ironpants and come and live with me.'

I shook my head.

249

Then I took another very cautious look outside. There was no way for us to get into the street from the front door without being seen. All kinds of thoughts went through my mind. I could make a diversion, try and tackle the two in the car and give Marti a chance to get away. That idea went out of my head when I turned round to see that she'd started packing another couple of cases.

'Do you think you need a Pickford's van?' I asked.

'I'm not leaving any of this stuff,' she said fiercely. 'You've got to get us out of here.'

'Get us out? We're not even going to be able to carry this.'

'I'd rather die now than give up my clothes,' she insisted, still relentlessly cramming clothes into cases.

'Maybe that can be arranged,' I told her. I tried the two largest cases. They weren't exceptionally heavy but the idea of fleeing into the stormy night burdened by four suitcases was so crazy that I didn't know why I was even considering it. I looked at Marti's determined face for a clue. She meant it all right. I didn't know whether to laugh or cry.

'Only one case,' I insisted.

'Come on, Dave,' she coaxed. 'You must be used to dealing with situations like this.'

'Just the one!'

She pouted at me.

'Who's in the top flat?' I asked.

'A young couple, and they have a West Highland terrier.'

'That rules them out, then.'

'I think it's an old man in the other ground-floor flat. He has the garden to himself.'

'He's favourite. Lend me your credit card. We'll have to get out through his back garden.'

'Wait,' she ordered. She bent down and began fishing under the bed.

'Don't say you've forgotten your slippers.'

'No just this,' she giggled, pulling out a large packet. It was full of money. 'Help yourself to a credit card,' she offered. 'I've found cash is best if you don't want to be found.' She then took a mobile phone out of the bag and transferred it and the money to the pockets of her coat.

I snatched her Gold Mastercard off her and set to work on the Yale lock of her neighbour's door. Marti started hauling her cases out into the hall. By the time I had the door open she'd got two cases out.

I pushed one back inside the flat.

'Bastard!' she whispered.

I put my head round the door I'd just opened. A thunderous snoring noise came from a bedroom to one side of the entrance. I opened the door wider and discovered a passage leading through to a French window that opened onto the garden. Fortunately the area was carpeted. The snoring never faltered.

'You'd think the noise we were making would have woken him up,' I whispered. Marti grabbed the door lock, but I pulled her away while I checked for alarms.

At that moment a ghostly shape appeared to sweep across us. I felt the hair on the back of my head rise. Marti gripped me in panic. I shook her free. The phantom shape was the dim light from the hall reflected by the door as it swung gently.

There didn't seem to be an alarm. Tiptoeing back, I closed the door by which we'd entered and then cautiously opened the outside door. Immediately a gust of wind swept through the flat. Papers blew about. The kitchen door started to swing shut but Marti grabbed it just in time. The sleeper snored on. Even as I hefted Marti's case through the door I got soaked. It was still chucking it down. We made a dash towards the end of the garden.

'What's over here?' I asked, gesturing at the seven-foot-high brick wall. The garden area was much darker than the front of the house. Visibility was about four feet. Rain was swilling down on us and my hair was plastered over my eyes. Marti had a Kangol beret jammed over her head and she was wearing a Burberry, which gave her more protection than my suit gave me.

'I don't know, more houses I suppose,' she said irritably.

That made sense. We'd get over the wall and then through the next garden and into the street beyond. That was my plan, anyway.

I lifted and pushed Marti onto the top of the wall and passed the case up to her. Then I hoisted myself up alongside her.

'Jump,' I advised, 'and I'll drop the case down.'

'You first!' she shrieked.

I released myself into the inky darkness.

The drop was at least twelve feet and felt more like twenty. Even worse, the wall bulged outwards at the bottom and I lost skin from my hands, arms and legs as I collided with it. My knees were driven upwards into my chest and every trace of breath was expelled from my lungs. The only consolation was that the ground was soft. I lay on the muddy earth struggling to breathe. Blue lights sparkled before my eyes. It was a moment before I discovered that although damaged I was in one piece.

'Dave, are you all right?' Marti howled from above. She was a vague dark shape against the background of the clouded night sky.

'Lower yourself and I'll catch you,' I said, struggling to my feet.

'No, how will I bring my case?' she argued.

'What's more important?' I bawled. 'Your life or your case?'

She released a volley of curses and then the case.

'You'll have to jump,' I urged when she gave no sign of following her baggage.

'I can't,' she howled. 'I might break my neck.'

'You didn't worry about me,' I shouted.

'I didn't know how high the wall was then,' she wailed.

'Lower yourself,' I suggested after stacking the case against the wall and standing on it. It was like one of those initiative tests. I managed to extend one arm far enough upwards to touch Marti's foot.

'Let yourself down,' I pleaded.

Instead, another volley of colourful curses descended on my head. The foot was raised above my grasp.

'Go back then,' I shouted. I felt my fingernails breaking against the wall as I scrabbled about for a grip. 'I'll meet you in the street but just remember I've got your suitcase here and it can stop here.'

That was the clinching argument.

'Damn you to hell, Dave Cunane,' she squawked.

This time she lowered herself fully until she was hanging from the top by her fingertips. I managed to grab her ankles and guide her down until I was supporting the whole weight of her body with one arm. Then we went over backwards as the case swayed away from the wall. It wasn't far for me to fall but Marti landed in the middle of a rhododendron bush.

I was guided towards her by her familiar braying laugh.

'Shut up!' I bellowed, which only made her laugh louder.

'Where the hell are we?' I yelled.

'I seem to remember a little park,' she said.

I shook my head. There didn't seem much point in saying anything. It could have been a railway cutting. For all Marti knew or cared, as the first to go down, I might have dropped onto a live rail.

We searched for her shoes but they'd disappeared, as had the beret. Then, with me lugging the big case, and Marti behind, we set off on a course perpendicular to the wall. After thirty steps we reached a path and broke through trees and overgrown bushes to street lights beyond and another road.

More by luck than design we made it to my car without meeting anyone. My painful scrapes and contusions were numbed by the cold. I struggled to stop my teeth chattering as Marti calmly fished a brush out of a pocket and fixed up her hair.

'I can hide you in Manchester,' I said.

'No, just drop me at the first taxi rank that we come across,' she said. There was something in her voice that discouraged argument.

'Where will you go?'

'I'm thinking about that,' she said vaguely. 'I'll send a message to the wine bar if we need to get in touch again.'

37

I had the heater at full blast but it didn't warm me as I drove
back up the M1. I wasn't entitled to feel any resentment
against Marti, but being me, I did. She had let me help her into
a taxi without a word of farewell or a sign of affection.

I don't know what I expected. A fond word wouldn't have
been out place, but there'd been nothing. It was an example of
'Love me, love my suitcases!' and I'd shown that I didn't love
them. But then would someone fleeing for their life make such
a fuss about luggage? I tried to come up with excuses for her
but I couldn't convince myself. The tiger of suspicion prowled
in my mind.

Was it my fault? Was my desire to dig for information too
insultingly transparent? Vanity said not.

These and other self-pitying, self-doubting thoughts
plagued me until Nature supplied a little distraction. Rain was
still lashing down. There was no sign of dawn. The mundane
task of keeping the Mondeo moving began to occupy more
and more of my attention as I left the suburbs of London
behind. I was desperately uncomfortable in my sodden
clothes, and that helped to keep me awake and alert. Water
thumping against the wheel arches as I drove through deep
pools and the incessant squeaking of the windscreen wiper
both became more pressing than questions about my love life.

Let's face it, I told myself, you're a selfish bastard who takes
what he can out of life.

As I drove northwards on the almost deserted motorway,
listening to radio reports of flooding with one ear and the
ceaseless drumming of the rain with the other, it was hard to
sustain any emotion. The thoughts that did seep through my
self-reproaches were that I was a fool, a man who couldn't

keep his emotions and his business interests in separate boxes, and that Marti had been lying through her teeth for at least half the time I'd been with her.

The crash came with devastating suddenness.

I was straining my eyes to bore through the billowing clouds of rain ahead when a rear impact almost jerked my head off my shoulders. There was no accompanying noise that I was conscious of but I knew I'd been rammed. My Mondeo spun off to the left across the hard shoulder and in a splintered second I caught a glimpse of a white van racing past before the world turned upside down. Now there was tremendous noise; so much noise, so loud and so varied that it seemed to press all the fear out of me. My airbag inflated and thumped me in the face and my head shot into the headrest as if a heavyweight boxer had landed a punch. I was still conscious and aware that the roof was about to be ripped off when the car flipped over again and I was cartwheeling towards a massive concrete bridge support. I just had time for one thought – who would care if I died, not with a whimper but with a bang? Then all the lights went off.

'Come on, Mr Cunane! David! David Cunane! Mr Cunane,' the words went on and on, over and over and over. Consciousness slowly returned and the first thing that came to me was that I was warm and dry and that it wasn't raining. I struggled to concentrate. I was flat on my back, there was a dim light filtering through but something was wrong with my eyes.

Then, like a record running down on an old-fashioned wind-up player, my consciousness slowly faded.

When I came back to the world the voice was still there: 'David, David, come on, Davie boy.' It droned on and on. I tried to concentrate on that voice. It belonged to a woman, one of those deep, phlegmatic Scots voices. 'David, David,' she crooned. I tried to move but nothing stirred, not a single muscle flickered. It was as if I was snuggling down at the bottom of a very deep hole with a mass of cotton wool pressing on me, restraining me. I struggled to move my lips but they wouldn't obey.

I stopped trying and concentrated on the voice again. There was comfort in it but not sufficient to distract me from my fears. I thought about my eyes. Was I blind? There was light but no vision. I seemed to overhear a whispered conversation to my left. It was maddening and the temptation to wallow in the self-pity that had almost overcome me in the car was overwhelming. I wanted to scream and howl. I felt as if I was slipping away from the world.

'Dave!' This time it was a male voice and it was right in my ear. It was as if a switch had been thrown. I moved my hand.

'There! What did I tell you?' the Scots voice said triumphantly. 'He's not in a coma. You Mancunians have thick skulls. Just a spot of mild concussion, that's all.'

Light flooded in. Whatever had been covering my eyes was removed. I still couldn't see. My eyes seemed to stay shut however hard I tried to open them.

'Dave, you've been in an accident,' the man said. I recognised the voice. It was DCI Brendan Cullen. I stopped trying to struggle up to full awareness. Cullen! What could he be doing at my bedside?

'Come on, mate! Wakey, wakey!' he said cheerfully.

'Bren,' I mumbled. My mouth felt as if it was full of battery acid. I tried to lick my lips but my throat was dry.

'Here, take this,' he said, putting the spout of a hospital water beaker to my lips. I sucked gratefully.

'Are you two all right for a minute?' the Scots nurse asked. 'He'll be OK. You're sure he's a friend of yours, Inspector? I'll be back to have a look in five minutes.'

Her departure distressed me. My emotions were fragile. I had to struggle to stop myself crying. The Scots nurse sounded immensely competent and capable. I didn't want her to go.

'Come on, Dave. No brain damage. That's what they say, but they don't know you like I do. Your brain was damaged to start with.'

'Thanks,' I croaked. To my ears the word seemed to come from a long way off.

'Do you want a fright?' he asked brutally.

'Oh, God! Haven't I had enough frights?'

'No, you need this one. Perhaps you might stop meddling in

256

things that don't concern you if you see the state you're in.' Cullen held a mirror in front of me. It took me a moment to realise that the mass of blue and purple I was staring at was my face. My eyes were swollen like two fat, double eggs. I felt like crying again but there was something in Cullen's voice that prevented that.

'He must have had perfect timing.'

'Who?'

'The guy in the van that copped you. It shot past us and gave you a deliberate nudge just as you were coming up to a nice solid concrete bridge and then away off the motorway at the next interchange before anyone could say boo. Whoever arranged it, I have to hand it to them. It was choreographed to perfection, balletic almost. Michael Schumacher couldn't have done it better.'

'You were following me?'

'Yep, and your fog lights were on, visible for miles. You were driving carefully on the inside lane, a steady sixty to seventy. I'm telling you, mate, that was no accident. If you'd been doing another ten miles an hour you'd be in the mortuary now.'

In my dazed state it seemed to take ages for my brain to work. I struggled to understand what Cullen was saying . . . the accident wasn't an accident. What did he mean? Then the thought that someone had been trying to murder me gradually took hold. It penetrated the miasma of self-pity that had been gathering round me even before the car went off the road. Anger began to give an edge to my thoughts.

'Why were you following me?'

'Operation Calverley. I told you. You're our principal lead. The only reason that you're not also our principal suspect is because I know the way you operate.'

'God!' I groaned. With vision, pain was returning too. Every part of my body had its own separate ache. I tried to move my arm and discovered that it was strapped across my chest.

'Displaced collar bone, concussion, suspected skull fracture, extensive bruising. Bloody lucky if you ask me. You should be a coffin job by rights.'

'Thanks,' I muttered and then lapsed into silence. The bed

felt very comfortable and I could have slept. Even without a near fatal road crash, I'd been on the go continuously for the last two days.

'Come on, Dave,' Cullen urged. 'I need to know what's been going on.'

'When you find out, tell me,' I groaned.

'Listen, we can do it here or at the nearest police station. This isn't an old pals' reunion. We were following you and you led us to Marti King, but now she's disappeared again. Where is she?'

'How do I know?' I asked.

'Oh, come on, Dave. She's been pulling your chain for weeks.'

'She's a client.'

'Like hell, she is. Do you spend the night with all your female clients?'

'That just happened.'

'Dave, baby, you're forgetting I can read you like a book. A pretty face and you'd believe anything she said. I can't afford to do that. I've got to check her out for the Olley and the Levy murders.'

'Marti didn't kill Olley!' I croaked.

'How do you know? I've seen that video a hundred times and I'll swear it was a woman.'

'It couldn't have been Marti.'

'How do you know? Are you just thinking with your balls or have you proof?'

'She's not like that.'

'Isn't she? Did you know that she had a passionate affair with the late Mr Lou Olley shortly before his demise?'

'I don't believe you.'

'Yes, and she was seen scrapping with him in a Manchester night club – Steptoes. We've got it on video. Lou wasn't a gentleman, not like you, Dave. He didn't give a shit about a lady's honour. She tried to slap him and he belted her in the eye.'

'Oh,' I muttered.

'Remembering something?' Cullen asked hopefully.

I shook my head. That was a mistake. The slightest movement reactivated all my aches and pains.

The Scots nurse returned.

'How are we getting on?' she enquired. 'Not tiring my patient, are you, Inspector?' While she was speaking she busied herself examining various intimate parts of my body. I realised that my many bruises were packed with ice. Florence McNightingale briskly adjusted everything. A tingling sensation told me that parts of my body that I'd given up as permanently lost were still functioning.

'No, sister,' Cullen said genially. 'Dave and I are old friends. We go back a long way, don't we, Dave?'

I didn't say anything but the sister was canny enough to ask: 'Is that right, Mr Cunane? My goodness, if you knew some of the tricks these policemen get up to . . .'

'Yeah, Mr Cullen's the least of my problems,' I managed to growl.

'Well, don't wear him out, Inspector,' she warned before bustling on to her next port of call. 'Concussion's a funny business, even for you thick-headed Mancunians.'

At that moment Cullen's mobile chirruped.

'Switch that off!' the sister ordered.

'Just my pager,' Cullen lied and then stepped out of the side ward.

His absence gave me time to think. My thoughts towards Marti King were not charitable, but she was a sort of client, and if I was going to emerge with any sort of dignity or reputation from this mess that was the story I had to stick to.

'I've got to go, Dave,' Cullen said cheerfully when he returned, 'but I'll be back. Let me just leave you with this one thought. We lifted several sets of prints from Sam Levy's house in Bowdon. Yours, Angelina's, the hairdresser's – and guess who else's?'

'Spare me the games, Bren.'

'Marti King's, that's whose. So just you think about that till I get back.'

38

After climbing walls attached to a huge suitcase and surviving a pile-up on the motorway, getting out of that hospital should have been child's play.

It wasn't.

I wasn't attached to any drips or monitors, so getting onto my feet was mainly a matter of suppressing the curses, groans and shrieks of pain that naturally arose when I moved my bruised and battered body. I swung my legs free of the bed and tried standing up. I did it, just. A wave of nausea swept over me but the thought of what Cullen and Operation Calverley had in store kept me tottering on my feet. Incredibly no bones appeared to be broken. I decided to write a letter of congratulation to the head of Ford UK if I survived the rest of the day.

I thought my luck was in when I spotted a blue plastic bag containing my clothes. I grabbed the bag and vainly tried to rip it open. The material seemed to be incredibly tough and it was sealed with swathes of tape. I struggled silently for the best part of five minutes without success.

In the end I managed to gnaw the bag open with my teeth and then extract the garments and lay them on the bed. My heart sank. They'd cut me out of my clothes. The only serviceable items were my shoes and belt. The trousers, jacket and shirt were there but all neatly filleted. I could have cried in frustration. I think I did cry. Then, when I was at the lowest point, I had a stroke of luck. Cullen had carelessly left his 'Man at C&A' mac slung over the chair next to the bed.

There was nothing in the pockets, not a nice handy warrant card or a spare £20 note, but it was long and it was about my size. That just left my legs. With my ugly face I could hardly pretend to be a female or even a stray hairy-legged Scot in a kilt. I had to do something. Cullen might be back at any moment. In every film I've ever seen about hospitals there's always a storeroom with a handy change of clothes. But this was real life and there was nothing.

I looked at my trousers slung forlornly on the bed. I draped them round my legs like two long skirts. In a way having open-plan trousers was an advantage because I was working one-handed. I still had a neck brace on and my left arm was lashed across my chest. Moving very slowly I managed to strip several long pieces of tape from the plastic bag and used them to fasten up the ends of my trousers. It didn't look too convincing, but then how many people were going to look at my legs with my face in such a mess? Getting the shoes on was a struggle. My feet appeared to have swollen by at least two sizes. Wallet, watch and broken mobile phone were in the bedside cupboard.

I don't know why no one stopped me. The first hundred feet were the worst. The side room I was in was on a corner and I managed to dodge into a main corridor with a minimum of fuss. Still, a man with a face like a bruised melon with trousers flapping round his legs . . . you'd have thought someone would have said something, but everyone who caught my eye hastily looked at something else. I was Mr Invisible. Probably it was because there was a large psychiatric hospital next door, but I walked along the corridor following the arrows for Exit, rolling from side to side like a drunken sailor, and no one said a word to stop me. The thought of Cullen's anger lent me strength.

When I got into the open air the rain had stopped. I painfully clumped along the hospital service road to a major road. I had no plan apart from putting distance between myself and the place where DCI Cullen expected me to be. It was hard taking in my surroundings. I could only swivel my head with the utmost difficulty. I was hoping that the hospital was in a big city, Birmingham or Coventry or somewhere, but it wasn't. There were green fields and trees in all directions. I scanned the road expecting to see a police car at any moment.

All that I did see were little knots of people waiting at bus

261

stops on either side. I went to the nearest group and stationed myself among them. Of those waiting I was probably the most convincingly dressed. The trend to dress as if expecting tropical conditions and then pretending that the weather was fine was being taken to absurd lengths by some, as they shivered in T-shirts and jeans. Ten anxiety-filled minutes later, a Stagecoach bus rolled up and I got my first clue as to where I was. The sign on the front said 'Rugby' and in my condition I felt that was totally appropriate.

'Rugby,' I said, handing the driver a ten pound note.

'Do you want the weekly saver?' he asked without even raising his eyes towards me.

I grunted a response which he took as affirmative because he put two pound coins and a weekly ticket into my hand. I considered struggling upstairs before deciding to haul my weary carcass to the rear seat. Again, the eyes of my few fellow passengers were carefully averted. Cullen's mac and the neck brace must have helped, but I presented a freakish appearance. Perhaps they were used to seeing twitchy vagrants emerging from the hospital.

Public transport has its advantages for the fugitive. The bus route was so winding and the journey so slow that if Cullen had discovered my disappearance by now, as he surely must have, he'd never have found me trundling towards Rugby on the slowest bus in the Midlands. As the bus jerked and slid its way along the country lanes I fell into a kind of twilight zone, halfway between pain and sleep. It was only when all the other passengers disembarked that I realised that I'd arrived in Rugby, a red brick town of small shops and narrow streets. I took a taxi to the station and then became probably the only person in the country to bless the name of Virgin Rail. There was a train to Manchester and it was due in twenty minutes.

It was almost six and already dark when I got out of a taxi at Thornleigh Court.

39

'Dave, are you insane?' was the question Janine understandably asked when I told her that we were starting the holiday in Blackpool right away.

'You're right, I am insane,' I said, 'but humour me. We can book into a hotel tonight and then look for somewhere else in the morning. My treat.'

'Oh, great,' Janine muttered. 'You turn up out of the blue looking like . . .' She paused and took a glance at the anxious faces of her children. Unlike the public, which had averted its collective gaze, they were studying my battered dial with the greatest interest '. . . like, I don't know what, and expect us to dash off into the night.'

'It's not so bad. We'll book in somewhere and then we can see the illuminations. The kids'll love it.'

'Oh let's go, Mum!' the children enthused in chorus.

'Stay here a minute!' Janine ordered Lloyd and Jenny. Then she linked my arm and marched me to the corridor.

'Who's after you?' she demanded in an urgent whisper. 'If you've put my children in danger this is the finish for us.'

'It's Cullen. He wants to question me about one of my clients and I've nothing to say to him.'

'It's that damned Marti King, isn't it?'

'Yes,' I admitted.

'Love, can't you see that she's going to get you killed? My crime editor friend reckons that Marti's a serious player in Carlyle's more nefarious enterprises.'

'He may be right,' I muttered between swollen lips. Janine kissed me. I winced, which she misunderstood.

'Why did you have to see her?'

'I wanted information.'

263

'Did you get any?'

'Some, but mostly lies.'

'Hmmmph!' Janine muttered with a trace of satisfaction. 'Did she have you beaten up?' Her words came out as smoothly as an assassin's dagger.

I'd have smiled if it hadn't been so painful. The matter-of-fact way Janine expected me to be routinely beaten up went a long way to explain why she was reluctant to scramble onto my bandwagon.

'I told you that was a car crash.'

'Oh, yes, and you just walked away from it? Don't expect me to believe that. The bitch! I'll see she gets what's coming to her.'

I looked at Janine helplessly. She gave me an encouraging smile. This was the moment when a completely honest man would have let it all hang out, but I didn't. I was selfish enough to think that one moment of stupidity shouldn't be allowed to put my life with Janine in jeopardy.

Janine looked me up and down for a moment. I wasn't dressed in shreds and patches any more. I'd managed to spend half an hour under the shower and I'd discarded the neck brace and the sling. I was still hurting everywhere but I told myself worse things had happened to me before. What I did know was that if I took to my bed now it would be a long while before I got the show on the road again, if ever.

'All right,' she said. 'You saw I sorted your flat out?'

'Thanks,' I mumbled, though I would have been happier if she'd left it.

'I packed a bag for you and we're all packed for an early start tomorrow, so I suppose we can go now if it's so urgent.'

'It is,' I assured her.

'Just promise me one thing, Dave . . . If there's a story in all this, you'll let me have it first.'

'Of course,' I said, 'and then you can share it with Clyde.'

'No!' she snapped. She then blushed to the roots of her hair. 'I'm not going to London with that oily rag. He was here last night.'

'Really,' I murmured.

'Don't look at me like that,' she said hotly. 'Clyde knows

how to flatter a woman. He said he'd like me to help him with his material.'

'I bet he did. What happened?'

'You don't own me, Dave.'

'Sorry, I shouldn't have opened my mouth,' I said. It was lucky that my face was so battered. My own guilty looks didn't show, but Janine couldn't hide hers.

'Don't kick off at me!' she warned. 'I won't be seeing him again. Do you know, he came round to the paper at lunch time? He took me to Nico Central for lunch. Talk about an octopus – you'd think he was old enough to walk down the street by himself without having to drape himself all over me. Then when we got to the restaurant he put his hand on my bottom. I don't take that from anyone.'

'What happened? Did you throw hot soup over him?'

'Let's just say I discouraged him,' she said.

I laughed delightedly, pain be damned.

'Blast you, Dave!' she snapped. 'What makes you think you're so superior? I bet you had it off with that drunken lush.'

'Touché,' I said, 'but seriously, Janine. You're the only woman for me, the only possible woman.'

'Hmmmph!' she snorted. 'And what's that supposed to mean? Sometimes I wonder about you, Dave Cunane.' She took my wrist and smacked my hand quite painfully. 'Evens?' she asked, giving me a kiss.

Whatever else it did, Blackpool didn't disappoint Jenny and Lloyd.

By the time we'd crawled into town behind an immense stream of traffic, found somewhere to stay and then installed ourselves on an open-topped tram to view the 'lights' in the teeth of a freezing wind, I was quite ready to call it a day. Not so, Jenny and Lloyd. They were in heaven. With their little faces reddened by the chill, they strained to see each illuminated 'tableau'. What with wind lashing their hair back, the tableaux straining at their moorings, and the screeching of steel wheels on rails, it was more like a scene from a survival movie than a visit to a place of entertainment, but the children loved every minute and sleep was the furthest thing from their minds.

When we got back to our red brick hotel on the North Shore, though, we all slept the sleep of the just, even those who weren't entitled to, like me. I woke before the others. Beside me, the light of a fresh day shone on Janine's regular features, all contentiousness smoothed away by sleep. I loved that face. She sighed and turned over. From the next room came the gentle hum of the children's breathing, like the purring of contented cats. Whatever else happened to me, this was the way I wanted life to be from now on. Any sacrifice was worth making, any danger worth facing to preserve this. I climbed out of bed quietly and tiptoed to the bathroom.

One look at myself in the mirror was enough to break the glowing romantic mood. I looked like a walking disaster zone. What right did I have to attach these people to me? I couldn't protect myself, let alone them. The next white van to zoom my way might wipe out the lot of us.

As I shaved, or rather directed my razor where it would cause least pain, I was able to study my battered features. A few more feet and it would have been solid concrete coming through that windscreen at me, not mud. I could almost visualise the funeral. Parents, a few close friends – a very few – a number of embarrassed-looking private detectives anxious not to be reminded of their own mortality, and that would be it. Janine and the children? They'd be well advised to stay away.

I shook myself. I wasn't going to get anywhere with these maudlin reflections.

Having time to think I came up with two alternative hypotheses. My first was that it was Marti King who'd ordered the attempted hit on the motorway. She'd had her mobile and it would have been perfectly possible to send someone up the M1 after me. The other option was that Marti hadn't directly arranged for the white van, but she'd parted company with me knowing well enough that I was in danger and hoping that I would lead the killers away from her. So that meant she was either murderous or lethally selfish; either way, she was bad news.

266

I had to find out more about Devereaux-Almond. A lot seemed to revolve round him. Olley was killed about four hours after I left Devereaux-Almond's house at Rochdale, and that same day someone else visited Devereaux-Almond and the gentleman nimbly cleared off to his yacht at Fleetwood. Levy was killed not long after he used a tapped telephone line to promise information about Devereaux-Almond. It also turned out that the same man had been involved in the mysterious adoption of problem-child Marti into the Carlyle family.

I tried to hold the ideas in my mind and work out what the connection was but the confidence with which I'd started the day drained away like the soapy water I'd just shaved in. Cullen was expecting answers from me. For all I knew I might find myself in the dock trying to explain to a judge and jury but the truth was that all I knew about any of these people was what they'd chosen to reveal to me.

I felt hot and angry with myself. My whole body ached and by rights I should still have been in a hospital bed. I strode over to the window and looked out. I was desperate to get out and start finding a few answers but now I was fixed up with a family. I had to wait for them. I pummelled my head. There must be something, something I'd seen or heard that would give me a start. I sat and listened to the breathing again. Gradually I became a little calmer. All right, I told myself, the big picture won't come . . . so start piecing together the small details that you do know.

I could phone Harry Sirpells, he might be in his office now. I crept round to Janine's side of the bed and took the mobile out of her bag.

I tiptoed to the door and let myself out. As I turned to close the door gently behind me Janine turned over and gave me a wave. I walked down to the hotel lobby, scene of many frantic political meetings. There were pictures of politicians all over the place. I found an empty armchair under the anxious yet combative gaze of Harold Wilson . . .

'Harry, it's Dave Cunane here,' I announced.

'Early bird aren't you?' he replied. The word 'bird' was pronounced 'bu-urred'. I should think it's impossible to get a broader Lancashire accent than Harry's without actually speaking Old English. 'It's only just gone nine.'

'This is urgent, Harry . . .'

'What's all this about you expanding?' he asked. 'You used to be a one man and his dog outfit like me.'

'Times change, Harry.'

This produced a longish pause.

'I found out some of what you want but it's going to cost you,' the Rochdale detective said gravely. He gave each word a good chew before he spat it out.

'I didn't expect you to work for nothing.'

'No, but that girl you have working for you seems to have funny ideas about expenses.'

'Oh,' I muttered.

'I've had to wine and dine several legal executives and clerks to get what I've dug up. They're vain little buggers, nothing but the best will do before they'll loosen their tongues for a bit of malicious gossip.'

'Harry, Devereaux-Almond . . . did you find something?'

'That girl of yours . . . I don't know.'

'Harry, cut to the chase,' I pleaded.

'Right, well, you'll be getting a bill for three hundred and I don't want any more quibbling.'

'Just tell me,' I begged. I felt as if I was burning up.

'Your man's ex-clerk, George Holmes, wasn't surprised when I came digging for stuff on his former boss. Hasn't a good word to say for him. Apparently Almond, as he was before he stuck the fancy handle on his jug, was the prize chump among the local legal fraternity, really bog-standard. He was the man you'd choose if you wanted someone to forget something. Forgot several important matters, did Mr Almond, and came within an inch of being struck off several times.'

'Do you mean he forgot things in the criminal sense? Like paid money into his own bank account and forgot to pay it out again?'

'No, he weren't actually dishonest, not sticky-fingered, like. He really forgot things, such as important papers for cases he'd been dealing with, even simple conveyances . . . he forgot to complete. According to Holmes, he was the one that conducted whatever business the firm did, not Almond.'

I listened intently. Somehow what the broad-spoken Rochdalian was saying didn't fit my expectations.

'Listen, Harry, this guy has a fifty-foot motor yacht and a huge house and he's retired well before the normal age . . .'

'I'm coming to that! Don't be so impatient, Dave. I don't know, you Manchester folk, you think we're hicks from the sticks up here, don't you.'

'No.'

'Aye, rubes down the tubes, that's what we are.'

'You're not a rube, Harry,' I assured him. 'You're an arse-hole!'

He laughed heartily at this. I could have done without the banter but I was desperate for more information. I felt my life depended on it.

'Right, monkey! Well, according to Holmes, Almond had trouble keeping his office open and paying Holmes his wages which was pretty poor stuff for a solicitor . . . you don't hear of many of them lads going belly up . . . then he got this case out of the blue. A murder case . . .'

'The King case.'

'Oh, you know about that, do you? Any road, this Almond bugger never looked back after that. He started handling the legal affairs of a big conglomerate . . . North West Mercian Investments . . . or at least he pretended he did.'

'Pretended?'

'Holmes reckoned that Almond once told him that all he got paid for was putting his name on documents. Nice work if you can get it, eh?'

'Yes,' I admitted with a guilty twinge. That was more or less what I did at Pimpernel these days.

'Holmes reckons that Almond's been on the inside of several very juicy property deals. You know . . . quite by accident he's bought up land that suddenly turned out to be very valuable.'

'Anything on this North West Mercian?'

'Nothing. Offices in Manchester apparently but I can do some digging at Companies House if you want.'

'Yeah, I do want.'

'Have you won the Lottery or something?' he asked.

'Something like that,' I murmured. 'I want you to do another thing for me.'

'I'm all ears, chief.'

'There's this cemetery, it's on Moston Lane, North Manchester.'

'Oh, aye. I know it,' he said.

'I want you to go there and find the Italian section and write down all the names on the graves beginning with C.'

'Are you losing it, boss?'

'Get the names down, all the ones beginning with C in the Italian section . . . even if they're Welsh or Irish or English or whatever, as long as they're in the Italian section I want them written down. I want a result by Monday.'

'This Almond isn't an Eye-talian and his name begins with A, anyway.'

I thought for a minute.

'Are you still there, Dave?' Harry Sirpells asked anxiously.

'Yes, and while you're at it you can do all the names beginning with A as well as the Cs.'

'This'll cost you. Weather's rough up here.'

'Oh, come on. It'll put some colour in your cheeks. Two hundred quid if it's on my desk by Monday morning.'

'I don't know. I'm a detective agency, not one of them blooming genetic places.'

'Genealogical, Harry. This is just a little historical enquiry I'm making.'

'Aye, happen you'd need to go where the bodies are buried for that.'

'That's just it,' I told him. I gave him the number of Janine's mobile and while I was looking up her number in the memory was interested to note that she had Clyde Harrow's office and home numbers stored.

My next call was to my own office on the off-chance that Celeste was in.

She was.

'Where've you been?' she shrieked. 'We're at panic stations here.'

270

'I was unavoidably detained yesterday. It was a test of your initiative.'

'Man! It was that daft dibble Cullen, wasn't it? He's harassing you, man. I can get my cousin to help you. He's on the Community Forum. The police'll have to listen to him.'

'I was in hospital, Celeste. A little accident.'

'Are you still there?'

'No.'

'This place is buzzing. You need to be here.'

I noted Celeste's deep concern for her employer's well-being. Presumably she thought that if I was well enough to speak to her I was well enough to be at work.

'Celeste, there were floods yesterday. You're not telling me that there was much observing to be done. Even insurance fraudsters would have been indoors.'

'It's not them. It's that Mr Cunliffe. He keeps phoning about your expansion plans. I told him you were in London and he just kept on phoning. He sounds frantic. He's sent round a load more cases. Some of them are in Wigan and Frodsham . . . all over.'

'That's great! If he phones this morning tell him I'm in conference with my bankers.'

'Are you?'

'Just tell him, Celeste. I'll be in next week.'

My call to Celeste terminated just as Janine came into the lobby with the children.

40

We started our day together with the Full English Breakfast.

Looking at the plate in front of me it came to me why those Full English of the past were so full of confidence. The large knives and forks, the extravagant quantities, the heavy white linen and the solid napkin rings, they all must have made the consumers of such breakfasts very sure of their place in the world.

Thinking of my own recent adventures, I didn't feel too secure and confident.

'You know, Janine, I think I should have got a job in a bank,' I said.

'What's brought this on?' Janine asked crossly. 'You wouldn't have stuck for more than a week.'

'Miss Seagrave says jobs in banks aren't very secure,' Jenny solemnly advised us. 'She says all that will be done by computers in a few years' time.'

Janine began grinding her teeth at the mention of her rival for Jenny's affection. I smiled placidly at her.

'I wonder if I could interest Miss Seagrave in a job at Pimpernel Investigations,' I said. 'She seems to have an answer for everything and I could do with the help.'

'Miss Seagrave says teaching children is the most noble job anyone can do,' Jenny replied.

'What about brain surgeons and doctors?' Janine countered.

'They need teachers to start them off,' Jenny said majestically.

'What does she have to say about journalists?' Janine asked. 'I suppose she thinks they're just useless ornaments.'

'I asked her that,' Jenny said without a trace of sarcasm. 'She says she's sure they have a very useful purpose but she doesn't know what it is yet.'

'That's it,' Janine snapped. 'If I'm going to get Miss Seagrave night, noon and morning I'm going home.'

Both children looked at her in alarm.

'Simmer down,' I said. 'Miss Seagrave's nothing compared to Paddy. He knows everything.'

The children bent their heads and began to polish off another round of thickly buttered toast. I poured out more tea for Janine and myself. I was about to try to soothe Janine when she suddenly disappeared in a mass of red roses. That is, I looked away for a moment and a waiter brought over a massive bouquet and more or less thrust it into Janine's face.

She gaped at me in surprise. I shook my head. Janine began opening the attached greetings card but she needn't have bothered.

'Permission to come aboard!' Clyde Harrow boomed in his ripest, fruitiest voice. 'Peace offering, ma'am,' he said cheekily. 'I was upset to think you might have misunderstood my little gesture yesterday.'

'Misunderstood?' Janine gasped. Then she began to look dangerous. The roses landed on the floor with a crunch of cellophane. 'Misunderstood! Why, you conceited, arrogant pig, how dare you come crawling after me?'

'He who dares, wins,' Harrow said loftily.

'Win?' I said. 'All you're going to win is a thump in the face.'

'Now then, young David, you seem to have cornered the market in bruises. I'm sure there are none left for me.'

'How did you find us?'

'Oh come. Your *petite amie* here told me that you were bound for our great coastal resort and there are few enough first-class hotels here.'

'Why, Clyde?' Janine asked angrily. 'What makes you think that you're entitled to burst into a private family holiday?'

'Holiday certainly, but a family holiday I would dispute. I was speaking to Henry Talbot just last week . . .'

'What!' Janine gasped. She suddenly looked stricken.

'Yes, the unfortunate chap is pining to see his offspring. I can sympathise. It's a position I've been in myself more than once. It was naughty of you to let me think that young David

273

here was the father of these delightful children.'

Janine responded by gathering up the children and heading for the stairs. 'Pay the bill, Dave, we're leaving at once,' she ordered.

'Clyde, you're a bastard,' I snarled at Harrow. 'I've never claimed that I was the children's father.' I pushed back my seat and stood up. Clyde recoiled. At nearby tables, knives and forks were lowered. Clyde, of course, was recognised wherever he went. How could he avoid it, dressed as he was like a clown escaped from the Tower Circus? People were gaping at him, but even assuming I could summon the energy I don't think the management would have been thrilled to see the famous celeb wrestling on the carpet on which Prime Ministers had so recently trodden.

'Now steady on,' he cautioned. 'We've been through all this stuff about bastards before. You don't want to make a scene and it was you I came to see, not Janine.' He then delved into the jacket of his gold lamé blazer and thrust a sheet of paper under my nose. 'Read this,' he commanded.

It was a letter from the board of Alhambra TV terminating Clyde's contract forthwith. It was dated yesterday. While I read, Clyde busied himself by devouring the substantial remains of our breakfast.

'There!' he said triumphantly, stuffing a rasher from Janine's plate into his mouth. 'I can read the guilt in your body language. I think some explanations are in order, don't you? All I could glean from the top floor is that Brandon Carlyle's demanding my poor old head on a dish. Something or somebody must have set him off. Somebody not a million miles from me now.'

I sat down heavily. The Full English Breakfast was congealing in my stomach.

'You've not made it a secret that you're after his job. One of your little female friends probably ratted on you.'

'I think not. The callipygian Lauren, my production assistant, has had her cards as well. Great is the lamentation in the house of Harrow.'

'Swallowed a dictionary, have you?'

'Callipygian, a girl who bears her charms behind her, to the rear, as it were. It's sad how poorly educated you younger men are.'

'What university did you attend, then?'

'The university of life, where I learned that the only way to deal with swine like Carlyle is to get your retaliation in first.'

'I see.'

'Yes, young David, and you needn't pretend that you're impervious to the claims of our lower nature. I saw you giving Lauren an appraising look.'

'Clyde, if you lay your mucky little fingers on Janine's nether regions again I'll break them off, always assuming that she doesn't do it herself.'

Unusually for him, Clyde coloured slightly at this. I didn't know what Janine did to him at Nico Central but it must have been humiliating.

'Let's get back to matters in hand,' he said quickly. 'Namely Brandon Carlyle . . . Unfortunately, he seems to have momentarily gained an advantage and you're involved in some way.'

'So you're no longer able to threaten to turn me into a public laughing stock.'

'Dear lad . . . at least you're a lad who's cost me dear . . . you'll be making a serious mistake if you underestimate the capacity of Clyde Harrow to bounce back from adversity. Now tell me, did you locate Marti King and put my proposition to her?' All the time he was speaking Clyde was industriously clearing Janine, Lloyd and Jenny's plates, vacuuming the left-overs down his outsize gullet.

'She must be the one who got you sacked,' I said. Then I told him about Marti's promise to have his show relegated to the wee small hours.

'Incompetent fool!' he spluttered, before starting on the remaining toast and jam. 'Your whole thesis that Ms King was at odds with her relatives must be at fault if she retains such influence with Brandon Carlyle.'

'Maybe,' I admitted, 'but you don't know it was like that. She may have mentioned it in passing and Brandon drew his own conclusions.'

'It'll cost him dear. He'll have to compensate me for my

remaining contract. Dave, my friend, do me a favour. Take your plate round the buffet again. I'm temporarily out of funds.'

I looked at his fat, creased face. There were flecks of egg yolk and jam round his lips. He flashed me a crooked smile. What do you do with someone who demands favours while insulting you?

'Get your own, fat boy,' I said, mildly enough.

Clyde looked far more upset by this rebuff than by anything I'd said so far. For a moment I thought he was actually going to cry. I signalled a waiter and asked him to put a breakfast for Clyde on my bill. Clyde was out of his seat before the words had left my mouth.

He returned moments later with enough food for a family of seven and proceeded to eat ravenously. I got up to leave.

'No, don't go,' he grunted. His cheeks were straining to contain the food in his mouth.

'I was going to take the kids to the zoo for a look at the animals being fed but now I don't think I'll bother,' I told him.

'Listen, pimpo-lad,' he said. 'I think light is beginning to dawn. I admit that by sending you along the primrose path of dalliance to Miss Marti I may have erred.'

'I didn't see Marti just on your say so and I'll have less about the path of dalliance if you don't mind.'

'Hah!' the fat old fraud said shrewdly. 'Do I detect an outbreak of guilty conscience here? You can't hide anything from a puff'd and reckless libertine like me. *Hamlet*, act one, scene three, sport.'

I tried to give him a hard stare but he smiled back at me so sweetly that I couldn't hold the frown.

'Clyde, I wish you'd mind your own business,' I muttered in exasperation, 'and leave off the Shakespeare.'

'I can't, old lad,' he said with a sigh. He then proceeded to chew the food in his mouth and swallow it, while shovelling more onto his fork. How he managed to eat and speak at the same time was something of a marvel. 'There's a divinity that shapes our ends, rough-hew them how we will, *Ham* . . .'

'. . . Thanks, that's quite enough ham for one morning,' I said, getting to my feet.

'Stay!' he pleaded. 'I'll keep it brief. I know it upsets you modern lads to be subjected to someone who has superior powers of expression.'

'Vanity of vanities,' I said, turning to go. 'That's in the Bible somewhere.'

'I apologise. Stay a moment, you may hear something to your advantage.'

'Do you really know Henry Talbot?' I asked. 'Or was that something a researcher dug up for you and you decided to throw in Janine's face?'

'My words may have been rash but the woman needs bringing down a peg. And yes, I have met Talbot. A sorry, miserable wretch he is too. Why the woman ever saw anything in him . . . he lacks the solidity that you and I share.'

'Speak for yourself, Clyde, and get to the point.'

'The point is this . . . I am turned out of a job in which I've demonstrated extreme competence, and turned out, I may add, by a man who could well be involved in two murders which the police show no signs of bringing home to his door.'

'So?'

'So, unless you, my young friend, are able to bring down this monster who sits enthroned amid his ill-gotten gains . . .'

'Which monster? Yourself?'

'You know who I mean.'

'And you're threatening me again, are you? I hope you remember what happened last time.'

'That was unfortunate, I admit that. I shouldn't have brought up the issue of abuse but at least it shows that Miss Marti is far from being at odds with the Carlyles. You yourself told me that you think Vince King holds some fatal threat over the accursed brood. Get him released and all may yet be well for me at Alhambra. I won't be the first to return in triumph to the scene of his disgrace.'

'I get him released, just like that?'

'You're my last hope.'

'Thanks,' I murmured. 'What was the threat you were going to use?'

'Threat?' he said vaguely. 'Oh, no threat, Dave. Henry Talbot is desperate for a chance to see his children. I offered to let him spend time with some of mine but apparently blood calls to blood. I advised him to take no hasty steps.'

For once, Clyde took his eyes off his food and held my gaze as he spoke. Beneath all the bluster and bragging he was a cool customer.

'I don't know whether to believe you or not, Clyde, but you'd better believe this. If Henry Talbot does harm to Janine because of something you've said it won't just be your fingers that get broken.'

'Strong words from a man who looks as if he's come off worst in an argument with a bus. All I'm asking is that you continue the course you've set and find something that puts Carlyle where he belongs. Lovely Marti must be blackmailing the family with the threat of her daddy being released. All you need do is find the proof that he's innocent and then you'll have the same hold she has.'

'I've thought of that.'

'With a single bound, you'll be free and so shall I.'

'Great.'

'Have you thought that friend Levy might have been the one who ordered the hit on Lou Olley? If Levy was more of a friend to Marti than he was to Brandon maybe he had Olley terminated before Olley could terminate Marti.'

'Rave on,' I told him.

The red roses remained forlorn and disregarded where Janine had flung them.

It took me twenty minutes to get Janine, the children and the luggage loaded into the car. There was no sign of pursuit from Clyde though we did spot Lauren chewing gum and leaning against his shiny new Toyota Land-Cruiser. She smiled at me. I pinched myself to make sure that I wasn't dreaming. What was I doing providing breakfasts for a man who drove around in a mobile sin-bin with room service attached?

'Don't say anything!' Janine said as we drove out of the car park. 'That pig, he's even brought his floozy with him. Look at the size of her arse, and then he's got the cheek to touch mine.'

'Cheek's the word, all right. Clyde's a one-off, but he may have stroked his last bottom. He's come a cropper at

Alhambra. They've flung him out and he expects me to help him get back in.'

'I hope you're not going to be soft enough to lift a finger for him.'

'No, dear,' I said wearily.

Say what you like about Blackpool, but I would advise anyone who's thinking of lying low to consider it. We were able to check into a self-catering flat in a palatial former miners' rest home within half an hour of leaving the hotel. There wasn't much fuss about names or identities when we paid for the week in advance.

'How would you fancy another tram ride,' I said to the children when we emerged onto the Promenade.

They both responded enthusiastically but Janine looked at me with narrowed eyes. 'You're up to something, aren't you?' she asked suspiciously.

'Just combining a little business with pleasure,' I said evenly.

She shook her head but then resolutely painted a smile onto her face. I knew she wanted to get the most out of her week at the seaside.

41

A few minutes later we were trundling northwards along the Promenade in one of the green and cream antiques that Blackpool Corporation considers suitable for public transport. We passed the North Pier and the miles of golden sand on our left. The day had improved but there was still a fierce breeze. Seagulls were having trouble staying air-borne. I knew how they felt. All my bruises seemed to have stiffened up. We clanked past sand-blown shelter after sand-blown shelter each with its complement of geriatric cases clinging to each other for protection from the wind.

I tried to harness the children's enthusiasm to my project by extolling the wonders of Fleetwood to them. 'There's a clock in the middle of the street, and fishing boats and a museum.'

'Is that all?' Jenny asked.

'They have these lozenges that the fishermen used to suck on cold nights called Fishermen's Friends. They're wonderful.'

'Why?' Lloyd demanded.

'They set your throat on fire. Really warm you up,' I explained.

He gave me a very sceptical look.

The children soon tired of listening to me. There was plenty to see along the eight miles between Blackpool and Fleetwood. The tide was out. The sun was gleaming on the foreshore and the children became completely absorbed in the passing scene.

'So what did that old maniac really want?' Janine asked me quietly. 'I know apologies are the last thing on his dirty little mind.'

'I don't know. You've certainly spilled some of the wind out of his sails. What did you do to him?'

'Nothing.'

'He's got it in for you. It can't be the first, or the five hundredth time, a woman's turned balky with Clyde but he's not taking it well.'

'Turned balky? What a nerve! I'm not a horse to be saddled and controlled by some man.'

'It was just an expression, Janine.'

'All I did was to pour some iced water down his trousers.'

'What?'

'His passions seemed to be inflamed so I pulled open those baggy trousers he wears and poured a large jug of ice-cold water onto the seat of his problem. I got a round of applause from the other diners.'

'Not from Clyde, you didn't. I don't know whether he was lying or not, but he seems to have been in contact with your ex-husband.'

'Why?' she asked miserably.

'Again, nothing's certain but I think he was implying that if I didn't help him with his problems he'd do what he could to make the situation with Henry worse.'

'What can he do?'

'Clyde could do a lot in a mean way. He isn't mean all the time but occasionally he lets his evil inclinations get the better of him.'

'But still . . .'

'Janine, he's been in your flat. He's talked to the children about their schools. He knows the situation between you and me. He knows we're here in Blackpool. The least he can do is to point Henry in the right direction. Worst of all, he knows how to put a spin on things so that we'll come out in a bad light. He's crafty behind that pose of his, and he's desperate.'

Janine was thoughtful for a while.

'I don't think the children are in any danger,' I told her. 'I'd take them to my parents' place if they were, but we registered under a false name and no one's likely to find us even if they were looking.'

'No,' she said. 'I'm sure you're right, but will you help Clyde?'

'It's not Clyde I'm helping but myself. For my own peace of

mind and maybe even personal safety I'd like to know what Marti King is up to.'

'Oh, come on, Dave! Ever the seeker after truth, aren't you? Pull the other one. You're interested in the woman, period!'

'No.'

'Obsessed, then?'

'No.'

'So, what happened in London?'

'When I met Marti she was very friendly . . .'

'Hah!'

'She was after something . . .'

'I'll bet she was.'

'She wanted to know if I had "Object X".'

'Spare me the Bondery, James!'

I spared her a thin smile. Object X was a surmise but I now knew that Marti hadn't summoned me to London just so she could look into my bonny blue eyes.

'That's my name for the thing Sam Levy was tortured for . . . the thing someone searched my flat and office for.'

'You never said your office was searched.'

'The alarms were by-passed and it was bugged as well. When Marti found I hadn't got the mystery object she turned the friendship off like a tap.'

Janine studied my face for a moment. I hadn't told any lies.

'What's your definition of being very friendly, Dave?' she asked. 'I take it that you mean she wasn't balky? Is that it?' She'd gone pale but there were two little red patches on her cheeks.

'It was only physical, it didn't mean anything,' I said unconvincingly.

'You and Clyde make a good pair,' she said angrily.

'Yes, and so did you and Clyde.'

'That was just a mistake. I soon put him straight but I bet you're still letching after Marti.'

'No.'

We rode on in silence past Thornton Cleveleys. We were nearing Fleetwood before she spoke again. 'It looks as if we're stuck with each other, Dave. Would it make any difference to you if we got married?'

282

'Yes,' I said.

'I'll think about it, then.'

'I can buy you a ring in Blackpool.'

'I said I'd think about it, Dave.'

'Right, only trying to show willing.'

We rode in silence for the rest of the way.

Fleetwood is as sweet and innocent a spot to commit murder in as any place you could find at the end of an eight-mile tram ride from Blackpool. The yacht 'Spirit of the Hills' was sitting at its mooring as quiet and empty as a fired gun. It was obvious that no one had been near it for some time.

I tried my luck at the Portakabin of the marina super-intendent. I told him that I was making enquiries on behalf of Almond's sister-in-law which wasn't exactly a lie but not the entire truth either. This is what I managed to glean . . .

Yachts were required to call the lock-head for clearance when sailing out of the port. Morton V. E. Devereaux-Almond was a keen weekend sailor. He wasn't regarded as inexperienced. No special notice was taken when he set off last weekend to do the Morecambe Bay triangle: Fleetwood, Piel Island, Glasson Dock and then back to Fleetwood. Sailing in Morecambe Bay makes particular demands on a yachtsman. The bay has vigorous tides with a big rise and fall and many shoals. The fact that he'd had his yacht berthed at Fleetwood for some years without getting into difficulties showed that Almond was a competent sailor with basic knowledge of tides and chart-work.

The marina superintendent assured me that he'd personally seen Almond at the helm of his yacht when it passed through the lock gates last Saturday. After some persuasion he phoned his colleague who'd been on duty on Sunday afternoon. At weekends yachtsmen radio the marina superintendent to check that there's sufficient water for them to enter the marina. The colleague remembered the call from 'Spirit' and it wasn't Almond who made the call. 'Spirit', with a draught of about two metres, wasn't an especially large yacht but there was one unusual thing. Whoever was steering the yacht on Sunday wasn't familiar with the channel leading into the Wyre estuary.

The channel was marked with buoys and lights and there was a bell called Fairway Number One where vessels were supposed to line up and follow the buoys along a more or less straight line into the estuary. In the past ships had been wrecked on King Scar or Little Ford, shifting grounds on either side of the deep channel. Last Sunday, whoever was steering the 'Spirit' had grounded it in under two metres of water on the east side of the channel and, rather than wait for rising water, had called the marina for a tow.

It wasn't Almond who paid the call-out fee in cash, but a short man, not a local and not much of a sailor according to the crew. He apparently didn't know that he could have raised the boat's keel and kept himself out of trouble. The crew didn't ask for his name or do any kind of check. There was nothing unusual about that. It isn't the practice to do a checklist of returning yachtsmen. The marina looks after the yachts and the people look after themselves. They have their own club and their own friends at the port. Berthing and storage charges for the 'Spirit' were all paid in advance for the year. For all anyone knew Almond might have been in the cabin sleeping off a drinking bout. It would have been possible for one man to crew the yacht. It was designed for short-handed ocean cruising but Almond usually took a friend from the yacht club with him when he went for an overnight cruise.

Persuading the superintendent to let me see the yacht was a lot more difficult. He explained that he was in a job's worth situation.

'OK, we'll just let the police handle it,' I said as casually as I could.

'There's all kinds of valuable gear on those boats,' he protested.

'We're hardly likely to make off with the anchor with two small children with us,' Janine told him.

He looked at her doubtfully and then came out of his cabin and locked the door.

'We've had pilferage from the yachts,' he explained. 'That's why we have the fence and the floodlights.'

'Search us if you like,' Janine retorted. 'I'm a journalist and I'm sure my paper would be interested in a feature on how unhelpful you were in locating a missing person.'

Grudgingly, the superintendent led us to where the 'Spirit' was berthed. He gestured us to keep back while he inspected the boat.

'That shouldn't be like that,' he said when he got on the deck. 'Someone's left the cabin door unlocked.'

I clambered aboard, all limbs aching, and he pointed to the cabin door. An unlocked padlock swung gently from its hasp. I pushed the door open. The cabin had been turned over from top to bottom.

'Right, I'm calling the police,' Janine said when I hauled myself back off the yacht.

'No, we'll call Cullen at Operation Calverley,' I said. 'If Devereaux-Almond's gone the same way as Levy, he'll have to know.'

Mention of Cullen's name had a powerful effect on me. I could feel the solid concrete moving under my feet. Then there was an overwhelming feeling of weakness and suddenly I was lying on the ground. When I came round only a moment later I could still hear things but as if from a way off. Janine was talking about me . . . 'He was in a bad car crash only the other day, I shouldn't have let him come . . .'

'Do you want me to get an ambulance?'

'No, if you could phone for a taxi I think I can get him back to where we're staying.'

'All this about the police that your friend was going on about . . . I think he's overwrought. These yachties often stay out overnight or come back on someone else's vessel. There's no need for all this drama. The chap Mr Devereaux-Almond hired to sail with him might have dropped him anywhere and then brought the yacht back to its mooring. If he sailed through the night and then back he could have reached the Irish Republic, North Wales, the Isle of Man, the Cumbrian coast, Liverpool . . . all in a day's sailing distance. Normally we wouldn't get worried about Mr Devereaux-Almond at all unless someone raises the alarm. I mean there was no distress call. He's a very competent yachtsman. Whoever was on the yacht with him would have raised the alarm if there'd been an accident.'

285

'But the mess in the cabin . . .'

'Yes, there is that,' the superintendent agreed, 'but I've seen a lot worse. There was quite a blow that weekend and the chap did run aground. He was probably suffering from exhaustion if he'd been sailing a long distance single-handed. He might have been trying to shift weight to get the boat off.'

'Janine,' I said feebly. It felt as if I was looking at the world through the wrong end of a telescope.

'Oh, Dave, you are a fool, you should be in bed and that's where you're going.'

42

It was Tuesday before I felt like getting out of bed.

'Dave, how do you feel about going home?' Janine asked as soon as my feet touched the floor. 'Celeste has been phoning me almost hourly and there are things to do in Manchester. Your business is going to pot while you're here. I've had to give her all kinds of instructions and I'd rather be back in Manchester.'

'But this is your holiday.'

'Fine holiday. First I'm threatened by Harrow and then my partner drags me off in search of yet another murder victim. I'd rather be at home.'

'Do as you please,' I muttered.

'Don't sulk, Dave. You're in no position to. What you've got to do is to accept that you're not superhuman. You can't get up and just walk away from a car smash like you did.'

'But I . . .'

'Shut up and listen for once.'

'I don't know if this Devereaux-Almond has come to a sticky end or not. I don't care. All I care about is you and the children and I'm not prepared to sit around waiting for someone to come and tell me that your next accident has been fatal.'

'I see.'

'Do you? I doubt it. What I'm telling you is to drop this whole thing and come back with me and we'll try and start again on a new footing. I know I've been difficult but so have you. You're obsessed with that tart King and her problems.'

For once in my life I felt too weak to argue. Janine took my silence as agreement. At least, I think she did. Ideas flickered through my weary mind. How could we be sure that whoever

287

had killed Devereaux-Almond, and I was sure he had been disposed of, would be satisfied to let things rest? Wasn't I next on the list? Would he be content to leave me as a near miss?

'Good, then that's settled,' Janine said briskly. 'There'll be no more trouble with Henry Talbot either. I'll arrange for him to have some visiting rights with the children, so you can forget about Clyde Harrow and his feeble blackmail attempts. Let that dirty animal stew in his own juice.'

I didn't see much of her for the rest of the week. It rained almost continuously and I spent the rest of the children's half-term sitting in front of the television with them. Jenny was happy enough with books and Lloyd liked watching the same videos over and over. Janine said nothing more about matrimonial plans and I felt in no position to remind her. It was the weekend before I was well enough to walk as far as the Meadows. On Sunday we all went for a bike ride that left me dripping sweat after half a mile.

However, the fact that I was worrying about fitness showed that I was on the mend and Monday found me feeling well enough for the office. There I discovered that if a week is a long time in politics, then it's an eternity in the life of a detective agency. I got an inkling of what had been going on when I saw two neatly dressed young men, one white and one Afro-Caribbean, letting themselves in from the street. I'd never seen either of them before but they both appeared to be completely familiar with Pimpernel Investigations. One of them looked at me oddly as I walked in after them, as much as to ask me what right I had to be there. They went through reception and on into the back.

The reception area was a shock. Only one thing was familiar. Sitting at her desk, a new larger desk, was Celeste. I noticed that she was wearing a pinstriped business suit. She looked as efficient and deadly as a Challenger tank waiting to go into action. The reception suite had been refurnished and decorated in vivid colours and the back rooms extended. My spacious quarters had been swallowed by a nest of small cubicles. There were six of them, each with a small desk, phone and filing cabinet. Celeste was in transports of joy as she showed me round.

'We got these office fitters in last Monday,' she explained, 'and they said there was room for six small offices and a receptionist in the communications room. We'll have investigators and they can see clients and write up their reports and do their work from their own little offices.'

'Celeste, when you say "we" decided this and "we" decided that, who do you mean?' I asked grudgingly.

She looked at me in surprise. 'Why, Ms White and me. I thought she'd discussed everything with you?'

'Oh, right,' I said feebly. 'But Celeste, where's my office?'

'Well, Janine ... er, Ms White, thought you could be out here with me if you wanted or you could have one of those offices,' she said awkwardly. 'She said you wouldn't be spending much time in here now. You'll be out getting new business and meeting influential contacts. I did tell her how you like to spend time on your own thinking about things but she just laughed and said you won't have much time for that from now on.'

'Yes, I'm sure she's right,' I said, struggling to take it all in. 'But tell me, these two guys, who are they?'

'Michael Coe, he's the younger one with the ginger hair. Your friend Mark Ross recommended him. He's an expert in all forms of electronic surveillance. He was in the army, Northern Ireland I think, but he won't say. He's got marvellous ideas for fixing up small cameras where people won't notice them. We can do all the surveillance we need without having squads of ex-plods everywhere.

'So you've given them their cards.' I spoke quietly, without any intonation.

'No cards, they're self-employed. But Mr Coe isn't, he's on a salary and so is Mr Snyder ... Peter, that is. He used to work for Investigations Unlimited, but they had to let him go ... we've taken a lot of their business ... and he's very well up with fraud investigations. Ms White used to know him. He's never been a policeman. He lives in Cheadle Hulme and he has four small children.'

As Celeste chatted on, confidently filling me in on the new managerial structure, I felt a wave of intense weariness sweep over me. From having a small one-man business that just

289

about supported myself and a teenage secretary, I now had a massive monthly salaries bill to meet. I wondered if I could cope.

Then a surge of annoyance told me that I could. Was I going to allow my girlfriend and a teenage secretary who'd done three months in evening college to organise me out of my life's work? No, I wasn't. It was still my name on the office door. I looked to check. Yes, there it was . . . D. Cunane, Proprietor.

Celeste followed my glance.

'Oh, yes,' she said proudly. 'Ms White's arranged for sign writers to come and do the outside of the office. She's got a designer to work on a logo for us. She thinks it's a good idea to keep the pimpernel theme but in smaller characters because customers might get the idea that we're some kind of wild cowboy outfit . . . you know, like the adventure novels . . . Sir Percy Blakeney and all that jazz?'

I nodded, determined not to give a hint of my stupefaction.

Giving me a warm smile she took a large card from behind her desk.

'Here's the new logo. Terrific, isn't it?' she said warmly.

'Great, just great,' I agreed.

Poor old 'pimpernel' had shrunk to tiny lowercase characters. It was the words INVESTIGATION AND PROTECTION that hit you in the eye. D. Cunane didn't appear at all.

I started laughing. I don't know why. The only thing I could think of was that the joke was on me.

'Are you all right, Dave, er, Mr Cunane?' Celeste asked. 'You looked as white as a sheet there for a while, if you don't mind me saying, er, I thought you were going to faint on me. Janine told me what happened to you.'

'I feel fine. I couldn't be better,' I said between wheezing laughs.

'I knew that Marti King was trouble. My sister's boyfriend, Lennie, has told her that Vince King has lots of mates on the outside here in Manchester. Men he was in the army with and men who've done time with him. They look up to him because he's never grassed.'

'Yes,' I said. As if on cue my two salaried employees emerged from their cubicles, anxious to see what was happening. I introduced myself and my near-hysterical laughter generated a mood of jollity all round. I could see we were all going to get on well and as a matter of fact we did. They seemed to know more about what they were doing than I did and I let them get on with it.

I just sat in the reception area for a while trying to get my bearings while Coe and Snyder went back to work. Celeste nervously busied herself sorting various pieces of paper.

'Celeste, I want you to know you've done a terrific job and that I probably wouldn't have a business if it wasn't for you,' I said.

'Ms White did a lot as well,' she said, beaming with pleasure.

'There's just one thing.'

'Yes?' she said anxiously.

'Harry Sirpells . . .'

'Oh, yes, he came in making an awful fuss. Demanding money and cursing, he was. I told him he'd get paid at the end of the month. He said there was no way he was going to do more work for you.'

'Good,' I said, breathing a sigh of relief. 'Did he leave anything?'

'There was an envelope,' she muttered doubtfully, 'but we've moved everything round so much. It must be here somewhere.' She began looking through her desk drawers.

'Celeste, it must be here. That envelope cost me a lot of money,' I said when she threw her arms up in defeat.

'Ms White went through everything on your desk and gave it to me to file. She didn't throw anything away. I was with her all the time.'

During the next hour and a half I discovered just how much rubbish I'd accumulated in a relatively short time. The envelope from Sirpells eventually turned up inside another file marked 'Miscellaneous' stuck at the back of a cabinet containing expenses claims. The words Devereaux-Almond Investigation were written on it in Sirpells' spidery handwriting. Obviously Janine thought that I'd spent enough time on Devereaux-Almond.

Seraphina Carlyle, 1928–1989, was buried in the plot next to an Eduardo Colonna, 1902–1973. There were two Carlyle infants buried in the same plot and there was space on her gravestone for further inscriptions. The inscription on Eduardo Colonna's gravestone also mentioned his wife Maria, and his brother Antonio, lost at sea on 2 July 1940. There were other Colonna gravestones, the earliest dated 1906. There were no Almonds but there were several Allemanos. One of the Allemano headstones recorded a Carlo Allemano, also lost at sea on 2 July 1940.

A separate piece of paper at the end of this report stated that North West Mercian Investments appeared to be a structure of interlocking companies like serpents trying to swallow their own tails. Who owned what had baffled Harry Sirpells and it baffled me. One of the companies involved was the Carlyle Corporation. Further investigation would require substantial payment in advance . . .

It all made a fine puzzle but there were several places I could make a start.

I looked up from the papers to scratch my head and discovered that Celeste was watching me intently.

'Is everything all right?' she asked.

I looked at her. As usual, it was difficult to read her expression. She'd spent a lot of time with Janine over the last week, long enough to have discussed my little peculiarities. I wondered if the question of the Sirpells file had come up and how long it would be before Janine learned that I was still investigating the links between the Carlyles and Devereaux-Almond.

'Everything's fine,' I said, suddenly deciding that I had quite enough on my plate without the Carlyles and Vince King. I needed a rest before I got involved with them again, if ever.

'Put this back where we found it, will you?'

Celeste smiled happily.

The next few weeks went by in a whirl.

I took on more staff. I had to, the work was rolling in. Janine's forecast was accurate; I didn't need an office of my own. The filing cabinets maintained by Celeste were quite sufficient. I spent most of my days out of the office interviewing bank managers and business consultants and accountants. It was strange but exhilarating, as if I'd begun a completely new existence with a fresh personality.

What I found really new and different was the atmosphere of success which seemed to trail behind me like a bad smell. Before, if I'd had an appointment with a bank manager I'd had to spend hours waiting to be seen and then usually sat with my eyes studying the carpet while I was lectured on the need for financial prudence. Now I was setting up salary structures and pension schemes and all was sweetness and light. It took some getting used to.

I met Ernie Cunliffe. Yes indeed, we had several intimate lunches at Nico Central rubbing shoulders with all the other movers and shakers on the Manchester scene. People I didn't know started giving me friendly nods or asking my opinion on matters I knew even less about. Ernie was timid, almost deferential. He kept recommending properties in the Wilmslow, Hale Barns area. 'Yes, Dave, there's some really nice developments at the moment in the three-hundred, four-hundred k range. I mean if you bought one as an investment you'd see a return on your capital in a very short time,' he said sagely.

'Right, I'll think about it,' I said, carefully pocketing the papers he gave me.

'You can't beat bricks and mortar as an investment, but have you thought about an annuity? The firm could let you have preferential terms, not that you're our employee or anything.'

I promised to consider it. I found the turn-around in my relationship with Ernie difficult to absorb. I still thought he was a rat but now, somehow, we were on the same side, both rats together. Ernie was nervous when other big insurance companies put work my way, as if his position now depended on keeping me sweet and available. I tried not to lose any sleep over it and as the weeks passed found myself more and more slipping into character as a man of business. It was so difficult not to. I met people in plush offices who were almost embarrassingly eager to share confidences. I occasionally listened to myself laughing and joking, swapping the latest buzz-words, grumbling about the quality of secretarial help. It was as if I'd suddenly become fluent in a new language. I knew things were getting serious when several of my new acquaintances offered to propose me for the Masons.

I suppose at the back of my mind I was relying on one person to bring me back to earth with a bump . . .

'Eeeh, David, you seem to have really landed on your feet here,' Paddy said when I showed him round the office.

I'd been waiting hopefully for the inevitable sarcastic comment to come but it didn't.

'You know, maybe I've been mistaken all these years,' he said with a sigh. 'Trying to push you into the police force, I mean. This is where the money is, no doubt about that. You'll never want for work while folk keep trying so hard to get something for nowt.'

I looked at him in sheer disbelief. Paddy misread the impression of shock on my face.

'Aye, lad,' he said. 'I don't mind admitting that you've got some smart folk working for you, some of them better qualified than they've got in the detective office over at Bootle Street, but then you pay your lot a damn sight more.'

Open-mouthed and at a loss for words I nodded agreement.

'That's it, you see, that's what's wrong with the Force these days . . . pay peanuts and you get monkeys, right?'

I looked at him, saddened to hear this heresy.

43

I think it was the non-censorious visit by my parent that set my old rebel juices flowing again. When he'd left the office I got Celeste to phone Bernadette Devereaux. Devereaux-Almond was not at home and had not been at home and he'd never been away for two months at a stretch before.

I sat at the small desk in the reception area, Celeste's old desk, that I used as my base. The office was very busy these days and it was difficult to think. Was Almond dead? The more I thought about it the more I realised that screaming murder at this stage would do more harm than good. The best way I could approach things was by taking up the cause of Vince King again. This time I would start at the top.

I took out a sheet of paper and began wrestling with my letter to the Right Honourable James McMahon, MP, Home Secretary. By the time I'd scrapped my first four efforts passers-by in the office began to take notice. It took me most of the day to hammer out this:

Dear Sir,
You will be aware of the case of Vincent King, presently serving life at Armley Jail for the murders of Dennis Musgrave and Frederick Fullalove in 1978.

I have been engaged by Mr King's family to investigate aspects of the case which give grounds for believing that his conviction was unsafe. No doubt as you were personally involved as Mr King's defence counsel you are well aware that his appeal on the grounds of material irregularity in the conduct of his trial was disallowed.

However I should inform you that I am in the process of collecting evidence that his solicitor Mr Morton V. E. Devereaux-Almond was not acting independently as the agent of Mr King but of a group

295

called North West Mercian Investments representing business interests in Manchester which were inimical to Mr King.

On enquiries being directed to Mr Devereaux-Almond as to the reasons why he, a solicitor never previously engaged in criminal work, took on the defence of Mr King, he not only took umbrage but appears to have left the country that same day without leaving a forwarding address.

I am certain that you will feel as I do that the double role played by Mr Devereaux-Almond constitutes sufficient grounds for you to refer the case to the Criminal Cases Review Commission.

Yours sincerely,
  D. Cunane.

I typed the letter on the firm's headed notepaper myself.

The reply which came in an amazingly short time of three weeks was brief and to the point.

Dear Mr Cunane,
The Secretary of State wishes me to inform you that he does not feel there are sufficient grounds for a referral of the case of Vincent King to the Criminal Cases Review Commission. He has considered the matter closely and feels that the question of Mr Devereaux-Almond's financial involvement with North West Mercian Investments for whatever reason has no relevance to the issues raised at Mr King's trial or subsequent appeal.

Yours sincerely,
J. K. Prendergast
Principal Private Secretary

This letter had scarcely hit my desk before Brendan Cullen arrived.

'Nice try, but no banana,' he said.

'What?' I said.

'Don't act stupid. You know what. You're not going to get your girlfriend's daddy out of prison so easily.'

'What girlfriend? What are you on about?'

Cullen looked round the crowded office. Celeste gave him a hostile stare from her corner. Two of my investigators swept in from the street and through to the back rooms. They looked at Cullen blankly. He could have been a Betterware salesman for all they knew or cared.

'God, you know I didn't believe it when they said you were expanding,' Cullen said with a shake of his head. 'It's like Piccadilly Station in here. How do you get any work done?'

'I manage when I'm not interrupted.'

'Well, tough! We need to talk. Come on, I'll buy you lunch or are you too prosperous now to be seen with a mere DCI?'

'Mr Cunane, do you want me to phone my cousin?' Celeste bawled from across the room. She'd recognised Cullen well enough.

'That's all right, love, I'm not arresting him,' Cullen said, turning to face her with his hands up in surrender. 'Not yet, anyway,' he said quietly when he turned back to look at me. The expression on his face was grim. He nodded towards the door.

I got my coat and we ended up at Pierre Victoire on Peter Street.

Brendan Cullen was well brought up. He waited until we were on the cheese course before he made any reference to the events surrounding my night with Marti.

'Are you still banging her? Marti, I mean,' he asked bluntly.

'I haven't seen her since that night.'

'Then do you mind telling me what the fuck you're doing sending bloody letters to the Home Secretary on behalf of her father?' he demanded fiercely. 'Didn't you hear me last time or were you too concussed? Marti's a definite suspect in both the Lou Olley and the Levy killings.'

'Bren, has anyone ever told you that you're boring?' I asked.

'Frequently,' he admitted with a trace of a grin.

'If Marti's such a major suspect why haven't you pulled her or anyone else in for questioning?'

'Because . . . because, we've nothing to go on,' he said in frustration. 'Trailing you down to London was really the last fling of Operation Calverley. The inquiry's being run on a care and maintenance basis now, a sergeant and two DCs.'

'Thanks,' I murmured. 'So you're not trying to trace the people who tried to kill me?'

'We found the van in Birmingham, another dead end. Anyway, why should we worry about people trying to do you in when you try so hard to kill yourself? Walking out of that hospital was a crazy stunt. I was sure somebody had lifted you until I saw that my coat was gone. You're an idiot.'

I made no reply to this. I didn't feel like apologising. Why should I? It's supposed to be a free country. They can't require you to stay in hospital if you don't want to . . . as long as you're not sectioned under the Mental Health Act, that is.

Brendan looked at me with an expression that said he thought I ought to be sectioned. Then he got to work on his Roquefort.

'Where is it anyway?' he said at last, jabbing his cheese knife at me for emphasis.

'What?' I said stupidly.

'My bloody raincoat.'

'I posted it to you, care of Bootle Street.'

'Great, it's probably in a bloody evidence box now,' he said gloomily. Then he started laughing. 'Christ, Dave, it's never dull when you're around. You really put the cat among the pigeons with that letter to the Home Office. I had the chief constable phoning me in the middle of the night demanding to know if this double-barrelled berk in Rochdale was the third victim in the Olley/Levy case.'

'And isn't he?'

'Of course not. He's just as entitled to go on his holidays as you are to walk out of hospitals.'

'He's dead, Bren. He's at the bottom of Morecambe Bay with an anchor round his legs.'

'That imagination of yours'll be the death of you, Dave,' he said with a grunt. He reached in his pocket and drew out a thick envelope which he threw down on the table. 'Go on, look,' he invited.

The envelope contained six postcards to Bernadette Devereaux all signed by 'Morton' and posted over the last two months. They were from holiday resorts in Florida; Miami, Fort Lauderdale, Palm Beach.

'There's nothing easier than to get someone to write out a load of postcards before you bump him off,' I said.

'Sticking to your story, are you?' Cullen said contemptuously.

'Yes. Look at the shaky, spidery writing. All done with the same pen too and nothing more specific than: "Having a nice time, wish you were here."'

'Yeah, well, even us blundering professionals thought of that. The writing matches other examples by Devereaux-Almond. His penmanship wasn't terrific.'

'No more than his legal work? How do you explain that he made so much money if someone wasn't paying him to keep quiet about King?'

'That is a mystery to me but then how do you explain that you're making so much money yourself? If everyone was rewarded on merit I'd be a millionaire and you'd be selling the *Big Issue.*'

'Ouch,' I muttered. 'But there was another thing. Someone brought his boat "Spirit of the Hills" back into Fleetwood Marina. You should be able to trace that man easily enough if he was a local.'

'Tell me something, Dave,' Cullen asked, 'why do you give a damn about Vince King or Morton V. E. Devereaux-Almond? I mean what's in it for you if you're not bonking pretty Miss Marti anymore?'

'I never was bonking Marti,' I said. It came out more vehemently than I intended. I believe I may even have blushed. Cullen raised his eyebrows in disbelief. 'Well, only that one time,' I admitted ruefully, 'and believe me I've paid a price for that.'

'But why, Dave? I mean letters to the Home Office, that's going it a bit, isn't it?'

'I think King is innocent and you still haven't convinced me that Almond's alive. Am I supposed to just ignore it when people I speak to disappear?'

'How very noble of you.'

'Don't sneer. You know you wouldn't be able to sleep comfortably if you thought King was innocent.'

'Dave, the man blew more safes than you've had hot dinners.'

'He's a little bastard and I wouldn't trust him further than I

299

could throw him, but the idea of him thinking that coppers like my dad were corrupt sticks in my throat. I believe that DI Mick Jones framed him.'

'Jones,' Cullen said with a weary shake of the head, 'he was a first-class shit, from what I've heard.' He began rapping the table with his finger. 'All right, there are one or two things . . . First, we haven't been able to trace whoever it was brought Almond's boat back and that's unusual. There's a small group of local men who do most of the crewing for the marina and the geezer on Almond's boat wasn't one of them. Secondly, I'm going to have a look at Jones on the q.t. The chief constable's desperate to avoid bad smells from any of Jones's cases, but that doesn't mean that I think your man King's got a cat in hell's chance of getting out unless he admits his crimes. Last of all, Dave, there's this. There *was* almost a third victim in the Olley/Levy killings and that was you! There's someone who's very determined that nothing should be raked up from what happened in 1978. Just watch your back.'

When Bren had gone a very strange thought went through my weary little head.

The chief constable was worried and Bren was doing a bit of sly checking. Did that mean that they suspected that it *was* coppers who killed Musgrave and Fullalove and that those bent coppers were still out there making sure that the case wasn't reopened? Then a still stranger thought crept into my mind. Bren Cullen had been on the spot when that white van hit me . . . Bren? Was it possible? I tried to shake off the idea but I couldn't.

44

The letter from Marti King arrived at my Chorlton flat.

Dear Dave,

I'm writing this to let you know that everything is going well for me now. I'm back with Charlie who's been taking aggression control therapy.

I enclose a cheque for the money you so kindly lent me in my hour of need and I can't thank you enough for everything that you did for me at that time.

I've seen my father at Armley Jail again. He asked after you and to tell you the truth I think he prefers you to Charlie. Anyway, that's all water under the bridge now. I've given up trying to persuade him to repent or recant or whatever it is he needs to do to get parole. He won't do it and it's no good trying. I know you did the best for him that anyone could have done but when a person doesn't want to help himself what can anyone do? Daddy's a hopeless case.

Relations with Brandon are very, very good and he's talked to me about you at length and hopes you are doing well and bear him no grudges. To show that there are no hard feelings he's asked me to invite you to the annual New Year party that the family put on at his home. (Please find the ticket enclosed.)

I hope you and your partner will be able to come. I'll be thrilled to see you both.

Best wishes,
    Marti Carlyle.

I studied the elaborately produced ticket: 'Mr Brandon Carlyle and his Family request the company of Mr David Cunane and partner at their New Year celebration . . . RSVP.'

In the spirit of the wary truce into which my relations with

301

Janine had settled I showed her the letter and the invitation expecting a scornful laugh. Janine and I had settled down to a period of mutual tolerance after the stresses our relationship had endured in the autumn. The offer of marriage which she'd made then hadn't been renewed but neither had it been retracted.

We were both incredibly busy, too busy to have much time for feuding. I was spending most of my days refereeing boundary disputes among my staff and it left me with little inclination for the old verbal sparring with Janine. Janine had found a child-minder to see Lloyd and Jenny back and forth from their private school in Didsbury, which relieved us both of a certain anxiety. Janine's threats of a move from Chorlton also appeared to have been shelved. Both Jenny and Lloyd were enjoying school and it seemed a shame to uproot them. So things were going on more or less as they had been. There had been the occasional letter from Henry Talbot about his offspring, but he hadn't taken it further.

'So little Miss Marti's landed back in the bosom of her family,' Janine said triumphantly when she read the letter. 'What did I tell you? A woman like that will never give up a wealthy husband like Charlie Carlyle until she finds someone equally wealthy, and let's face it, flower, even with your current affluence you're never going to fill that bill.'

'Thanks,' I muttered.

'No really, Dave, all she ever wanted was to use you to work Charlie up into a fit of jealousy, and look how keen she is to get dear old Daddy out of the calaboose? It looks like he's had his chips now that she's all right again.'

'I take it that I should rip this ticket up?' I asked.

'No fear, we're going. I wouldn't miss this for anything.'

'I'm not going if you're going to make a scene.'

'Don't flatter yourself, Dave. Why would I make a scene? Women fighting over a man, that belongs to the Middle Ages. I'm a journalist, and half the people worth knowing in Cheshire and Manchester will be at this bash. This chance is too good to miss.'

'What chance?'

'Dave, just because your business has taken off it doesn't

mean that I'm going to be content to stay a journalist on a local paper for the rest of my life. I have to meet the people who count, and so do you.'

I looked at her in surprise. I knew she was ambitious, but she'd only ever discussed the so-called 'Cheshire Set' in terms of the utmost contempt, and in her articles for the paper she maintained a radical, populist tone when she wasn't preaching strident feminism.

'Dave, get real!' she ordered.

'Yeah, real is as real does,' I said, retreating to my own flat to send the reply to Brandon Carlyle.

Life is never perfect. Not having to worry about where the next pound was coming from had robbed life of a certain flavour, and now Janine was showing signs of becoming 'adult' and 'realistic'. I wasn't sure that I liked the change, but my recent close brush with death had induced a mood of acceptance. I scribbled hasty replies to the invite and to Marti's letter.

Christmas came and went in a blur, and on a very wet New Year's Eve I found myself driving down the Cheshire lanes past Nantwich towards Brandon Carlyle's mansion. South Pork was hard to miss: a lot of other traffic was heading in the same direction and crowds of onlookers were waiting at the gates. They peered into our car but turned away when they saw that we weren't celebs or footballers. I flashed my ticket at the uniformed security man and he waved us on. The black and gold gates slid open.

'The gates of hell,' I muttered, 'suitably wide and open.'

Janine suppressed a laugh, but I was more than half serious.

'What have you got us into?' I said to her. 'This is worse than Blackpool Illuminations.' All the garden 'features' – busty Greek maidens, industrial-sized barbecue areas, water works and tinkling little dells – were lit up like a fairground. The glaring white lights and the lashing rain created a weird effect in the dismal night.

'Lighten up, Dave,' she said crisply. 'This is the place to be. I can't wait to get in. Think of the column inches.'

'Lighten up,' I echoed sourly. 'Is that what you've been doing all week?' Janine had spent the days after Christmas in

303

a frenzy of preparation – skin, hair and dress, all had had a complete and expensive makeover. 'It's only a New Year's party at the Carlyles, not a command performance at Buck House.'

'You sound more and more like your father with every day that passes,' she countered, proving that she knew how to wound.

We joined the queue of cars heading for the mansion and proceeded slowly along the drive. Janine was unable to resist the temptation to snatch her pocket recorder out of her bag and begin making a few notes. It was certainly worth it. The pillared portico alone demanded a paragraph – few new homes for the wealthy in this part of the world are complete without a pillar or two, but this place had them in spades. There were even free-standing pillars lining the drive. All the mansion lacked was a massive neon sign on the roof saying 'FABULOUSLY WEALTHY'. I had to admit that Brandon Carlyle was no hypocrite. He wanted everyone to know that he was rich. There was no half-apologetic cringe from him, no fake olde worlde reticence.

When we arrived we found the entire coaching and playing staff of the Pendlebury Piledrivers standing in the brilliantly lit entrance courtyard like slabs of rock from Stonehenge. Each man was wearing a grey suit. The fountain was blasting away and iridescent spray was being blown towards the impassive sportsmen who doggedly stood their ground. I wondered if they were drugged. The sight of them irritated me intensely.

When I pulled up by the portico one of the slabs stepped forward for the car keys. His smile revealed a lack of front teeth. He had the sort of shoulders they invented wide-screen TV for.

'Still in a Mondeo, Cunane?' Charlie Carlyle said. He was standing under the pillared entrance of the mansion greeting guests as they detached themselves from their cars. It was true enough that most of the other cars were in the luxury class. There was an edge of contempt in Charlie's voice. 'I'd have thought you could have gone a bit more upmarket.'

'At least it's mine,' I said aggressively. I found that the desire to bust his fat lip was as strong as ever. Janine gripped my arm fiercely and tried to steer me away. I resisted the firm tug she gave me. 'Tell me, Charlie, did your dad get a job-lot on the suits for his livestock?' I asked, gesturing towards the ranked rugby league players.

A middle-aged couple pushed up behind us, waiting to be greeted by the son and heir. The man coughed impatiently.

'Why? Do you want one?' Charlie asked. 'No deal, I'm afraid, but I think the old man could have a word with a car dealer if you were thinking of something classier than an old Ford.'

'Well, I wouldn't have to ask my daddy for a sub to buy it,' I gibed.

Charlie's face darkened and he stepped forward.

'It's time somebody put some manners on you, Cunane,' he snarled.

'Are you volunteering?' I asked. 'Or are you only tough with women?'

This time I'd pressed the right button. Charlie pushed against me with his face glowing like a red stop-sign and I barged back at him. Janine gasped. It looked like the party was over.

'Here, what's all this?' the middle-aged man behind me asked in a querulous tone. He stepped between us, rain glinting on his horn-rimmed specs. A few feet away the rugby squad began stirring.

'What's it to you, Jack?' I asked the horn-rimmed individual.

'I'm the chief constable of Cheshire.'

At that precise instant there was a detonation of uncontrolled laughter that stopped us all in our tracks. Marti stepped forward. 'You two boys! What are we going to do with them?' she said to Janine, and then kissed my partner as if she was a long-lost sister. Marti linked herself to Janine and me and led us into the house.

'Just a bit of fun, an old friend,' Charlie explained to the policeman, as Marti drew us away into the entrance hall. There were crowds of people in the atrium standing about in that awkward way people do before booze is flowing freely. Janine and I both snatched a drink from the waiter as Marti whisked us past. Marti declined the offer herself, sharing a knowing smile with me. I drained my glass, heedless whether it was expensive champagne or cherryade. I looked Marti firmly in the eye. She stared back unflinchingly. She was wearing a red balldress of very economical design. On a starlet on the beach at Cannes it would have been described as daring. In this domestic setting it looked as if she'd come in her skimpiest underwear. I could feel pressure from my partner's fingers as Marti's breasts almost bobbled loose from their flimsy restraints barely a foot from my nose. They were like a pair of frisky Shetland ponies.

'Isn't he naughty?' Marti said to Janine, who clenched her teeth in reply. 'But wouldn't you rather have him as he is than like a neutered tomcat? Speaking of useless animals, come and meet my in-laws.'

Janine seemed to be struck dumb. The best she could manage was an awkward little squeak of agreement as we followed Marti. I wasn't overflowing with sympathy.

Taking my eyes off Marti, I scanned the room. Familiar faces of people who were completely unknown to me met my glance on every side: soap stars, footballers, weather bimbos, politicians beaming at everyone, and lots of people I'd never seen before. It was a big room. You could have held a basketball game in there and got quite a few spectators in as well. In one corner, a chamber orchestra was gallantly flogging polite music out of their instruments. There was a bar along the whole of one wall with six uniformed staff behind it slinging out drinks as fast as the thirsty guests could collect them. It resembled a scene from the Wild West where some lucky prospector was standing drinks for the whole town. In its usual contrary way, my thirst disappeared. Brandon Carlyle had told me that I was snotty nosed the last time I was here. He was right. I scanned the heaving mob with contempt. This was no charity do. All these good folk were here for what they could grab.

The in-laws, that is the Carlyle brothers and sisters, all nine of them, seemed a pretty nondescript bunch, all variations on the same theme as Charlie – flabby faces, blobby noses. Some were fatter, some smaller (but none taller) and some of the men had thinner hair. Their ordinariness came as a shock after Marti's earlier description. Assorted wives and husbands were present, all wearing an odd fixed expression not so much of boredom as of expectation. Possibly they all felt that marrying a Carlyle entitled them to some form of compensation.

Marti introduced me as the son of an old acquaintance of their father's and they favoured us with weak smiles but no curiosity as to who their daddy's old mate was. Thinking about their father, I realised that this was probably down to early training, not ignorance. While shaking hands I felt a sudden desire that the earth would open and swallow me. What was I doing here when I could be somewhere else? The Pimpernel staff were having a New Year's party in a club. I could have been with them. I should have been with them.

The way it was, I felt like a prize animal at a cattle show as Marti led us to each of her in-laws in turn. She was expert at introduction and I soon found myself discussing the prospects of the Pendlebury Piledrivers with Bungalow. He didn't seem especially thick or any more interested in rugby league than I was, and he had no trouble stringing a polite sentence or two together. I couldn't help glancing at his shoes. They didn't have any laces. The wives and sisters, not at all the ugly monsters that Marti had led me to expect, pressed forward in ranked battalions and soon Janine's ears were buzzing as she downloaded information.

Other couples in the room looked at us enviously as we seemed to be monopolising the company of the favoured family. Again, I got a sensation of unreality as heady and sudden as a narcotic rush. Why should people feel excluded because they couldn't chat with Brandon Carlyle's offspring? I'd have paid good money to be somewhere else. The room was crammed with party decorations, masses of cheap tinsel put up by some firm and not out of place in that setting. There was nothing in the room more than a couple of years old. Here and there along the ceiling line, on the overarching dome and behind ornaments and fixtures I caught a glint of reflected light. CCTV cameras were recording the scene for posterity.

Maybe Bungalow was as thick as Marti had claimed. Certainly his attention span wasn't what you'd call long, but perhaps that was just me being boring. He informed me in vague terms that there was a jazz group in the gym and a famous Manchester boy-band in the covered swimming pool.

I was exchanging further inanities with him, saying whatever came off the top of my head and looking round for more drink, when someone touched my sleeve.

'I'm so glad you could come,' Brandon said. He reached round and took hold of my hand. He didn't shake it, just took it and led me away from the noisy female crowd. He looked neither right nor left at any of his offspring. The multitude parted in front of him and we seemed to be in a little island of quiet. Janine looked at me and raised her eyes pleadingly but she was attached to the little group of Carlyle females, now chattering about children and the price of eggs, and stood by helplessly as Brandon removed me.

As I left the main reception area I took a backward glance, hoping to spot my partner. Instead my eyes fleetingly met those of Insull Perriss. He looked startled to see me and then his expression contorted, whether with hatred or fear I couldn't tell at that distance.

'Come through here,' Carlyle invited, leading me to a side door. 'I need a chat with you and you're a hard man to pin down.'

'You should have no trouble pinning anyone down with all these slabs from the Piledrivers here,' I said.

'Never stop making jokes, eh?'

'Not really, I'm not feeling very humorous.'

'Have you had a good year? I'm told you're prospering.'

'So-so,' I agreed grudgingly.

Turning his back on me, Brandon punched numbers on a security pad by another door, made of reinforced steel. Bolts shot back and he ushered me through.

'I come here when I want real privacy,' he said roguishly. The room was dominated by a series of garishly coloured boxes which I recognised as an old-fashioned mainframe computer. It took up at least half of the room. 'That's a souvenir,' he explained, 'like the ice-cream cart downstairs.'

'That's not, though, is it?' I said, pointing to the mass of screens set along the opposite wall. I watched fascinated for a moment. Janine was on one screen. On another I could see the rapidly receding back of Insull Perriss. He was attempting to make a stealthy exit through the French windows.

Following my glance Brandon touched the controls and we got a close-up of Perriss's fat neck. A fold of flesh hung over the businessman's collar. His hair was cut in a neat straight line. I could hear the sounds of his struggle with the door lock.

'Do you know him well?' I muttered.

'A business acquaintance. He seems to want fresh air.'

'Perhaps he's sick.'

Carlyle touched a button and on various screens Pendlebury Piledrivers all touched their ear-pieces at the same time.

'Let him go,' I said.

Turning to me, Carlyle gave an elaborate shrug – hands, arms, whole body in motion.

'It's a free country,' he murmured, chuckling as he turned back to his screens. This time he put a finger on a large touch screen showing a plan view of the ground floor. The window that Perriss was by now attacking frantically sprang open. A light began flashing on the monitor. 'I was only opening the door so he could get out,' he explained. 'It's all controlled from here. I shall have to tell the stewards to close it and escort him off the premises if he wants to leave. You know, I've got the kit here to keep a track on everybody.'

He spoke into a mike and Piledrivers began moving. If only their on-field manoeuvres were as well co-ordinated.

'Nice way to run a party,' I commented.

'Ha! I detect a note of scorn,' Carlyle said with a grin. 'Security, that's what this is. You can't do anything without security these days. You should know that. No one can get within five hundred yards of this house without being electronically scanned. I have important people here tonight . . .'

'I saw the chief constable.'

'He's small fry . . . the local head bobby. I said important people.'

'Nice to know where one is on the pecking order.'

'Oh, stop being the detective for once, Mr Cunane. Can I call you David?'

309

'Call me Shit-for-brains if you want, because that's what I must be.'

'You know why I like you? Your refusal to be impressed is impressive.'

'I'm deeply touched.'

'David, I think it's time you and I got on the same side. Good and evil, all that tiresome old stuff – nobody goes for that any more.'

'Don't they?'

'No! Look, sonny, they've sent ships into space. There's nothing up there. No heaven. When did you last go to church? Churches are empty. People want what they can see and touch.'

He flicked his hand towards the screens.

'Let me show you.'

He sat at the console and began working the controls again like an organist at a Wurlitzer.

'There you are!' he said triumphantly. A screen showed a couple copulating vigorously. The man's shiny bald head reflected the light into the camera as Carlyle zoomed in for a close-up.

'Stop it,' I muttered. The screen showed the woman's face. Carlyle switched to another screen showing a man snorting a line of coke in a cloakroom.

'No, this is reality. If you can't fuck it, or see it, or eat it, or smoke it, or put it up your nose, then it doesn't exist. Those two know what life's about.'

'I thought you were a family man?'

'I am! Marti's back with her husband – what a blessing, eh? You're doing well in your business. I'm doing well and my children seem to have settled their differences. This is a time of goodwill.'

'Do you include Clyde Harrow in your goodwill? I heard he's been declared bankrupt.'

'A foolish man; but forget him – your future, that's what you should be thinking about.'

'Mr Carlyle . . .'

'Brandon to you, David.'

'I only came tonight because my partner thinks she's going

310

to get a good story out of this party.'

'You know, I like you, David. You don't beat about the bush. Straight from the shoulder, eh? Shall we see what she's up to?'

He fiddled with his controls again and picked out Janine. She was speaking to one of the soap stars. Carlyle zoomed in on her hands. As we watched, Janine slipped her hand into her bag and switched on her tape recorder.

'Ha!' Carlyle cackled. 'That'll do her no good. It'll be wiped electronically before she leaves. I can fix up an interview for her, if you like.'

'*Brandon*,' I said scornfully, 'it's fine by me if you want to stop beating about the bush. Why did you invite us here? The last time I was here, you made all kinds of bloodcurdling threats.'

'Be fair! That was when you were poking your nose into things that didn't concern you. We've all come on a bit since then. Marti's settled down at last, and even that mad father of hers seems to accept that he's not going to walk from prison till he admits his crimes.'

'Mr Carlyle, or should I say Colonna, there are still several outstanding crimes unsolved, or had you forgotten?'

'Oh, so that's it? The dreaded Mafia, eh? I'm proud of my Italian heritage and for your information my family doesn't come from Sicily. My grandfather and a friend walked here from Italy in 1891, right across Switzerland and France, they came. They were both good Catholics who didn't want to serve in the King of Italy's anticlerical army. Grandfather came from a small village near Genoa and I still have relatives there. I'll tell you another thing. When they reached Manchester they found lots of Irish bullies waiting to oppress them but my grandfather wouldn't let anyone get the better of him.'

'Meaning what?'

'Meaning that it's you and your father who're the ones keeping up a vendetta, not me. You wouldn't take a reward for not dropping me in it over poor Sam's death. I respect you for that, but won't you at least shake hands and let bygones be bygones?'

It seemed churlish to keep my hand behind my back. I was in his house after all.

311

'If you sup with the Devil you need a long spoon, eh?' he joked, punching my arm playfully. 'Cautious man!' Carlyle's grip was surprisingly firm. I wondered just how soon he would turn over the reins to Charlie and Marti. They might be in for a long wait. He looked full of vitality, set for a telegram from the Queen.

'You know that film? *The Godfather?* I've cursed it many a time, but there's just one true thing in it. In my world you never know where your enemy is coming from. The guy that smiles and says he's your friend, he's the one you've got to look out for. That's why I like you. You scowl at me when you shake hands.'

'So it's just a coincidence, you being a Colonna?'

'Hell! There's a guy here tonight called Capone,' he said with a laugh. 'Now Scarface Al wasn't a fictional creation. Do you think I should check this possible relative out for a tommy-gun?'

The way he put it, my suspicions seemed crazy. Still, these things are sent to warn us, as my granny used to say. I tried to stop scowling.

'Your grandfather went into the ice-cream business, did he?'

'So what?'

'Mine was a copper.'

'How did I guess that?' he asked with a smile. 'For us it was ice cream, barrel organs or working in the mill. We've come a long way, and it hasn't been easy in this country. My own dear uncle was killed by the British government, murdered really.'

'That was Antonio, was it?'

Carlyle looked at me with narrowed eyes.

'Been doing some research, have you?'

'A little,' I agreed.

'So you know that my uncle and my father were interned during the last war. Marched off at a moment's notice, they were, leaving me and my mother with not a penny between us. They weren't dragged off to a death camp, I'll admit, but don't let anyone tell you that it was only the Germans who rounded up innocent people in the dead of night. Yes, a great big fat Irish copper came and banged at our door at four a.m.'

312

'Nothing to do with me,' I said.

Carlyle looked at me with an expression of burning anger in his face. He waited for me to contradict him again and when I didn't he gave a satisfied little nod and went on.

'Uncle Antonio was unlucky. He and Dad were sent to be interned in Canada on board the *Arandora Star*. It was sunk by the Germans in the Atlantic and Antonio was among those who drowned. More than six hundred lives were lost out of fifteen hundred on board. Don't hear much about that these days, do you? Do you think they let my dad go home when they pulled him from the sea half choked to death with oil? No, not they! They shipped him back to the Isle of Man and kept him there till the end of the war, which was almost two years after Italy had surrendered. Nice way to treat people who'd only ever worked their guts out trying to earn an honest living, wasn't it?'

I shook my head. Carlyle seemed intent on his story. His face coloured with remembered fury. I think he forgot it was me and not Winston Churchill that he was talking to. He radiated a sense of grievance.

'And another thing! You won't believe this! I got my call-up papers in 1944. Yes, I was required by His Majesty to leave my mother on her own with spiteful neighbours howling for bombs to be poured down on Italy and go off to defend the people who had my father under lock and key. That was fair, wasn't it?'

I shook my head, frightened to say anything in case his fury against Anglo-Saxon and Irish bullies got the better of him.

'When they finally let him and the other very dangerous Italian ice-cream sellers go, my dad got sick of listening to planks telling jokes about the reverse gears on Italian tanks and he changed our name. Don't you think he earned that right?'

'I'm sure he did, but that's not the whole story, is it?'

'What do you mean?'

'You didn't get to where you are now on the proceeds of ice cream.'

'Nice to see that your father's still as garrulous as ever. I suppose he told you that I made my money from crime?'

313

I shrugged.

'I made my money with what I've got up here,' he said, proudly tapping his forehead and smiling.

'There was something else though, wasn't there? Vince King knows something, or why else was he able to make you rescue Marti from that hell hole she was in?' I was watching him closely and his expression changed from geniality to something far more predatory. His eyes were focused on the mainframe computer, not on me. I looked at it with greater interest.

It was an ICL 2966, which meant nothing to me. It consisted of four large separate cabinets, each about six foot high and three foot wide. They were an ugly orange colour. Behind those cabinets were two further cabinets, one with a tape machine and one with a disk drive. All the cabinets stood on a raised dais, and thick cabling ran from under this to a conduit and fuse box on the wall. This was no souvenir. It was fully functional.

'Nothing will stop you shoving your nose where it's not wanted, will it?' he said bitterly. 'What's your father told you about me and King?'

'My father's told me nothing. You see, I broke with the family tradition. I'm not a policeman and he's not at liberty to tell me what he thinks.'

Carlyle laughed at this. There was nothing genial about his laugh this time.

'That's very lucky for you both then. See that you remain in ignorance,' he said, leading me to the door.

45

I was hardly out of Brandon's fortified den before Marti linked her arm into mine. This time Janine was not around to make it a threesome.

'Caught you!' she said triumphantly.

'I don't think so,' I said, unlinking my arm firmly.

'I see. It's like that, is it? I thought with you accepting the invitation . . .'

'That I was ready for a little more recreational sex? And don't give me that guff about you only ever having made love to Charlie boy.'

'All bitter and twisted, aren't you?' she asked with a wide smile. 'I only came looking for you to make sure you don't miss Charlie's fireworks. There aren't any windows in Brandon's room, and by the way, do you realise how highly honoured you are?'

'No.'

'Brandon never lets any of the family in that room.'

'Great.'

'Come on, Dave. We weren't so bad together, were we?'

'No, not so bad. I just love being used, and while we're at it, was it your idea to send that van to kill me after our night of passion?'

'Don't be disgusting. You've got a nasty puritanical streak in you, Dave Cunane. To hear you talk anyone would think I forced myself on you, and as for wanting to kill you, the fact that I've invited you here shows that that's rubbish.'

'Does it? If I've learned one thing it's that normal rules don't apply when you're around. I ought to send you a bill for damages. Working for you almost proved to be the most expensive mistake I've ever made.'

'Has the dragon-lady been stamping her tiny foot then? Is that what this phoney rage is all about?'

'Leave Janine alone . . .'

'No, why don't you? Anyone can see she's got her claws into you. You don't need her . . .'

'I'll decide that.'

With Marti nothing was ever predictable. She turned and blocked my path out of the narrow corridor and then, focusing those green eyes of hers on me, she draped her arms round me. I struggled to avoid a response . . .

'You still fancy me, don't you?' she said.

'Who's forcing herself on someone now?'

'You want me, Dave. I can tell. I could see it in your face as soon as you laid eyes on me. Janine's a cold fish. She doesn't need you or any man.'

'You would know, would you?' I asked scornfully.

'I know her sort. She only wants you around as a convenience. She'll never let you go now she's got you where she wants you.'

'Funny, Janine said something very similar about you never leaving Charlie and it looks like she was right.'

'You're a fool, aren't you? But I'm not. I'm supposed to leave Charlie, am I? And give up a fortune running into hundreds of millions, a fortune that I've as much right to as any of Brandon's children, if not more.'

'So what is it, Marti? Money or love?'

'Grow up, Dave, you sound like Barbara Cartland. If we play our cards right for a few more months we can have both. You've done well so far, dropping all that stuff about getting Dad out of prison. That made Brandon nervous, but he really likes you, and do you know why? Most of the people he meets try to flatter him. Even his own sons and daughters, they lay it on with a trowel, but you just say what you think. He likes that.'

'I take it that all this recent affection for your in-laws is purely temporary then?'

She tossed her head back and gave that laugh of hers. The echo had hardly died away before Charlie put his head round the door leading from the main reception area.

'What are you doing in here, you little shit?' he shouted at me. Then like a big stupid animal he stared at Marti and took in the situation. She had her arm linked into mine again and was making no move to unclinch. 'You, you bitch!' he roared at her. 'Up to your old tricks, are you?'

Without another word he charged at us.

'Charlie!' a high-pitched voice shrieked from behind me. It was the old man.

Fortunately Charlie's rage disabled him. He swung a blow at me and I ducked, pulling Marti down with me.

'Will you let me go!' I shouted at her. Charlie came close and attempted to wrestle me to the floor. I fended him off. It was like something out of a primary school playground. I'd had enough. I pushed Marti at him and she slowed his progress. He wrapped his arm round her and attempted to throw her in the direction of Brandon. Marti was laughing wildly. She landed on her behind in front of the old man.

'Charlie! Charlie!' Brandon yelled. 'Stop it! It's not what you think. I saw the whole thing.'

Charlie was well past reasoning with. He hurled himself at me. Part of his aggression must have been fuelled by drink, because although willing to strangle me, he wasn't capable. I sidestepped and left my foot in his path. He went down like a forest giant. On the way his head slammed into the wall. He hit the carpeted floor, bounced, and then rolled over, groaning and clutching his head. His suit was split up the back.

My heart was in my mouth. This was just what I needed . . . an assault charge with the Chief Constable of Cheshire on the premises and half the local press outside with their ears burning for a juicy story. I may have groaned a little myself.

'It looks like Charlie's had his fireworks display for this year!' Marti said, laughing as she hauled herself to her feet and leaning on her father-in-law. For all the cover the clothes she was wearing gave her she might as well have been stark naked. I looked at her in dismay. She smiled, licked her lips and then turned to Brandon. 'Got the old *Candid Camera* tapes running, have you?' she asked. He gently pushed her away, shook his head and went to his son, who was now attempting to sit up, cradling his head and mouthing a stream of curses.

317

'Shut up, Charlie!' he ordered in a voice as cold and cutting as a March gale. 'Is this what I sent you to Ampleforth for?' The sharp tone must have got through because Charlie stopped his whimpering for a moment and looked up at his father. His eyes were glazed over.

'Mr Cunane, David,' Brandon continued. 'Please accept my apologies. You've behaved like a gentleman which is a hell of a lot more than I can say for my expensively educated son.'

I had the presence of mind to nod my head. Brandon seemed to have a dimmer view of his son than I had. Usually when some maladroit hits the deck as a result of my ministrations I'm immediately surrounded by a chorus of his relatives baying for blood and compensation. Brandon's attitude made a refreshing change, but I didn't intend to linger and outstay my welcome. I turned to go.

'Stay a moment and help me,' Brandon pleaded in a soft voice. I turned. Brandon cut a dignified figure in his dark Savile Row suit, as he indicated his son with an economical gesture. He seemed to be suggesting that the mess on the floor, Charlie, was an affliction of nature. I felt sympathetic. Brandon looked fragile, not exactly King Lear naked on the stormy heath as Clyde Harrow would have put it, but definitely in need of assistance. 'I don't want his brothers to see him like this. God knows, there's already enough spite flying round in this family to fuel a Balkan War without them seeing him like this, fool that he is.'

He sighed.

'You, woman, help him,' he said, turning to Marti as I obediently grabbed Charlie by the shoulders. She suppressed a snigger and gave me a hand in getting her half-stunned husband to his feet. Between us we dragged and carried him into Brandon's bedroom, which was next to his computer room but lacked the elaborate electronic locks that secured that place. Charlie moaned again when we dropped him on the bed.

'You'll live,' Marti said unsympathetically. She wrapped ice from a small fridge in a towel and dumped it on Charlie's head. He winced. 'He's not damaged,' she said to Brandon. 'His skull's far too thick for that.'

'You see what I have to put up with,' Brandon said to me in a low voice. 'What's going to become of this family when I'm out of the picture? I wish I'd met your mother before your father did,' he confided, patting my arm.

'What!' Marti said with a barely suppressed shriek of her mad laughter. 'You wish Dave was your son?'

Brandon gave an expressive sigh and held his arms up in a gesture of dismay. 'God knows,' he muttered, 'he couldn't be any worse than the collection I've got.'

Marti gave me a knowing look. I hurriedly let myself out of the room before Brandon renewed his offer to alter my paternity.

46

'Where have you been?' Janine gasped when I rejoined the main party. My suit was slightly disarrayed. 'You've been having it off with that tramp, haven't you?' she demanded. 'I saw her sneaking out after the old man took you away.' The throng of Carlyles had dispersed and she was sitting on the arm of a sofa with an indefinable expression on her face.

'You could say that,' I said with a laugh, straightening my collar and smoothing my hair back. Looking round the room I was having trouble adjusting to how normal the scene was. 'I've certainly just bedded someone, but it was Charlie Carlyle, not Marti.'

'Dave!'

'He came looking for trouble but he got a bit more than he bargained for,' I said smugly. Stupidly enough, I was feeling quite satisfied with myself.

'Had we better get out before they come for us?' she asked, looking round the room as if the Piledrivers were suddenly about to converge on us.

'It's all right, Brandon saw the whole thing and he blames Charlie,' I told her.

'And I suppose that hooker had nothing to do with it?'

'What hooker?'

'You know who I mean.'

'Marti was there,' I admitted, 'but there was nothing going on. Ask the old man if you want.'

Janine looked distracted, as if she was trying to work something out. 'Do you think he'd give me an interview?' she asked eventually. 'I could do an extended profile on him.'

'He might if I ask. He looks on me as a son.'

'Don't be funny, Dave!' she said hotly.

320

I laughed.

We circulated among the other guests for the next hour. I looked round for Insull Perriss but there was no sign of him. True to my craft for once, I didn't ask after him. It was moderately interesting to watch Janine ply her trade. She backed a Swedish footballer, a central defender, and his pregnant girlfriend up against a wall. He was possibly the most famous Scandinavian to hit these parts since they named the ford at Knutsford after Knut but the girl was just a local hopeful. Janine cajoled and coaxed details of their love life out of them using methods that would have turned my father's hair white if they'd crossed his mind back in the days of Judges' Rules. Apart from giving other guests the third degree as opportunity offered, there was little to do. I was depressingly sober. We both sampled the lucky prize draws that were on offer but neither of us won. The next person to try it after me plucked out a Rolex.

'I hope that's not bent,' I said sarcastically as the guest, a TV producer I recognised from the company box at Old Trafford, enthusiastically ripped the paper off his gift. He grimaced and then carefully put the watch away in an inside pocket.

'Jazz in the gym or pop in the pool?' I said to Janine.

'Let's stay here,' she said.

We'd worked our way through the big reception hall and into a large room which opened onto the fields at the back of the house when Janine suddenly gave a little shriek of fright.

'Dave! Look who's over there,' she said urgently.

'Who?' I asked, looking at the tall, seemingly gormless individual she was indicating.

'It's him . . . it's Henry!'

I looked again. Henry Talbot was half turned away from us talking to a short, middle-aged woman with very flabby upper arms and a low-cut blue evening dress. He had a shock of greying dark hair hanging over his forehead, a scrawny neck with a prominent Adam's apple and a long, thin nose like the prow of a ship, but his most striking feature was his lips. They were full and pendulous and gave his face an ugly cast. I could see no resemblance between him and either Jenny or Lloyd.

321

Stooping over the plump lady to catch her remarks above the din of conversation, he resembled a vulture.

'Let's go,' Janine whispered, but, in the mysterious way that a shout doesn't attract attention in a crowded room while a whisper does, Henry heard her. He turned and gave a gesture of recognition. At the same time uniformed caterers came to summon us to the buffet.

'He's seen us,' Janine moaned.

'Do you want me to go?' I asked.

'Stay!' she snapped. 'For God's sake, you can be infuriating at times, Dave. Why should I want you to go?'

I stayed and we both watched Talbot grease his way towards us with a fixed smile on his oily mug. He didn't appear to be with anyone. There were people hurriedly moving past us to get at the food.

'Be civilised,' Janine warned as she struggled to compose her face into a smile.

'Aren't I always?' I said.

Then Talbot was on us. Clearly he didn't have polite chit-chat on his mind, pushing up close to us, closer than either of us was comfortable with.

'Who's looking after my children?' he demanded, the forced smile never leaving his face.

Janine flared up, but I spoke first. 'What's it to you? It's late in the day for you to come the concerned father, isn't it?'

'Oh, it speaks, does it?' he asked Janine cheekily, ignoring me. 'Perhaps you'd like to tell it to mind its own business.' He deliberately loomed over Janine, dominating her, almost stepping on her feet. Janine was no wilting plant. She put her hand on his chest and pushed.

'Get away from me!' she gasped. For a second Talbot seemed ready to resist as she thrust him back. Although the smile never left his face there was a suggestion of malevolence about him which was far more compelling than anything poor Charlie Carlyle had managed. A wrestling match among the vol-au-vents appeared to be imminent.

I stepped into the breach.

'Keep your distance,' I growled.

People were pressing all around us, attention completely

focused on the magnificent spread which the caterers had just revealed by sliding open a partition wall. None of them picked up on our unfolding little drama.

'Please do oblige me by smashing my face in,' Talbot said with a sneer. He had the fruity accent typical of expatriate Brits who make their living in the States by amusing the Yanks with their quaint mannerisms. 'I know you have a talent for violence and I'm sure the courts would be delighted to hear all about it.'

'Would they?' I muttered. 'Then we'll have to give them something to chew on, won't we?'

Janine pulled me back. 'Come away, Dave, he's up to something.' Under her make-up Janine's face had turned dead-white and she seemed to be struggling for breath.

'That's right, Jannie,' Talbot smirked. 'I'm up to something, as you so artlessly put it. I'm going to see if an English court will recognise that I'm a more responsible person to bring up two children than a feminist freak and her criminal boyfriend.' There was a depth of hatred in his words which shocked and frightened me more than the actual message. The big smile was still there, and there was something reptilian about the way those fleshy, rubbery lips folded over the prominent, unnaturally white teeth – teeth like a display of porcelain in a china shop window, just waiting to be smashed. Then, before either of us could reply, Talbot turned and joined the mass attack on the food.

I pulled Janine back. She was limp.

'He's bluffing,' I said confidently.

'I don't think so,' she said grimly. 'He's got very good connections in the legal profession. His grandfather was the Lord Advocate of Scotland and his father's a High Court judge in England who only retired this year. When Henry makes a threat he usually carries it out. I should know. He beat me black and blue often enough.'

'That's it!' I said. I could feel my neck swelling with anger. 'You never told me he'd hit you. It's time somebody gave bloody Henry a few lumps of his own.'

'Stop it, Dave. That's just what he wants.'

'But he hit you. You let him!'

'I didn't tell you before because I knew you'd be like this.'

'Too right, I am. I'll twist his ugly head off his shoulders.'

Janine smiled at me. 'You mean well, but though I'm tempted to let you try, violence would only make things worse. I'm not anybody's "little woman". I don't need you to fight my battles.'

I started to laugh. I know that I'm mad, but the anger drained away as swiftly as it had flooded over me. Maybe I'd caught something off Marti, but my laugh was almost a fair match for hers.

'Dave!' Janine whispered. 'People are looking.'

They were. Talbot turned round to stare. I gave him a mock salute and a derisive smile. He quickly turned away with an angry frown on his face.

'He called you Jannie. Please, Ms White, can I call you Jannie?'

'No thanks,' she murmured. 'Daft, silly Jannie lived in another time and another place.' She kissed me. 'I'd much rather be Mrs Cunane than that selfish, stupid, in-bred twit's Jannie!'

There didn't seem to be much for me to say. It didn't take a genius to unpick Janine's elliptical phrase. I was practised at it. As usual, Janine hadn't said that she actually *wanted* to be Mrs Cunane, in a right-now, let's name the date sort of way; just that such a state was preferable to life with wife-beating Henry. My only consolation was that little word *much*.

Food was the last thought on my mind or on Janine's, but we stood for a moment watching the battle for sustenance. I've been in soup kitchens where the starving homeless showed more manners than some of Brandon Carlyle's guests. There may have been a slightly censorious expression on my normally bland and pleasing features as I scanned the scene. The thought of Brandon Carlyle recording every tiny detail was obscene. I spotted the chief constable greedily struggling to overload his plate with quail's eggs and venison. He returned my glance with a beady-eyed glare and then turned back to the buffet. There was enough there to claim anyone's attention: venison, pheasant, whole fresh salmon piled up in ranks, moules, lobster, king prawns, crab meat, bass, swordfish, monkfish, as well as more commonplace articles like chicken, sausages, ham and turkey.

Marti was right when she said I have a puritanical streak. I do and so does Janine.

'Let's go home!' we both said together.

As we turned we bumped into Marti and Charlie. He was in a tracksuit and she was wearing a coat over her non-dress.

'Just the people I wanted to see!' Marti said. 'You've got to come and help Charlie light his fireworks. The poor man's disabled. I don't know what can have happened.'

Charlie gave us a thin, sullen smile. My amazement grew when he spoke.

'Sorry about the misunderstanding,' he said between clenched teeth. 'I'm in therapy for rage control.'

'That's OK,' I said loftily.

'Perhaps you could put Dave in touch with your therapist,' Janine suggested.

'This is Dave's significant other,' Marti trilled.

Charlie showed considerable interest in Janine's attractions.

'Come on, you two,' Marti said, chivvying us through the grazing crowds towards the open spaces beyond. 'There are wellies and a golfing umbrella out here. You can hold the torch, Janine.' She led us out onto a paved patio area and Charlie limped behind us, Quasimodo style.

'Perhaps you can tell us why Henry Talbot's here?' I asked Marti when Janine dropped back to help Charlie stumble across the grass.

'Henry? Who he? . . . Oh, yes, him,' she replied nonchalantly. 'He's putting together a production package with Alhambra and the Arts and Entertainment Network in the States. It's a ten million pound deal to do a costume drama, Maria Edgeworth's *Castle Rackrent*. They're looking at Meryl Streep to play the lead.'

'Really?' I murmured.

'Yes,' Marti said firmly. 'It's a prestige production. Bags of Irish-American interest, of course. It'll go down like a bomb in Boston. They say the Senator's interested, and Brandon's quite keen on it. We have to do a few high-budget jobs along with all the suds and sex to make sure we don't lose the franchise.

There's still a lot of firming-up to do yet.'

'So Henry wasn't here just to upset Janine and myself?'

'Don't be paranoid, Dave.'

'Can I quote you about the production?' Janine asked, catching up with us.

'Quote away, but now come and help this poor man of mine to light his sparklers. He looks forward to this all year and he'd hate it if one of his brothers muscled in to help. It could all be done electronically but he's like a big kid about it.'

Charlie's sparklers turned out to be a major fireworks display with all kinds of electrical and mechanical means of ignition. I was on my guard lest Charlie ask me to shove my head down a mortar tube while he set it off but nothing happened, apart from the fireworks, that is. Charlie really did need my help; he'd strained his spine.

Eventually, when polite applause from the patio reached us through the clouds of drifting smoke we began to make our way back. I was separated from Janine for a moment and Marti drew alongside.

'Dave,' she said, in a far from light-hearted voice. 'Henry Talbot can be on the next plane back to LA as soon as you say the word. There's just one thing. You've got to promise me that you've forgotten everything about Vince, even his name.' She pressed a small piece of paper with a phone number written on it into my hand.

47

'Dave, just do what the woman wants,' Janine ordered.

We were discussing Marti's parting comment.

'No way! I let her pull my strings this time and where will she stop?'

'I can't stand this stupid male pride. Henry . . .'

'Don't compare us!'

'. . . will drag me through the courts. You've no idea how vindictive he is. His family were terribly possessive about the children, as if my sole purpose in life was to continue the Talbot bloodline. That's what's started all this up again. Lloyd's the heir of the Talbots. And Henry and his precious father don't want to see Talbots being brought up in the slums of Manchester.'

'They aren't.'

'You may think that but not Henry. Anywhere north of Watford that isn't a stately home counts as a slum to him. He's already told me off because Lloyd has a Manchester accent.'

'God!' I groaned. 'I can't phone her.'

'Why not? You've done nothing about Vince since your accident.'

I had not told Janine about my letter to the Home Secretary, and I wasn't about to tell her now. 'Since the murder attempt, you mean,' I corrected her.

'All the more reason to let her know that you're having nothing more to do with Vince.'

'I don't let anyone tell me what to do.'

'Stupid pig!' she muttered, and things went downhill from there.

We were barely on speaking terms when the brief holiday period came to an end. By unspoken agreement we avoided

327

the King issue until Monday morning came round. It was one of those miserable, cold, damp days with the cloud cover hovering at head height. The children were in their rooms getting their school things together and I was about to leave for work.

'Are you going to phone her?' she demanded.

'No. It's a bluff.'

'How do you work that out, mastermind?'

'Henry will never get custody. All you have to do is tell them that he hit you. Anyway, he deserted you.'

'I can't get through to you, can I? Henry was educated with half the lawyers in the country and his father had the rest in chambers with him. He'll have the best silk in the country arguing his case and he'll say that he moved heaven and earth to get me to come to the States with him.'

'Did he?'

'He suggested it but I already knew he was having an affair.'

'Well, then.'

'They'll bring up things about you.'

'What things?' I said.

'Marti King knows you killed those two men and she only has to tell Henry.'

'She won't tell him that because she doesn't know enough to back it up. All she knows is what she heard you bawling that day.'

'I don't bawl.'

'You are doing now.'

'Phone her!'

'No,' I said.

'Dave, I've finally worked out why you're going to all this trouble and putting my children at risk. It's not to get Vince King free. It's because you want the fame and kudos of freeing a hopeless case.'

I was late getting into the office. As I opened the door it struck me that I hadn't the faintest idea how I'd got myself there. Everything since leaving Janine was a blank. I sat in the outer office like a thundercloud waiting to burst.

Insull Perriss arrived shortly after I did, accompanied by two minders. Despite the cold morning, torrents of sweat were pouring down the fat industrialist's face.

'I can see how you make your money,' he blustered.

'Do I know you?' I said.

'You can stop that, you dirty little blackmailer,' he shouted. He was frantic. The minders looked nervous and embarrassed, as if they'd forgotten to bring along Perriss's straitjacket.

'What's the problem?' I said, trying to coax a smile out of paralysed jaw muscles – not easy after the way I'd parted from Janine.

'You're the problem, you filthy scumbag, Cunane. You gave your word that there'd be no comeback from those dirty swine trying to blackmail me, and then what do I see but you hand in hand with that disgusting old man.'

'I don't know what you're talking about and I suggest you leave,' I said.

'I'm going to hound you out of business. I'm going to ruin you,' he shouted. He showed no signs of leaving.

'Call the police,' I said to Celeste.

This produced a bark of laughter from Perriss. 'I'd like to see you dare,' he scoffed.

'Go on,' I said to Celeste when she looked at me for instructions. 'We've no facilities here for dealing with the insane.'

'You daren't,' he said, 'not after what you've done.' He watched disbelievingly as Celeste spoke into the phone. 'You can get years for blackmail and conspiracy.'

'I don't know you and I don't know what you're on about,' I said, giving him a last chance to draw his horns in. The deal with him was that I forgot everything and I was keeping to it. 'If you're accusing me of something, perhaps you'd like to explain what it is.'

He stood where he was with an evil expression on his face. The minders flanked him like a pair of statues.

I looked at my watch. Police response time was supposed to be about five minutes round here.

Two minutes later police sirens began wailing nearby, not

329

necessarily for us.

Perriss mopped his brow but stood his ground.

'Oh, forget it!' he said abruptly a minute later and dashed to the door. His companions followed.

'Do you know him?' Celeste asked.

'Never seen him before,' I snapped. 'Call off the police.'

She turned to her task but the set of her body told me that she didn't believe me.

The thunderstorm that had been brewing inside my brain finally burst. This was what I got for messing about with the Kings and the Carlyles. There was no way I could alter the past but I could unravel myself from it, starting with Insull Perriss. The truth was I was reaching boiling point. It wasn't just with Janine, or Marti, or Perriss; it was with myself. I was getting sick of constantly being the stupid half of my own 'smart woman/stupid male' advertising routine.

I decided that enough was enough. I was tired of being manipulated.

I got to my feet. Celeste looked at me in alarm.

'Where are you going?' she said as I grabbed my coat.

'I'm going to sort that guy out.'

'But you don't know where to find him,' she warned as I shut the door behind me.

I did know. I drove straight to Trafford Park and the factory where Perriss manufactured obscure little bits of machinery that went into aircraft. Perriss was in a fairly large way of business. His firm had branches in Birmingham and London and abroad. When I got there Perriss's Bentley was in the car park. I went to reception.

'Tell Mr Perriss that Mr Cunane wants to see him,' I said curtly.

The girl looked at me fearfully. She must have touched the security button because a uniformed member of the Corps of Commissionaires was on the scene in seconds. I was arguing the toss with him when there was a rumbling sound from the stairs leading to the first-floor offices. Perriss appeared, trailing three young suits who were trying to restrain him.

'You filthy animal!' he screamed when he saw me and

330

launched himself from the third or fourth step. Unfortunately for him but happily for me, Perriss's days of athletic leaps were long over. He landed up by my feet like a deflated balloon amid an awkward tangle of limbs and administrative assistants. His fall didn't quite knock all the spite out of him.

'Hit him!' he shrieked at the commissionaire. 'He's a criminal!' Those were the few words that made sense among an inchoate stream of curses.

The commissionaire looked at me uncertainly and then at his employer. Assaulting members of the public probably wasn't in his job description. I folded my arms and smiled. By this time overalled workers from the shop floor had arrived to see what was happening. Quite a crowd was gathering. Perriss was foaming at the mouth, quite literally raving.

'Hit him, beat him!' Perriss continued to yell as he struggled to his feet. Rough hands were laid on me and I made no effort to resist.

'Perriss, do you want me to tell them about your habits?' I shouted as the cursing and the manhandling went on. 'I only want a private word.'

The transformation from indignation to trepidation was startling. In seconds Perriss was shooing the throng away and storming up to his office. My handlers now drew back into a circle around me.

'What's he done?' the commissionaire demanded. 'Are you the police? We know he has his funny ways but there's hundreds of jobs depending on him.'

'Keep these people back,' I said. 'I only want to speak to him. It's about something that's better not discussed.'

Reluctantly the commissionaire complied. I heard people grumbling about warrant cards and IDs but formed the impression that this wasn't the first hysterical scene that Perriss had been involved in. Maybe he'd had to pay off others. I went up the stairs, and found a warren of closed offices. Perriss's was at the end of a short corridor. I knocked.

'I only want to speak to you,' I shouted. 'I'm not here to do you any harm.'

'I'm going to end it all,' Perriss wailed. 'I've had enough.'

The door was locked but it yielded to my shoulder. Perriss

was behind his desk. As I burst in he snapped a double-barrelled shotgun shut. There was an open box of cartridges on the desk. Perriss was sweating and crying and his hair was all over the place. There was something phoney about it all, though. To me it looked like ham acting, a part he'd played before. He levelled the gun at me. I kicked the door shut behind me.

'Good!' I shouted. 'You might as well shoot me as well as yourself because I don't know what you were on about at my office.'

This seemed to take him by surprise.

'You've got a cheek,' he sobbed, lowering the gun. 'If Carlyle's sent you for money you can tell him he's squeezed me dry. There's no more money or anything else. It's all I can do to keep the firm from the receivers.'

'Why the hell should I want money, and what's that got to do with Carlyle?'

'You're in with him, aren't you? I saw him patting you as if you were his favourite lap-dog.'

'I don't work for him,' I said indignantly.

'You soon will do, I've seen it before. He sucks people in. I made one mistake years ago and he's used it to bleed me ever since. You've given him copies of that stuff, haven't you?'

Perriss was drowning in a sea of self-pity. He kept toying with the shotgun. I began to wonder if his sense of drama needed a violent conclusion to the proceedings. Behind me I could hear noises as people pounded up to the office. I turned and pulled a cupboard against the door.

'No one's coming in here until you tell me just what's been going on,' I announced. 'Either use that gun or put it down.'

He lowered the gun.

It took thirty minutes to calm Perriss down. Brandon Carlyle had been blackmailing him for money and information off and on for twenty years. Seeing me with Carlyle at the New Year's party had tipped him over the edge. By the time I left, the factory nurse had him stretched out on a couch with his shirt off. He accepted that I wasn't a blackmailer. At least I think he did. When I reached the foot of the stairs, a buzz of whispered conversation came from the office area, and I could have sworn that I heard the word 'paedophile' more than once. No one stopped me leaving but I got some curious looks. Perriss's vice probably wasn't as big a secret as he believed.

I drove back to the office by a different route. That isn't difficult in Trafford Park where there are so many round-abouts and all the roads look the same. By the time I'd threaded my way out of the giant industrial estate my mood hadn't become calmer. If anything it was worse. My feelings against Marti and Brandon Carlyle were similar to those of Insull Perriss against me. When I got to the office I summoned Michael Coe and Peter Snyder to my desk.

'But Dave, er, Mr Cunane, they're on other enquiries,' Celeste protested when I told her.

'Page them now, Celeste,' I ordered.

'This means you'll have to find other people to cover the work they're supposed to be doing,' she argued.

'Fine, you do that,' I said.

Celeste began rummaging noisily in the papers on her desk. I found the sound extremely irritating. 'And when you've finished that you can phone the estate agent and see if there are any first-floor offices available in this street. I can't go on working down here, people get the impression that I'm your assistant.'

'Yes, Mr Cunane,' she said, with a smile.

'It doesn't need to be anything grandiose, just private.'

'Right.'

There must be some people who enjoy being manipulated by the likes of Brandon Carlyle and Marti King. The problem is, I'm not one of them. OK, I'd let things slide. Apart from the letter to the Home Secretary I hadn't made any moves in the Vince King case. I was busy, I was recovering from the 'accident' and there were no obvious leads to follow apart from Devereaux-Almond – and he was no longer on the scene.

That letter, though, was like a stone thrown into a still pond. It had produced ripples. If the Manchester police knew about it then it was safe to assume that Brandon Carlyle also knew. Hence the invitation to the New Year party where the patriarch did his best to show me that he had tender feelings

333

for me while Marti tried blackmail. Brandon was offering the carrot and Marti was offering the stick.

As far as I was concerned they'd over-reached themselves. One or other might have been amusing, but both were too much. The sheer nerve of the pair was enough to convince me that, even if not innocent, Vince King deserved to have his case reconsidered. There must be something they were desperate to hide, and I'd never be safe until it was out in the open. The family obviously needed copper-riveted guarantees from me; guarantees that I couldn't give without becoming their tame spaniel. Insull Perriss had already wrongly guessed that I was hand-in-glove with Brandon. How long would it be before I was faced with that as my only alternative? How long before Brandon decided that I was a detail that needed tidying up just as Lou Olley and Sam Levy had been tidied up?

I could either reopen the investigation and get the Vince King case finally sorted before it was too late or I could knuckle under. My decision had already been made when I told Janine that I wasn't going to phone Marti. James McMahon surveying matters from his lofty position had decided, no doubt correctly, and under advice from his civil servants, that evidence that King's solicitor was involved in some kind of chicanery wasn't enough to reopen the case. So I'd have to find evidence that was sufficient to convince. The thing was in official channels now. It would be awkward for McMahon to ignore new evidence if I could find some.

With Devereaux-Almond out of the picture, dead or fled, that left Dr Sterling Sameem and the bent copper, Mick Jones, as the only possible sources of new information about the case. I had to get to them before they disappeared like the Rochdale solicitor.

I decided to put Snyder on to finding Dr Sameem and Coe on to ex-Detective Inspector Jones. It was better that way. Coe was a single man, so it would be easier for him to fly out to Spain than Snyder whose wife in Cheadle Hulme expected regular hours. I briefed them when they turned up and neither thought there was anything unusual about the jobs. When I'd seen them on their way I took myself off to Bolton to confer

334

with Paddy. Celeste asked me who was to be billed for Coe and Snyder's time.

'Me,' I said, 'and while you're at it, Celeste, I'd like you to give your solicitor cousin Marvin a ring. I want him to write an official letter to the Home Secretary for me.'

My father wasn't looking particularly well when I arrived. He was stretched out on a sofa, which was very unusual for him, and he was wearing his dressing gown. Normally by mid-morning he'd have been at work on some project for hours.

'Talk to him,' my mother said, 'he's in a funny mood.'

Paddy tossed the *Daily Telegraph* to one side when I walked into the room. 'Load of bloody rubbish!' he said.

'What, the *Telegraph*? I thought it was your bible?'

'I can't bear to read newspapers these days. Some of these journalists just have no idea how this country's really run.'

'I'm taking up the case of Vince King again,' I said. 'I'm certain he was fitted up and the only question is by whom, the Carlyles or your lot.'

This announcement didn't produce the explosion of anger that I'd been expecting.

'I expect he was,' Paddy said wearily. 'I expect Carlyle and Jones both had a hand in it, but that's not why King's still inside.'

'Why then?'

'I've already told you. I can't tell you things that are covered by the Official Secrets Act.'

'I don't see how that applies. We're talking about a criminal case here.'

'I can't tell you.'

'Even though someone's out to kill me? They've already had a damn good try.'

'David, you brought this on yourself, and others besides you would be in danger if I told you. It isn't as if you aren't used to people getting rough with you.'

'Getting rough! They tried to run me into a motorway bridge.'

Paddy shook his head but he didn't speak.

'Great! So my own father won't help.'

335

'David, no one's forcing you to take up the cause of Vince King. If he didn't kill a copper he's done plenty of other things.'

'Enough to serve more than twenty years for?'

'Plenty of safe-crackers got that and more in my young day.'

'That may ease your conscience but it doesn't do anything for me,' I snapped.

I walked out. My mother came out with me to the car and I told her what had happened. Perhaps I was expecting sympathy, but I didn't get any.

'And what does Janine think of all this?' was her reply.

'Janine? She agrees with the former detective chief superintendent. She wants me to drop the whole thing.'

'There you are,' Eileen said. 'You're just like your father. Peas from the same pod! You're both stubborn to the point of stupidity and always ready to pursue a principle no matter who gets hurt. I always knew you were too like each other ever to get on. That's why I was glad you didn't join the police. I think you'd have quarrelled even more than you have done.'

'Huh!' I muttered.

'That's right!' she said. 'Proof of the pudding. You don't like the truth about yourself any more than your father does.'

'Thanks.'

Later that afternoon I got a message from Michael Coe. He'd had a lucky break. He'd found the address in Marbella where ex-DI Mick Jones was living only to discover that Jones was no longer among the living. Just two months previously the ex-copper had been killed by a hit and run driver while crossing a street he used every day when he went for his morning papers. The car, which was stolen, was found burnt out in a side street six blocks away. The Guardia Civil didn't hold out much hope of finding the culprit and had it listed as an accident.

It was one of those days. When I reached my flat that evening I found a pile of junk heaped up against the door. I recognised all the objects belonging to me that had somehow ended up in Janine's flat: cups, plates, and odd bits of underwear. She'd even dumped the kids' cycling kit.

I went to her door. There was no reply so I tried my key. She'd changed the locks. I tried shouting through the letter box but the only answer was an echoing silence. It wasn't until I went down to look up at her windows that I noticed the For Sale sign.

Janine had finally moved out.

48

I spent the next two days at home feeling sorry for myself. The business ran itself. I was coming to the conclusion that things went better when I wasn't around. Janine, as usual, had done a thorough job when it came to distancing herself from me. Phone calls to her office met with guarded replies and no information about her current whereabouts and it was similar, but worse, at the children's school. There, the woman who answered gave me the distinct impression that she thought Janine was on the lam from a bout of domestic violence. My blood boiled and I longed to go and sort her out as I'd done with Insull Perriss, but there are limits. Schools are harder to get into than factories these days – anyway, what could I say? I was discarded but I wasn't the children's father. I had fewer rights than Henry Talbot.

I could have put someone on to tracing her but pride prevented me.

It was Celeste who brought me back to earth.

'Are you coming into work today?' she drawled over the phone on Thursday morning. 'I mean, if you're ill don't bother, but Peter Snyder found that man you sent him to look for and he'd like to know what you want done next.'

'So would I,' I replied. 'Tell him I'll be in by ten.'

Dr Sterling Sameem was now a resident of an old people's home in West Cheshire.

I decided that a hands-off approach was best. I sent Peter Snyder down to see the old man after briefing him for the best part of an hour. Then I did my best to get back into the groove. Somehow, it all seemed artificial. I found it hard to summon up the interest to talk to clients about their problems, but I forced myself, and by Friday afternoon it was getting easier. I was in no rush to hurry home – the prospect of an empty weekend yawned in front of me like a dark crevasse.

Peter had spent the best part of Thursday trying to persuade the staff at the nursing home to allow him in. On Friday, I sent him back for another attempt.

'I can't believe those people in West Cheshire,' he said when he returned just after five. 'It's like you're back in the Middle Ages. Half a mile away from the motorway and you're in the bush.'

'Come on, Peter.'

'No, I mean it! Dense hedges and trees everywhere, and the natives! Wow! I don't think some of them have ever seen a black guy. Talk about suspicious! This nursing home, Chalfont Hall? I think they thought I was casing the joint for a robbery, though what they'd have worth taking I don't know. It's a weird old Victorian building with everything in the wrong place, you know? Like somebody got the plans and read them upside down. The stairs lead up from a pantry next to the kitchen and the old folks get out into the garden through a window.'

'French windows have been around a long time, Peter.'

'No, that's what I mean. It isn't a French window. It's an ordinary window in the dining room that they've got wooden steps up to and steps outside.'

'What about Sameem?'

'Right, sorry! It's just that I'm not used to dealing with these natives. I saw Sameem. Funny thing is, with him it helped that I'm black . . . He's actually an Irishman, funnily enough.'

'Really?'

'Yeah, sorry. I mean . . . anyway . . . he's not one of these Cheshire bushmen – you know, the inbred ones with the single eye on their foreheads? He had a Lebanese father and Irish mother, was born and brought up in Ireland and worked in England all his life. The sister in charge reckons he has something she calls selective Alzheimer's, meaning that he turns it on and off as it suits. Last month two guys came to see him and he cracked on that he couldn't speak at all – didn't know his own name, soiled himself while they were with him.'

339

'Who were they?'

'Very anxious to see him about a legal matter, something to do with his pension, the sister said . . . Anyway, Sameem turned on such a performance, crapping himself and gibbering and drooling, that they left after half an hour and haven't been back. Very polite they were, she said.'

'So he's no use to us, then?'

'Yes, he is! I told you . . . First he wanted to know if I was connected to the police, the Crown Prosecution Service, or the Carlyle Organisation. Very cagey he was, only opened up when I told him that I was representing the interests of Vince King. He was reassured because I'm black.'

'You already said that.'

'Sorry, boss, but it's true. He wanted to talk about the King Case, especially about the carpet fibres which are supposed to prove that King was in the room where Musgrave and Fullalove got shot. It turns out that there was a bit of fiddling with the forensics.'

'How come?'

'Sameem testified that the fibres on King's trainers were unique to a carpet in the room where the bodies were found – same dye, same weave, same shape and composition, etcetera, thus placing King at the murder scene, right?'

'Right,' I agreed.

'Wrong!' Snyder gasped excitedly. 'That was only the first, provisional finding. DI Jones managed to lose the later finding, in which Sameem said that the first evidence was useless because A, the carpet wasn't unique to the Post Office as first thought and B, King had a matching piece of carpet on the floor of his van!'

'So why didn't this come out at the trial?'

'Undue influence, guv!'

'I'd rather you didn't call me guv, we aren't a police soap opera,' I said snootily and regretted it as soon as I spoke. I sounded like a real stuffed shirt.

'Only my joke, guv . . . er, Mr Cunane.'

'Get on with it,' I growled, to hide my embarrassment.

'Sameem went to Salford all ready for the biggest fucking row of the century. He was going to get Jones fired for

340

deliberately suppressing evidence. Instead Jones showed him some photographs in which Sameem was having a little kiss and a cuddle with a fifteen-year-old lad at a gay cruising area in Worsley. Jones threatened to do him for it unless he kept silent about the second finding.'

'So he did?'

'He did. Like you say, this wasn't a police soap opera where everything comes right in the end. Sameem feels guilty now, claims he was the only support of a widowed mother and that he was ready to tell the truth at the trial if he'd been asked.'

'But you're not saying that the present Home Secretary, James McMahon, knew about this?'

'Of course not, no more did the prosecution. All they knew was that fibres had been found on King's shoes which matched those in the murder room. Sameem went into that witness box convinced he was going to be crucified. When the prosecution asked him if the fibres were *identical* he saved himself from perjury by saying they were *similar*. That was true, they were similar. Only they were from a roll of carpet that, far from being unique to the GPO, had been sold to thousands of customers. Sameem expected that McMahon would come down on him like a ton of bricks for using the word similar but he didn't. He just said he had no further questions for the witness. Sameem says it's all there in the transcript. McMahon must have thought attempting to shake Sameem would only strengthen the prosecution case.'

I leaned over to the filing cabinet where I had put the trial transcript and fished it out. It only took a moment to confirm what Peter Snyder had said.

'OK, but we've only got Sameem's word for all this. Is there documentary proof?'

'In spades, guv! . . . Sorry!'

'No, it's all right, Peter. Call me what the hell you like. I should have done this months ago.'

'You've had other things to do.'

'Maybe. So what's this documentary evidence?'

'Sameem has a copy of the original report he sent to the Salford police. He kept a copy of the suppressed report to cover himself, and there's another copy in the police case files.

341

He made sure of that. Those files are in the basement of the old Salford police HQ.'

'So why the change of heart?'

'He's been diagnosed with cancer – inoperable. He'll be going into a hospice soon. He wants to check out with a clean sheet.'

'Right!' I said. 'We get an affidavit from him at once.'

'Tomorrow?' Peter said hopefully.

'No, now – this evening. If there are two other characters nosing around we don't know what might happen. Who are these guys anyway?'

'I dunno. The sister didn't keep the card they gave her. They definitely weren't Mancunians. The sister says they were quite refined, by which I think she was trying to tell me something.'

'So that proves it?'

'You know what I mean. She said she thought they were lawyers, a couple of fancy white dudes in nice suits.'

'And what does Sameem say?

'He claims he can't remember. Highly selective memory, he's got.'

'Right! It's hardly a coincidence that they turned up just after I wrote to the Home Secretary. You get yourself back down there with Celeste's cousin and you get Sameem to say all this on tape and video in nice legal fashion and you get some of the pointy-headed Cheshire natives to act as witnesses if you can stand to be in the same room with them.'

'That was only a joke, guv . . . nothing racial, you know.'

'Don't worry, I don't think being a Cheshire native counts as an ethnic group. I shouldn't think they can do you for it.'

Peter looked at me for a moment, unsure of whether I was serious, and then he laughed but not very loudly.

'All right, Peter, you've done a great job. Phone your wife and tell her you'll be late. You can have overtime or time off in lieu, whatever suits.' He smiled and hurried to his office.

'Celeste!' I shouted. 'Get your cousin Marvin lined up. I've got a job for him. I want him to get an affidavit from a witness.'

'Are you going?' she said.

'No, just Peter and Marvin. You heard what Peter said – this

342

old guy doesn't trust us white folks.'

She gave me an odd look but phoned Marvin.

Waiting for my two emissaries to return from deepest Cheshire was the hardest thing I'd done for weeks. All I could do was trust them. I've given up smoking but I regretted it now as I found myself chewing my fingernails.

I phoned Janine's mobile again to see if I could appease her but she still wasn't answering. I felt frustrated. Surely she would see that I'd done what had to be done?

I walked down Deansgate to get a pile of sandwiches to sustain my troops when they returned. I paced the office. I began to think that I wasn't suited to the managerial role.

The waiting at least gave me time to think of what I was going to do next.

'Got it!' Peter said when he and Marvin arrived back well after midnight. 'It's all on tape and video and witnessed by two of the staff and another patient. He's made a written statement for Marvin and he's given us the copy of the report he sent to Jones which was countersigned by a junior forensic scientist who now lives at Mitchell, South Dakota, USA.'

He put the tapes and papers down on the table. I snatched them up as if they might evaporate and hurriedly sealed them in a large envelope. I sent Peter off to bung them into the night-safe of the Midland Bank on King Street on his way home.

'Marvin, I'd like you to write a letter to the Right Honourable James McMahon humbly requesting that he refer the case to the Criminal Review Board in the light of new evidence that renders the conviction unsafe.'

'Are you sure he'll act, with him being personally involved and the Home Secretary and everything?' Marvin asked.

'Why, do you think he'll try to cover it up?'

'It puts him in a bad light.'

'No, not unless you or Peter leak any of this to the press first. There's nothing to say that McMahon's done anything other than defend a man who had overwhelming evidence against him, evidence that we can now show was rigged. If we give McMahon the opportunity to act without trying to blacken his

343

name or make political points he's bound to do the right thing. This is England, not Upper Volta.'

'Even so . . .'

'The fact that he was directly involved in the original trial will make him act quickly to avoid any suggestion of a cover-up. You'll see! King will be out in no time. All it needed was the evidence.'

'Right, man!' Marvin said. 'But do you want this done tonight?'

'I do, and we're both going to see King tomorrow. I'll phone Armley Jail first thing and ask them to leave us two visiting orders at the gate.'

Marvin, who was small, chubby, and sported a curiously unsolicitor-like haircut of short back and sides with bleached mini-dreads on top, now looked very serious, with an owlish expression on his face. He was in his late twenties, dressed in trainers, loose baggy blue jeans and a red zip-up fleece. He was wearing glasses and now he took them off and twisted them nervously in his fingers.

'Er, Mr Cunane,' he said, 'there's a snag.' My heart sank.

'It's just that Celeste, you know, sometimes she exaggerates. She told you I'm a fully qualified solicitor, but I'm not. I've passed my exams for legal executive at night school but I'm not even a fee-earner in a legal firm yet. I'm a paralegal and I could become a solicitor, but I haven't got a job.'

'You've got a job now, you bugger!' I said recklessly. 'Consider yourself employed. We'll work out your salary with you tomorrow.'

'Thanks,' he gasped. The nervous expression disappeared.

'And all that about you being on the Community Forum and the police being scared of their own shadows when you walk past, is that exaggeration too?'

'I'm trying to get on the Forum,' he said stiffly.

'Right,' I said.

'There may be a problem on the legal side,' Marvin said, all learned and legalistic now. 'We've got one witness to with-draw part of the evidence with which the Crown convicted King. It could be that the Appeal Court will regard the other evidence as being strong enough to override this doubt. From what I've heard, the Police Federation would kick up the mother and father of all rows if McMahon lets King out.'

'You're forgetting that McMahon is personally involved. He'll bend over backwards to avoid the impression that he's sweeping the case under the carpet to hide his own incompetence. The letter I had from him was signed by the top civil servant in the Home Office. Believe me, they'll have to act.'

'But shouldn't we wait until Michael Coe gets back from Spain?'

'Would you like to wait if it was you in Armley Jail?'

Marvin gave a little nod and turned to Celeste's word processor. It took us three hours to come up with a draft that I was satisfied with – barbed, yet polite.

'Do you want me to post this?' Marvin asked.

I thought for a moment.

'No, we'll speak to King before it goes in the post,' I said cautiously.

49

On my way home to Chorlton in the small hours to snatch a few hours' sleep I felt elated but suspicious of my success. Somehow it all seemed too easy. Then I told myself that Sameem's evidence had been there all these years, just waiting for the right person to come along.

As I turned into the car park of Thornleigh Court I got a shock. The place was full of lights and cars and vans and men and women moving about – uniformed men and women; the police were out in strength. I parked my car in the usual slot and as I got out strong hands were placed on my shoulders.

'David Cunane?' the uniformed sergeant said.

I nodded.

'I'm arresting you on suspicion of the abduction of Jennifer Elizabeth Talbot and Lloyd Henry Talbot. You need not say anything . . .'

I listened in a daze as the sergeant droned through the standard caution. Lights were being shone in my face and I found it hard to grasp what was happening. It was as if I'd fallen into a play where all the actors except me knew their lines. All that penetrated my brain were the confused noises off. I heard my name being shouted from person to person. 'He's here!' There seemed to be a sort of ripple effect as news of my presence passed among the milling mob of law enforcers. My name circulated among them as in a game of Chinese Whispers, and as a backdrop to all this every light of every window in the flats was lit. I could see row upon row of faces peering down at me. I thought, 'This is how it felt when the Romans threw a victim to the lions.'

'Is he cuffed?' someone asked, and immediately my wrists

were jerked up and a pair of those unpleasant newfangled rigid cuffs clamped on as tightly as possible.

'Get him up here,' someone else barked and then two strong arms jerked me forward to the entrance of the flats and up the stairs. There seemed to be coppers everywhere. I hadn't seen so many police in one place since the Lord Mayor's Procession. I was passed, or rather shoved from hand to hand, until I arrived outside my own door. Two sweating officers in shirtsleeves were vainly struggling to break it down with sledgehammers. They lowered their hammers and looked at me with expressions that can only be described as hate-filled. A hush descended on the whole group. The air of sweat and expectation was so strong that you could have sliced it with a knife and sold it in aid of the Police Benevolent Fund.

'Have you got them in there?' a uniformed inspector demanded peremptorily. 'It'll go better for you if you tell us now.'

'Got who in there?' I asked stupidly.

Then a figure emerged from among a knot of policewomen. It was Janine.

'Dave, how could you?' she shouted, pressing forward with her fists raised.

'Do what?' I shouted back as the policewomen enveloped her in their arms.

'Take my children, you monster!'

I hung my head and turned away. I didn't want to look at Janine's face. It was contorted with malice and rage and fear.

Unfortunately my gesture was observed by those who had me in custody and an interpretation placed on it. It seemed as if every copper in the narrow hallway started talking at once and then a half silence fell and in that partial hush I heard a male voice say, 'They must be dead, we've made enough noise to rouse them.'

Janine heard it too. She threw her head back and howled. The men holding me involuntarily tightened their grip and the pair with the sledgehammers raised them for action.

'You're doing no good with that,' an authoritative voice commented from the rear.

'We need a drill.'

'Explosives, more like,' one of the sledgehammer wielders said.

'We could get the Brigade up to the outside windows,' another suggested.

To me it was lunacy. The astonishment was so great, it deadened my nerves like a powerful narcotic. I couldn't believe what I was hearing. It was like being in your coffin and listening to the undertaker and a mortician discuss what shade of embalming fluid to use on your corpse. I struggled to find words but they didn't come easily.

'I've got the key!' I shouted at last. I couldn't reach my trouser pocket because of the cuffs and the restraining arms.

'Let him go!' Janine said. 'He must have the keys.'

I extracted the key only to have it snatched out of my hand. The hammering, whilst insufficient to do more than dent my armoured door, had distorted the lock. A brawny constable managed to insert the key but they had to produce a metal bar to give it some turning movement before he could undo the lock. Then the door sprang open. I was held when I tried to go forward.

A male and a female constable entered with batons raised. I don't know what they were expecting but they went in there in great dread. It looked absurd to me.

'I've not done anything to Jenny and Lloyd,' I said. 'Would I, or could I? Janine, tell me what's happened.'

She buried her face in her hands and wept. The two officers emerged shaking their heads. The inspector behind me propelled me forward with his hand on the small of my back. I'd had enough of that. I turned and shoved him as hard as I could. This led to a Keystone Cops-type collective stumble among the crowded masses in the hallway. No sooner had they begun to lurch than the lights went out, plunging us into near total darkness. I winced in agony as a police boot came into contact with my ankle and as my head went forward I heard the whistle of disturbed air as a baton was flicked near my face. The next thing I can remember is the sharp pain as a baton came into contact with my head.

The poor old fuzz had an awful time with me after that. The

blow had split my scalp and blood flowed freely. It ran down over my eyes and into my mouth and for some reason it wouldn't stop. I didn't lose consciousness at all, but for some time I lost interest in any events apart from the efforts to stem the blood flow. It wasn't just trickling, it was spurting.

'Christ! What's the matter with you?' the policewoman trying to administer first aid asked crankily as she crammed yet another wound dressing onto the top of my head. 'You haven't got haemophilia, have you?'

'I don't know,' I mumbled.

'Aids?'

'No!'

I was frightened. My blood has flowed often enough, but never this profusely. It was a Niagara of gore. There was an odd, pulsing, throbbing ache in my head. I nervously recalled the crash on the motorway. Was there something seriously wrong that had been overlooked?

'We'll have to get him to hospital,' she said.

'It's only a drop of claret,' a senior voice said. 'It'll stop in a minute and then he can tell us where he's hidden the children. The ME can see to him at Bootle Street.'

But the bleeding didn't stop. The pile of soaked wound dressings increased. I began to feel faint.

'I can't take responsibility if this prisoner isn't hospitalised at once,' the female officer said. Her tone was panicky, heightening my own fears.

'Shit! The bastard's doing it on purpose,' I heard someone whisper fiercely, but they hauled me downstairs and soon I was listening to the wail of a siren from the inside of an ambulance. The cuffs stayed on but the paramedics had plugged me into plasma as soon as they rolled up.

It was six a.m. before the blood stopped flowing, by which time the staff at Wythenshawe Hospital had transfused more than five units into me. The baton blow had severed an artery in my temple and it required a surgeon to repair the damage. He likened the wound to a cut from a sword. I felt too feeble to get seriously annoyed but I promised myself that I would. Marvin's number was on my mobile and I got a nurse to phone him. Poor bloke! I thought. He starts work at Pimpernel Investigations and he ends up taking a dying deposition, writing to the Home Secretary and then having to turn out to rescue his employer all in the same night.

Marvin arrived at the same time as DCI Brendan Cullen. They had me in a side ward with a burly sergeant to keep me company. More officers were clustered outside, getting in the way of the staff.

As soon as Marvin arrived I felt tongue-tied. I didn't even know his surname. I needn't have worried. Fronting up to the police was a skill Marvin shared with his cousin.

'This is an outrage!' he yelped in a penetrating voice. 'I demand that Mr Cunane be released from custody at once.' The bevy of uniformed officers answered with a collective honk of dismissal, like sea-lions seeing off a newcomer on some Arctic beach. 'It's an offence to hold a seriously injured man in hand-cuffs. I'll see that the officers responsible are called to account.'

'Honk, honk, honk!' they chorused, at least that's what it sounded like.

Somehow Brendan Cullen insinuated himself to my bedside in the midst of this drama.

'Get rid of this clown, will you, Dave,' he suggested quietly, 'and then I can sort this lot out. It's all down to a simple misunderstanding.'

'Marvin's not a clown. He's the chief legal officer of Pimpernel Investigations,' I said.

'I don't care if he's the fucking Pope of Rome, get him out of here!'

'I'll get rid of my clown when you get rid of your clowns,' I snapped, 'but he isn't.' The effort of saying this made me feel dizzy. I lay back on the pillow.

'Listen to him. He's just getting people's backs up.'

The honking was reaching pandemonium levels.

'Marvin,' I muttered weakly.

My adviser appeared at the opposite side of the bed to Bren. His teeth were bared and he was ready for action against any odds. I felt proud of him. He bent over to receive instructions. 'Mr Cullen's going to sort things out,' I whispered. 'You don't need to make a fuss.'

Marvin, however, was made of tough metal. He stayed, willing to outface any number of coppers. The uniformed branch took the cuffs off me and retreated. Cullen chatted while Marvin watched him like a hawk from his side of my bed.

'Some geezer snatched the kids from outside their fancy school in Didsbury at about three-forty yesterday,' Bren said. 'Right on the main road, it is, couldn't be handier for a snatch. The child minder who normally rounds them up wasn't there. The kids must have been standing at the gates looking for her when they were snatched, but nobody saw a struggle or anything. That's why we thought he must be someone who knows them – the abductor, that is.'

'Mr Cunane was in his office with my cousin and several other witnesses at the relevant time,' Marvin chipped in.

'Hell's teeth! Don't you think I know that? Heads are going to roll over this one.'

'They certainly are, Inspector,' Marvin said. 'My client couldn't possibly have been involved.'

'The cunning bastard who snatched the kids arranged for the child minder not to be there.'

'Oh God!' I muttered. I could feel the stitches in my scalp pulling tight.

'Not you, Dave. Don't worry,' he said, nervously smoothing my pillow.

'Fine, I won't worry. Jenny and Lloyd have disappeared but now I don't need to worry because the police don't think it was me.'

'No need for sarcasm, Dave. There've been mistakes all round and not least by Ms White. Apparently she thought the child minder would be looking after the kids until six this Friday.'

'What happened to the child minder?' I asked.

'I'm coming to that.'

'Has no one heard of mobile phones?' I murmured.

'Ms White had hers switched off for some reason. She says that's your fault.'

'Oh,' I muttered.

'Ms White didn't get nervous until she arrived at the child

351

minder's house at six in the evening to collect her kids. It was hysterics all round then because they weren't there. A male phoned at three p.m. and told the child minder's fourteen-year-old daughter that he was picking up the Talbot children and the minder didn't need to bother. The child minder assumed that it was you. Up until recently you often picked them up.'

I grunted by way of assent.

'I gather you and Janine have split up, Dave. I'm sorry, but that phone call seems to be the main reason why you were in the frame. Sorry, mate.'

'That's all right, Bren. I probably needed a CAT-scan and a brain operation.'

'Joke if you like, but things happen fast in a child abduction case. You know that. By the time one of the geniuses outside thought to ask the child minder's daughter to describe the voice of the man who phoned her it was four a.m. and you were already in here being operated on. The child minder's kid says the man had a "well-spoken" voice, upper class like Prince Charles, so that rules you out, Dave. We've now interviewed the kids who saw Jenny and Lloyd getting into the car. They say the bloke had a thin, hatchet-like face and a big nose and was driving a BMW, so that lets you out again, doesn't it?'

'Wouldn't it have been simple enough to check if I was in my office?'

'They did, but you were out.'

'Only for a few minutes while I got some sandwiches.'

'This was an urgent enquiry, mate. Someone slipped up. They thought the office was empty.'

'I'm making a note of all these blunders, Inspector,' Marvin said menacingly. 'My client's in hospital because of crass police stupidity.'

'You do what you want, sunshine,' Bren told him.

'Racial abuse now! Just wait!'

'I'm sorry, Marvin, can you leave that for now?' I pleaded.

'Don't let them take an inch, Mr Cunane. That's what we've learned in the community.'

'I'm sorry,' Bren said. 'I call everyone sunshine; black, white or polka dot.'

'Institutional racism!' Marvin snorted before shutting up.

'Why did Janine think I would have harmed the children? I can't believe it.'

'You'll have to ask her yourself. She's asked to see you if that's OK with you.'

'But she was so venomous. She wanted to scratch my eyes out.'

'Dave, you've got to understand what she's been through. There's more . . . When Jenny and Lloyd were reported missing we did a search of the local area . . .'

'Which is where?'

'Sorry, you'll have to ask her that. I'm not permitted to tell you. A search was done to check that they weren't playing in the streets or at a friend's house. Then Ms White said they might have gone to the flat at Thornleigh Court if they were wandering outside school. They don't know the district where they're living now. When uniformed branch got to Thornleigh Court they found that someone had stuffed two bloodstained school shirts into Ms White's letter box.'

'What sort of sicko does that?'

'I dunno, I was hoping you might have some ideas. They're checking the blood groups. Anyway, the next thing is, they come up against the armoured door of your flat. I'm sorry, Dave, but all these young constables have seen lots of horror films – they started jumping to conclusions.'

'They'll be jumping to more than that when I put in our claim for damages,' Marvin said.

'Will you see her?' Bren asked, ignoring Marvin.

I nodded my head. He went out and Marvin followed him.

50

Janine looked shattered.

Her hair was lank with sweat. There were lines on her face that I'd never noticed before, and her eyes seemed to have sunk into their sockets. You'd have put her age nearer to sixty than thirty if you hadn't known.

She stood at the door looking at me for what felt like an age. I wanted to go and hug her but I couldn't move. I was embarrassed because my bandage-swathed face was so inexpressive. I didn't know what to say.

'Janine . . .' I mumbled. I felt as guilty as hell.

She didn't speak. I didn't want her to speak. Her eyes were filled with tears.

Finally, she came close and looked at my wound for a moment. Then she put her hand over her mouth. 'We can't go on meeting like this, Dave,' she said and then gave a nervous laugh.

'I'm so sorry,' I said. 'I should never have taken this risk. This is my fault.'

'No, it's Henry and that bitch Marti. They're in a different league from us. Nobody could expect they'd be so cruel.'

'It's still my fault.'

'Cullen says they thought they were going to lose you.'

'It looks worse than it is.'

'Dave! They had to pump more than three pints of blood into you and it's all because I was certain you'd taken Jenny and Lloyd to spite me. I got the police so wound up that they were bound to lash out. An inch or so lower and they'd have had your eye out.'

'I've had worse.'

'Cut out that stiff-upper-lip nonsense, Dave. You've been

354

horribly injured. It's because I'm so stupid. Be told, and stop being so noble.'

'Sorry, Janine.'

'Stop apologising and get angry with me.'

'I can't. This is all my own fault, not yours.'

'Dave, I didn't come here for a self-abasement contest with you.'

'What did you come for?'

She stuck her chin out and flicked her hair back in that characteristic way. 'Cunane, you big ape! I came to tell you that I need you more than anyone except the children. I won't be able to cope if you die as well as Jenny and Lloyd.'

'Jenny and Lloyd aren't dead.'

'How can you be so sure?'

'Who has a key to the entrance of Thornleigh Court besides you and me?'

'Henry. I thought of him first, but we were all so certain that it was you who picked the kids up.'

'It *was* Henry and it *is* my fault more than yours. That stunt with the bloody shirts is just what a geek like Henry who's been in Hollywood for years would come up with. He's trying to throw you off the scent while he gets the children out of the country. He wouldn't harm his own children, would he?'

'I don't know,' Janine said uncertainly. 'I don't think he would, but suppose that horrible woman has made him hand them over to her so that she can blackmail you into leaving her father in prison . . .'

'Janine, love,' I said gently. 'Marti's a piece of work all right, but I don't think she'd harm the children. Henry's acting on his own.'

'How can you be sure? She threatened you at the New Year party.'

'I'm a fool. I should have agreed to have nothing more to do with the Vince King case when she offered to ship Henry back if I let it drop . . .'

'Why didn't you?'

'I couldn't have known this was going to happen. You told me that Henry Talbot comes from a legal background. I couldn't have known he'd snatch his children off the street. I

355

thought that the worst that could happen was a court case that you were bound to win.'

'You're so stubborn! You weren't going to let any woman tell you what to do, whether it was me or Marti.'

'It's not like that. You can't let criminals dictate your life to you.'

'Oh, so she's a criminal now, is she?'

'I've found proof that the evidence at King's trial was rigged. She knows it, and Brandon Carlyle knows it. That's why they don't want Vince out. They're scared he'll upset their lucrative little empire.'

'The great detective triumphs and I lose my kids!' Janine said bitterly.

'Don't be like that. The two things are unrelated. We'll sort Henry Talbot out.'

'What are you going to do?'

The question was so ridiculous that we both managed a grim smile. I hadn't enough energy to blow up a balloon, let alone sort anybody out.

'I'm going to do nothing but I know someone who will take action.'

'Who?'

'Clyde Harrow.'

'Him!' Janine's face turned crimson. 'Why should he lift a finger to help us?'

'I'll come up with a few reasons, don't worry.'

'Shouldn't we tell the police?'

'What police?' I asked. She turned and looked at the corridor. Where moments before there'd been a platoon of coppers now there was just space.

'Where've they all gone?'

'They've gone off shift, love; and someone's decided that the disappearance of your children's just a domestic problem now they know their father's got them. You haven't got any kind of court order forbidding Henry from seeing the children, have you?'

'I have full custody. Henry's visiting rights were just a voluntary agreement, but there's no court order preventing him from seeing them.'

356

'So there you are. I expect he's thinking of taking them back to the States.'

A determined expression came back into Janine's face and the wan, fatalistic air of tragedy that she'd brought into the room with her faded. She snatched out her mobile and then remembered where she was and went out for the telephone trolley.

'Will you phone him or will I?' she asked.

'Better me . . .'

'How nice to hear from one's friends when sunk in adversity. I don't think I got your Christmas card this year,' were Clyde's first words when I eventually reached him, 'but if this is about Henry Talbot, forget it. He's a very dear friend of mine.'

'Now what makes you think I want to talk about that creep?'

'I don't know,' he said evasively. 'I just thought you might.'

'Did you know I've split with Janine?'

'Oh, should I commiserate or congratulate?'

'Neither, it's just one of those things. I wanted to discuss a little deal with you but I'm temporarily incapacitated. I was hoping to put a little money your way, seeing as you're so hard up.'

'Cunane, pimpo-boy, if you're phoning at this hour in the morning, or indeed at any other hour, to gloat over my dim financial prospects you're wasting your time.'

'Hmmm,' I said, 'I can probably do something to improve your cash flow if you get your arse into gear and come down to Wythenshawe Hospital.'

This produced a profound sigh at the other end of the line.

'I can forgive your crudity, just; but to tantalise a man groaning beneath a mountain of debt is unforgivable,' he said, 'and am I to assume that you've undertaken paid employment with the Health Service? Possibly you're hiring yourself out as a trial piece for trainee surgeons?'

'The way things are going, I might as well do.'

I told him about my injury.

'Nothing too life threatening, then,' he said airily. 'I mean

357

the skull, pretty tough part of your anatomy I should have thought.'

'I'm here because of police brutality and I was hoping that you could use your media contacts to see that the incident gets maximum publicity,' I lied. My voice sounded feeble even in my own ears and I hoped that it added some veracity to my pitch.

'Pimpo-lad! Is this really a case of "Good night, sweet prince"? *Hamlet*, act five, scene two. I must say I find the thought of your deathbed curiously attractive.'

'I thought you might.'

'In normal circumstances I'd be happy to publicise your dying declarations gratis, and for nothing, but now that you have mentioned cash flow I find myself even more drawn by the melodramatic possibilities. Have you any idea of the sort of compensation the police are handing out in these cases? I'd be happy to work for a suitable percentage.'

I gave an increasingly eager Clyde directions on how to reach me. Bankruptcy notwithstanding, he was still in possession of his 4WD vehicle and, to judge by the noises off, also not without a companion to share his debtor's couch, the lovely Lauren no doubt. I was just about hanging on for all this. I felt attenuated, as if some force was stretching me like those machines they use to make toffee or seaside rock. I lay back on the bed and closed my eyes . . .

'I never knew you could be so crafty,' Janine whispered.

'Er, Dave,' I heard Janine say, 'Clyde's coming. I don't like to wake you but . . .'

'Get behind the door,' I ordered. 'He mustn't see you until he's in the room, and then make sure he doesn't get out.'

Janine darted off.

I'd been asleep for an hour. Curiously the effect of the massive blood transfusion wasn't enervating. Maybe the blood had come from paratroopers or members of some other aggressive force, but I felt more than ready to tackle the problems of the day.

'Clyde, old fruit . . .'

'No, young man, I may be temporarily separated from my

358

electronic pulpit but I will not be addressed as "old fruit",' he replied grandly and then turning as if to leave he caught sight of Janine.

'Hah! A subterfuge, I should have expected as much,' he said theatrically. Janine took a menacing step towards him and he drew back. 'What, no iced water, madam? No handy bedpan to drench poor Clyde with?'

'Oh, stop it!' Janine bellowed.

'All right, Mr Harrow, sir, let's get serious,' I said. 'I want to know everything you know about Henry Talbot. There might well be a cash reward for the right information.'

'No, Clyde Harrow is not come down to this!' he snapped indignantly. 'Trading a friend for a handful of small change! You assume too much. A temporary sojourn in Carey Street is not sufficient to transform me into a turncoat.'

'OK, forget it. I was probably clutching at straws anyway. You don't know anything about Talbot.'

'But I do! Even a debtor such as myself is entitled to question the creditworthiness of those offering inducements. The last time I saw you, your face was a swollen mass of yellow and purple bruises, and you now appear to have had the top of your head surgically removed. When the time comes for me to collect my reward, will I be standing at a graveside in some chilly cemetery watching your remains disappear for ever?'

'Janine, you know where I keep my frozen assets. Will you give them to this fraud even if his prophecy comes true?'

She nodded.

'It's not a matter of cash. I'm not a hireling,' Clyde insisted. 'I don't take money out of the soiled fist of a private detective, living or dead. Only a position of honour could compensate me.'

'You want your job back?'

'How prescient of you! Use your influence with the Carlyles to restore me to my former degree and I will deliver Talbot trussed, stuffed and ready for the oven.'

'Pig!' Janine snapped. 'You know where he is and what he's done but you bargain with my children.'

'I can do without emotional outbursts from you, dear lady,'

Clyde replied coldly. 'Your last assault severely damaged my waning credit in Manchester but your summary of the position is essentially accurate. Where you go wrong is in your assumption that Henry Talbot is any less capable of bringing up his children than you are. He intends to make an entirely new life for them in America under an assumed name, and as a mere man myself I don't see why he shouldn't be allowed the chance.'

'Cut the cackle, Harrow,' I said. 'Do you know where Talbot is likely to be now?'

'Within a mile or two,' he bragged.

Janine looked as if she was about ready to explode. I signalled her to rein back her anger. She got the message and left the room.

'I'll do what I can on the job front . . .'

'Sorry, not good enough! Promises won't pay my alimony cheques. I will require personal assurance from one of the Carlyles before I move a finger.'

'You'll have it,' I promised.

51

The trouble with head injuries is that you can't always control what's happening around you. I told Clyde that I would get him his job back, and there may have been some idea in the back of my mind of trying to blackmail the Carlyles over Vince's release, but no sooner did I start thinking on those lines than I got a blinding headache. I lay back and must have fallen asleep again.

When I came round this time it was with an abrupt shock.

Janine was wrestling on the floor with a young woman. I thought I was dreaming but the crash of equipment as they rolled over and over was all too real. The woman, who was clad in an Adidas jogging suit and wearing a plastic face mask, was trying to pull something out of a bum-bag and Janine was straining every muscle to prevent her.

'Dave!' she gasped. 'Stop her!'

I tried to struggle out of bed. It was like a waking nightmare. Trying to move was hell. I felt as if I was becalmed in a sea of molten tar.

Janine's attacker had rolled on top and she was tugging at something shiny and metallic in her bag. It was a gun. I couldn't move to save my life. I may have shouted. With a yell of triumph the attacker freed the gun and pointed it at me. At that moment Brendan Cullen dived into the room and hit her like a ton of bricks. The gun flew out of her hand and she was hurled against the steel leg of my bed. Her head hit it with a sickening thud and she rolled onto her back.

'Lucky for you I came back, isn't it?' Cullen said mildly when he picked himself up and dusted off his trousers. 'I wonder what we have here?' He studied the woman on the ground. Nurses and hospital security staff arrived and in seconds the small side ward was crammed with bodies. The would-be assassin was hauled onto a trolley, still alive but breathing with an ominous snorting noise. Cullen phoned for reinforcements and Janine squirmed through the mob to my bedside.

'Dave, you were asleep again and I was out getting a cup of coffee. I came back and I saw her bending over the bed and pulling that gun out. She was here to kill you.'

'That's right, old cock,' Cullen said cheerily. 'Did you recognise her?'

'Recognise her? I can hardly see you now, let alone her!' I said grumpily, fingering the bandages which enveloped my head.

'All right, Dave, keep your hair on.'

'I'm glad someone finds this amusing,' I said. One side of my head had been shaved for the operation.

'All I meant was that she might have been the last thing you ever saw. I'd have thought her face was etched on your memory,' Cullen shot back.

'She was wearing that mask,' I croaked.

'So she was,' Cullen agreed. Using tweezers he picked the mask up from the corner where it had been kicked and placed it in an evidence bag. 'I should wait for forensics, but with so much coming and going in here the place is bound to be contaminated anyway.'

'What problems you have. I'm still waiting for an explanation as to why I was attacked in a supposedly secure hospital.'

'So am I, sunshine,' he said grimly. 'So am I. I wonder what kind of mask this is?'

'I can see you've never played ice hockey,' Janine volunteered from her corner of the bed. 'That's a goalkeeper's face mask. I know because I've taken Lloyd to the Arena to see the Manchester Storm.'

The mention of Lloyd started her weeping.

'Don't worry,' I said. 'We'll find him and Jenny. At least we know it's not a child molester who has them.'

That was no comfort to her.

'I've told you Henry used to like beating me up,' she said.

362

'Goodness knows what he'll do if Jenny starts being difficult.'

'He'll be on his best behaviour, love, believe me,' Cullen interjected.

'How do you know?' Janine demanded.

'It figures,' he continued. 'He'll want the kids on his side at least until he gets them out of the country. He's probably smothering them in ice cream and sweets and videos and whatever else kids of that age want.'

'No!' Janine wailed. She collapsed into the armchair and buried her face in her hands.

'Bren, if that's the best you can do . . .' I muttered fiercely.

'Right, let's have a look at the gun then,' he said, ignoring my words.

Partly numbed by drugs as I was I still felt a shiver of horror as Bren lifted the weapon up by placing a pencil in the barrel. I watched fascinated as he took out a pen and pressed the button to eject the magazine.

'Uh-oh!' he muttered, as the magazine fell onto the bed.

'What?' I asked anxiously.

'Special bullets, that's what. Point-two-two LR Stinger bullets, just like the ones which killed Lou Olley.'

'What are they?' Janine asked, looking up from her private grief. I felt a surge of pride that she could go on being professional in the circumstances.

'This gun's a Star Model Target Pistol, made in Spain and no doubt smuggled into this country in some holidaymaker's baggage. It fires ten point-two-two calibre Long Rifle bullets, but these particular bullets weren't made in Spain. They're Stinger bullets, made in the USA, and specially modified to increase their stopping power to make up for the small calibre. Each bullet inflicts maximum injury. It doesn't pass through the target and out the other side. All the energy is released inside the body. A single bullet is powerful enough to stop an elk. Even you wouldn't have survived a hit from one of these, Dave.'

His words sounded intentionally brutal. I remembered the warning he'd given me that morning when he'd been at Lou Olley's PM. The effect was to render me speechless for once. Janine crumpled. She slumped forward and would have fallen on the floor if Bren hadn't caught her. He helped her back into her chair.

'It seems to me that the lady with the lump on her head who tried to do you, Dave,' he continued, quite unconcerned, 'is the same female who killed Lou Olley. At least, the chances of there being two female assassins who pack point-two-two target pistols loaded with Stingers is pretty slight. So it looks like the idea of Operation Calverley – keeping an eye on you – has finally paid off.'

'Paid off!' I croaked indignantly. 'It's pure chance that she didn't succeed. Don't try to twist this round into a great success for yourself. Janine deserves the credit. I wouldn't be here if she hadn't had the guts to tackle that woman.'

Cullen gave me a wistful look.

'I suppose you deserve some credit,' I admitted.

'Does this mean it's all over?' Janine asked. 'You'll catch the people who're behind all this now, won't you?'

'Maybe, love, but if she's a pro it's unlikely she has any idea who paid her to kill Dave.'

Janine looked ready to be sick at this concept. She struggled to keep her emotions under control. I lay back and prayed for unconsciousness but it didn't come.

'This hasn't got anything to do with Henry taking my kids?' Janine asked almost in a whisper.

'Lady, if it was anyone else but Dave involved I'd say no, but where he's concerned anything's possible. Do you want to know how many times I've warned him that the Carlyles play for keeps?'

'He doesn't listen,' Janine agreed wearily, 'but my children, what about them?'

'I've put out an alert to all ports and airports to stop Talbot taking them out of the country but I'm afraid I'd be fooling you if I told you that was likely to be one hundred per cent effective.'

'What will I do?' Janine enquired forlornly.

'Keep your fingers crossed that someone spots them, that's all we can do,' Bren said sadly.

'But we were going to find out from . . .'

While speaking Janine was looking at me. I shook my head

364

as vigorously as circumstances permitted. Janine looked surprised. Her voice faltered.

'Yes, love?' Bren prompted.

'How did that killer know Dave was here? How could she know?' she improvised.

'There are people who spend all their time listening to the police radio, and if whoever organised this didn't find out that way there must be dozens of people who saw Dave being carted off in the ambulance.'

'Not to mention that some of Manchester's finest don't mind making a dishonest bob or two,' I said.

'Oh, you can speak, can you?' Bren said with a curl of his lip. 'I must be off to see if there's any sign of your mate's friends.'

'Thanks for the protection.'

'Better late than never. You know I had a feeling that if I stuck close to you I'd crack this case.'

'Nice to know you care.'

'Yeah, well don't wander off,' he said with an ironic glance at my various attachments. 'You as well, Ms White. I'll need a statement.'

'What are we going to do?' Janine wailed as soon as Cullen's broad back was round the corner.

'Janine, I've got a strong feeling that we don't need to get in touch with the Carlyle family. I think they know exactly where we are.'

I spent an interesting morning being poked and prodded when I wasn't napping and being told how lucky I was that the blow wasn't a millimetre in another direction. Medical opinion was tending to agree with Clyde that I had a thick skull. It was nice to know that there was one part of me that was useful.

We both made statements about the shooter to Cullen's oppo, Detective Sergeant Munro, who made no effort to hide his distaste. I also made a statement about my 'accident' to an inspector from West Yorkshire who assured me that the fullest investigation would be made into the near fatal circumstances but that I wasn't to expect an early result as all batons concerned were now very clean, indeed polished, and no one was admitting anything; and didn't I think it possible that I hit my head on the steel door lintel as I fell, and that the whole thing was just an unfortunate accident.

I didn't, but I left him with a strong hint that my interest in vengeance would be considerably lessened if efforts to find Jenny and Lloyd were expedited.

Marvin also paid a visit. He handed me a card with his surname on: *Marvin Desailles*. He was wearing a dark three-piece suit. It was at least one size too big but that didn't prevent Marvin from conveying an impression of great dignity and seriousness. I introduced him to Janine as the firm's legal representative.

'Are they still harassing you?' he asked, with a nod at the armed police standing by my doorway.

'Oddly enough they're supposed to be protecting me, but it's more a case of shutting the stable door than anything. Janine saved my life.'

'Sorry about your troubles, ma'am,' he said to her formally, and then, 'The other matter, sir, shall I proceed?'

It took me a minute to work out what he meant. He sounded more like an old-fashioned English butler than a streetwise lawyer.

'No, give me the letter,' I said after a moment's thought. 'Mr King may have to stay in jail a little longer.'

'Are you sure?' he asked. 'I mean there will have to be action, won't there?'

'Postponed for the present,' I said.

Marvin left soon after and I then had my work cut out persuading Janine that charging off to Manchester Airport would do no good. We were talking when there was a knock on the door and the uniformed officer opened it. Tony Hefflin stood beside him, hair as bouffant as ever, and wearing a cashmere jacket and slacks. He looked as if he was off for a visit to Tarn Golf Club. His crinkly skin was the colour of tanned leather. He must have spent hours under the lamps.

'Excuse me, this gentleman says he's a friend of yours,' the copper said disapprovingly.

Hefflin's reputation had obviously gone before him.

366

'He is and I was expecting him,' I said. 'Come in, Tony.' The armed doorkeeper frowned but admitted the emissary from Brandon Carlyle.

'Cunane,' Hefflin said grouchily, 'a little bird tells me that a copper put you in here. That's good to know.'

I smiled at him and he responded with a puzzled frown. He gave Janine the barest of nods.

'What! No chocolates?' I said. 'How's Brandon?'

'You won't learn, will you? How many times have you been told to keep your nose out of the family's business?'

'Whoa! Family now, eh? What's happened? Has Brandon adopted you?'

'And does your warning mean that you accept that it was the family who sent an assassin to kill Dave?' Janine demanded.

'I know nothing about any assassin, though I can't say I'm surprised. Lover-boy here's trodden on more toes than a blind elephant at a ballet dancer's picnic.'

'What have you come for, then?'

'I'm here to see that Cunane gets the message. Stay out of our business and be told!'

'I'm going to deck the next person who tells me to "be told",' I said.

'Look at you,' Hefflin mocked. 'You couldn't raise a hand to save your life.'

'But I can,' Janine said angrily, stepping forward to confront Hefflin. 'I want my children back.'

'That's nothing to do with us.'

'The Carlyle Corporation employed Henry Talbot and brought him into the country. It's got plenty to do with you,' I said.

'I know nothing about that.'

'Then you'd better be a good little errand boy and find out,' I suggested. 'I'd also like to hear about the "or else".'

'What are you on about? Are your brains scrambled?'

'I've to stay out of the family's business. What's the "or else"? Another hit?'

'I've told you, that was nothing to do with us. You've already had your payoff from the family. Why the hell do you think your little no-hope business suddenly got so prosperous? Now you're reneging. We hear someone's been to visit Dr Sameem. What the fuck do you think you're playing at? You'll be back in the gutter before you get out of that bed if Mr Carlyle lifts his hand.'

'I don't think so. It would be hard to manage anyway, being in the gutter and in bed at the same time.'

'The great joker, eh? I want your word that you'll drop whatever you were up to and then Mr Carlyle may think twice about dumping you in view of the efforts by unknown parties to kill you. The publicity might not be good for the firm.'

'That's not going to happen either,' I said confidently. 'You listen, Hefflin. You tell Brandon that I can have Vince King released from prison within the next forty-eight hours. See how that grabs him.'

'Now I know you've really lost it. King's staying in jail till he rots. I didn't pay my subs to the Police Federation all those years to see a cop-killer walking free.'

'He'll walk,' I said smugly.

Despite himself Hefflin was curious.

'Oh, yes?'

'Yes. The Home Secretary will have no alternative when I send him the proof that evidence was suppressed.'

'What evidence, dickhead?'

'Evidence that the carpet fibres which placed King in the murder room could have come from somewhere else. Evidence that DI Jones blackmailed the forensic scientist to cover up.'

'You're making this up.'

'No, it's all down in black and white, signed, sealed and waiting to be delivered to James McMahon.'

'He'll ignore it.'

'He can't. The permanent secretary knows all about it. King will be out while the unsafe conviction is investigated by an outside police force. McMahon will have King out of that prison so fast that you'll miss it if you blink. He'll do it to protect his own and the Government's reputation and also because King really is innocent.'

'You sod!' Hefflin cursed. He turned on his heel, but when

he reached the door thought better about the dramatic exit. 'I'll be back,' he said furiously and then shut the door quietly behind him.

52

With all the nimbleness of his rat-like nature Hefflin slipped back into the room about five minutes after he'd left. Perhaps it was unfair to say the disgraced former copper was rat-like but I wasn't feeling generous. There was a suaveness and a sure-footedness about the way the man moved that specially grated on me in my present bed-bound state.

'She'll have to go,' he said, pointing to Janine.

'It's the fate of my children you're discussing!' Janine said indignantly.

'This isn't a fucking press conference. I'm not saying what I have to say in front of any sodding journalists,' Hefflin said smoothly. I could see he was enjoying winding Janine up. He was brimming over with barely concealed spite. It wasn't hard to imagine what his conversation with Brandon had been like.

'They're my children and I'm staying.'

'OK, so I'm going,' Hefflin announced.

Janine tried to block him at the door. Hefflin was foolish enough to try to push her aside. The result was that, experienced copper though he may once have been, he found himself flat on his back with Janine trying to use his abundant wavy hair as a handle to bang his head repeatedly against the carpeted floor. Apart from a few piercing gasps the struggle took place entirely in silence.

'Janine, we need him if we're going to get Harrow to help us,' I warned, but to no avail. The pair rolled over in furious battle, with Hefflin cursing monotonously under his breath. It was only the arrival of a nurse that stopped them. She yelled for security as soon as she opened the door and took in the scene. It took two hospital security men to get Janine off Hefflin. Then an armed police guard crowded the former copper into a corner while the hospital security men stood with the panting, wild-eyed Janine. I noted with satisfaction that Janine was clutching a handful of Hefflin's hair. He looked well battered. His face was a dangerous shade of puce.

Moments later a hospital official in a suit arrived to read the riot act. He was accompanied by the surgeon who'd treated my wound.

'The hospital management can't tolerate this kind of rowdiness,' the official, a mild-looking man with a moustache, told us. I could see that he suffered from an intimidation deficit and that he was having trouble working himself up to the right degree of indignation. Surveying Hefflin's cashmere jacket, now sadly in need of some invisible mending, and Janine's torn blouson, he shook his head and tut-tutted. 'Really, we don't expect this class of behaviour from people of your sort. It's bad enough in A&E on a Saturday night with the drunken yobbos, but we don't expect this kind of thing in an intensive care unit. I'm told you're a journalist, Ms White. I wonder how your editor would like to hear that one of his employees was rolling round on the hospital floor in a savage attack on this gentleman?'

'I did no such thing,' Janine said gamely. 'He attacked me. I'm sure my editor doesn't mind his journalists defending themselves.'

Hefflin started spluttering indignantly at this.

'I'm not here to sort out the rights and wrongs. There's already been an extremely serious incident in this room. The management will have to assess our ability to cope with the treatment of Mr Cunane if incidents on this scale are going to reoccur. We have the safety of other patients and staff to think of.'

The suited official pursed his lips and looked at me sourly as if I was a particularly unwelcome cuckoo in his nest. That made my mind up for me.

'Never stay where you're not wanted, my old granny used to say,' I said, swinging my legs out of bed. Even that small action drained my strength but I kept a brave smile on my face.

'Just where are you proposing to go?' Janine demanded.

371

Having shaken off the two guards she was now standing at the foot of my bed with her arms akimbo. Also with arms akimbo and matching frowns were the official, two nurses, the surgeon and even the security guards. From my perspective, the whole group of akimbos looked like a mob working themselves up for a lynching.

'There's no point in staying here,' I said. 'They obviously want me out.'

'No, Dave, that's not fair,' Janine said. 'It wasn't you that was fighting . . .'

'Mr Cunane, you're my patient,' the surgeon said proprietorally. 'You need complete rest and calm. There's always a danger of blood clotting after an operation like yours. You might not be so lucky next time as you were last night.'

'Oh, let him take his chances,' Hefflin said contemptuously. 'He's too stupid to know when he's well off.'

'I must insist you stay in bed,' the surgeon said.

'And I must insist on getting out of here,' I said, struggling to my feet. 'There's too much at stake.'

'Listen to that,' Hefflin snorted. 'Don't try sounding so noble, Cunane. We all know you're only in this for the money.'

'Yeah, that's right,' I agreed. 'Time is money and I can't afford to hang around here. Get out, Hefflin, I'll meet you in the car park.'

Hefflin left. The security men went with him. Janine came over to me.

'Dave, you can't do this,' she said quietly. She laid her arm on my shoulder.

'If we're going to have any chance of catching up with Talbot I've got to go,' I whispered. Her face was a study in conflicting emotions and after a moment she withdrew the arm with which she'd been pushing me back to bed.

I started fidgeting with the drip that ran into my wrist. The medical staff intervened and twenty minutes later, after signing in triplicate forms absolving the hospital of all blame in the event of my sudden death, I was free.

'Mr Cunane, you must avoid all exertion and keep on taking the anti-coagulants,' the surgeon said. 'Come back if you feel unwell. You've lost a lot of blood.'

He was right. I did feel bloodless. It was as if my body had somehow been stretched. My feet and legs felt so detached from the rest of me that they might have been twenty feet away from my brain.

When we got to the car park Janine went to her own car and I went over to Hefflin's Jaguar.

'I hope you do snuff it,' he said spitefully as he leaned across the seat to open the passenger door for me. 'You deserve it for the trouble you've caused. How much are you asking to keep Vince King where he is? I can go up to six figures but I can't guarantee that the old man will let you stick around to enjoy it.'

'I wasn't thinking of cashing in my chips just now,' I said. 'All I want from Brandon Carlyle is a guarantee that Clyde Harrow will get his job back.'

Hefflin looked confused. He tried to work this out. 'Is Harrow blackmailing you in some way?' he asked eventually.

'And I won't be letting Vince King remain as a guest of Her Majesty for much longer either.'

'What! I thought . . .'

'You thought I was a little sleaze bag just like yourself. No, you can tell Brandon that if he plays ball with Harrow I can give him a day or two to get himself sorted and then my evidence is going to James McMahon.'

'You're crazy!'

'Maybe,' I admitted, 'but tell your boss that if he has any idea of getting rid of me it won't do him a scrap of good. The truth about the Vince King case is going to come out whatever he does.'

'The truth! You wouldn't know that if it hit you in the face,' Hefflin snarled as I got out and walked over to Janine's car.

53

Hopes of a quick departure from Wythenshawe Hospital soon faded as negotiations bogged down. Two hours later I was still in Janine's car while Clyde Harrow and his agent shuttled between ourselves and Hefflin with offer and counter-offer. A couple of executives from Alhambra TV had arrived to support Hefflin. Marvin and Celeste had joined us. Security guards from the hospital hovered nearby but perhaps remembering various incidents, they kept their distance. I felt as if I was about a hundred years old. All the aches and pains from my previous 'accident' seemed to have been reactivated. I tried to keep a brave face on things.

Finally everything was settled. That is, I knew things weren't really settled between myself and Brandon Carlyle, but they were settled to the satisfaction of Clyde Harrow and the odious Hefflin. Clyde was given a new contract and the promise of a new series and I promised to delay action on King's release for four days, time that would allow Brandon to make his plans to minimise any side effects.

'Are you set then?' Clyde Harrow asked. 'I shall personally lead you to Henry Talbot's lair.'

'You could have saved us all a lot of trouble by giving us the address hours ago,' I said.

'But then where would I have been?' he asked plaintively. I almost detected an edge of apology in the egomaniac's voice.

'Clyde, you don't believe that Brandon Carlyle's going to tolerate your presence in his organisation for a moment longer than necessary, do you?' I asked wearily.

'It's all down in black and white. I have cast-iron guarantees,' he muttered defensively.

'I expect Lou Olley thought he had guarantees,' I said.

'You don't really think I'm in danger, do you?'

'All I know is Brandon Carlyle has ways of getting what he wants – ways that aren't always legal. Anyway, we'll see you get a nice funeral.'

'Stop it!' Clyde ordered.

'Where's Talbot? Take us to him,' I snapped back.

'Ah, the "frown and wrinkled lip and sneer of cold command", I think I like you better in this mode, Pimpo-lad. That's from . . .'

'Shelley,' interjected Janine, ' "Ozymandias". Can you two stop picking at your personalities for a moment and lead me to my children?'

'Sorry, I was only attempting the extramural education of your partner,' Clyde replied coldly.

Janine didn't dispute Clyde's description of my status, which heartened me slightly.

'The children are with him in a caravan on Anglesey which belongs to the parents of my dear little companion, Lauren.'

We both looked at Clyde in dismay. I'd been expecting him to name some hotel in Manchester.

'God!' Janine groaned.

I looked at my watch.

'We can be there in two hours,' I said.

'He's intending to slip across to Ireland,' Clyde informed us. 'He has the children's passports and he needed somewhere to lie low until it was safe for him to catch the Holyhead ferry.'

'Why, Clyde?' Janine asked bitterly. 'What have I ever done to you that justified this?'

He coloured slightly but then rallied. 'My dear woman, I know that we live in an age of women's rights, but why shouldn't a mere man such as myself seek some psychic recompense for insults offered? You chose to humiliate me in public, I chose to help a loving father to recover his children. I think that makes us even.'

'You bastard!' she hissed.

'I've already discussed the question of my ingeneration at tedious length with lucky Dave,' he said, glancing at my bandages with a sly smile, 'but as you choose to spend time trading insults when you could be pursuing your unfortunate offspring, may I say that your own behaviour needs careful examination. A truly loving mother would have had her children with her when Henry came in search of his paternal rights. You made it easy for him.'

Janine began to get out of the car. She was breathing fire. I held her back.

'We haven't time for this,' I said. 'Clyde, you go in front in the Toyota, and believe me, if you're playing games I'll phone Carlyle to tell him the deal's off.'

Clyde turned with a scowl and headed for his top-of-the-range Toyota Land-Cruiser without another word. Lauren was doing the driving. We followed her out of the car park and onto the M56.

My estimate of two hours for the journey to Anglesey was wildly optimistic. It seemed as if half the population of northern England was en route for Wales, but eventually we crossed the Menai Straits onto the low-lying island. Janine concentrated on her driving but I could tell that Clyde's comment had found its mark. She was too quiet.

Lauren's parents' caravan was in a vast park behind sand dunes overlooking the western side of the strait. We peered through the windows: the caravan appeared to be empty.

'They were here,' Clyde said defensively. 'You can see the place has been disturbed.' For once he looked nervous as he watched me fingering Janine's mobile phone.

'I have the key,' Lauren informed us. Janine snatched it off her and ran to the door of caravan, a massive semi-static affair. Once inside it was obvious that the children had been there.

'This stove's still hot,' I said. 'You tipped him off, didn't you? You told him we were coming.'

'No, he must have spotted the car,' Clyde said quickly.

'The passports are still here,' Janine said, opening a drawer, 'and their luggage.'

'Perhaps they just went to the beach,' Lauren suggested.

'In the car?' I asked. The car port at the side of the caravan was empty.

'No, you're right. It's only a short walk,' Lauren said. I looked out of the window. It was an overcast mid-winter day.

376

A penetrating wind was sweeping in from the sea. The trees and bushes were bending against the strong breeze. It wasn't the sort of day for the beach. While the caravan park was by no means deserted, what people there were were indoors. You could see them through the large bay windows relaxing in front of televisions. I went to the door. I could hear seagulls and the wind beating against the dunes.

'Clyde, you're an evil rat,' Janine said in a low voice. 'You dared to tip him off.'

'No,' Clyde muttered.

'You dared . . .'

'. . . "I dare do all that may become a man" . . .'

'Don't quote Shakespeare at me, you filthy windbag!' she screamed, and before the words were out of her mouth, she snatched up an empty pan from the stove and struck Clyde a resounding blow over the head.

'Jack that in!' Lauren yelped, springing to Clyde's defence. 'It's true. He never used the mobile.'

'Liar!' Janine roared. She was beside herself with frustration and rage. It was just as well for Clyde that there were no knives handy. As it was, his partner helped him to stagger towards his car, more or less in one piece.

'That wasn't too clever,' I commented. 'He might have told us more.'

'I'm not feeling clever. I want my kids back,' Janine said, clenching her fists. Then we both watched the Toyota, driven by Lauren, creep around the corner and off the site.

As we stared into the vacant space another car appeared.

'Oh, God! It's them,' Janine gasped.

'Quick, shut the door and hide,' I said.

A moment later the car pulled up alongside the caravan. The doors slammed and Janine sprang into action.

The punishment she'd handed out to Clyde was mild compared to what Henry got. He was holding a carrier bag which hampered his defence when Janine launched herself from the caravan steps. In a second he was on the ground and Janine was pounding his face with her fists. She grabbed a loose stone and, feeble though I was, I managed to wrest it out of her fingers before she killed him. In the second of opportunity that provided, Henry scrambled free and dashed into the caravan, slamming the door shut behind him.

There was a general mêlée as the children flung themselves at Janine.

'Mummy! Mummy! Mummy!' was all I heard.

Janine gathered herself up and led the children to her car. They went without a backward glance until they were seated in the car.

'Daddy bought us sweets and drinks,' Jenny said. 'They're in that bag. Can I go and get them?'

Janine accelerated out of the caravan park.

54

The next two days are missing from my personal calendar. This time the staff at Wythenshawe Hospital kept me confined in a first-floor room with a 'No Visitors' sign fixed on the door and strictly adhered to. Not that I could have managed a conversation even if there'd been one on offer.

The first sign I got that anyone cared about my continued existence was a visit from Brendan Cullen and his sidekick Munro on the Tuesday morning. They more or less conned their way into the unit by claiming urgent police business.

Munro went through the motions of taking a statement from me about the attempt on my life by the female assassin but when I'd put my poorly scrawled signature at the bottom of the page Bren signalled the younger man to leave us.

'Janine's back at the flat, and the kids are OK. I thought you'd like to know.'

'Yeah, she phoned.'

'She's not been round then?'

'She can't leave the children. They're terrified of being left.'

'Or is it her that's terrified of leaving them? She didn't look too good when I saw her. Henry Talbot's still in custody but they'll be letting him out shortly on condition that he returns to America.'

'So attempted murder's not a crime any more?'

'It seems not,' Cullen agreed. 'It's all wrapped up in psychological jargon, but what the statement from the North Wales CPS amounts to is that no action will be taken if Talbot promises to leave the country and not come back.'

I shrugged. I wanted to sleep but he seemed in no hurry to leave.

'Words to the wise, Dave?' he said, tapping his nose with his forefinger.

'I've had so much good advice lately that I'm thinking of starting my own agony aunt column,' I replied.

'Don't get peevish, sunshine,' Bren said with a smile. 'Speaking of sunshine, did you know he's gay? Your legal representative, that is?'

'So what,' I said fiercely.

'It's nothing to me. It's just that he's not got a snowball's chance in hell of ever getting on the Community Forum as the lovely Celeste keeps hinting.'

'Tough! I'm sure we'll all survive that disappointment.'

'OK, Dave, don't get on your high horse. Everyone's getting so politically correct these days that you daren't say boo to a goose down at the nick.'

'My heart bleeds.'

'Yeah, that's what I was coming to. The lady who wanted to stop your clock? She's a nut.'

'I'm sure she is.'

'No, I mean she's not a professional assassin. She's strictly an amateur. That's not to say what she might have turned into if she'd got away with doing you in. She's a South African student studying here in Manchester. She was majoring in town planning at the Metro Uni and she's turned to killing as a lucrative sideline.'

'Now you're joking.'

'No, her name's Ulrike Reichert and she's a South African of German ancestry. It seems that back home in the Republic she and her whole family are gun nuts, armed to the teeth day and night. We've had the greatest difficulty getting her to talk about anything except guns. That's what led her into her new sideline.'

'I can see you're itching to tell me.'

'Right, we've made enquiries among her friends and at her hall of residence, and it seems that all she talks about is guns and how soppy we Brits are in not allowing every citizen to have an armoury. She even tried to join the university officer's training corps but they saw the strange light gleaming in her eyes and turned her down. Anyway, to cut a long story short, she's been talking like this in various pubs in both Hulme and Salford, boasting about how she could hit the Ace of Spades at fifty paces, and someone approached her to do the job on Lou Olley.'

'Who?'

'That she won't or can't say. It wasn't Hefflin or Marti, if that's what you're thinking. The vague description she gives could fit dozens of ageing villains.'

'So she was just recruited in a pub?'

'I know it sounds unlikely, but if you wanted a hit man or a hit woman, you'd hardly go down to the Job Centre and leave an ad, would you? I believe it. She talked too much and eventually the wrong person, or the right person from his point of view, heard her spiel. She wasn't being paid in money. They offered to let her keep the gun and they threw in a mobile home as well.'

'You're joking!'

'I said she was a nut.'

'What was she offered for the job on me?'

'You should be flattered. A top of the range BMW sports car.'

'Great.'

'She says she knows nothing about what happened to Sam Levy, and as all the instructions were given over untraceable mobile phones it doesn't look as if we're going to get any more juice out of her.'

'There's no way you can link her to the Carlyles?'

'I've told you. We haven't a scrap of hard evidence against any of them. It could have been old Levy himself who organised the Olley hit. He had good contacts with the local underworld.'

'I can't believe that.'

'Yes, think about it. Suppose Olley was coming to sort out Marti. Sort her out fairly permanently, I mean, for besmirching the Carlyle honour with you. Who would she turn to for protection but dear old Sam? It's a possibility. Levy gets Olley killed and then some of Olley's mates do Levy.'

'They're thieves. They'd never leave a box of pearls lying about.'

381

'I only said it's a possibility. We might never know what happened, but what puzzles me is what's suddenly become so urgent about slotting you? And why is that arsehole Clyde Harrow looking so pleased with himself, and why was Tony Hefflin sniffing round here?'

Suddenly I didn't feel very well. My head was throbbing again. I lay back and closed my eyes.

'Dave, you're a mate, but I shall want some answers in the morning,' Bren said quietly before leaving me alone.

I must have slept for several hours. It was dark and the hospital was relatively quiet when I woke up. A woman was holding my hand.

'Janine,' I murmured.

'Hah! It's not Ironpants,' my visitor said sharply.

'Marti!'

'Lucky guy, aren't you, with two women fussing over you? Which one of us would you rather it was?'

I said nothing and then in the darkness I heard the air being sucked into her lungs for that familiar tidal wave of laughter.

'No!' I gasped.

She managed to confine the eruption to a mere chuckle. She switched on the night light.

'You know, you've made more waves for the Carlyle Corporation than even I managed at my peak. Is it true you've got proof that my dad was innocent?'

'Yes.'

'Make sure you keep it somewhere safe, then. I wouldn't give tuppence for your chances of surviving next week. If you knew the trouble I've been to over the last year trying to keep you alive . . .'

'Nice of you.'

'Yes, it was,' she agreed, 'and it's time you paid me back.' She kissed me and slipped her hand under the sheets for a quick grope.

'Marti!' I muttered. She wasn't deterred and somehow I couldn't find the energy to stop her or to scream for help. The flimsy gown I was wearing didn't offer much of an obstacle to her advances. All my responses were normal.

382

'I wouldn't have done it for anyone else,' she said conversationally as she unbuttoned her blouse, 'but you're the first man who ever did anything for me without knowing I was Vince King's daughter or connected to the Carlyle family.'

'Really.'

'Yes,' she grunted, pulling the sheets completely off the bed. In rapid succession, several of her garments joined the blouse and the sheets on the floor.

'This isn't the time or the place,' I protested.

'It is. I might never get another chance,' she said climbing onto the bed and straddling me.

'Someone might come in.'

'The door's locked.'

By this time neither Marti nor I was wearing much apart from a pleasant expression. I know I should have chinned her or something but I didn't.

'You're pretty fit for a hospital patient,' she commented a few minutes later. 'I bet old Ironpants wouldn't have done that for you.' She was sitting on the bed beside me, trying to twist the hair sticking out from under my bandages into a plait.

'She's got other things on her mind as well, you know,' I said, untangling her fingers from my hair. 'It was you who arranged for Talbot to come back on the scene, wasn't it?'

'If it's worth fighting over a man, it's worth fighting dirty,' she said with a laugh.

'Don't start!' I pleaded.

She laughed again, not her full air-raid siren but loudly enough. I felt certain that someone would come banging on the door, but no one did. As if she could read my mind Marti started getting dressed. I watched as she tethered her breasts in her bra. At least she hadn't come to put a bullet in my head – or had she?

'You haven't exactly been straight with me, have you?' I said truculently, while trying to arrange the hospital gown to protect what remained of my modesty. 'Was it you who sent that white van after me when I was coming back from Finchley?'

'Of course not! Nor did Brandon or Charlie. I haven't a clue who that lot were.' She was now fully dressed and she picked up the hospital bed-linen and slung it at me. 'Dave,' she said seriously, 'Charlie tried to do you but his effort was as feeble as everything else about him.'

'When did he try?'

'Right from that first day at Tarn he's been breathing fire whenever your name comes up. You mocked his accent or something. He's very sensitive, is Charlie. He broods on things. I managed to dissuade him then but when he found we'd been to see Vince and that I was seeing you he had a go at you with a Jeep. You were running on the Meadows or something. Poor Charlie, he couldn't hit a hole in the road.'

'Poor Charlie! Maybe I should have helped him by lying down.'

'Don't start me off,' she warned as she tried to suppress her laugh. 'He probably would still have missed you.'

I fixed her with a stern look.

'And what about the hit on Lou Olley? I just do not buy it that you don't know who was responsible. Time to spill the beans, Marti.'

She pouted.

'Oh, I suppose you might as well know. Remember I told you about Charlie's attempt to finish Brandon off by fixing the electric doors at South Pork, and how Brandon caught him at it? Well, Brandon told him then that he had to get shot of me or leave the business. Poor old Charlie asked Lou Olley to handle the job. Lou had a soft spot for me . . .'

'You mean, you'd bedded him!'

'Could be, but the stupid lump was soft enough to tell me that he was coming to pick you and me up at your office.'

'And as far as you were concerned it might just as well have been a suicide pact for one person only – me?'

'It didn't work out that way, did it?'

'Did you get Olley killed?'

'Not me personally, but I know how it was done. What do you expect, Dave? Olley wasn't the sort of man you stop with a slap on the wrist. It's horrible. I don't want to talk about it.'

I looked her in the face and she opened her green eyes wide. She looked truthful and sincere enough to set a High Court judge raving about fragrant English roses. Oh well, the late Olley was unlamented. Why should I push it? On the other hand, I was neither late nor unlamented . . . yet!

'Marti,' I said softly, 'someone tried to run me into a motorway bridge. That wasn't clumsy Charlie! Another few inches and I'd have been strawberry jam.'

'I know,' she replied, sounding so honest and serious that almost every particle of me wanted to believe her.

'How do you know?' I asked angrily.

'Dave, get real. The family knows everything about you that the police know. Did you think Hefflin was the only cop on Brandon's pay roll?'

I shook my head in despair.

'There's someone else involved besides the Carlyles. Brandon's scared stiff. I'm not certain but I think they tried to break into his house. I had an idea they were after me too, that's why I cleared out so fast when I clocked them in Finchley.'

'Sounds likely!' I said sceptically. 'As well as the Carlyle clan, someone else is out there looking for our blood.'

'Just your blood, Dave,' she murmured, stroking my hand. 'It was you they were after that night in London. I found that out when they went after you and not me. I'm straight with Brandon. When I ran off to London he thought I was going to grass . . . I mean, Charlie had arranged for Olley to kill me, but Brandon knows now that I never would've grassed. We don't do things like that in my family.'

'You're a joke, Marti! Sending Olley to kill you is just a social blunder but grassing's the worst crime in the book. Let me get Brendan Cullen here and you can tell him all this.'

'Now you're pissing me off, Dave.'

'But why? Don't you see this is your best way to dump Charlie?'

'You're talking like a copper. Face it, Dave, grassing is worse than a crime. I'd never do it. Why, if Vince came out tomorrow he could go to a dozen different places where they'd have a whip round for him. But grass on your own and no one wants to know you. It's just something no decent person ever does.'

I gaped at her. She sounded like an outraged matron who'd just been asked to strip by a bunch of lager louts. I tried to suppress a laugh.

'I see,' I said between giggles. Marti didn't see anything funny.

'No, really, after you gave Charlie that alibi for Lou it put me in the clear with the family. They knew I'd learned my lesson and that there wasn't going to be any comeback for Charlie's little mistake. He tried to kill me and I played away for a while with a good-looking guy. These things happen in families. It's a fact of life – look at the Royals . . . Brandon really trusts me now.'

'And you trust him? And Charlie, how can you stand having him near you?'

'Dave, you're a lovely man, so straight! I'd move in with you tomorrow if I thought you'd live a bit longer, but really! You don't pull in enough to keep me in shoe leather, whereas Charlie . . .'

'Whereas Charlie arranged for you to be bumped off.'

'There is that,' she admitted and her face darkened. 'This is all such a mess, Dave. If only I'd never got you involved with Vince. Brandon won't live for ever and we could have got it together . . .'

'Nice!' I muttered.

'Dave, there's something I must tell you. You know that day you rescued me at Tarn Golf Club?'

'How could I forget it?'

'It put the idea of how to kill me in Charlie's head. They were going to fake an accident. You'd be driving and I'd be drunk, and we'd both be dead because the car would have burnt to a cinder with us in it.'

'Sounds complicated.'

'No, it would've been easy. They had a car rigged to set on fire. When he was shot Olley was on his way to pick you up. I'm not sure what he would've said, but they'd have got you behind the wheel of that car with me in it and then bingo!'

'No wonder Charlie wanted to see me afterwards. It's time someone sorted him.'

'No, Dave, that's useless. This is how things are. The first

386

day I was in the children's home I learned that everyone's out for themselves. You don't think there's somebody up there writing everything down in a big book, do you?'

I shrugged my shoulders uncomfortably. She looked at me for an answer. 'The accounts have to be balanced sometime,' I muttered eventually. In Charlie's case that might be sooner rather than later, but I didn't say that.

She breathed in sharply and I thought she was going to laugh, but suddenly her eyes were brimming with tears. 'That's what Sam Levy used to say, and look what happened to him,' she said. 'His whole family was killed, his sister got cancer and he was tortured to death.'

'Don't you think the people who tortured him should pay for it?'

'It wasn't Brandon. I know that.'

'You mean you've persuaded yourself.'

'I know, because it was me that got Lou done and that caused Sam's death.'

'How?'

'Do you ever speak in sentences of longer than one word?'

'No.'

'OK, man of few words. Let's just say that Charlie isn't the world's greatest conspirator. I had a good idea what he was up to and I made my own moves.'

'Marti, this is an interesting story but at the time Lou was killed you were in the Renaissance Hotel, dead drunk.'

'I didn't say I killed him myself. I got him done.'

'How?'

'It's not like you think. Olley kept coming on to me. We'd had a fling but he wouldn't accept it was over. It was him gave me the black eye that time. I knew what was in the wind. I told Sam Levy . . .'

'Who just happened to have a South African contract killer in his top pocket.'

'How did you know?' she asked in a shocked voice.

'A little bird told me,' I said.

'It was him who arranged for Lou to have his surprise.'

'Nice man!'

'He was. He'd been wanting a straightener with Lou Olley

387

for a long while. Sam couldn't stand Olley. He reckoned poor Lou had ideas above his station. It was Sam who got him started, after all. Sam tried to get Brandon to sack Olley, but Brandon sacked him instead. Leah died soon after he got the heave-ho and I think Sam thought her death was something to do with that. He felt he'd done as much to build up the business as Brandon. When I told him Charlie was going to get Olley to do me he said he'd sort it. I thought he just meant he'd have a word with Brandon – maybe he did, but we know what happened next – no more Lou Olley.'

'That's a lovely theory, Marti, but the same woman who shot Olley was in this room the other day trying to kill me.'

'Yes, but don't you see? That's why they tortured Sam.'

'Who did?'

'The people that Brandon's scared of, the ones who ran you off the motorway.'

'Marti, do you think I still believe in fairies? It was Brandon who sent her. Hefflin was just coming to check that she'd done the job.'

'It wasn't Brandon. I was with him when he heard that the police had done you. He sent Hefflin round to make sure you knew to keep shtoom about Charlie's alibi.'

'They must be very convenient for Brandon, this mystery gang who go round killing people who upset the Carlyle Corporation.'

'It's all true. Don't you see, they tortured Sam and found out about this woman. Then they stashed her away for future use.'

I laughed.

'Brandon knows who they are but he won't tell,' Marti insisted. 'I think it's something to do with his big tickle.'

'Big tickle!' I scoffed. 'This isn't a joke.'

'Brandon's not laughing. I'm not laughing. Dave, the main reason that Brandon's not in prison is that he knew when to stop. He had this big tickle, made enough dosh to set himself up for life. My dad was involved but neither he nor Brandon will say what it was. After that Brandon went more or less legitimate, or at least he keeps the mucky end of the business at arm's length. My dad didn't know when to stop. He's always been a chancer and that's why he's banged up now.'

'Why should this tickle still be causing trouble twenty-odd years later?'

'It was something heavy, something really big, something that made the Train Robbery or the Brinks Mat job look like rubbish. Look how well Brandon's done ever since. It could be that one of these London firms still has its nose out of joint and wants to share Brandon's good luck.'

'How come there's been nothing in the papers about this job?'

'Maybe the authorities decided to keep it quiet.'

'There seem to be a lot of ifs and maybes, Marti.'

'I can't make you believe me, but why do you think they left that box full of pearls when they did Sam? That was to show Brandon that they weren't after chickenfeed. Brandon might have killed Sam but he'd never have tortured him.'

I shrugged.

'OK, be a dickhead then! Don't believe me. You've ruined everything. You're like my old man, you don't know when to stop.'

'How do you work that out?'

'You can get my dad out of prison, which is something Brandon would like rather less than the abolition of money, right?'

'Right.'

'I mean, that's why I started this whole thing about my dad – to get even with Charlie and Brandon.'

'I see, so what am I doing wrong?'

'Dick! If you'd asked Brandon for a million in used notes to keep Vince inside he'd have paid up with a smile. He wouldn't have been pleased but he'd have respected you. He might even have let you live, especially if you'd cleared off with me afterwards. But what do you do? All you ask for is Clyde Harrow's job back! Brandon's got to think that you're a crazy who needs to be put down like a mad dog.'

'Mad dog I may be, but I'm not crazy enough to make bargains with murderers.'

'I keep telling you, Brandon hasn't murdered anyone yet – well, no one that you know.'

'All right, say I believe you about Sam Levy and the attempt

389

to kill me on the motorway and that it was all down to some other bunch and not Brandon, what about Morton V. E. Devereaux-Almond? Someone topped him.'

'Says who?'

'Me.'

'Brandon doesn't like loose ends but I can't believe he did old Almond. Almond's his cousin.'

'Name of Allemano?'

'Martin Victor Emmanuel Allemano is what it said on his birth certificate. Martin for his dad and Victor Emmanuel for the King of Italy. Yes, you've been a busy boy, Dave, finding things out, and look where it's got you. No, it must be those other people who did for him.'

'Do you expect me to believe that?'

'It doesn't matter what you believe now. Brandon's certain to kill you and there's nothing I can do about it. I expect he's already put the contract out on you.'

'Do you know that?'

'He won't say "Kill Cunane" to anyone. He'll just put the right words in the right ears and they'll know what to do. It's business with him now, not sentiment. Letting Harrow have his job back was just to put you off your guard.'

'You know some charming people, Marti.'

'It's not my fault. It's always been like that, but when you came along in that car park and put Charlie in his place I thought there might be a chance for something else.'

I looked at her. She was smiling now. I wasn't. According to her thesis, my goose was cooked whoever came out on top.

'Right!' she said. 'That's what I really came to say. It'll make no difference now what you do about Vince, so you might as well spring the old fool.'

Hysteria can be catching and this time it was my turn to laugh. Marti joined in. Then she gently turned the lock on the door but to my surprise didn't leave that way. Instead she went over to the window, opened it and started climbing out. We were on the first floor.

'Whose daughter am I, then? Get my dad out, eh?' she said with a cheeky grin. 'Goodbye, Dave. I won't wish you luck because I think you've used yours up and I need all my own.'

390

Then she was gone. The last I saw was her hand as she closed the window behind her and clambered onto the fire escape.

I lay back on the bed with my head in a whirl. Was Marti now so well in with Brandon that he sent her on trawling expeditions to see what I knew? Or was it all about her father?

My reverie was interrupted a few moments later when one of the night sisters entered the room.

'My goodness, Mr Cunane, what have you been up to? The bed's like a ploughed field and you're all sweaty.'

She took my pulse. 'That's high,' she said. 'You haven't been doing press-ups or something, have you?'

'I've never left this bed,' I said.

55

When I drifted into sleep for the final time that Tuesday I had
a vague idea of signing myself out of the hospital again in the
morning. I didn't fancy another question and answer session
with Brendan Cullen, particularly as there were still more
questions than answers in my own mind.

As it turned out I was going nowhere. A mild sedative the
night sister had supplied, the exertions of Marti's visit, the
feeling of excitement and disappointment combined; all
resulted in a profound and unfeigned weariness. I was barely
conscious when Bren came round. He stood by my bedside
and grumbled for a few minutes before leaving. As far as I
knew no one else visited me that day and I got some rest.

It was only on Thursday morning when the chaplain called
that I began to regain some interest in the vertical world. It hit
me then that they had me down as a serious possibility for
cashing my chips.

'Your mother's been in touch,' the priest, a red-haired
Irishman called Mulligan, said. 'She's very anxious that you
get yourself right with God.'

'No thanks,' I mumbled. I think I was more frightened of
that prospect than of the combined intervention of the Carlyle
family and a whole platoon of South African hit women. Fr
Mulligan shook his head sadly, gave me a blessing and left.
However, fear's a powerful stimulant and by Thursday
afternoon I was distinctly perkier.

I felt cosy, lying there and setting the wheels of justice in
motion to right a wrong, cosy but slightly nervous. I was hot.
Plotting revenge is sweaty work. I knew that most of what
Marti had told me was open to interpretation. Brandon
Carlyle had certainly suspected that Charlie or Marti had had

a hand in the demise of Lou Olley, but where did that leave me? Could I outmanoeuvre Brandon? He had spent a lifetime dodging and weaving to come out on the right side of things. Should I just go and throw myself on his mercy and plead ignorance? Or should I run for cover?

No, that wasn't the way things were going to go. I found the idea that Brandon was behind the success of Pimpernel Investigations gut-wrenching. Was it true? I'd probably never know, but what I did know was that I had as much right to a place in the sun as any of the Carlyles. The thought filled me with anger. The gall of that old man to patronise me! Feeble though I was I wanted to lash out. I should have pounded Charlie to jelly when I had the chance. Who were these people? It was time somebody got the better of them – but how?

As a private detective it wasn't my job to go round righting wrongs, and there was enough of my father in me for me to know that Vince King had probably got away with lots of unpunished crime for which his 'unearned time' could be seen as just retribution in the higher scheme of things. Still, the idea of King on the streets was the one thing which seemed to give Brandon Carlyle something to worry about, and the more he had to worry about the better were the chances of survival of myself and Pimpernel Investigations.

It took all the energy I'd accumulated to persuade the nurse to bring the phone.

'Marvin,' I said. 'Send the letter to the Home Secretary.'

He promised to do it at once and I slumped back into my sheets to await developments.

They let me out of hospital at the weekend and I was well enough to take part in the triumphant release of Vince King on the following Monday. The top of my head was still bandaged, and if you look at the television footage of Vince's release, which Celeste's mother thoughtfully videoed for us, you can just get a glimpse of a white football bobbing about at the back of the scrum. Marvin and Celeste did all the talking and they had plenty to say about the miscarriage of justice. I was very happy to leave it all to them. As for the man himself, he was surprisingly sombre when we got him back to Manchester.

Vince showed no interest in calling on Marti or even going out on his own. He stayed in my flat. I put this down to reaction at first, but when he was still insisting on having myself or Peter Snyder around with him at the end of the week I began to wonder . . . Talking to him was a strain. He had an odd attitude to me, as if I was a partner in crime. He kept discussing various criminals, mostly dead ones, as if I'd known them personally, but showed no interest in a visit to his old haunts. He spent a lot of time by the window scanning the street.

I asked him who he was expecting but got a blank look in reply.

The news about the death of Mick Jones produced a grimace of mild irritation, but the only topic he showed any interest in was my description of the Carlyle home.

'Cameras and beams and sensors, eh? You know what I've always found? The more electronics they have, the sloppier they are.'

'I'll remember that,' I muttered. If Vince fancied an unauthorised tour of the Carlyle premises, who was I to stop him?

'You know what one of the most popular study courses in prison is?'

I shook my head.

'Electronics.'

He went over and over my description of South Pork as if building a picture in his mind. I tried direct questions about his past and about Marti's theories but got the blank stare treatment again.

I'd been tempted to lash him to a chair and toast his feet in the oven but my condition ruled out anything strenuous; besides, Vince was a media celebrity, at least for the moment. The phone at Pimpernel Investigations rang almost continually with requests for interviews. Otherwise Vince King made an undemanding guest at Thornleigh Court. He expected everything to be done by numbers as in prison and if I wasn't around to entertain him was content to stare at the road or the telly. The only break in my normal routine was that he insisted on having the TV tuned to racing the whole time.

394

'You berk!' he yelped when I pressed for an explanation. 'I was safer inside than out. The least you can do is stick with me for a few days until I find my feet.'

'The only time I've seen Brandon Carlyle lose his temper was when I said that I was looking for a miscarriage of justice in your case,' I said, trying to provoke a reaction.

'I bet that got up his nose,' King said laconically.

'What is it? Does he owe you money, did he fit you up or what?' I was getting irritated. I could hardly tell him that it would be nice if he went and stuffed Brandon Carlyle immediately.

'Leave it out, son,' King said with a smile. 'I've been wound up by experts. I've waited years to sort things with Brandon Carlyle and I'll do it when I'm good and ready.'

'Meanwhile, what are you waiting for?'

'I've got lots of friends here in Manchester, people who'll take their time before contacting me.'

'Why?'

'They'll want to check if I've grassed to get out. But when they find that I haven't they'll be in touch and then Mr High and Mighty Carlyle can start worrying,' he said mysteriously.

He wouldn't say who his friends were and that was all I got out of him until on Sunday afternoon I got a distress call from my mother. 'Dave, your dad's taken a turn for the worse,' she said.

I felt a hand squeezing my heart.

'He hasn't eaten or spoken since they let that Vince King out of prison. It's as if he's decided to die. You've got to do something.'

The expression on my face when I put the phone down must have told King that it was bad news.

'What?' he grunted.

'Later,' I said, going into the bedroom to make another, more private call.

'So what was all that about, sweetheart?' he said sarcastically when I came back into the living room thirty minutes later. 'Woman trouble?'

'My father,' I said, 'he's gone into a decline since they let you out.'

'The old bastard! Is he going to croak?'

'Not if I can help it. I think it's time we had a few explanations, don't you?'

'What do you mean?'

'It would be nice to know why you spent twenty-odd years doing time for a crime you didn't commit. You must have known that Morton Almond and James McMahon weren't exactly the "dream team" when it came to your defence. Just what is it between you and Brandon Carlyle?'

King's green eyes sparkled with fun and he laughed out loud.

'If you think I'm going to lose any sleep because some barmy old copper decides to die you can think again. I'll send a cheap wreath to his funeral but that's it.'

'That's not it. You're going to come with me and we're going to unravel exactly who did what to whom all those years ago.'

'And who's going to make me?' he asked.

'I am,' Brendan Cullen said quietly. He'd let himself in from the hall. Vince King knew Bren's profession at a glance.

'What the fuck have you got the Old Bill here for?' he bawled. 'I didn't grass before and I'm not grassing now!'

'That's all right,' I said evenly. 'Nobody's asking you to grass. If you don't want to come with me, DCI Cullen here will take you to see your daughter at the Carlyle place. It's curious that such a fond daughter as Marti hasn't even phoned to see how you are, let alone visited, so we thought we'd help the family reunion along.'

'I've told you. I'll see her and her in-laws when I'm good and ready.'

'You'll see them now,' I said.

'That's right, sunshine, you come with me,' Bren said.

'Fuck off!'

'Dear me, we're only asking you to come and see your loving daughter and all your rich in-laws,' Bren taunted.

Vince began grinding his teeth at this.

'Rich, are they? Wait till you see what they're like when I've done with them.'

'Why all this aggro?' Bren asked with that infuriating smile of his. 'Marti is your daughter, after all.'

'She's disowned me. I don't blame her, she's family, but them!'

'You're going to see the Carlyles or you're going to see Dave's dad, and we're going to hear the full story. Make your mind up, and you can forget about incriminating yourself. Nobody's going to bang you up again after all this media circus about an innocent man doing twenty years. Christ! You're that bloody innocent you'd have to shoot the Prime Minister before the Home Office and the CPS would agree to you being banged up again!'

King gave a crooked grin at this.

'I'm not going to see the old bugger and you can't make me. I'm safe here. If Carlyle tries anything I can see him coming at me. Out there in the sticks anything might happen.'

'Maybe this will persuade you,' I said, taking out the Walther PPK 9mm automatic that had been concealed behind the water heater in the bathroom.

King's eyes widened but he didn't seem particularly impressed. 'Get stuffed,' he said. 'You'd never use that, not with a copper here.'

'Use what?' Bren asked blandly.

My first shot missed his ankle by a millimetre and thudded into the woodwork of the chair he was sitting on, sending splinters flying.

'Persuasive, aren't you?' King said, getting out of his chair. 'Never did get on with me own relatives. Is it far to the old copper's drum?' he asked cheekily.

There was snow on the ground when we reached the West Pennine Moors and the track down to the cottage was almost impassable. Jake Carless poked his head round his door when we slithered past his shack but he withdrew it with a malicious scowl when he saw me. There was a distant thump of explosives from a quarry further back in the hills.

The change in my father was shocking. His face and his whole body seemed to have shrunk and there was a grey pallor over him as if death had already claimed him.

'He's been brooding about the Carlyles and that DI Mick

397

Jones ever since you got involved with them, Dave,' my mother said. Her tone wasn't accusatory but we both knew what was at the back of her mind. 'When they let that Vince King out and there was all that on the television about police corruption and incompetence it was more than he could cope with.'

'This is Vince King,' I said.

She clapped her hand to her mouth in horror. 'What are you trying to do? Kill Paddy outright? He's sinking fast as it is.'

'Dave and I think that Vince owes an explanation, particularly to Paddy, and that when Paddy hears it he may feel better,' Bren said.

Eileen struggled to take this in. She was looking haggard. She'd lost that sprightliness that had kept her looking young for so long. I wasn't in any doubt that if Paddy died she wouldn't be around for much longer either. But then Eileen showed why she'd been able to put up with Paddy, and perhaps with me as well, for so long.

'Look at us!' she cackled suddenly. 'The Cunane family! Him upstairs, taken to his bed with melancholy because they're laughing at his beloved police force and him not even personally involved, me brooding myself into the grave years before my time and our son going round with his head in a bandage like Pudsey Bear, and you want to bring a convict into the house!'

'I wasn't guilty!' Vince King bridled.

'Not of what they got you for,' Eileen corrected.

He laughed at this. 'You're all right for a copper's wife,' he said. 'OK, lead me to the old bast . . . er . . . the old man.'

'Who are you calling a bastard?' Paddy snorted when King entered his bedroom. 'Tell us how Brandon Carlyle got away with it.' He sat up in bed impatiently.

56

'Who's been talking?' King snarled.

'Actually, it was Marti,' I said. 'She has some idea that you persuaded Carlyle to take her out of that children's home they had her in because you threatened to grass on him.'

'Never, I'd never grass!' King said. Denial was a conditioned reflex as he seemed to realise himself. A slow grin spread over his sharp features. 'At least, I'd never grass unless it suited me to.'

'It was you did the bloody police computer room, wasn't it?' Paddy said fiercely. I looked at him in fright. A blue vein was standing out on his emaciated forehead.

Cullen looked at me in puzzlement. I shook my head. I was no wiser than him.

'Never got me for it though, did you?' King crowed. 'I've never been done for my real work.'

'Tell us,' Bren invited.

'Make us comfortable first!' King snapped.

Paddy took the hint and fished a whisky bottle out from under his sheets.

'And I thought you were dying!' Eileen screeched, but she bustled round and soon we were all seated.

'How did you get in?' Paddy said eventually.

'One of yours, how else?' King replied smoothly.

'Jones?'

King shrugged his shoulders. 'I don't know about that, but I do know it was bloody tight in those crawl spaces.'

'The police computer room . . . it was supposed to be manned twenty-four hours a day and to be one of the most secure places in the country,' Paddy explained. 'Your friend here stole a blackmailer's treasure chest from it.

Enough to set Brandon Carlyle up for life.'

'But I didn't know that for a long time, did I?' King said. 'I only did it as a favour. It was a bloody dangerous place as I found out later. I was let in but then I had to hide. They didn't tell me that there was a fire damping mechanism that flushed the whole place with an inert gas at the first sign of fire, did they? I was on the point of lighting up before I realised that. It wouldn't have done much good for me, that gas. They had these banks of bloody big computers, ICL 2900s, and there was me under the raised floor in the crawl space. Good job I didn't light up. They'd only have ever found me by the nasty smell.'

'I shouldn't be telling you this but it doesn't seem to matter now,' Paddy said. 'The police in Manchester had a copy of the so-called Round Up list. That's what chummy here stole. I think a branch of the security service has been going round tidying things up recently.'

'They don't know what you're on about, cocker,' King said. 'They were still in short pants when all this was going down.'

'They were expecting a war with the USSR at any time,' Paddy said conversationally. His gaze went beyond us to the bleak snow-covered hills outside. A chill had crept into the room. As if in confirmation of our thoughts there was the boom of a distant explosion. 'Blasting again,' Paddy commented before continuing . . . 'Right into the eighties a nuclear exchange was considered to be a fair possibility. Naturally the police were involved in the Government's precautions.'

'You sound like a bloody civil servant,' King complained.

Paddy shrugged. 'Part of those precautions involved rounding up the many hundreds of subversives who'd been trained in the Soviet Union to make maximum trouble in this country in the event of war. Lists of suspects had been prepared by the security service and they were to be taken into preventive detention as soon as the Russians made a move – emergency powers. Hah! You'll laugh now, but it wasn't so funny at the time. They'd designated the football and cricket stadiums at Old Trafford as one of the primary collection points: political militants and CP sympathisers were going in the football ground, and agents of influence and saboteurs were to go in the cricket ground.'

400

'Where were they going from there? I asked.

Paddy looked shy for once. 'They didn't tell us that,' he said quickly.

'Oh, I see.'

'Dave, it was serious,' he said angrily. 'What are you supposed to do with convicts and prisoners in a nuclear war? NATO believed that the Warsaw Pact intended to cause massive disruption in this country prior to a ground invasion across the north German plain. There were plans for feeding the prisoners for the first couple of weeks but after that it was down to the politicians. I think it depended on how rough things got. If they'd dropped nuclear bombs on Britain or the Russkies had invaded I think they were going to get the option of recanting or standing in front of a firing squad.'

'Firing squads at Old Trafford . . .' I murmured. 'Bit drastic, wasn't it? I thought you were in the CID anyway?'

'It was expected that some of the most dangerous subversives would make themselves scarce as soon as things began to look sticky. That was where the CID came in. I was one of the senior officers let into the secret.'

'Bloody important, weren't you!' King sneered. 'But you weren't able to protect your big secret well enough. Brandon Carlyle must have heard a whisper, not that he was a communist or anything. Far from it! But he was sensitive, what with his dad and his uncle having had such a bad time in the last lot. It was him who had the idea of nicking the list. They gave me a tape to replace it with, a reel about a foot in diameter in a case with clear plastic sides and a plastic housing round the rim to keep it from unravelling. I crept out from my hidey hole with it. Bloody noisy place it was; air-conditioning roaring away like the clappers, printers chattering, tape decks whirring. Nobody saw me switch the tapes. Then I slapped this big red button on the wall. I thought it was a fire alarm but it powered down all the computers. Talk about pandemonium! Nobody noticed me getting back in my hole.'

'As a matter of interest, how did you get out?' Paddy asked in a bored voice.

'I hid for a whole day. Had me sandwiches with me, didn't I? Come four a.m. there was only a technician on duty. He

401

went to the loo and left the outer door open. I walked right out, free as a bird.'

'And who did you give the tape to?'

'That would be telling, wouldn't it?'

It was at that precise moment that the first billow of smoke gushed up the stairs and into the bedroom.

'Hell-fire and damnation!' Paddy shouted at Eileen. 'Have you left the chip pan on, woman?'

'Of course not,' she snapped back.

I stood at the top of the circular metal stairway. The room below was filled with dense black smoke.

'This way,' Paddy bellowed, leaping from his death-bed as nimbly as a teenager.

It was lucky that he did because the words were hardly out of his mouth before a pillar of flame like the jet from a blast furnace shot up from the stairwell. It bounced off the ceiling on to the bed and where we'd been sitting. If we'd still been there, we'd have been dead. Like scorched rabbits coming out of a hole with a ferret behind them, we scrambled through the large bedroom window and out onto the roof. Grey smoke was already puffing up between the tiles and we'd barely escaped from the inferno in the bedroom before black smoke with the consistency of treacle poured out of the house windows.

'This way! Follow me,' Paddy yelled and he led us off the side roof of the house onto the garage roof and then down to the ground. My mother's face was completely blackened with soot and she was struggling for breath. I wasn't feeling too boisterous myself. Paddy organised us. He got us to a safe distance and then told Cullen to use his mobile for the fire brigade, not that they'd be able to do much. People poured out of neighbouring cottages to help, even Jake Carless arrived with a filthy horse blanket which he proceeded to drape over Paddy's bony shoulders.

'What is it? Your Calor gas gone up then?' Jake asked with glee.

'Has it, hell! This was deliberate,' Paddy snarled, desperate at being caught at a disadvantage by his chief tormentor. 'Look sharp, man, or that bloody ramshackle barn of yours will go up as well.'

402

Jake's jaw dropped. Even as we watched the wind was driving showers of sparks towards the old hay barn that adjoined Carless's farm. He dashed off screaming for help, and some of the able-bodied men did make a move in his direction but with such marked reluctance that the barn caught fire before they could do anything, and then all the rest of the rambling farm buildings went up.

'I've been expecting this for years with the slovenly way that man takes care of his farm,' Paddy said, not without a trace of satisfaction, 'but for it to start at my cottage!'

The fire brigade and police arrived at the upper road, their sirens helping to further madden the cattle and sheep struggling to escape from the stricken farm. Access for the fire engines was impossible. The steep track resembled an Alpine ski slope, but the brigade made their way down on foot.

'Casualties?' they asked. 'Anyone still in the buildings?'

Heads were shaken all round, but then Bren came over to me.

'Have you seen Vince King?' he enquired.

57

'They've searched the ruins,' Brendan Cullen said later that evening when we were all gathered back at Thornleigh Court. 'There's no obvious trace of any human remains but the fire investigation officer said that the blaze was so fierce that a body could have been totally consumed.'

'I'm telling you, he pushed past me when I was getting Eileen out,' Paddy said angrily.

'I didn't see him,' Brendan said.

'You were looking after yourself. It's only natural. It was hard to get your footing on that roof. Luckily Eileen and I had it off pat as part of my fire drill.'

Cullen looked at Paddy with an expression of wonder on his face. I could sense the comment coming but he suppressed it.

'Was it arson?' Paddy asked forlornly.

'They can't tell yet. You did have a lot of paint and DIY material lying about, didn't you?'

'Oh,' Paddy said, and then stared at me as if to say it was my fault. I hung my head. Everyone I knew seemed to come to grief.

'Listen, lad,' Paddy said quietly, 'I've always known it was dangerous . . . knowing about the Round Up list, that is. It's not your fault really. I've had this hanging over me for years. That's why I knew no good could come of you getting involved with Vince King and the Carlyles.'

'Why didn't you explain?' I asked bitterly.

'I couldn't. I did take an oath of secrecy, after all.'

'But Dad, there've been two serious attempts to kill me besides what happened today and I didn't have a clue what it was all about.'

'I'll tell you what I know,' he said grimly, 'but there isn't much more than I've already told you. That toe-rag King stole a top secret list which Carlyle's been fattening on ever since.'

'But Mr Cunane, why would that lead to someone trying to kill us?' Bren asked.

'I can only guess at that,' Paddy said, glaring at me. 'There's sleeping dogs that are best let lie, but some people don't know that.'

'Gee, thanks, Dad!' I said.

'I've told you often enough,' he said firmly.

'Er, can we get back to why someone wants us dead?' Bren asked mildly. From the way his eyebrows were struggling to nest on top of his scalp I could see he didn't believe a word.

'Right, the first thing is this: that robbery that Vince King described – him hiding under the computers and everything – officially, that never happened.'

'Yeah, it's a new one on me,' Bren said coolly.

'Yes, that's right. Us four and King and Brandon Carlyle are the only ones who know that the theft of those Round Up tapes was an ordinary robbery. Presumably the late Mick Jones also knew, if it was him who helped King.'

'Tapes? King said there was only one,' I interjected.

'King's a born liar. He wouldn't tell you the right time of day unless he knew you had your own clock . . . There were two, one as back-up.'

'Was the rest of what he said lies?' Bren asked. His eyebrows had drooped, but his tone suggested that he could think of more interesting ways to spend a Sunday evening.

'No, he's vain is King,' Paddy said confidently. 'I'm sure it happened much as he said . . . It was the worst moment in my career when they found that the tapes had gone. As one of the few in the know at the Manchester end they had me down as the prime suspect. I'll never forget them asking me if I'd ever been to Moscow on my holidays.'

'Apparently they cleared you,' I said. I wasn't feeling sympathetic.

'Those MI5 men were mostly public school and university types. Their minds were completely focused on the USSR. I mentioned the possibility of a local thief and they laughed their socks off. Luckily for me they decided that it had to be

405

some super-spook in London who'd done the switch.'

'This still doesn't tell us why someone tried to knock us off this afternoon,' Bren said wearily.

'It does. There was no suspicion of Carlyle at the time – small-time local villain, he was. Crafty with it, but small-time. What's happened since then? Brandon Carlyle's become very, very rich. Seventh richest man in the country if you believe what you read in the papers – and how's he done that? Because he's blackmailed men in PLCs and banks whose names were on the list to tell him when to buy and when to sell. That's attracted attention all right – inside information. How did he get all those shares in Alhambra TV – bought well before it was announced that they were getting the franchise? A lucky gamble like he said, or did he know?'

'Still . . .' I said sceptically.

'You don't know how these security outfits work, secret services and what not. It's all done on computers these days. They do research on people like Carlyle. By now there's someone sitting in Moscow or Tel Aviv or Washington – or even, God help us, Baghdad! – who has a fair idea how Brandon Carlyle got rich. There've been enough questions about him in this country. Maybe Carlyle convinced them that he destroyed his tape, or maybe he did a deal with them to share it, but now they think that Dave's muscled in on the act and that he's got the other tape, the one Carlyle's partner, Sam Levy, must have had.'

'You haven't mentioned the British Government. Surely if they'd had an inkling that Carlyle had secret information they'd have arrested him,' I said.

'Can you imagine the row if thousands of prominent people found that their names were on an official death list?'

'OK, I'll give you that,' I said, 'but why hasn't anything leaked out about all this before?'

'Because for months after King's little exploit MI5 was walking on eggs, frightened that there'd be a press conference in Moscow,' Paddy said. 'The Government had to be in a position to deny everything. They destroyed all copies of the tapes and wiped out all references to the plan. People like me were warned to keep our mouths shut.'

'They could have killed Carlyle,' I argued.

'They didn't know about him. He must have played his cards very carefully, and he went after information, not money. Contrary to what you might think, a lot of the names on that list were rich quislings who wanted to be sure they were backing the right horse in case the Russians took over.'

'Were there any coppers on it?' I asked.

'I don't know. I was only told in general terms what to expect.'

'What about Vince King?'

'Work it out . . . you're quick enough with your theories most of the time. Carlyle, Levy and Jones discover what they've got – the biggest pile of blackmail material anyone could ever imagine – and thanks to Jones they know they're in the clear. Think of the names there must have been on that list: civil servants, legal officials, businessmen and industrialists, wealthy people, even ordinary people who were just scheming for a Soviet takeover. Everybody's forgotten about it now, but back then there were lots of people who really did believe that life was better under the Soviet system. Christ! They must have been mad. I remember seeing this piece on the news. There were all these people in this Russian butcher's shop, queuing like zombies they were, and then this policeman arrives, he dumps a pile of sausages down on the counter, horsemeat sausages and that's their ration for the week – one sausage each . . .'

'Always did like your steak, didn't you, dear? And no queuing either,' Eileen interjected.

'Stick to the topic of Vince King,' I said. 'The Soviet Union's history now.'

'No thanks to some of the people whose names were on that list. It stands to reason that Carlyle and co. must have seen Vince as the weak link. He was a pro criminal, liable to get arrested on his next job. They must have thought that he'd blab.'

'But he wouldn't, you heard what he said – he'd never grass.'

'We know that now but they didn't. He'd never been arrested before. Back in the seventies you had all those "super

407

grasses" in London falling over themselves to shop their mates. It was natural for them to try to kill King. My best guess is that Jones knocked King out first and then he was arranging the best method of executing King and Musgrave so that it looked like there'd been some kind of argument between them.

'Fullalove was a keen young officer. I think Jones had told him to stay in the car but he didn't. He was just too curious to see what was going on. He crept into that room just after Jones had shot Musgrave in cold blood. He protested. Perhaps he went to the phone, so Jones shot him as well. Then he heard other officers arriving so he just had time to shove the gun into King's hand before they arrived.

'They must have conned King before the trial saying that he'd get the best defence money could buy arranged by Brandon's own solicitor, and then they saw that Vince wasn't going to grass after all. So they let him go down for the one crime that he hadn't committed.'

'But they forgot about Marti,' I said. 'She was the one thing that King really loved. When Social Services brought Marti to see Vince in jail he must have flipped. He phoned Carlyle and told him he'd be singing like a canary if they didn't do something for Marti, and so the very next day Brandon Carlyle practically adopts her. She'd be a useful piece of security for him to make sure Vince kept quiet. They kept her in the family all those years and even let her marry Charlie . . .'

'King's a natural survivor, or at least he was. It's poetic justice if he's gone up in smoke, now.'

'But if he's not, where does that leave Marti?' Brendan Cullen asked. 'She must have been the one he was waiting to get in touch with when it was safe, and God knows what the pair of them are plotting to do to Brandon and Charlie.'

'Don't worry about them,' Paddy said confidently. 'The devil looks after his own.'

'I wish I could be that confident,' Bren replied.

I looked at Paddy. Although emaciated, he'd lost the frightening death's-door pallor that he'd had in the afternoon. I think he looked on the opportunity to rebuild his ruined cottage as a challenge.

'How do we know that we're not still targets?' I asked. 'I

mean, if this renegade secret service group or foreign intelligence or whatever is still out there, what's to stop them targeting us?'

'Take a look out of the window, Dave,' Brendan offered laconically.

I did. The Press were encamped in force outside Thornleigh Court. Two uniformed policemen were holding them back from the entrance. We'd already seen the headlines on Sky News: 'FREED EX-CON VANISHES FROM EX-TOP COP'S BLAZING HOME'. The story had all the ingredients to keep the Press outside for days.

'They're hardly likely to try something with them there, and the Press are also the reason I'm being forced to play nursery maid now,' Bren said wearily. 'We'll have to come up with some convincing story that throws them off the scent . . . something on the lines of how King met a tragic accident while visiting an old friend.'

'Thanks, but forget the old friend bit,' Paddy said. 'King was in for killing a copper, you know.'

'We'll have to come up with something.'

'Forget the Press. They can only tell lies about us. These secret buggers can kill us all very dead,' I said.

'That's you all over, Dave,' Paddy said. 'Throw a damper on the proceedings like you always do! Suppose they were looking for the actual list itself, that tape in the plastic box. I mean, if someone was going to break things in the Press – perhaps a nosey private detective with a girlfriend who was always on the lookout for a big story – that person would need the list itself as proof, wouldn't he? They must know it's gone up in smoke. You're quite safe now.'

With that optimistic thought Paddy went to join Eileen in the guest bedroom. There was something unnatural about Paddy. He seemed to flourish in adversity whereas I felt sick, and not just through smoke inhalation.

'Cheery old sod, in't he?' Bren said, when my father had shut the door. 'Considering . . . How did you stick it, growing up with him? He's such a "take charge" bugger. God, he had us out of that bedroom like shit through a goose. Just as well though, eh?'

'I wish I could feel as safe as he makes out.'

'You are. Your South African friend was probably hired by one of your business rivals and she won't be trying again.' I looked at him. He had that friendly but enigmatic smile that didn't give a clue about what he was thinking. Had I imagined the visit from Marti and her warning? I didn't think this was a good moment to tell him about that.

'Bren, are you certain King's dead? That bit Paddy said about him being a natural survivor, I mean . . .'

'King died in the fire.'

'Bren,' I muttered. 'You know the snow was melting all round the house?'

He nodded. The heat had been intense.

'When you told me that Vince King was missing I walked round looking for him. Before the snow melted I saw a single set of tracks heading across the field towards that hill opposite the house, not on a path or anything, just across the field.'

'What's in that direction?'

'Nothing really, just the quarries at Egerton.'

'I see,' he said quietly. 'Highly significant, Dave. The old geezer just walks into a quarry and helps himself to a pile of explosives and detonators, yeah? Sorry, but it doesn't happen like that. Quarries use emulsion explosives these days and they come in ruddy big tankers. King's curled his toes up.'

'I don't think so.'

'Yes,' Brendan insisted. 'They'll turn up his teeth or his lucky safe-key or something tomorrow, you'll see.'

'What about the tapes?'

'Oh,' he grunted. 'I'm sorry, mate, but I don't buy any of that. I used to think you had a vivid imagination until I met your dad. He's been brooding on the King fiasco and it's made him a bit strange.'

'King told us . . .'

'He told us what he thought your father wanted to hear. He picked up on what Paddy said. The rest was pure fantasy . . . humouring a sick man or just lying for the sake of it.'

'But what about the way Brandon Carlyle made his fortune?' I protested. 'You've got to admit that's real.'

'Listen, Dave, Carlyle made his loot by buying up small,

410

undervalued companies, finding the bits that were worth something and then selling them on. The only unusual thing about him is the speed of the turnaround. He's made plenty of enemies in the process. They've complained to the financial authorities both here and in America often enough and, believe me, if there was any blackmailing going on it would have come out years ago. I'll believe in those lists when you put them in my hands. Round Up lists! If I don't go and round up my own family I'll have no home to go to.'

There must have been something in my expression.

'Dave! I'm sorry about King. It was rough. You get him out and your father char-grills him, that's tough! But you've had a serious blow on the head. Stop worrying about King or your father and start thinking about yourself or you'll be back in hospital,' he warned.

58

The mob of reporters waiting by the ground-floor exit of Thornleigh Court dispersed during the night. Was that down to the hidden hand of Brandon Carlyle or merely due to fatigue and deadlines being passed? I didn't know and I didn't care.

I took Brendan Cullen's advice and went back to work on Monday morning, hoping to start putting my life back together. The business showed no sign of imminent collapse – if anything we were busier than ever. There were no reports of quarries being broken into. The Vince King story was a one-day sensation in the media. That was all it had ever been. Miscarriage of justice cases were two a penny these days. There was a paragraph or two on the fire in the local papers and that was it. Paddy was already talking about having plans drawn up for a new house and had decided to rent a cottage for himself and Eileen. I found it chilling the way people I met joined the ranks of the late and unlamented without anyone turning a hair. I suppose I was getting middle aged.

I wanted someone official to start ranting and raving: Where's Almond? . . . Why's King dead? . . . Why did someone try to kill Dave Cunane? But nobody did. DCI Cullen didn't show his face. I had a letter from the Police Complaints Authority telling me that investigation into the alleged assault against me was still proceeding but that it was considered too early to come to any conclusions.

Janine phoned and suggested meeting for lunch, so I took that as a starting point in my struggle to claw my way back to normality.

'I can't seem to settle to work,' she complained over the soup course.

I refrained from saying 'Snap!'

'It seems pointless writing a story about some starlet's love life or her boyfriend's drug habit when I can't stop thinking and worrying about my own children all the time.'

After what I'd been through, comforting Janine didn't come easily, but I tried. 'Henry's back in America, they'll be OK now,' I told her confidently.

'I'm not so sure,' she said, biting her lip. 'They have these professional child kidnappers over there. He might try again.' She looked tense. There were lines in her forehead that I hadn't seen before.

'I can supply you with a bodyguard if you like,' I offered with a smile.

'I know, but he or she would be so expensive,' she said, still with that same worried, intelligent expression that she seemed to have been wearing for weeks. Janine's no raving beauty but there's a depth and intensity about her that draws me. I think her capacity to jump to the wrong conclusions must be similar to my own.

'I don't know, you can sometimes find a good bodyguard who'll work for pocket money and all-found,' I said in the same serious tone she'd used. She seemed to consider my words. 'You know, supply him with bed and board, especially bed,' I said.

'Dave!' she exclaimed. 'You've got a one-track mind. I've not even finished my soup and you're propositioning me! Clyde Harrow had the decency to wait until I was fed.'

I pulled a small piece of bread off my roll and flicked it at her.

'We'll have no ice-cold showers over my marriage tackle, lady,' I warned.

She laughed and her frown lines faded for a moment. Then the serious look returned.

'I'm thinking about you all the time but it'll take me a while to get back to normal in that department. I can't stop seeing an image of you on the floor with your head covered in blood. Perhaps we could take things a step at a time. The children keep asking about you. Jenny's doing this science project – maybe you could come to the Science Museum with us this weekend?'

413

I was perfectly happy with that. We made a firm date to meet. I hardly had the strength to insist on anything these days. Although still hanging around like an unwanted lodger, my libido hadn't been very active in recent days. That was one thing that inclined me to believe that my midnight tryst with Marti had been a fantasy. I could have found out by phoning her but that didn't seem a very clever idea. My best friend already believed that I was ready for a trip to the funny farm and I could do without spreading the impression even more widely. As for Brandon Carlyle having a contract out on me, well, that isn't the type of thing that a credit checking agency will normally find out for you.

By Thursday afternoon I was back into a more or less normal routine . . . truthfully, a less than normal routine. I missed Janine and the children.

'Urgent phone call for you, boss,' Celeste said, 'line three.'

There were times when I still found it hard to credit that Pimpernel Investigations had multiple phone lines.

I picked up the phone. 'Dave, have you heard the news?' Janine asked breathlessly. 'No, of course you haven't. It's only just come in here. There's some kind of hostage situation going on at the Carlyle place and they think there are casualties. My editor's letting me go because I know the layout.'

'Hold on, Janine. The police won't let you get within half a mile of South Pork.'

'I've prepared for this story and I'm not going to miss it.'

'Keep me posted.'

Janine was as good as her word but there wasn't much for her to report, and anyway the event was covered by national TV and radio. The identity of the hostage-takers wasn't known and the media played a delightful game of speculating which outfit was holding the Carlyle family to ransom. Every acronym in the terrorist lexicon was considered. The police were notably tight-lipped. A minister at the Home Office issued a statement on behalf of the Home Secretary calling for a peaceful surrender by the terrorists.

414

I had my own opinions and even hopes, but I'd been told that they were fantasies, so I kept my mouth shut. I wasn't tempted to speak to Brendan Cullen, and Paddy didn't even give me a phone call.

The break came at about four a.m. I was rolling over in my bed trying to get myself comfortable for the remainder of the night when I heard a helicopter hovering low overhead. That wasn't unusual. Like most of the inhabitants of South Manchester, I have rather sour feelings about the police helicopter. The boys in blue like playing with their toy at odd hours. They have to, if only to keep up with the demand for material for TV shows. I tried to wrap a pillow round my head to drown out the noise and drifted back into a half sleep only to be stirred a few minutes later by pounding on my door.

'What the hell!' I said when I opened it to admit Brendan Cullen.

'Get dressed, sunshine, you're coming in the big fly bird,' he announced. His face was flushed and his eyes shining with excitement. I hadn't seen him so full of bounce for months.

'You're joking!' I said dismissively. 'The GMP should open an office in these flats, you're here so often!'

'Losing your beauty sleep, are you? Listen – the Carlyle siege? It's Vince King who's behind it.'

'Oh no, he's dead. You told me,' I said, struggling to sound as bored as possible.

'Yeah, sorry about that, but he's got the Carlyle place rigged with enough explosive to blow half of Cheshire to kingdom come and he's demanding that you turn up as a mediator.'

'No way, Brendan. He couldn't possibly have explosives. You put me straight on that.'

'He didn't bring any explosives with him or rob any quarries, if that's what you mean. It turns out that Carlyle Junior keeps enough fireworks at Moat House Farm or South Pork or whatever it's called to light up South Cheshire for a month. King's rigged up dozens of booby traps and he's using a firework display computer to control them. The bugger's as tricky as a bagful of snakes.'

'He's an old man, a throwback.'

415

'No, he's had help. There were at least three with him, but he's on his own now.'

By this time the brief flare of adrenaline caused by the banging on my door had fizzled out. I looked at Cullen. For once he'd lost that irritatingly superior expression he usually wore in my company.

'I'm sorry, Bren,' I said, 'but I'm tired and I'm going back to bed.'

'Don't joke, Dave. You've got to come. I looked the other way when you pulled out your illegal shooter.'

'What shooter? Tell me what legal right you have to haul me off on some wild escapade in the middle of the night,' I said. I was thoroughly enjoying myself now.

By way of reply Bren pulled open my dressing gown.

'Dave, you'll wear a wire,' he replied, ignoring my protests. 'I want a recording of everything that's said. This is our best chance to crack the Carlyle racket.'

'There is no Carlyle racket. How many times have you told me?'

'All right, have your fun. You're entitled. I told you months ago that the Carlyles were getting so much protection that it could only be down to national security. Well, you and your old man have more or less unravelled that, but I could hardly give chapter and verse to a pair of civilians, because that's all you are.'

'But now I'm the civilian you need to pull your chestnuts out of the fire,' I said. I hope I kept any note of gloating out of my voice. 'So what's King done?'

'He wanted the Home Secretary in there to hear Brandon Carlyle confess to fitting him up. We managed to argue him out of that but he's going to blow up the place at dawn unless you turn up. He wouldn't let a copper in to see him at any price but he'll put up with you for some reason. He's expecting you to be wired up, but be careful. There've already been three fatalities – those bodyguards of Carlyle's have more guts than sense and King's got the survivors penned into the gym. He's serious. He claims that Carlyle will have him killed anyway and that he's nothing to lose by getting his two penn'orth in first.'

I hurried to dress. Bren ushered a technician into the room who taped a radio mike to my chest. The transmitter was placed in the small of my back. Moments later Bren and I were crammed into the small police helicopter which had landed on the Meadows and then we were away over the sleeping suburbs and small towns, heading towards the solitary splendour of South Pork.

'You!' Brandon Carlyle snarled when I finally made my way into the atrium where he, Charlie and Marti were imprisoned. It wasn't easy. The many large glass and pottery flower pots now contained cans of black gunpowder. Trailing wires led towards the atrium. Three corpses lying near the gym door in pools of congealed blood demonstrated the lethal effects of shrapnel.

'Yeah, it's me, and don't think I'm here by choice,' I replied.

'You've got some face on you, Cunane,' Brandon growled, 'coming here.'

'No,' King snapped, 'I want him. Keep your big trap shut until you're told to speak, Carlyle.'

Brandon Carlyle began laughing.

'You're small-time, King . . . small mind and small ideas. First you demand the Home Secretary in person, but then you settle for a Manchester private detective. What a joke!'

There was nothing funny about King. He was wearing army-style camouflage clothes and, judging by the smell, he was also wearing the surface layer of several cow pastures. He'd made various alterations to Brandon's fancy décor. Except for the one I'd come in by, every door was blocked with piles of furniture. In the space created there was a massive pile of fireworks. I had some trouble adjusting. Fireworks were associated with happy occasions in my mind.

King had lugged the electronic firework console into the room. It was now installed on one of the marble-topped tables. He turned to it. 'I've only to touch a key and young Charlie here's going to be needing a peg-leg,' he said quietly. 'So shut up, or you'll see how funny that is.'

I looked at Charlie. He was bound, gagged and festooned with fireworks from head to foot. The word 'fireworks'

417

doesn't convey the right picture. These were massive, thick tubes attached to Charlie's body with duct-tape. He looked terrified. Sweat was dripping off his fleshy face. There was no sign of anyone else. Marti was sprawled on a sofa next to her father-in-law. The sofa itself was draped with explosives and they were both lashed together with duct-tape.

King watched me scrutinise his hostages. He seemed proud of the situation.

'Don't think I'm going to let Marti go because she's my daughter. She's as bad as Brandon. Told me it was my duty to stay in prison so she could enjoy a nice standard of living, that's what she did!' King sounded very near the edge.

'Can't you let her go?' I pleaded.

'Don't get any wrong ideas, Cunane. You're just here to listen to the fine birds sing. Come here!' he ordered.

I walked over to him and he patted me down. I felt his hand touch the radio transmitter. He looked me in the eye before speaking.

'There we are,' he said. 'Clean as a whistle. No wires. We can talk as if we're among friends, and the first thing you do, Marti, is tell this clown of a detective how many times you've tried to kill him.'

'Dad!' Marti said. For the first time since I'd met her there was a note of genuine pleading in her voice.

'No, he's entitled to know. You tell him.'

'I won't,' she said.

Vince touched the keyboard and the windows rattled as a powerful explosion shook the building. Flakes of plaster landed on us.

'The next one's in here,' he said. 'I've had a full day to do this, you know. Who'd have ever thought Charlie would come in useful for something? Handy him having a container-load of illegal Chinese fireworks, wasn't it?'

Charlie's eyes rolled pathetically as he struggled to speak through his gag. Marti scowled at his recumbent form but she still looked stubborn.

'Was it you who sent the white van after me on the motorway?' I prompted. I didn't share Marti's apparent confidence that her father meant her no harm.

Marti looked as if someone had suggested she have teeth extracted without anaesthetic. She made a short motion with her head.

'Tell him, you bitch!' King snarled. 'Or your meal-ticket's dancing days will be over.' If the look of savage fury on King's face was a pretence, he was the world's best actor. His fingers hovered over the console.

'I already know about it, Marti!' I coaxed.

'Not so thick as you look, are you?' she asked sarcastically. 'I gave you every chance to leave Ironpants but you're too stupid. You didn't think I was going to let you get away with that, did you?'

'How did you do it?'

'Paul Longstreet knows people. It was them in the street outside. They were looking after me.'

'What about the mysterious London firm that wanted a share of Brandon's big tickle?'

She laughed, mad as ever. Brandon nudged her furiously.

'It doesn't matter,' she told him. 'Can't you see Vince is going to do us whatever we say?' Then she turned to me. 'Dave, you're a gullible fool. You're ready to believe anything.'

'Not quite anything,' I muttered. 'It was you who killed Sam Levy, wasn't it?'

She laughed, this time the full thunderclap. Tears rolled down her cheeks. We all waited patiently for the disturbance to subside.

'I was wondering how long it was going to take you to work out that the trains between London and Manchester run in both directions. I came back when Brandon told me that Sam was trying to get in on the act after Lou Olley had his comeuppance.'

'So you did that as well?'

'Of course. I had some help with me. Paul was very obliging.

'Did you think I was really drunk that day at the Renaissance? Brandon and Charlie here had worked out that a permanent separation would be cheaper for them than a divorce. I found that Reichert woman myself. All she wanted was a mobile home. It's no secret that I wanted a lot more. What I told you about Sam's nose being out of joint on account of Olley was true enough, but Sam was far too cautious to go round offing people. He thought he'd try to cosy up with you and worm his way back into the organisation that way, but I couldn't let him do that. Besides, he had something I wanted.'

'Shut up, you mad whore!' Brandon shouted. He looked frantic.

King laughed. 'Getting near the knuckle now, are we?' he sneered.

'We can still sort this,' Brandon said. 'Let me go and I can cut a deal for us both.'

'I've had enough of your deals,' the crazy ex-convict taunted. 'The last one cost me twenty years of my life.'

'This is all your fault, Cunane,' Brandon said with a curse. 'We should have sorted you the first chance we had.'

'Everyone makes mistakes,' I said.

'Sam had protection,' Marti said. 'He needed it. You don't retire from the Carlyle Corporation any more than you get divorced from it. He told me all about the tapes one afternoon. I always knew there was something. Sam had one Round Up tape, Brandon the other. That was the sort of business relationship they had – trusting. The silly old fool should have given it me when I asked, but he wouldn't. He was so stupid. He could have cleared off to the Philippines and spent his declining years in a brothel, the dirty old pig, but he wouldn't give me what I wanted.'

'Did you find it?' I asked.

'No,' she said with a smile. 'I thought he might have given it to you. He babbled about you enough.'

'We're all dead now,' Brandon groaned, 'now you've mentioned that tape. If Cunane opens his big mouth they'll never let us live. They'll kill us like they killed my uncle. That includes you as well, Cunane.'

'Who'll kill us?'

'The same people who killed my uncle,' he said with his eyes rolling in fear.

'The German Navy?' I asked sarcastically.

'You know who I mean. The secret service. They've only

420

held back all these years because they knew I'd never go public.'

'You're dreaming,' I said, more contemptuously than I felt. 'There's not a single person in the secret service who was there when you stole those tapes. You're the killer. You killed Devereaux-Almond and Mick Jones, didn't you?'

'I had to,' Brandon moaned. 'I had the family to think of. Morton was on his own apart from that crazy sister-in-law of his, and Jones always knew what the risks were.'

'That's enough of your troubles,' King snapped. 'Tell him how you fitted me up.'

'Vince, I'm pleading with you. End this now and we can all get out if you let me speak to the right people first. They'll make that mess with the Piledrivers look like an accident. We can still make a deal, the tape for our silence.'

'What you can do is sing like a fucking canary, or I'll blow your son's head right into your fucking ceiling,' King replied with a chuckle. I knew he meant every word. So did Brandon.

'It was Jones who knew about the tapes,' Brandon admitted in a half-whisper. I hoped the radio mike was picking it up. I moved nearer to him. 'He told me and I had to know whose names were on it. I was stupid really. I should have realised that it wasn't Italians they were after this time, but I kept thinking about my uncle. Vince had no idea about how valuable the tapes were, but Mick Jones said we ought to get rid of him because there was always the chance that he'd grass if he got caught . . .'

'You wanker!' King snarled.

'. . . I tried to get Vince to come into the business but he liked robbing too much . . .'

King gave a hollow laugh at this.

'You slimy bastard! The first I knew about what was on those tapes was when Cunane's crazy father told me. You said they were plans of bank vaults.'

Although restrained by his bonds, Brandon managed one of his expressive shrugs. I was impressed.

'In the end I couldn't allow the risk to my family,' he continued. 'The trouble was we didn't have Fullalove straightened. He knew there was something not quite right.

421

He barged in before Jones and knocked King out, then Jones came to tidy up. He shot Fullalove and Musgrave, moved some of the plunder and was about to arrange King in an artful pose before shooting him with another gun, when he heard police sirens. Jones must have set off a hidden alarm or something. Later, I did what I could for Vince. I took Marti into the family.'

'When he threatened you, you mean!' Marti retorted.

'Right, that's your lot, you old bastard,' Vince King said in triumph. 'Get out, Cunane. I'll give you two minutes.'

'Kill yourself if you want, but I'm not going without these three and those men in the gym. The law can sort the Carlyles out,' I said piously.

'Hark at you,' he mocked. 'Thanks for the invitation to kill myself but I've no intention. You can stay and be blown up with these bastards if you like.'

'The death penalty's been abolished. You've no right to do this,' I said. 'At least let Marti and the Piledrivers go.'

'I have to give you marks for trying,' King said. 'Marti's her mother's daughter. Do you know how many times she visited me in prison? I've spent more time with you than I have with her. Anyway, I'm off,' he said. With that he tapped a sequence into the keyboard and loped towards the doorway. There was a distant sound of explosions.

'He's set the sequence running!' Marti yelled.

'Where's the off-switch?' I asked nervously. The console consisted of a laptop computer fixed into a specialised docking panel with a mass of circuitry underneath for connections to be made. There was a complicated diagram on the display screen. Given a month or so I might have worked it out.

'Ask Charlie!' she said in panic.

I ripped the tape off Charlie's mouth. A strip of his skin came with it but he made no complaint.

'You can't turn it off. He's disabled the programme.'

'What about these?' I said, pointing to the loose wires trailing everywhere.

'If you rip the wires out everything will go up at once. It's programmed to set off fireworks in sequence with a carefully timed music programme. There are remote units as back-ups and accidental disconnection may send the whole lot up at once.'

As he spoke my fingers were tearing at the duct-tapes which fastened the fireworks to him. In a moment he was free.

'How long have we got?' I gasped.

'Just seconds,' Charlie said. 'I don't know which displays he's programmed to go off first.' Then as Charlie tottered to his feet he took a swing at me. His face was an encyclopaedia of aggression. Startled though I was, I pushed him away and he lurched towards the pile of fireworks.

'The tape, Charlie. Get the tape!' Brandon shrieked. Charlie looked undecided for a second but then he stumbled off to do his father's bidding. He started wrenching furniture away from the blocked interior door. He was still strong. The noise he made slinging furniture about matched the din from outside.

'Thanks for untying me,' Marti commented sarcastically as Charlie headed for the computer room. I started frantically trying to unravel Marti from her bonds. It was impossible to free her without also freeing Brandon, but I didn't do it willingly. Over my shoulder I glimpsed the surviving Piledrivers leaping over the bodies of their colleagues as they headed for freedom. I doubt if any rugby league spectator had ever seen them move so fast. They certainly didn't spare us a second glance. The whole area round the building was being lit up by exploding fireworks, all skilfully tampered with so they caused maximum damage. I didn't fancy my chances in the open, but the house was piled with the stuff.

'Come on!' I said to Marti. 'We can make it.'

'Not without that tape!' she screamed. Brandon had plunged into the interior of the building. I tried to grab her and pull her after me but she slipped free. The explosions were much nearer now. The windows in the house began to cave in. Glass was flying everywhere. I looked around again and Marti was gone.

I legged it.

As I ran, the 'features', Brandon's prides and joys, went up all around me. Vince had really done a job. Green and golden flames flickered. Explosions thumped. The former SAS man had taped powerful skyrockets onto plastic statues. They went up in sparks and then showered the area with molten plastic. I tried to cover my face. I ran and ran. There was no sign of firemen or safety ahead.

It wasn't until I was almost at the main road that I spotted Brendan Cullen.

'They're still in there,' I gasped, 'King's trying to escape.'

'I know,' he said helplessly, 'but we'll never catch him while this is going on.'

We both looked back at the mansion. The shape seemed to waver. Flames shot out of windows and then with a dull roar the whole place blew up. I started to go back but Brendan held me.

'It's no use,' he shouted above the roar. 'She must be dead.'

Epilogue

Neither Brandon nor Charlie survived Vince's hellish firework display. Their bodies were found later in the wreckage of Brandon's computer room. No trace of Marti or Vince was found at South Pork – not that their part in events played any part in the story the police put out.

Still keeping to the line that Brandon Carlyle was a respected businessman – after all he was the seventh richest man in the country and we live in an enterprise culture – they attributed the destruction of South Pork – Moat Hall Farm – to a burglary that had gone tragically wrong when Charlie's illegal containerload of banned Chinese fireworks went up. There were no allusions to Brandon's criminal past or mentions of Vince King. It was all down to unknown burglars who were still being sought.

Even in death, Brandon Carlyle was able to manipulate the media. There are many unanswered questions, and one day, perhaps, there'll be a no-holds-barred biography of Brandon Carlyle, but not yet.

The Cheshire Police handled all the publicity, or at least they appeared to. There may have been more experienced hands than theirs at work.

There's been no mention whatever of any secret tapes, nor reference made to other killings. A body that could have been that of Morton Devereaux-Almond was washed up at Bray in the Irish Republic but identification was uncertain. Anyway, his death was down as an accident.

Needless to say, my name wasn't mentioned at all, and there wasn't even a secret commendation from the sour-faced Chief Constable of Cheshire. No doubt he was peeved that there would be no more quail's eggs at New Year.

I found that I could live without the gratitude of the police. I managed to live quite well.

Brandon's prediction that our own security services would kill me to silence any potentially dangerous voices hasn't come true – and I don't think it will. About two weeks after Brandon's death a parcel was delivered to me at the office. It came from a solicitor acting for the estate of Sam Levy and contained a spool of tape of the type described by Vince King. After some thought I turned it in to Brendan Cullen. He said nothing about it and no one else has made any comment. I suppose if one is looking for a conspiracy of silence by the security services, the limp-wristed efforts to catch Vince and Marti provide some evidence.

I was grateful, though.

Janine and I see each other at weekends. We're like an old couple. We both need each other but I've never dared to suggest a closer relationship. I still see Clyde Harrow occasionally. He's a shit, but he can be a laugh at times. His career in television survived the fall of the House of Carlyle, as did Pimpernel Investigations.

I was with him at Old Trafford one Saturday when something very curious happened. We were fighting our way towards the car park after the match. The crowds were almost shoulder to shoulder when someone put a hand on my arm. I say that, but of course there were dozens of people touching me in that press of bodies. There was something special about that hand on my arm, though; electricity or something. I whirled round and I caught a glimpse of an attractive blond before the crowd swept us apart. She looked vaguely familiar, as if in disguise. That sound, though, that wasn't disguised. I could hear the inimitable laugh of Marti King growing ever fainter behind me.